NORA ROBERTS

Dear Reader,

Welcome to the fictional kingdom of Cordina, where intrigue and royal romance abound! In this very special 2-in-1 volume, we are pleased to bring you books three and four in Nora Roberts's beloved Cordina's Royal Family series. And if you've read *Cordina's Royal Family: Gabriella & Alexander*, you won't want to miss how Princess Gabriella's brother – as well as her daughter – find love when they least expect it!

The Playboy Prince is exactly whom Lady Hannah Rothchild must avoid when she goes undercover at the palace. But when Prince Bennett discovers her true identity, he realises the lady he has fallen in love with is a force to be reckoned with.

In *Cordina's Crown Jewel*, Princess Camilla is tired of royalty. So she runs away, ditches her guards and takes off on a road trip. All she wants is to get lost and escape the press – but instead she finds the most unlikely man of her dreams!

We hope you enjoy these two fabulous takes of unexpected love by the master of romance.

Happy reading!

The Editors
Silhouette Books

NORA ROBERTS

Cordina's Royal Family
BENNETT & CAMILLA

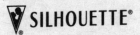
SILHOUETTE®

*Silhouette and Colophon are registered trademarks of
Harlequin Books S.A., used under licence.
Silhouette Books, Eton House, 18-24 Paradise Road,
Richmond, Surrey TW9 1SR*

CORDINA'S ROYAL FAMILY: BENNETT & CAMILLA
© Harlequin Books S.A. 2006

*The publisher acknowledges the copyright holder of the
individual works as follows:*

The Playboy Prince © Nora Roberts 1987
Cordina's Crown Jewel © Nora Roberts 1992

ISBN: 978 0 263 85840 2

025-0507

*Printed and bound in Spain
by Litografia Rosés S.A., Barcelona*

CONTENTS

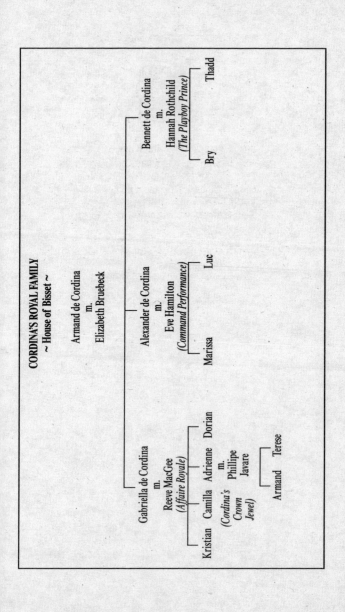

CORDINA'S ROYAL FAMILY
~ House of Bisset ~

Armand de Cordina
m.
Elizabeth Bruebeck

Gabriella de Cordina
m.
Reeve MacGee
(Affaire Royale)

Kristian Camilla Adrienne Dorian
(Cordina's
Crown
Jewel)
m.
Phillipe
Javare

Armand Terese

Alexander de Cordina
m.
Eve Hamilton
(Command Performance)

Marissa Luc

Bennett de Cordina
m.
Hannah Rothchild
(The Playboy Prince)

Bry Thadd

THE PLAYBOY PRINCE

For Tara Bell,
with hope that her wishes come true

Chapter 1

The stallion plunged over the crest of the hill, digging hard into the earth and kicking up dust. At the peak, he reared, powerful forelegs pawing the air. For an instant, horse and rider were silhouetted against the bright afternoon sky. One looked as dangerous as the other.

Even as hooves touched earth, the rider's knees pressed to the stallion's side and sent them both recklessly racing down the sheer incline. The track there was smooth, but hardly gentle with a wall of rock on one side and a drop into space on the other. They took it at full speed and gloried in it.

Only a madman rode with such arrogant disregard for life and limb. Only a madman, or a dreamer.

"*Avant*, Dracula." The command was low and challenging as was the laughter that followed. The tone was one of a man who considered fear a banquet and speed the wine.

Birds, startled by the thunderous pounding of hooves on dirt, flew from the trees and bushes on the cliff above to wheel screaming into the sky. Their noise was soon lost in the distance. When the path veered to the left, the stallion took it without a pause. The edge of the road gave way to cliffs that spilled sharply for seventy feet to the white rocks and blue sea. Pebbles danced off the dirt to shower soundlessly into the empty spaces.

The rider glanced down but didn't slow. He never even considered it.

From that height, there was no scent of the sea. Even the sound of waves crashing was indistinct, like thunder far off and still harmless. But from that height, the sea held a danger and mystique all of its own. Every year she claimed her tribute in the lives of men. The rider understood this, accepted this, for so it had been since the beginning of time. So it would continue to be. At times like this he put himself in the hands of fate and backed his bet with his own skill.

The stallion needed no whip, no spur to drive him faster. As always, his master's excitement and confidence were enough. They tore down the twisting path until the sea roared in their ears and the cry of gulls could at last be heard.

To the onlooker, it might seem the horseman was fleeing from devils or racing to a lover. But anyone seeing his face would know it was neither.

If there was a gleam in the dark eyes, it wasn't one of fear or anticipation. It was challenge. For the moment, and the moment only. Speed whipped the man's dark hair as freely as the horse's dark mane.

The stallion was fifteen hands of coal-black energy,

wide at the chest, powerful at the neck. The horse's hide glistened with sweat, but his breathing was strong and even. Astride him, the rider sat erect, his tanned, narrow face glowing. His mouth, full and sculpted, was curved in a smile that spoke of both recklessness and pleasure.

As the path leveled, the stallion's stride lengthened. Here, they passed whitewashed cottages where clothes flapped on lines in the sea breeze. Flowers crowded for space in tidy lawns and windows were opened and unscreened. The sun, still high in the sky after noon, flashed its brilliant light. Without slackening, without needing his master's light hands on the reins to guide him, the stallion sprinted for a hedge as high as a man's waist.

Together, they soared over it.

In the distance were the stables. As there were danger and deadly attraction in the cliffs behind, so were there peace and order to the scene ahead. Red and white, and tidy as the lawns surrounding them, the buildings added another touch of charm to a landscape of cliffs and greenery. Fences crisscrossed to form paddocks where horses were being exercised with far less drama than Dracula.

One of the grooms stopped circling a young mare on a lead when he heard the stallion's approach. Crazy as a loon, he thought—but not without grudging respect. This horse and this rider, merged together in a blare of speed, were a common sight. Even so, two grooms waited at attention for the stallion to slow to a halt.

"Your Highness."

His Highness, Prince Bennett of Cordina slid off Dracula's back with a laugh that echoed the recklessness. "I'll cool him down, Pipit."

The old groom with the slight limp stepped forward.

His weathered face was passive, but he passed his gaze over both prince and stallion, checking for any sign of harm. "Your pardon, sir, but a message came down from the palace while you were out. Prince Armand wishes to see you."

Not without regret, Bennett handed the reins to the waiting groom. Part of the pleasure of the ride was the hour he normally spent walking and brushing down the stallion. If his father had sent for him, he had no choice but to forgo pleasure for duty.

"Walk him thoroughly, Pipit. We've had a long run."

"Yes, sir," said the groom who'd spent three-quarters of his life with horses. Among his duties had been seating Bennett on his first pony. At sixty, with one leg game from a fall, Pipit remembered the energy of youth. And the passion. He patted Dracula's neck and found it damp. "I'll see to it myself, Your Highness."

"Do that, Pipit." But Bennett loitered long enough to loosen the cinches. "Thanks."

"No thanks necessary, sir." With a quiet grunt, Pipit hefted the saddle from the stallion's back. "Isn't another man here who has the nerve to deal with the devil." He murmured in French as the horse began to dance in place. In moments, Dracula settled again.

"And there isn't another man I'd trust with my best. An extra scoop of grain wouldn't hurt him this evening."

Pipit took the compliment as no less than his due. "As you say, sir."

Still restless, Bennett turned to walk from the stables. He could have used the extra hour to cool himself down as well. Riding fast, riding reckless, satisfied only part of his thirst. He needed the movement, the speed, but most of all, he needed the freedom.

For nearly three months he'd been tied firmly to the palace and protocol, the pomp and procedure. As second in line to Cordina's throne, his duties were sometimes less public than his brother, Alexander's, but rarely less arduous. Duties, obligations, had been a part of his life since birth, and were normally taken as a matter of course. Bennett couldn't explain to himself, much less anyone else, why some time during the last year he'd begun to fret and chafe against them.

Gabriella saw it. Bennett thought perhaps his sister even understood it. She, too, had always had a thirst for freedom and privacy. She'd gained a portion of that two years before when Alexander had married Eve, and the weight of responsibility had shifted.

Still she never shirked, Bennett thought as he passed through the palace's garden doors. If she was needed, she was there. She still gave six months of every year to the Aid for Handicapped Children while keeping her marriage vital and raising her children.

Bennett dug his hands into his pockets as he climbed the stairs that would take him to his father's office. What was wrong with him? What had happened in the last few months that made him want to slip quietly out of the palace some night and run? Anywhere.

He couldn't shake off the mood, but he managed to tame it as he knocked on his father's door.

"Entrez."

The prince wasn't behind his desk as Bennett had expected, but was seated beside a tea tray at the window.

Across from him was a woman who rose to her feet at Bennett's entrance.

As a man who appreciated women of any age, of any form, he took an easy survey before turning to his father. "I'm sorry to interrupt. I was told you wished to see me."

"Yes." Armand merely sipped his tea. "Some time ago. Prince Bennett, I would like to introduce Lady Hannah Rothchild."

"Your Highness." Her gaze swept down as she curtsied.

"A pleasure, Lady Hannah." Bennett took her hand, summing her up in seconds. Attractive in a quiet way. He preferred less subtlety in women. British from her accent. He had an affection for the French. Slim and neat. Invariably, the more voluptuous caught his eye. "Welcome to Cordina."

"Thank you, Your Highness." Her voice was indeed British, cultured and quiet. He met her gaze briefly so that he saw her eyes were a deep and glowing shade of green. "Yours is a beautiful country."

"Please, sit, my dear." Armand gestured her back to her chair before he lifted another cup to pour. "Bennett."

Hannah, with her hands folded in her lap, noticed Bennett's quick look of dislike at the teapot. But he sat and accepted the cup.

"Lady Hannah's mother was a distant cousin of yours," Armand began. "Eve became acquainted with her when she and your brother visited England recently. At Eve's invitation, Lady Hannah has agreed to stay with us as Eve's companion."

Bennett could only hope he wouldn't be expected to escort the lady. She was pretty enough, though she dressed like a nun in a gray, high-collared dress that came a discreet two inches below her knees. The color did nothing for her pale, British complexion. Her eyes saved her face from being plain, but with her dark blond hair pulled back so severely from her face, she put him in mind of the old Victorian companions or governesses. Dull. But he remembered his manners and treated her to an easy, companionable smile.

"I hope you enjoy your stay as much as we'll enjoy having you."

Hannah gave him a solemn look in return. She wondered if he was aware, and thought he was, of how dashing he looked in casual riding clothes. "I'm sure I'll enjoy it immensely, sir. I'm flattered the Princess Eve invited me to stay with her while she awaits the birth of her second child. I hope to give her the companionship and help she needs."

Though his mind was on other matters, Armand offered a plate of frosted cookies. "Lady Hannah has been very generous to give us her time. She's quite a scholar and is currently working on a series of essays."

Figures, Bennett thought, and sipped at the hated tea. "Fascinating."

The smallest of smiles touched Hannah's lips. "Do you read Yeats, sir?"

Bennett shifted in his chair and wished himself back to his stables. "Not extensively."

"My books should be here by the end of the week. Please feel free to borrow anything you like." She rose again, keeping her hands folded. "If you would excuse me, Your Highness, I'd like to see to the rest of my unpacking."

"Of course." Armand rose to lead her to the door. "We'll see you at dinner. Be sure to ring if you require anything."

"Thank you, sir." She curtsied, then turned to extend the courtesy to Bennett. "Good afternoon, Your Highness."

"*Bonjour*, Lady Hannah." Bennett waited for the door to close behind her before dropping onto the arm of his chair. "Well, she should bore Eve to tears within a week." Ignoring the tea, he took a handful of the small iced cookies. "What could Eve have been thinking of?"

"Eve became very fond of Hannah during her two weeks in England." Armand walked to a scrolled cabinet and, to Bennett's relief, took out a decanter. "Hannah is a well-bred young woman of excellent family. Her father is a highly respected member of the British Parliament." The brandy was deep and rich. Armand poured it sparingly.

"That's all well and good, but—" Bennett stopped abruptly as he reached for the snifter. "Oh good God, Father, you're not thinking of trying for a match here? She's hardly my type."

Armand's firm mouth softened with a smile. "I think I know that well enough. I can assure you Lady Hannah was not brought here to tempt you."

"She could hardly do that in any case." Bennett swirled the brandy, then sipped. "Yeats?"

"There are some who believe literature extends beyond equestrian handbooks." Armand drew out a cigarette. There was a knot of tension at the base of his neck. He forced it to concentrate there rather than allowing it to spread.

"I prefer the useful rather than poetry about unrequited love or the beauty of a raindrop." When that made him feel small and ungracious, Bennett relented. "But in any case, I'll do whatever I can to make Eve's new friend welcome."

"I never doubted it."

His conscience soothed, Bennett moved on to more important matters. "The Arabian mare should foal by Christmas. I'm betting it's a colt. Dracula will breed strong sons. I have three horses that should be ready to show in the spring, and another I think should be taken to the Olympic trials. I'd like to arrange that within the next few weeks so that the riders will have more time to work with the horse."

Armand gave an absent nod and continued to swirl his brandy. Bennett felt the familiar push of impatience rising and fought it down. He was well aware that the stables weren't high on his father's list of priorities. How could they be with internal affairs, foreign affairs, and the very tricky politics within the Council of the Crown?

Yet, didn't there have to be something more? The horses not only gave pleasure, but added a certain prestige when the Royal House of Cordina possessed one of the finest stables in Europe. For himself, it was what he considered his only true contribution to his family and country.

He'd worked for the stables as hard and as menially as any groom or stable boy. Over the years, he'd studied everything he could about breeding. To his delight, he'd found within himself a natural skill that had added spark to his education. Within a short time, Bennett had turned a good stable into one of the best. In another decade, he was confident it would have no equal.

There were times when Bennett needed to discuss his horses and his ambitions with someone other than a stable hand or another breeder. Still, he understood, and always had, that that person would rarely be his father.

"I take it this isn't the time to discuss it." Bennett took another small sip of brandy and waited for his father to reveal whatever weighed on his mind.

"I'm sorry, Bennett, I'm afraid it isn't." The father felt regret. The prince could not. "Your schedule this next week. Can you tell me about it?"

"Not really." The restlessness was back. Rising, Bennett began to pace from one window to another. How close the sea seemed and yet how far away. He wished for a moment that he was on a ship again, a hundred miles from any land, with a storm brewing on the horizon. "I know that I have to go into Le Havre at the end of the week. The *Indépendance* is coming in. There's a meeting with the Farmers' Cooperative and a couple of luncheons. Cassell fills me in each morning. If it's important I can have him type up the highlights for you. I'm sure I'm cutting at least one ribbon."

"Feeling closed in, Bennett?"

With a shrug, Bennett tossed off the last of his brandy. Then the easy smile returned. Life, after all, was too short to complain about. "It's the ribbons that do it. The rest, at least, seems worthwhile."

"Our people look to us for more than governing."

Bennett turned from the window. Behind him the sun was high and bright. Whatever he might sometimes wish in his secret heart, the royalty he'd been born with cloaked him. "I know, Papa. The problem is I don't have Alexander's patience, Brie's serenity or your control."

"You might need them all soon." Armand set his glass down and faced his son. "Deboque will be released from prison in two days."

Deboque. Even the name caused fury to churn in Bennett's stomach. François Deboque. The man by whose orders his sister had been kidnapped. The man who had planned assassination attempts on both his father and his brother.

Deboque.

Bennett pressed a finger to the scar just below his left shoulder. He'd taken a bullet there, and the trigger had been pulled by Deboque's lover. For Deboque. By Deboque.

The bomb planted just over two years before in the Paris Embassy had been meant for his father. Instead it had killed Seward, a loyal assistant, leaving a woman widowed and three children fatherless. That, too, had been Deboque's doing.

And in all the years, nearly ten now since Gabriella's kidnapping, no one had proved Deboque's involvement in the kidnapping, the conspiracies or the murders. The best investigators in Europe, including Bennett's brother-in-law, had been brought in, but none of them had proved that Deboque had pulled the strings.

Now, within days, he would be free.

There was no doubt in Bennett's mind that Deboque would continue to seek revenge. The Royal Family was his enemy if for no other reason than he'd been held in a Cordinian prison for over a decade. Neither was there any doubt that during that decade, he'd continued to deal in drugs, weapons and women.

No doubt, and no proof.

Guards would be added. Security would be tightened. Interpol would continue its work, as would the International Security System. But both Interpol and the ISS had been trying to nail Deboque with murder and conspiracy to murder for years. Until he was gotten under control and the strings to his organization severed, Cordina and the rest of Europe were vulnerable.

Hands in pockets, Bennett strode out to the garden. At least they'd dined *en famille* that evening. It had relieved some strain, even though little could be said in front of Eve's new friend. He doubted if anyone that quiet and prim would have picked up on any tension around the table. She had answered when spoken to and nursed one glass of wine throughout the meal.

He would have wished her back to England a dozen times if he hadn't seen how good she actually was for Eve. His sister-in-law was three months pregnant with her second child and didn't need the additional strain of talk of Deboque. Two years before she'd nearly been killed protecting Alexander. If Lady Hannah could keep Eve's mind off Deboque, even for a few hours a day, it would be worth the inconvenience of having her in the palace.

He needed to talk with Reeve. Bennett drove his balled fists into his pockets. Reeve MacGee was more than his sister's husband. As head of security, he would have some answers. And Bennett certainly had the questions—dozens of them. More was being done than the placing of extra guards. Bennett refused to go through the next weeks blindly while others worked to protect him and his family.

Swearing softly, he looked up at the sky. The moon was cloudless and half full. Another time, with the scents of the garden wafting around him, he would have itched for a woman to watch the sky with. Now, filled with frustration, he preferred the solitude.

When he heard the dogs bark, his body stiffened. He'd thought himself alone; he'd even been sure of it. In any case, his aging hounds never barked at family or familiar servants. Half-hoping for a confrontation, Bennett moved quietly toward the sound.

He heard her laugh and the sound surprised him. It wasn't quiet and prim, but rich and delighted. As he watched, Hannah leaned down to stroke the dogs, which pressed against her legs.

"There now, what a lovely pair you are." Smiling she bent farther still to nuzzle. The moonlight slanted over her face and throat.

Instantly, Bennett's eyes narrowed. She hardly looked plain and subdued at the moment. The moonlight accented the hollows and contours of her face, enriching the soft English skin and deepening the already deep green eyes. He would have sworn that he saw both strength and passion there. And he was a man who recognized both in a woman. Her laughter floated out again, as rich as sunlight, as sultry as fog.

"No, you mustn't jump," she cautioned the dogs as they circled her. "You'll have mud all over me and how would I explain that?"

"It's usually best not to explain at all."

She snapped her head up as Bennett spoke. He saw

surprise, or thought he did, but it passed quickly. When
she straightened, she was the calm, unremarkable Lady
Hannah again. He chalked up the passion he'd thought
he'd seen to a trick of the light.

"Good evening, Your Highness." Hannah took only a
moment to curse herself for being caught unaware.

"I didn't know anyone else was in the garden."

"Nor did I." And she should have. "I beg your pardon."

"Don't." He smiled to put her at ease. "I've always
felt the gardens aren't enjoyed nearly enough. Couldn't
you sleep?"

"No, sir. I'm always restless when I travel." The dogs
had deserted her for Bennett. She stood beside the flow-
ering jasmine and watched him stroke them with strong,
capable hands. She was well aware that numerous ladies
had enjoyed the same easy touch. "I'd seen the gardens
from my window and thought I might walk awhile." In
truth, it had been their scent, exotic and alluring, that had
urged her to loiter after she'd noted the layout of the
space.

"I prefer them at night myself. Things often look different at night," he continued, studying her again. "Don't
you think?"

"Naturally." She linked her hands together just below
the waist. He was marvelous to look at, sun or moon.
When he'd strode into his father's office that afternoon
she'd thought that riding clothes suited him best. The dogs
came back to press their noses against her joined hands.

"They like you."

"I've always been fond of animals." She unlinked her
hands to stroke. He noticed for the first time that her hands

were delicate, long and slender like her body. "What are their names?"

"Boris and Natasha."

"Suitable names for Russian wolfhounds."

"They were given to me as puppies. I named them after characters in an American cartoon show. Spies."

Her hands hesitated only a heartbeat. "Spies, Your Highness?"

"Inept Russian spies who were forever after a moose and squirrel."

He thought he saw it again, the flash of humor that lent something special to her face. "I see. I've never been to America."

"No?" He moved closer, but saw nothing but a young woman with good bones and a quiet manner. "It's a fascinating country. Cordina's become closely linked with it since two members of the Royal Family have married Americans."

"A fact that disappointed a number of hopeful Europeans, I'm sure." Hannah relaxed enough for a cautious smile. "I met Princess Gabriella several years ago. She's a beautiful woman."

"Yes, she is. You know, I've been to England several times. It's strange we never met."

Hannah allowed the smile to linger. "But we did, Your Highness."

"Boris, sit," Bennett commanded as the dog lifted a paw toward Hannah's dress. "Are you sure?"

"Quite sure, sir. Then you'd hardly be expected to remember. It was several years ago at a charity ball hosted by the Prince of Wales. The Queen Mother introduced you to me and my cousin Lady Sara. I believe you and Sara became…friendly.''

"Sara?'' His mind backtracked and zeroed in. His memory, always good, was faultless when it came to women. ''Yes, of course.'' Though he remembered Hannah only as a vague shadow beside her glamorous and bold cousin. ''How is Sara?''

"Very well, sir.'' If there was sarcasm, it was well coated with manners. ''Happily married for the second time. Shall I send her your regards?''

"If you like.'' He dipped his hands into his pockets again as he continued to study her. ''You were wearing blue, a pale blue that was nearly white.''

Hannah lifted her brow. She didn't have to be told that he'd barely noticed her. The fact that he hadn't, yet still remembered the color of her gown gave her a moment's pause. A memory like that could be useful—or dangerous.

"You flatter me, Your Highness.''

"I make it a policy not to forget a woman.''

"Yes, I can believe that.''

"My reputation precedes me.'' The frown was there, then gone, to be replaced by a careless smile. ''Does it concern you to be alone in the garden, in the moonlight with—''

"The Royal Rake?'' Hannah finished.

"You do read,'' Bennett murmured.

"Incessantly. And no, Your Highness, I'm quite comfortable, thank you.''

He opened his mouth, then laughed and shut it again.''Lady Hannah, I've rarely been put so neatly in my place.''

So he was quick—another point she'd have to remember. "I beg your pardon, sir. That certainly wasn't my intention."

"The hell it wasn't, and well done." He took her hand and found it cool and steady. Perhaps she would prove to be a great deal less dull than he'd anticipated. "I should beg your pardon for baiting you, but I won't since you obviously hold your own so well. I'm beginning to see why Eve wanted you here."

Hannah had learned long ago to block off any form of guilt. She did so now. "I became very fond of her in a short time and was delighted with the opportunity to stay in Cordina for a few months. I confess, I've already fallen in love with little Princess Marissa."

"Barely a year old and she's already ruling the palace." Bennett's eyes softened as he thought of his brother's first child. "Maybe it's because she looks like Eve."

Hannah withdrew her hand from his. She'd heard the rumors that Bennett had been half in love, or possibly more than half in love, with his brother's wife. It didn't take even so talented an observer as she to hear the affection in his voice. She told herself to file it away. It may or may not have its uses later.

"If you'll excuse me, sir, I should go back to my room."

"It's still early." He found himself reluctant to let her go. It was unexpected that she would be easy to talk to, or that he would find himself needing to talk to her.

"I'm in the habit of retiring early."

"I'll walk you back."

"Please don't trouble. I know the way. Good night, Your Highness." She merged quickly with the shadows while the dogs whined a bit and thumped their tails against his legs.

What was there about her? Bennett wondered as he bent to soothe his pets. At first glance she seemed almost bland enough to fade into the wallpaper, and yet... He didn't know. But as he walked back toward the palace with the dogs at his heels, he resolved to find out. If nothing else, probing a bit beneath Lady Hannah's quiet breeding would keep his mind off Deboque.

Hannah didn't wait to see if he followed her, but walked quickly through the garden doors. She'd been born with the talent to move quietly, so unobtrusively she could easily be missed in a group of three people. It was a talent she'd honed to a skill and which served her well.

She moved up the stairs without a sound, never looking back. If you had to check whether you were being followed, you were already in trouble. Once inside her own room, she locked the door and slipped out of her practical pumps. Because the woman she professed to be would never leave her clothing scattered, Hannah picked them up, and with only a brief look of distaste, placed them neatly in her closet.

Checking only to see that her curtains were drawn, she peeled off the unflattering cocktail dress.

Although she thought it deserved its day in the garbage, she carefully hung it on a padded hanger.

She stood now, a slimly curved woman with milk-pale skin and long legs in a skimpy lace-edged teddy. Drawing the confining pins from her hair, she let it fall heavily to her waist with a sigh of pure pleasure.

Anyone who knew Lady Hannah Rothchild would have

been stunned by the transformation, so complete, so ingrained was the role she'd played for nearly ten years.

Lady Hannah had a passion for silk and Breton lace, but confined it to nightwear and lingerie. Linens and tweeds were more fitting to the image she'd worked hard to create.

Lady Hannah enjoyed reading a pot-boiling thriller in a steamy bubble bath, but she kept a copy of Chaucer on her nightstand and if asked, could quote and discuss a handful of obscure passages.

It wasn't a matter of split personality, but necessity. If she'd given it any deep thought, Hannah would have been able to state that she was comfortable with both of her selves. In fact, more often than not she thoroughly liked the plain, polite and marginally pretty Hannah. Otherwise, she could never have tolerated the sensible shoes for extended periods.

But there was another part to Lady Hannah Rothchild, only daughter of Lord Rothchild, granddaughter of the Earl of Fenton. That part was not quiet and unassuming, but shrewd and sometimes reckless. More, that part had a taste for danger and a mind that absorbed and stored the most minor detail.

Combined, those parts of Lady Hannah Rothchild equaled an excellent and highly skilled agent.

Ignoring her robe, Hannah opened her top drawer and drew out a long, locked box. Inside was a strand of pearls handed down from her great-grandmother with matching earrings her father had had reset for her twenty-first birthday. In the drawers of the box were several other pieces of jewelry befitting a young woman of her class.

Hannah pulled a notebook out of the false bottom and

taking it to the rosewood writing desk, began to write her daily report. She hadn't gone into the garden merely to smell the roses, though she had lingered too long because of them. Now she had the complete layout and no longer had to rely on the information fed her. She took the time to draw a sketch of the palace, including the doors and windows most easily accessible. By the following day, or the day after at most, she would have a schedule of the guards.

It had taken her little time to form a friendship with Eve. Securing an invitation to the palace in Cordina had been as easy as asking for one. Eve missed her sister and the familiarity of her own country. She'd needed a friend, one she could talk to, one who would share her delight in her daughter.

Hannah had obliged.

She felt the quick trickle of guilt again and ignored it. A job was a job, she reminded herself. She couldn't let the fondness she felt for Eve interfere with a goal she'd begun to work toward two years ago.

With a shake of her head, she made her first notes on Bennett. He wasn't completely what she'd expected, Hannah thought now. Oh, he was as charming and as attractive as his dossier had said, but he'd given the dull Lady Hannah his time and attention.

An egotistical womanizer, Hannah reminded herself. That had been her own conclusion after doing her research on him. Perhaps he was a bit bored and entertained thoughts of distracting himself with a vulnerable and accessible woman.

Narrowing her eyes, Hannah looked back on the way he had smiled at her. A man of his looks, position and experience knew how to use that smile or a soft word to enchant a woman of any age and any class. The fact that he'd done so, with astonishing regularity, was well documented. Perhaps he would try to add another jewel to his crown by seducing her.

She remembered the way he'd looked in the moonlight, the way his eyes had warmed when she'd bantered back with him. His hand had been firm and hard when it had taken hers—the hand of a man who did more than wave regally to his people.

With a shake of her head, she brought herself up short. It wouldn't do to consider a dalliance with Bennett for enjoyment, but for its usefulness. Thoughtfully, she tapped her pencil on the pad. No, a romance with Bennett would only lead to complications, no matter how advantageous it might be in the long run. She'd keep her eyes down and her hands folded.

Carefully, Hannah hid the notebook again and replaced the false bottom. The box was locked, but left in full sight if anyone searched her dresser.

She was in, she told herself with a growing sense of anticipation as she looked around the room.

When Deboque walked out of prison in two days' time, he'd be very pleased.

Chapter 2

"Oh, Hannah, I'm so glad you agreed to visit awhile."
With her arm hooked with her new friend's, Eve strolled
behind the backdrop at the theater. Her body remained
slender during the early months of her pregnancy, but her
dress was cleverly cut to conceal even the slight weight
gain. "Alex doesn't find it as necessary to pamper me to
death now that you're here. He finds you so sensible."

"I am sensible."

Eve's low chuckle flowed into her easy Texas drawl.
"I know, that's the beauty of it, but you're not always
telling me to sit down and put my feet up."

"Men sometimes look at pregnancy and childbirth as a
traumatic disease rather than a fact of life."

"That's it exactly." Delighted with Hannah's dry wit,
Eve drew her into her office. With Gabriella so often in
America and her own sister visiting only rarely, Eve had
indeed yearned for another woman to relax with. "Alex

keeps expecting me to faint or get overly emotional. I never felt better in my life, except perhaps when I was carrying Marissa.''

Tossing back her fall of dark hair, Eve perched on the edge of her desk. Here, at least, she could still claim some measure of the privacy she'd given up when she'd married a prince. Though she never regretted the sacrifice, she always enjoyed stealing a bit of her own back.

''If you hadn't come, I'd have had to fight him tooth and nail to continue working. He only agreed because he felt you'd keep a close eye on me when he's busy.''

''Then I won't disappoint him.'' Hannah took quick stock of the office. No window, no outside access. With a smile, she chose a chair. ''You know, Eve, I really admire you. The Fine Arts Center always had a good reputation but since you took over here, this theater has become one of the most important in Europe.''

''It's what I've always wanted.'' Eve looked down at the diamond-encrusted band on her finger. Even after two years it sometimes astonished her to find it there. ''You know, Hannah, some mornings I'm almost afraid to wake up; I think that I'll find out it was all a dream. Then I look at Alex and Marissa and think, they're mine. Really mine.'' Her eyes clouded a moment with both fear and determination. ''I won't let anything or anyone hurt them.''

''No one will.'' Eve's thoughts were on Deboque, Hannah surmised. The princess was bound by duty to keep some fears to herself. ''Now, not to pamper, but I think we could both use some tea, then you can show me what sort of job I can do around here.''

Eve brought herself back with an effort. Nightmares of Deboque, a man she'd never seen, continued to plague her. "Tea's a wonderful idea, but I didn't bring you to the Center to work. I just thought you'd like to see it."

"Eve, you of all people should understand that I need something to do or I'll be bored to death."

"But I'd hoped this could be a vacation for you."

The guilt shimmered a bit. "Some people aren't meant for vacations."

"All right then. Why don't you watch rehearsals with me for an hour or two and give me an honest opinion?"

"I'd love to."

"Great. I'm worried about the opening. We only have a couple of weeks left and I've had nothing but trouble with this playwright."

"Oh, who is it?"

Eve rose and took a deep breath. "Me."

Hannah drank her tea and stayed in the background. It didn't take long for her to see that Eve was respected not only as the wife of the heir, but for her knowledge of theater. She noted too that guards, unobtrusive but in force, were always close at hand. When the princess was in the theater, every entrance was blocked, every interior door was double guarded. Hannah was also aware that a special unit of security checked the Center daily for explosives.

While seated mid-theater with Eve, Hannah watched the rehearsal. She'd always had an affection and respect for actors, as she understood the effort and skill that went into characterization. Now, while lines were cued and staging set, she matched the members of the troupe with the information she already had compiled on each of them.

They were certainly talented, Hannah thought as she

found herself drawn into the rhythm and emotion of Eve's play. The sets were still incomplete, but the players needed no more than Eve's words and their own skill to make a statement. Each one of the actors had a reputation in theater and a complete security check.

But it had been an actor—Russ Talbot—who'd nearly carried out Deboque's revenge two years before. Hannah couldn't forget that it was a strong possibility that someone other than herself had been planted. Deboque was known for covering his bets.

"She's wonderful, isn't she?"

Drawn back, Hannah looked over at Eve. "I beg your pardon?"

"Chantel O'Hurley. She's exquisite." Shifting in her chair, Eve leaned on the seat back in front of her. "She rarely makes a stage performance, so we're lucky to have her. I'm sure you've seen her films in England."

"Yes." Hannah gave her full attention to the curvy blonde center stage.

Chantel O'Hurley. Hannah paused to recollect everything she'd read in the actress's file. Twenty-six. American film star. Residence, Beverly Hills. Daughter of Frances and Margaret O'Hurley, traveling entertainers. Sisters, Abigail and Madelaine. Brother, Trace.

Hannah frowned and continued to watch. She had full background information on the entire O'Hurley family, except the brother. There her sources had closed tight. In any case, Chantel O'Hurley was a talented actress with an impressive list of screen credits and no known affiliation with any political group. Nonetheless, Hannah would keep an eye on her.

"She's found the heart of it," Eve murmured. "I'd finished the play and was trying to work up the courage to produce it, when I saw her in her last film. I knew immediately she'd be the perfect Julia.'' On a long breath Eve leaned back again in an unprincesslike slouch. ''I can't believe she's here, reciting my lines. There isn't an emotion that voice can't pull out.''

''I'm sure she's honored to be performing in a play written and produced by Princess Eve of Cordina.''

On a half laugh, Eve shook her head. ''If the play had been lousy, I could have been Empress of Europe and Chantel wouldn't have accepted the part. That's what I'm hanging onto.''

''A member of the Royal Family doesn't write lousy plays.''

At the sound of the voice behind her, Eve was springing up and reaching out. ''Alexander! What are you doing here?''

''I, too, have an interest in the Center.'' He kissed the hand he held before turning to Hannah. ''Please, sit, I didn't mean to disturb you.''

''No.'' Eve sighed and glanced back at the stage where rehearsals continued. ''You meant to check up on me.''

It was, of course, the truth, but Alexander only shrugged. In the dim light, Hannah saw his gaze sweep over his wife's head to the guards placed at several strategic points. ''You forget, *ma mie*, that I am still president of the Center. In addition to that, my wife's play is in rehearsal. I have a small interest there as well.''

''And you came to be certain I wasn't staying on my feet.'' Over the frustration came the tug of love. Eve rose to her toes to kiss him. ''Thank you. Hannah, tell His Highness I've been taking care of myself in the four hours and forty minutes since he last saw me.''

"Your Highness," Hannah began dutifully, "the princess has been taking excellent care of herself."

A smile softened his features, but he continued to stand protectively near his wife. "Thank you, Hannah. I'm sure the credit goes to you."

With a low laugh, Eve tucked her hand through Alexander's arm. "Hannah, you can see that I wasn't joking when I said that Alex thinks I need a keeper. If you hadn't come I have no doubt he'd have hired a two-hundred-pound wrestler with tattoos."

"I'm glad I could save you from that." What was this? Hannah wondered. A tug of envy? Ridiculous as it seemed to her, she recognized the emotion as she studied Alexander and Eve. So much in love, she thought. The power of it all but cast an aura around them. Did they realize, could they realize, how rare a thing they'd found?

"Now that I've interrupted," Alexander was saying, "I was hoping to convince you to join me for my luncheon with the American senator."

"The Yankee from Maine."

With a smile, Alexander stroked her cheek. "My dear, it continues to fascinate me how your country divides itself into sections. But yes, the Yankee from Maine. We should be finished by three and be back at the palace when Marissa wakes from her nap."

"But you had a meeting this afternoon."

"I canceled it." He brought her hand to his lips. "I wanted to spend some time with my family."

The glow of pleasure all but lit up the theater. "Give me five minutes to get my things. Hannah, you'll join us?"

"If it wouldn't inconvenience you, I'd really like to stay and watch the rest of the rehearsal." Her mind was already shooting ahead. Alone, she could take a casual tour of the complex. If there were vulnerabilities, she'd find them.

"Of course, stay as long as you like." Eve bent down to kiss her cheek. "We'll have a car wait for you at the stage door. Five minutes," she repeated to Alexander before she dashed off.

"What do you think of the play?" Alexander asked Hannah as he took the seat beside her.

"I'm hardly an expert on the theater, Your Highness."

"In private, please call me Alexander."

"Thank you," she murmured, aware that this gave her an intimacy rewarded to few. "There's an intensity, an immediacy in the dialogue that makes one care deeply about the characters. I don't know the end, but I find myself hoping Julia wins even while I'm afraid she won't."

"Eve would like to hear that. The play—and other things—have her very tense right now."

"You're worried about her." In a gesture that was pure instinct, Hannah placed a hand on his. "She's very strong."

"I know that, better than most." But he'd never been able to block off the memory of how her body had stiffened, then gone limp in his arms when a bullet had struck her. "I haven't told you before how very grateful I am that you came to be with her. She needs friendship. I changed her life, selfishly perhaps because I couldn't live mine without her. Whatever can be done to give her a sense of normalcy, a sense of peace, I'll do. You understand the obligations of royalty. The limitations. Even the risks."

"Yes, I do." Hannah left her hand on his another moment before removing it. "And I understand a happy woman when I see one."

When he turned to her then, Hannah saw the strong resemblance to his father. The lean, almost scholarly face, the aristocratic lines, the mouth that was held firm. "Thank you, Hannah. I think perhaps you'll be good for all of us."

"I hope so." She looked back at the stage, at the players, at the roles. "I do hope so."

Alone, Hannah watched for another half hour. Yes, the play was good, she decided, even gripping, but she had other games to play.

The guards remained, but with no royalty present they were more for the purpose of keeping others out than monitoring those already in. Lady Hannah was already established as the princess's confidante and companion. Trusted by Prince Armand himself, she wasn't followed when she rose and slipped through a side door.

There was a miniature camera concealed in a lipstick case in her handbag, but she didn't use it now. Her training had taught her to rely on her powers of observation first, her equipment second.

A building the size of the sprawling Center wasn't easily secured. Hannah found herself giving Reeve MacGee a nod of respect as she walked through. Heat sensors as well as hidden cameras. But the sensors were activated only when the Center was closed.

Security passes were required at the door for members of the cast and crew. On the night of a performance, however, entrance could be gained for the price of a ticket. Deboque would step from behind bars in a day's time.

As she walked, leaving one corridor for the next, Hannah drew a blueprint in her mind. She'd studied the layout of the Center on paper before, but preferred to walk in it, to focus on it, to touch the walls and floor.

Too many blind corners, she thought. Too many small rooms used for storage. Too many places to hide. Even with Reeve's expertise, the building could be vulnerable with the right plan of attack. But then, Hannah believed any building could be.

She turned into Wardrobe, pretending a casual interest in the costumes. Did the guard at the door know everyone by sight? How easy would it be to replace one of the technicians? A photo was affixed to the pass, but makeup and hairpieces could take care of that. How often had she, or another like her, gained access to a place by faked credentials or a clever disguise?

Once inside, a man could disappear easily. If a man on the security panel could be bribed or replaced, so much the better.

Yes, she'd put that scenario in her report and let her superiors chew on it awhile. She'd add to that the fact that no one had checked her bag. A small plastic explosive could be easily carried and easily planted.

She walked from Wardrobe into a rehearsal hall walled with mirrors. With a little shock, she stared at her reflection on all sides. Then, as she had in the garden, she let out a low, easy laugh.

Oh, Hannah, she thought, how miserably dull you are. Turning to the side, she shook her head. No, maroon did nothing for her, and the high-necked jacket with its bulky belt only made her look unattractively thin. The skirt came well below the knee to hide her legs. She'd braided her hair today, tightly, then had circled the braid at the base of her neck.

Being a part of herself, it was the best cover she could have conceived. She'd been too skinny as a child, with unmanageable hair, and knees that were forever scraped. Her facial bones had been prominent even then, but in the young girl's face had seemed too sharp, too angular.

Then when the other girls had begun to bloom and curve, Hannah's body had remained stubbornly straight. She'd been bright and athletic and cheerful. Boys had patted her on the back and called her a good sport, but they hadn't been interested in taking her to any dances.

She'd learned to ride, swim, shoot skeet and to put an arrow in a bull's-eye from a hundred paces, but she hadn't dated.

She'd learned to speak Russian and French and enough Cantonese to surprise even her father, but she'd gone alone to her own graduation ball.

When she turned twenty, her body changed, but Hannah hid the late blossoming under dull clothes. She'd already chosen her path in life. Beauty turned heads and in her field it was always best to go unnoticed.

Now, she looked at the results in the wall of mirrors and was satisfied. No man would desire her. It was human nature to look at the physical shell and draw emotion from that long before you dipped beneath to the intellect or soul. No woman would envy her. Dull was safe, after all.

No one would suspect a plain, bookish woman of excellent breeding and quiet social manners of deception or violence. Only a select few were aware that the woman beneath was capable of both.

For a reason she couldn't name, that thought made her turn away from her reflection. Deception had been with her all of her adult life, and yet she couldn't quite dismiss the twinges of guilt she felt whenever Eve looked at her as a friend.

It was a job, Hannah reminded herself. No emotional attachments, no emotional involvements were permitted. That was the first and most important rule of the game. She couldn't afford to allow herself to like Eve, to even think of her as anything but a political symbol. If she did, everything she'd worked for could be lost.

The envy had to go as well, Hannah reminded herself. It was a dangerous lapse to let herself look at the love between the prince and Eve and wish something similar for herself. There was no room for love in her profession. There were only goals, commitments and risks.

There would be no prince for her, royal or otherwise.

But before she could prevent it, her thoughts turned to Bennett and the way he'd smiled at her in the moonlight.

Idiot, she told herself and began tightening a few loose pins. He was the last person she should think about in a personal way. If for no other reason, there was his dossier and the astonishing list of women who'd been part of his life already.

Use him, certainly, her mind went on. But don't think about him as anything but a means to an end. Romantic fantasies had ended for her at sixteen. Ten years later, in the middle of her most important job, was hardly the time to begin to weave them again. She would do well to re-member that the stiff-lipped, proper Lady Hannah would never see His Royal Highness Prince Bennett de Cordina in a romantic light.

But the woman within dreamed and for a moment strained against the confines she'd built herself.

Hannah turned to look back at the mirrors when she heard the footsteps.

Immediately alert, she cast her eyes down and walked from the room.

"Ah, there you are."

At Bennett's voice, Hannah gave an inward curse, but curtsied. "Your Highness."

"Taking the grand tour?" He walked closer, wondering why she looked as plain as a maiden aunt and continued to intrigue him.

"Yes, sir. I hope it's all right."

"Of course." He took her hand, willing her to look directly at him. There was something about her eyes.... Or perhaps it was her voice, that cool, always composed British tone. "I had some business in town. Alexander suggested I swing by when I'd finished to see if you were ready to go back."

"That's very kind of you." And oh, how she would have preferred a silent, anonymous driver who'd have given her the opportunity to assimilate her report on the drive back.

"I was here." He felt the restlessness layer over him as she drew her hand back to her side. "If you'd like to see more, I'd be happy to take you around the rest of the Center."

Hannah weighed the pros and cons in a matter of seconds. Another quick look might add something, but she'd already gone through the main theater twice, once with Eve and once alone. It might begin to look odd if she went through again with Bennett.

"No, thank you. It is a fascinating place. I've never seen a theater from this side."

"Eve's territory. I confess I prefer front row center myself." He took Hannah's arm and began to lead her down the hall. "If you hang around her for any length of time, she finds something for you to do. With me, it's usually moving boxes. Heavy boxes.''

With a laugh, Hannah slanted him a look. "That's one of the best uses a woman can find for a man."

"I can see why Eve took to you." He'd come simply to do his sister-in-law a favor, but now found himself glad. Outward appearance aside, Lady Hannah was anything but dull. For perhaps the first time in his life, Bennett was beginning to look beneath the physical. "Have you seen much of Cordina yet, Hannah?"

She noticed he'd dropped her title, but decided to let it pass. "Only snatches so far, sir. Once I'm a bit more familiar with Eve's routine, I plan to explore a bit. I've heard your museum has some excellent exhibits. The building itself is reported to be a fine example of post-Renaissance architecture.''

He wasn't interested in exhibits, but in her. "Do you like the water?"

"Of course. Sea air is very beneficial for the constitution.''

With a half laugh, Bennett paused at the top of the stairs. "But do you like it?"

He had a strange talent for looking at a woman as though he were seeing her for the first time. And looking as though it mattered. Despite her training, Hannah felt her pulse rate accelerate. "Yes. My grandmother has a place near Cornwall. I spent several summers there as a girl."

He wondered what she would look like with her hair down and the sea wind teasing it. Would she laugh as he had heard her laugh in the garden? Would he see that light flash in her eyes again? Then he realized it didn't matter how she looked. He went on impulse, knowing he might regret it.

"I have to go into Le Havre in a couple of days. The drive runs along the coast. Come with me."

If he'd asked her to step into the storage room and neck, she would have been no less surprised. Surprise turned quickly to caution and caution to calculation. But beneath it all was the simple pleasure that he wanted her company. It was the pleasure that worried her.

"It's kind of you to ask, Your Highness, but Eve may have plans."

"Then we'll check with her first." He wanted her to go. He found himself already looking forward to spending a few hours with her away from the palace. Perhaps it was for the challenge of it, the challenge of picking away at that prim, proper exterior and finding what, if anything, lay beneath. Whatever the reason was, Bennett didn't question it. "Would you like to go?"

"Yes, I would." Hannah told herself it was because it would give her the opportunity to study him more closely, for professional reasons. She told herself it would give her the chance to see how well security worked away from the palace and the capital. But the truth was as simple as her answer. She wanted to go.

"Fine, then we'll fix it, and you can stand through the long and wordy welcoming ceremony with me."

"Hate to be bored alone, do you?"

Laughing, Bennett took her hand again. "Yes, I can see exactly why Eve brought you to us." Her hand was an inch from his lips when the murmur of voices came from below. Glancing down, more than a little annoyed, Bennett spotted Chantel.

"The anger has to show," she was insisting, walking

so quickly the director had to lengthen his stride to keep
up. "Julia is not a passive woman. She doesn't hide what
she feels no matter what the consequences. Dammit, Mau-
rice, I'll make it subtle. I know my job."

"Of course you do, *chérie*, that I don't question. It is
simply that—"

"Mademoiselle." From the top of the stairs, Bennett
looked down. Hannah had a firsthand glimpse of how he
smiled at a truly beautiful woman. Without thinking, she
drew her hand from his and linked her fingers together.

Chantel, reaching one hand up to draw back her pale
blond hair, tilted her head back. Even so dispassionate an
observer such as Hannah had to concede that few women
could claim such a combination of glamour, beauty and
sexuality. Her lips curved. Her eyes, a deep, dreamy shade
of blue, smiled with them.

"Your Highness," Chantel said in her rich, smoky
voice as she dipped into a formal curtsy. She started up
the stairs and Bennett started down. In the middle, they
stopped, then Chantel reached up to touch his face before
bringing him closer for a lengthy kiss. Above them, Hannah felt her teeth snap together. "It's been a long time."

"Too long." Bennett cupped her hand in both of his.
"You're lovelier than ever. It's astonishing."

"It's genes," Chantel claimed, and grinned at him.
"My God, Bennett, what a beautiful man you are. If I
wasn't a cynic, I'd propose."

"If I wasn't terrified of you, I'd accept." They em-
braced again with the ease of old friends. "Chantel, it's
good to see you again. Eve was turning handsprings when
you agreed to take the part."

"It's a good play." Chantel gave a matter-of-fact
shrug. "Even though I adore you, I wouldn't have come

all this way to take a role in a bomb. Your sister-in-law's a talented woman.'' Chantel cast a look over her shoulder at the director waiting respectfully at the bottom of the stairs. ''You might mention to her that I'm fighting to preserve the integrity of her Julia.'' As she turned back, she spotted Hannah standing on the landing. ''Friend of yours?''

Glancing back, Bennett held out a hand. ''Hannah, come meet the incomparable Chantel.''

The stiffness in her movement only suited her character, Hannah told herself as she started down. All unremarkable women tensed up when slapped in the face with great beauty. She stopped on the step beside Bennett, but kept nearly a foot of space between them.

''Lady Hannah Rothchild, Chantel O'Hurley.''

''How do you do?'' Formal and proper, Hannah held out a hand. Chantel kept her face passive as she accepted it.

''I do fine, thank you.'' As a woman, as an actress who understood angles and role-playing, she wondered why someone with such good bone structure and a flawless complexion would deliberately make themselves appear plain.

''Lady Hannah is keeping Eve company for a few months.''

''How nice. Cordina's a beautiful country. I'm sure you'll enjoy it.''

''Yes, I already am. I also enjoyed watching you rehearse.''

''Thanks, but we have a way to go.'' Chantel tapped a finger on the banister and wondered why she felt such instant distrust. Dismissing it as overwork, she turned back to Bennett. "I have to run. Try to make some time for me, darling."

"Of course. You're coming to dinner Saturday with the rest of the cast?"

"Wouldn't miss it. I'll see you there, Lady Hannah."

"Goodbye, Miss O'Hurley."

After giving Bennett a quick pat on the cheek, Chantel descended the stairs again and let the director trail behind her.

"She's quite a woman," Bennett murmured.

"Yes, she's very beautiful."

"There's that, too." Without looking at her, Bennett took Hannah's arm again. "I suppose I've always admired her willpower and ambition. She's determined to be the best and isn't afraid to work for it. Every time I see her on the screen, it's breathtaking."

Hannah dug her fingers into her purse and reminded herself she was supposed to be unassuming. "You admire ambition, Your Highness?"

"Nothing's changed for better or worse without it."

"Some men still find ambition in a woman unflattering, or at least, uncomfortable."

"Some men are idiots."

"I couldn't agree more," Hannah said dryly, dryly enough that he lifted his brow as he gazed at her.

"Why am I never quite sure whether or not you're insulting me, Hannah?"

"I beg your pardon, sir, I was simply agreeing with you."

He stopped again. From the stage came the murmur of voices, but the hall was deserted. Bennett took her chin in his hand, ignoring her jolt of shock, and studied her face. "Hannah, why is it when I look at you I'm not convinced I'm seeing all there is?"

Alarm bells went off in her head. Her face paled a bit. She knew it, but thought, hoped, he would take that as natural. Not by another blink did she show concern. "I don't know what you mean."

"I wonder." He moved his thumb over her jawline, then just beneath where the skin was softer yet, and warm. "Yes, I wonder more than I should about you, Hannah. Do you have an answer for that?"

There were amber flecks in his eyes, turning what might have been plain brown into something tawny and compelling. He had the mouth of a poet and the hands of a farmer. Hannah wondered how it was possible to combine the two as her heart, always so steady, began to drum against her ribs.

"Your Highness—" It was both the lady without and the lady within who fumbled.

"Do you, Hannah?"

He saw her lips part. Strange, he hadn't noticed how attractive her mouth was before—soft, just a bit wide and beautifully shaped without cosmetics. He wondered if it would taste as cool as her voice or as rich as her eyes.

She had to stop this, here and now. The yearning building inside her could only be destructive. Even as she longed to reach out, she cast her eyes down. "No, sir, except that many times men are intrigued with a woman simply because she's not what they're accustomed to."

"We'll see." He backed off, though the effort it cost him was a surprise. "I'll take you back now, Hannah, and we'll both give it some thought."

Chapter 3

Hannah was given free run of the palace and the grounds. She had only to ask and her bath would be drawn or her bed turned down. If she developed a craving for hot chocolate at three a.m., she could pick up the phone beside her bed and request it. As a guest of the Royal Family, she was afforded every amenity the palace could offer.

And as a guest of the Royal Family, she was afforded her own guards.

Hannah considered them only a slight nuisance. It was a simple enough matter for someone of her talents to make them think she was tucked safely away in her rooms while she was somewhere else entirely. However, the fact that she was being watched made it difficult to set up a meeting with her contact on the outside.

Using the palace phones was out of the question. Too many extensions made it a risk that even a casual, coded conversation could be overheard. She'd briefly considered smuggling in a transmitter, then had rejected the notion. Transmissions could be traced. She hadn't spent two years of her life to get to this point to see it all wiped away because of some electronic foul-up. In any case, she preferred meetings of such importance to be face-to-face.

Two days after she arrived in Cordina, she mailed a letter. It was addressed to an old family friend in Sussex who didn't exist. Its destination was one of Deboque's many branches throughout Europe. If for any reason the letter was intercepted and opened, the reader would find nothing more interesting than a chatty note describing Cordina and the weather.

Once the letter reached its destination and was decoded, it would read differently. Hannah had given her name, her rank in the organization and had requested a meeting, detailing the time, date and place. The information would be fed back to the Cordina contact. All she had to do was get there, alone.

One week, Hannah thought once the letter was on its way. In one week she would well and truly begin what had been started so long ago. She had plenty to do to keep her busy in the meantime.

Princess Gabriella and her family were visiting the palace that evening. The staff had been in an uproar for the better part of the day, more, Hannah guessed, because the children were descending than for any other reason. Hannah had heard that the priceless collection of Fabergé eggs was to be put out of reach.

She spent the day quietly enough, visiting Eve and Marissa in the nursery, lunching with several members of the Historical Society, and in the lull of late afternoon, exploring the cellars for vulnerabilities.

Now, she clipped on her pearls and prepared to join the family in the main drawing room. It would be interesting to see them all together, she thought. In that way she could judge the interactions as well as the individuals. Before too much time had passed, she had to know them all as well as she knew herself. One mistake, one bad judgment call, and all could be lost.

"Come back here, you little demon!"

Hannah heard a loud laugh, a thud, then rushing feet. Before she had a chance to open the door to see for herself, it burst open. Barreling through it was a small boy with a thatch of dark hair that may or may not have been combed in the last week. He gave her an amazing grin, showing more than one gap before he scooted under her bed.

"Cachez-moi, s'il vous plaît!" His voice was muffled by the skirt of the spread before he disappeared.

Hannah opened her mouth again only to see Bennett filling the doorway.

"Did you see a small, miserably mannered boy?"

"I, ah—no," she decided on the spot and folded her hands. "I did think I heard someone go running past. What are you—"

"Thanks. If you see him, lock him in a closet or something." He started off down the hall. "Dorian, you nasty little thief, you can't hide forever."

Hannah walked to the door and looked out to see Bennett turning the corner before she closed it. Moving back to the bed, she crouched down and lifted the skirt. "I think it's safe now," Hannah told him in French.

The dark hair poked out first, then a sturdy little body dressed in short pants and a white linen shirt that were streaked with dirt. If Hannah hadn't already seen his picture, she would have taken him for one of the servants' offspring. But he was royal.

"You are English. I speak excellent English."

"So you do."

"Thank you for hiding me from my uncle." Young Prince Dorian bowed. Though he wasn't yet five, he executed it perfectly. "He was angry, but he doesn't stay that way long. I'm Prince Dorian."

"Your Highness." Hannah curtsied. "It's a pleasure to meet you. I'm Lady Hannah Rothchild." Then unable to resist, she bent down to his level. "What did you steal?"

Dorian glanced at the closed door, back at Hannah, then grinned. Digging into his back pocket he pulled out a yo-yo. It might once have been blue, but now it was the gray of old wood with a few chips of brighter paint still holding. Hannah studied it with appropriate respect.

"This is Bennett's—His Highness's?" Hannah corrected.

"*Merveilleux, n'est-ce pas?* He's had it since he was five." Dorian turned the toy over in his hand, marveling that it had once been new and shiny when his uncle had been just the age he was now. "He gets angry when I go into his room and play with it, but how else am I going to be able to make it work?"

"Good point." Hannah barely resisted the urge to ruffle the royal head of hair. "And one would doubt he plays with it himself very often."

"He keeps it on a shelf. It isn't that he really minds me looking at it," Dorian explained, loyal to the core. "It's just that when I try to make it work, the string gets all tangled and knotted up."

"It takes a little practice."

"I know." He grinned again. "And I can only practice if I steal it."

"Your logic is flawless, Your Highness. May I see?"

Dorian hesitated only a moment, then graciously handed it over. "Girls usually aren't interested in such things." He made a grimace of masculine disgust. "My sisters play with dolls."

"Everyone has different tastes, I suppose." Hannah slid her finger into the loop, wondering how long it had been since Bennett's had fit there. The string wasn't as old as the toy itself. By her guess, it would have been replaced more than a dozen times over the years. On impulse, she let the yo-yo slide down, dangle, then brought it neatly up.

"Oh, nicely done." Charmed, Dorian watched her with wide eyes.

"Thank you, sir. I used to have one of my own. It was red," she remembered with a half smile. "Until my dog chewed it up."

"Can you do any tricks? I tried Round the World once and broke a lamp. Uncle Bennett scolded me, but then he tossed out the pieces himself so no one would know."

Because she could picture it so well, Hannah smiled. A loud roar, but little bite, she decided and wished she didn't like him the better for it. "A trick?" As she considered she took the yo-yo up and down. Then, with a quick flick of her wrist took it Round the World. When it snapped back in her palm, Dorian laughed and climbed on her bed.

"Do another, please."

Calling on memory, Hannah Walked the Dog and had the young prince bouncing on the bed and calling out for more.

"Well done, Lady Hannah," Bennett said from the doorway. "Obviously you have hidden talents."

Hannah had to bite off an oath as she brought the yo-yo back. "Your Highness." Toy in hand, she curtsied. "I didn't hear you knock."

"I didn't." Bennett pushed away from the doorjamb he was leaning on to walk to the bed. Unrepentant, his nephew grinned up at him.

"Isn't she wonderful, Uncle Bennett?"

"We'll discuss the Lady Hannah's attributes later." He gave Dorian's ear a twist before turning around. "My property, if you will."

Fighting to keep a straight face, Hannah handed it to him.

"This might seem to be nothing more than a simple child's toy," Bennett began as he slipped it into his pocket. "But in fact, it's an heirloom."

"I see." She cleared her throat on the laugh, but it escaped anyway. Hoping she looked contrite, she stared at the floor. "I beg your pardon, sir."

"The hell you do. And he was in here all along wasn't he?" Bennett pushed his nephew flat on the bed and sent him into a fit of giggles. "You let me go running off all over the palace looking for this petty thief when all the time he was hiding behind your skirts."

"The bed skirts to be honest, sir." She had to clear her throat again, but managed to speak calmly. "When you rushed by with so vague a description, I had no idea you were looking for Prince Dorian."

"I admire a good liar," Bennett murmured as he moved closer. For the second time he caught her chin in his hand. But for the first time, she saw all of the arrogance he was capable of and felt all of its attraction. "And I grow only more intrigued."

"Lady Hannah can do a double Round the World."

"Fascinating." Bennett slid his hand away slowly as he turned back to his nephew. If he'd listened for it, he might have heard Hannah's slow sigh of relief. "I thought we had an agreement, Dorian."

Dorian's head drooped, but Hannah didn't notice that the light in his eyes dimmed in the least. "I only wanted to see it. I'm sorry, Uncle Bennett."

"Sure you are." Bennett hauled him up by the armpits, scowled, then kissed him soundly. "Your mother's downstairs. Don't slide in the halls on the way to the drawing room."

"All right." On his feet again, Dorian bowed to Hannah. "It was a pleasure meeting you, Lady Hannah."

"And you, sir."

He sent her a gap-toothed grin before he dashed off.

"Sweet talker," Bennett muttered. "Oh, you might think he's all charm, but he has a black heart."

"Strangely enough I was reminded of you."

With one brow lifted, Bennett rocked back on his heels. "Indeed, my lady, that is strange."

"He's a scoundrel, without question. And you love him."

"That's beside the point." Bennett stuck his hand in his pocket. "As to the matter of the yo-yo."

"Yes, sir?"

"Try to wait until I'm five feet away before you laugh in my face."

"As you wish, Your Highness."

"It was a gift from my mother when I was ill one summer. I've bought the little devil a dozen of them, but he keeps stealing mine. He knows if I don't get a son of my own by the time he's ten I'll make him a gift of it.''

''I have a redheaded doll my mother gave me when I broke my wrist in a fall. I kept it when I outgrew all the others.''

It wasn't until he'd taken her hand that she realized she'd told him something he didn't need to know, something she'd never told anyone else. Even as she warned herself such lapses were dangerous, his lips brushed her fingers.

''You, Lady Hannah, have a kind heart as well as a clever tongue. Come, walk downstairs with me and meet the rest of my family.''

Reeve MacGee would be a formidable obstacle. Hannah had thought so before, but seeing him with his family, she was sure of it. She knew his background from the time he'd entered the police force as a rookie through his less publicized work for the United States government.

His involvement with Cordina and the Royal Family had the ring of romance, but Reeve was no poet. He'd come out of a self-imposed retirement at Prince Armand's request when Gabriella had been kidnapped. Though she'd escaped, her time in captivity had left its mark. Amnesia had plagued her and Reeve had been enlisted to protect her, and to investigate.

There had been no doubt that Deboque had been pushing the buttons, but though his lover had been captured and imprisoned, she'd never implicated him. Like other powerful men, Deboque inspired loyalty. Or fear.

During the time that Gabriella was struggling to regain her memory, she and Reeve had fallen in love. Although Reeve had refused to accept a title when they married, he'd agreed to head security in Cordina. Even with Reeve's experience and skill, the palace had been infiltrated once again.

Two years ago, Alexander had nearly been assassinated. Since that time, Reeve had managed to block any and all attempts on members of the Royal Family. But Deboque was about to walk out of prison. With freedom would come more power.

Hannah watched Reeve now, seeing a quiet, introspective man who plainly adored his wife and children. He would use everything available to protect them from harm. So much the better.

With her hands folded and her skirts smoothed, Hannah sat and listened.

"We all know your play's going to be a wonderful success." Gabriella, with her hand caught loosely in Reeve's, smiled at Eve. Her rich red hair was styled with casual chic around a face that remained delicate and lovely. "That doesn't mean we don't understand you have to worry about it."

"I'm at the point now where I wish it was over." Eve drew Marissa into her lap.

"But you're feeling well?"

"I'm feeling fine." Eve let Marissa climb down again. "Between Alex's pampering and Hannah's eagle eye, I can hardly lift a finger without a doctor's certificate."

"It's so good of you to come." Gabriella smiled at Hannah before she sipped some sparkling water. "I know firsthand how comforting it is to have a friend nearby. Are we keeping you happy enough so that you're not homesick?"

"I'm very happy in Cordina." Hannah kept her back straight against the sofa.

"I hope you'll come out to the farm while you're here."

"I've heard a great deal about it." Gabriella had been kidnapped there while it had still been an overgrown plot of land. "I'd love to see it for myself."

"Then we'll arrange it." Reeve spoke quietly as he lit a cigarette. "You're enjoying your visit so far?"

"Yes, I am." Their eyes met and held. "Cordina is a fascinating country. It has a fairy-tale aura perhaps, but it's very real. I'm particularly interested in visiting the museum."

"I think you'll find we have some very unusual exhibits," Armand put in.

"Yes, sir. I did some research before leaving England. I have no doubt that my time in Cordina will be an education."

Marissa toddled over, still a bit unsteady on her year-old legs, and held her arms up. Hannah placed the child in her lap.

"Your father is well?" Reeve asked her through a haze of smoke.

Hannah jangled her pearls to entertain the baby. "Yes, thank you. It often seems that the older I get, the younger he gets."

"Families, no matter how large or how small, are often the focus of our lives," Reeve said quietly.

"Yes, that's true," Hannah murmured as she played with the baby. "It's a pity that families, and life, aren't as simple as they seem when we're children."

Bennett sat relaxed in his chair and wondered why he thought if he could read between the lines, he'd discover a great deal more than small talk.

"I wasn't aware you knew Hannah's father, Reeve."

"Only casually." When he leaned back, his smile was easy. "I heard that Dorian stole your yo-yo again."

"I should have locked it in the safe when I heard he was coming." Bennett patted the slight bulge in his pocket. "I'd have given the little devil a run for his money, but he had an accomplice." He turned his head to look at Hannah.

"I'll have to apologize for my son," Gabriella's lips curved as she lifted her glass again. "For drawing you into his crime, Lady Hannah."

"On the contrary, I enjoyed it. Prince Dorian is charming."

"We call him other things at home," Reeve murmured. The woman was a mystery, he thought. The harder he looked for chinks, the fewer flaws he saw. "With that in mind, I think I'll go out and look for the bunch of them. Adrienne's at the age where you can't be sure she'll mind them or urge them to wade in the fountain."

Bennett glanced toward the terrace doors. "God knows what havoc they might have wrought in the last twenty minutes."

"Wait until you have your own." Eve rose to take Marissa from Hannah. "You'll spoil them rotten. If you'll excuse me, I want to go up and feed Marissa."

"I'll go with you." Gabriella set her glass aside. "I thought we might talk over the plans for the Christmas Ball. You know I want to help as much as I can."

"Thank God I don't have to beg. No, Hannah, please, sit and relax," Eve continued as Hannah started to stand. "We won't be long."

"See that you're not." Bennett took out the yo-yo to pass it from hand to hand. "Dinner's in an hour."

"We all know your priorities, Ben." Eve bent to kiss his cheek before she left the room.

"I could use a walk myself." Rising, Alexander nodded to Reeve. "I'll help you round up the children." They were barely out the terrace doors when a servant appeared in the doorway.

"I beg your pardon, Your Highness. A call from Paris."

"Yes, I've been expecting it. I'll take it in my office, Louis. If you'll excuse me, Lady Hannah." Taking her hand, Armand bowed over it. "I'm sure Bennett can entertain you for a few moments. Bennett, perhaps Lady Hannah would enjoy seeing the library."

"If you like to look at walls of books," Bennett said when his father was gone, "you can't do much better."

"I'm very fond of books." Taking him at his word, Hannah rose.

"All right then." Though he could have thought of a dozen better ways to while away an hour, he took her arm and led her through the corridors.

"It's difficult to believe that the museum could have finer paintings than you have here in the palace, Prince Bennett."

"Le Musée d'Art has a hundred and fifty-two examples of Impressionist and Postimpressionist paintings, including two Corots, three Monets and a particularly fine Renoir. We've recently acquired a Childe Hassam from the United States. In return my family has donated six Georges Complainiers, a Cordinian artist who painted on the island in the nineteenth century."

"I see."

Noting her expression, Bennett laughed. "As it happens, I'm on the board of the museum. I may prefer horses, Hannah, but that doesn't preclude an affection for art. What do you think of this?''

He paused in front of a small watercolor. The Royal Palace was beautifully, almost mystically painted. Its white, white walls and turrets rose behind a pink mist that enchanted rather than concealed the building itself. It must have been dawn, she thought. The sky was such a delicate blue in contrast to the deeper sea. She could see the antiquity, the fantasy and the reality. In the foreground were the high iron gates and sturdy stone walls that protected the palace grounds.

"It's beautiful. It shows love as well as a touch of wonder. Who was the artist?''

"My great-great-grandmother.'' Pleased with her reaction, Bennett drew her hand into the crook of his arm. "She'd done hundreds of watercolors and had tucked them away. In her day, women painted or drew as a hobby, not as a profession.''

"Some things change,'' Hannah murmured, then looked back at the painting. "Some things don't.''

"A few years ago I found her work in a trunk in one of the attics. So many of them had been damaged. It broke my heart. Then I found this.'' He touched the frame, reverently, Hannah thought. She looked from his hand to his face and found herself caught up in him. "It was like stepping back in time, generations, and discovering yourself. It could have been painted today, and it would look the same.''

She could feel her heart moving toward him. What woman was immune to pride and sensitivity? In defense, she took a small step back. "In Europe, we understand that a few generations are only a blink in time. Our history stands before us, centuries of it. It becomes our responsibility to give that same gift to each new generation.''

Bennett looked at her and found her eyes almost impossibly deep. ''We do have that in common, don't we? In America, there's an urgency that can be exciting, even contagious, but here, we know how long it takes to build and secure. Politics change, governments shift, but history stands firm.''

She had to turn away from him. It would only cloud the issue if she thought of him as a caring, sensitive man rather than an assignment. ''Are there any others?'' she said with a nod toward the painting.

''Only a handful, unfortunately. Most were beyond repair.'' For reasons he could only be half-sure of, he wanted to share with her things that mattered to him. ''There's one in the music room. The rest are in the museum. Here, have a look.'' With his hand guiding her again, he took her down the hall into the next wing, their footsteps echoing off the mosaic tile.

Leading her through an open door, Bennett took her into a room that seemed to have been fashioned to accent the white grand piano in its center.

There was a harp in the corner that might have been played a hundred years before, or last week. In a glass case were antique wind instruments and a fragile lyre. The flowers were fresh here, as they were in every room in the palace. Trailing blossoms of jasmine spilled out of glossy, Chinese red urns. A small marble fireplace was swept and scrubbed clean with a pile of fresh kindling stacked as though inviting the match.

With Bennett, she walked across an Aubusson carpet to look back in time. This painting was of a ball, festive in bright colors and bold strokes. Women, gloriously feminine in mid-nineteenth-century gowns, were whirled around a gleaming floor by dashing men. There were mirrors that reflected the dancers and doubled them while a trio of chandeliers glistened overhead. As Hannah studied it, she could almost hear the waltz.

"How lovely. Is this room here, in the palace?"

"Yes. It has hardly changed. We'll have the Christmas Ball there next month."

Only a month, she thought. There was so much to be done. In a matter of hours Deboque would be out of prison, and she would soon learn if her groundwork had been clever enough.

"This is a beautiful room." Hannah turned. Keep your conversation light, she warned herself. Keep your mind light, for now. "In our country house there's a small music room. Nothing like this, of course, but I've always found it so relaxing." She wandered to the piano, not so much to examine it as to give herself distance. "Do you play, Your Highness?"

"Hannah, we're alone. It isn't necessary to be so formal."

"I've always considered the use of titles as proper rather than formal." She didn't want this, she thought quickly. She didn't want him to close that gap of rank between them.

"I've always considered it annoying between friends." He walked behind her to touch her lightly on the shoulder. "I thought we were."

She could feel his hand right through the neat linen of her dress, through the skinny silk strap beneath and onto her flesh. Fighting her own private war, she kept her back to him. "Were what, sir?"

He laughed, then both hands were on her shoulders,

turning her to face him. "Friends, Hannah. I find you good company. That's one of the first requirements of friendship, isn't it?"

She was looking up at him, solemn-eyed, with the faintest blush of color along her cheekbones. Her shoulders seemed so strong under his hands, yet he remembered how soft, how delicate the skin along her jawline had seemed.

Her dress was brown and dull, her face unpainted and unframed. Not a hair was out of place and yet he got a flash of her laughing, her hair unbound and her shoulders bare. And the laughter would be for only him.

"What the devil is it about you?" Bennett muttered.

"I beg your pardon—"

"Wait." Impatient, as annoyed with himself as he was with her, Bennett stepped closer. As she stiffened, he held his hands up, palms out as if to reassure her he meant her no harm. "Just be still a moment, would you?" he asked as he lowered his head and touched his mouth to hers.

No response, show no response. Hannah repeated it over and over in her head like a litany. He didn't press, he didn't coax or demand. He simply tasted, more gently than she'd had known a man could be. And the flavor of him seeped into her until she was all but drunk with it.

His eyes remained open, watching hers. He was close, so close she could catch the scent of soap on his skin. Something that brought images of the sea. Hannah dug her fingers into her palms and fought to keep from showing him the turmoil within.

God, she wanted. How she wanted.

He didn't know what he'd expected. What he found was softness, comfort, sweetness without heat or passion. Yet he saw both in her eyes. He felt no driving need to touch her or to deepen the kiss. Not this first one. Perhaps he already knew there would be others. But this first one showed him an ease, a relaxation that he'd never looked for in a woman before.

He was man enough, experienced enough, to know there was a volcano inside of her. But strangely, he had no desire to push it to the eruption point, yet.

Bennett broke the kiss simply by stepping back. Hannah didn't move a muscle.

"I didn't do that to frighten you." He spoke quietly, for it was the truth. "It was just a test."

"You don't frighten me." He didn't frighten the woman he could see, but the one within was terrified.

It wasn't quite the answer he'd wanted. "Then what do I do to you?"

Slowly, carefully, she unballed her hands. "I'm afraid I don't understand what you mean, Your Highness."

He studied her another moment, then spun away. "Maybe not." He rubbed a hand along the back of his neck wondering why such an unassuming, placid woman should make him so tense. He understood desire. God knows he'd felt it before. But not like this. Never quite like this.

"Dammit, Hannah, isn't anything going on inside of you?"

"Of course, sir, a great number of things."

He had to laugh. He should have known she would put him in his place with logic. "Call me by my name, please."

"As you wish."

He turned back. She was standing in front of the glistening white piano, hands folded, eyes calm and quiet on his. He thought it the most ridiculous thing, but knew he was very close to falling in love. "Hannah—"

He'd taken no more than two steps toward her when Reeve walked into the room. "Bennett, excuse me, but your father would like to see you before dinner."

Duty and desire. Bennett wondered if he would ever find a full merging of the two. "Thank you, Reeve."

"I'll take Lady Hannah back in."

"All right." Still, he paused and looked at her again. "I'd like to talk with you later."

"Of course." She would move heaven and earth to avoid it.

She remained where she was when he left. Reeve glanced over his shoulder before he came closer. "Is there a problem, Lady Hannah?"

"No." She drew a deep breath, but didn't relax. "Why should there be?"

"Bennett can be…distracting."

This time when her eyes met his, she made certain they were slightly amused. A layer, the thinnest of the layers of her outer covering was dismissed. "I'm not easily distracted, particularly when I'm working."

"So I've been told," Reeve said easily enough. He was still looking for flaws and was afraid he might have found the first in the way she had looked at Bennett. "But you've never worked on an assignment quite like this one."

"As a senior agent for the ISS, I'm capable of handling any assignment." Her voice was brisk again, not the voice of a woman who'd been moved, almost unbearably, by a kiss. "You'll have my report by tomorrow. Now I think we'd better join the others."

She started by, but he took her arm and stopped her. "There's a great deal riding on this. On you."

Hannah only nodded. "I'm aware of that. You requested the best, and I am."

"Maybe." But the closer it came, the more he worried. "You've got a hell of a reputation, Hannah, but you've never come up against anyone like Deboque before."

"Nor he anyone like me." She glanced toward the hallway again, then lowered her voice. "I'm an established member of his organization now. It's taken me two years to get this close. I saved him two and a half million by seeing that that munitions deal wasn't botched six months ago. A man like Deboque appreciates initiative. In the last few months, I've been planting the seeds that will discredit his second in command."

"Or get your throat cut."

"That's for me to worry about. In a matter of weeks, I'll be his right hand. Then I'll serve him to you on a platter."

"Confidence is an excellent weapon, if it isn't overdone."

"I don't overdo." She thought of Bennett and strengthened her resolve. "I've never failed with an assignment, Reeve. I don't intend to begin with this one."

"Just make sure you keep in contact. I'm sure you'll understand when I say I don't trust anyone."

"I understand perfectly, because neither do I. Shall we go?"

Chapter 4

Hannah's plans to avoid driving with Bennett to Le Havre were neatly demolished. She'd justified her decision by convincing herself she could detail more useful information by concentrating on the palace. In order to remain behind, she'd come up with the credible, if unoriginal excuse of a headache.

Hannah had deliberately waited until Alexander had finished breakfasting with his family so that she could speak to Eve alone. It took Eve less than ten minutes to turn it on her.

"It's no wonder you're not feeling yourself." Eve sipped tea in the sunny nursery while she looked over her schedule. "I've kept you cooped up ever since you arrived."

"Don't be silly. The palace is the size of a small town. I've hardly been cooped up."

"However big it is, it still has walls. A nice drive along

the coast is just what you need. Bernadette.'' She glanced up at the young nurse who was preparing to take Marissa for her morning walk. ''Would you see that Princess Marissa has a hat? It's a bit breezy out.''

''Yes, ma'am.''

Eve held out her arms for her daughter. ''Have a nice time, darling.''

''Flowers,'' Marissa said, and laughed at her own voice.

''Yes, pick some flowers. We'll put them right here in your room.'' She kissed both of Marissa's cheeks then let her go. ''I hate not being able to take her for a walk this morning, but I have a meeting at the Center in an hour.''

''You're a wonderful mother, Eve,'' Hannah murmured when she saw the concern in Eve's eyes.

''I love her so much.'' With a long sigh, she picked up her tea again. ''I know it's foolish, but when I'm not with her I think of dozens of things that might happen, that could happen.''

''I'd say it was normal.''

''Maybe. Being who we are, what we are, just magnifies everything.'' Unconsciously, she rested her hand where even now her second child slept. ''I want so badly to give her a sense of normalcy, and yet...'' Eve shook her head. ''There's a price for everything.''

Hannah remembered Alexander saying almost the same thing in referring to his wife.

''Eve, Marissa is a lovely, healthy and happy child. I'm not sure they get any more normal than that.''

Eve stared at her a moment, then dropped her chin on her open palm. ''Oh, Hannah, I'm not sure how I got through the last two years without you. Which brings me right back to where we were.'' Briskly, Eve refilled Hannah's cup. ''You came here to visit and so far I haven't given you a moment's free time unless you were handcuffed to me. That makes me feel very selfish.''

''The reason I'm here is to be with you,'' Hannah reminded Eve, as she felt herself rapidly losing ground.

''The reason you're here is because we're friends. As a favor, take the day, relax, enjoy the sea air. I promise you Ben can be wonderful company. I guarantee that five minutes after you're in the car, your headache will disappear.''

''Someone have a headache?''. Ben asked as he strode in. He was wearing the white dress uniform with the red insignia that stated his rank as officer in the Cordinian Navy. On the left breast pocket was the royal seal that proclaimed him prince. Hannah had always considered the opinion that women fell for men in uniform nonsense. Until now.

He looked so…dashing, she admitted, though her practical side searched for a less dramatic word. The snowy-white jacket accented his tan and the dark contrast of his hair. He grinned at her, making Hannah aware that he understood his effect. Automatically she rose to dip into a curtsy.

''Bennett, I'd forgotten what a heartbreaker you are in dress whites.'' Eve tipped her face up for a kiss. ''Maybe I should tell Hannah to take an aspirin and stay behind after all.''

''I think Lady Hannah can take care of herself. Can't you, *chérie?*''

Hannah decided then and there that if she had to fence with him, she would wield her foil well. ''It's always been the case.''

"You are a bit pale." He touched a finger to her cheek. "Are you really not well?"

"It's nothing." She wondered if he could feel her blood stir at the casual contact. "And Eve assures me that a drive along the sea is exactly the right prescription."

"Good. I'll bring her back with roses in her cheeks."

"If you'll give me a moment, I need to get my bag."

"Bennett." Eve stopped him before he could follow Hannah out. "Am I wrong, or did I see something just now?"

He didn't pretend to misunderstand her. "I'm not sure."

"Hannah's lived a very sheltered life. I suppose I don't have to tell you to be…well, careful?"

Though the sunlight streamed in behind him, his eyes cooled. "No, I don't have to be reminded who a man in my position can and can't have an affair with."

"I didn't say that to annoy you." Instantly Eve was on her feet, taking his hands. "We were friends long before we were family, Ben. I only ask because I'm fond of her and I know how irresistible you can be."

He softened, as he always did with Eve. "You always managed to resist."

"You always treated me like a sister." Eve hesitated again, torn between two loyalties. "Would I be pushing if I said she's not your usual type?"

"No, she's not. Perhaps that's what baffles me. Stop worrying." He bent to kiss her brow. "I won't damage your proper British friend."

"It could be I'm just as concerned about you."

"Then don't be." Giving her cheek a careless stroke, he walked to the door. "Tell Marissa I'll bring her some seashells."

Calm and resigned to her decision, Hannah met him at the top of the stairs. "I hope I didn't keep you waiting."

"We've plenty of time. I can promise the drive will be worth the pomp and speeches on the other end."

"I don't object to pomp and speeches."

"Then we're fortunate. Claude." Bennett nodded to the tall, sturdy man who waited beside the main doors.

"Good morning, Your Highness. Lady Hannah. Your car is ready, sir."

"Thank you, Claude." Bennett steered Hannah through the doors knowing the simple statement meant that the road between Cordina and Le Havre had been secured.

Hannah saw the car the moment they stepped outside. The zippy little French convertible sat at the foot of the steps flanked by two solid sedans.

"Do you drive that?"

"Looks like I should wind it up, doesn't it?" Bennett touched the shiny red hood with affection. "Handles like a dream. I've had her up to one-twenty on a straight."

She thought of how it would feel, speeding beside the sea with the wind on her face. Hannah pushed aside such wishes and tried for an uneasy look. "I hope you don't intend to try to break your record today."

With a laugh, he opened the door for her himself. "For you, I'll drive like a grandfather."

Hannah slipped into the seat and nearly sighed with pleasure. "It is rather small."

"Big enough for two." Bennett rounded the hood. Claude already had his door opened.

"But surely you don't travel without your security or an assistant."

"Whenever possible. My secretary will be in the car behind us. Let's give them a run, shall we?" He switched on the ignition. From the rich sound under the hood, Hannah decided it was filled with engine. Before she could draw a breath, Bennett sent the car speeding down the long, sedate drive. He drove the way he rode a stallion. Full speed.

"They're muttering already, I imagine." He gave the guards at the gates an easy salute. "If Claude had his way, I'd never go over thirty kilometers. I'd also be closed up in a bulletproof limo wearing a suit of armor."

"It's his job to protect you."

"A pity he has so little humor about it." Bennett downshifted, then sent the car squeaking around a curve.

"Did your grandfather live a long and fruitful life?"

"What?"

"Your grandfather," Hannah repeated as she folded her hands neatly in her lap. "I wondered if he lived a long life. It seems unlikely if he drove like this."

The wind was blowing his hair around his face as he turned his head to grin at her. "Trust me, *ma belle*, I know the roads."

She didn't want him to slow down. It was the first time she'd felt true freedom in months. She'd nearly forgotten how sweet it tasted. The sea shimmered blue and white beside the road as they traveled down from the heights of the capital. Palms twisted their way toward the sky, bending and swaying in the stiff breeze. Lush red flowers burst out of bushes that grew helter-skelter along the roadside. The air smelled of sea and perpetual spring.

"Do you ski?" Bennett asked her as he noticed her watching a man glide over the water behind a low-slung boat.

"I never have." It looked wonderful. "I'm sure you have to be fairly athletic. I'm more at home in libraries."

"One can't read all the time."

She watched the skier take a somersaulting tumble into the water. "I think perhaps I can."

Bennett grinned and roared though a lazy S-turn. "Life's hardly worth the trouble without a few spills. Don't you ever have the urge for adventure, Hannah?"

She thought of the last ten years of her life, of the assignments that had taken her from castles to ghettos and everywhere in between. French alleys. Italian waterfronts. She thought of the small-caliber pistol she carried in her bag and the pencil-slim stiletto tucked like a lover against her thigh.

"I suppose I've always preferred my adventures vicariously, through books."

"No secret dreams?"

"Some of us are exactly what we seem." Suddenly uncomfortable, she shifted away from the topic. "I didn't realize you were a naval officer." Another lie, she thought. But her profession was built on them.

"I served a couple of years. At this point, it's more of an honorary rank. Second sons are traditionally bound for the military."

"So you chose the navy."

"Cordina's surrounded by the sea. Our fleet is smaller than yours, certainly, but it's strong."

"And these are uneasy times."

Something came and went in his eyes. "In Cordina we've learned that all times are uneasy times. We're a peaceful country, and because we want to remain so, we're prepared always for war."

She thought of the pretty white palace with its exotic gardens and fairy-tale turrets. Inaccessible by sea, with a cliff-top view that scanned miles with the naked eye. She sat back as the sea rolled by. Nothing ever was as simple as it seemed.

Le Havre was charming. Nestled at the base of a long hill, it clustered together with small white-washed buildings and clapboard cottages. Fishing and sail boats swayed quietly at neat docks at one curve of the harbor. Around the seawall of old stone, hardy blue flowers pushed their way through cracks. There were lobster traps and nets spread and drying in the sun. The scent of fish was heady and oddly pleasant in the early morning air.

At a glance, it could have been taken for any tidy fishing town that survived on and with the sea. But as they rounded the harbor the docks became more expansive, the buildings larger. Cargo ships with men hauling freight down gangplanks flanked an ocean liner. Like much of Cordina, Le Havre was more than it seemed. Through location and the skill of its people, it was one of the finest ports of call in the Mediterranean. It was also the center of Cordina's naval base.

Negotiating the narrow, winding streets, Bennett drove through a set of gates. He slowed only long enough to be acknowledged by the guards with snappy salutes. There were bungalows here painted a faded pink that reminded Hannah of the inside of a seashell. Palms and flowers grew in profusion, but she recognized the structure and order of a military facility. Moments later, Bennett drew up in front of a stucco building where seamen in whites stood at attention.

"For the next few hours," he murmured to Hannah, "we're official." Bennett reached in the back and picked up his hat. Even as he set it on his wind-ruffled hair, one of the seamen reached the door to open it for him. With the brim shading his eyes, Bennett returned the salutes.

He knew the sedan had already pulled up behind him, but didn't look back as he guided Hannah into the building.

"First, we have a few formalities," he warned her, tucking his hat under his arm.

The formalities were a group of officers, from admiral down, and their wives and attachés who were waiting to greet and be greeted by His Royal Highness.

Hannah acknowledged the introductions and pretended not to see the looks of speculation. *Not the prince's type.* She could read it easily in every eye that met hers. She fully agreed.

They were given tea and a tour of the building—for her sake. Hannah feigned an ignorance of the equipment shown her, asking the proper questions and looking properly polite at the simplistic answers. She could hardly mention that the radar and communication systems were as familiar to her as they were to the trained operators. In a pinch, she could have rigged the equipment to contact the ISS base outside London or Deboque's headquarters in Athens.

She walked by display cases, listening with apparent fascination as an admiral explained to her the difference between a destroyer and an aircraft carrier.

The pomp and circumstance continued as they were escorted outside to await the docking of the *Indépendance*. The band, their white uniforms blinding in the sun, struck up a rousing march as Bennett stepped onto the dock. Crowds of people cheered from behind the military barricade. Babies and small children were held up so that they could catch a glimpse of the prince.

Hannah counted off a dozen security people mingled with the crowd in addition to the two men who were never more than an arm's span from Bennett's elbow.

Deboque is out, she thought. Everything is a risk.

The battle-gray destroyer maneuvered into position while the crowd applauded and the band continued to play. Seamen on the dock stood at attention as did seamen on deck. After six months at sea, the *Indépendance* was home.

The gangplank came ponderously down. The pipes were sounded. The captain strode down to salute the officers and bow to his prince.

"Welcome home, Captain." Bennett offered his hand, and the crowd cheered again.

There was, as there always was on such occasions, a speech to be made. Hannah kept her face attentive while she slowly scanned the crowd.

It was no surprise to find him there. The small, slightly stoop-shouldered man was on the edge of the crowd holding a small Cordinian flag. In his plain work clothes and quiet face, he would never be noticed or remembered. He was one of Deboque's best.

There would be no move on Prince Bennett today, she thought, though the back of her neck itched. Her successful planting at the palace had been one of her highest contributions to Deboque's organization. The working order now was for care and cleverness rather than a rash assassination attempt.

In any case, she knew Deboque wasn't as interested in Bennett as he was in Alexander, and in Alexander not so much as in Armand. He wouldn't settle for the second in line to the throne after so long a wait.

Still, she closed her hand over the handle of her bag. She shifted, only a matter of inches, but Bennett's body was now more than half shielded by hers.

Had the man been sent with a message for her? Hannah

wondered. Or had he simply been ordered to stay close and watch? Instinct told her it was the second. Casually, she swept the crowd again. Her eyes met his and held for only a fraction of a second. There was an acknowledgement, but no signal. Hannah let her gaze move on, knowing they'd meet within a few days at the museum.

The pretty ceremony with its brisk military music and banners continued with a tour of the ship and an inspection of the crew. Hannah walked with the admiral's wife as Bennett was led down the line of officers and seamen. Now and then he stopped to comment or ask a personal question of one of the men. More, she saw that he listened to the answers. Even a casual observer could have seen that he was given more than respect due his rank by the men he greeted. There was love, the kind Hannah was aware only men could give men.

Though she was certain Bennett had seen enough of ships to last a lifetime, he toured the bridge, the officers' quarters and the galleys with apparent fascination. The ship was as neat as a parlor, utilitarian certainly, but freshly scrubbed and without a sign of peeling paint or rust.

Bennett moved quickly through the ship, without seeming to hurry over the decks. There were questions that had to be asked, compliments that were deserved, but he knew duffel bags were packed and waiting. He clasped hands with the captain again, aware that the man had every right to be proud of his ship and his men. As he started down the gangplank, the cheers rose up again. Bennett had to wonder if they were for him or because the ceremonies were finally over and the men could go ashore.

Protocol demanded that he be escorted back through headquarters. It was here that Hannah began to sense his impatience to be off. Still, he was gracious, shaking hands, kissing hands, exchanging a last pleasantry. It wasn't until he was seated in his own car again that he let out a low oath.

"I beg your pardon, sir?"

Bennett merely patted Hannah's hand before he started the engine. "Four hours was a long time to keep you on your feet. Thank you for bearing with me."

"On the contrary, I found it fascinating." Nothing had ever seemed more wonderful than the wind blowing on her face again as the convertible picked up speed. "The tour of the ship was particularly educational. It was clever, wasn't it, for the ship's cook to frame a recipe for crepes where the flour was measured in pounds rather than cups?"

"Food becomes a priority after a few months at sea." He glanced over, surprised she'd been so well entertained by a ship and several pompous speeches. "If I'd known you were really interested I wouldn't have hurried things along quite so much."

"I suppose it becomes all routine and a bit boring for you after a while."

"I was thinking of the men. All they really wanted was to get ashore to their wives or lovers—or both." He was grinning when he turned his head toward her. "You can't imagine what four months at sea is like when the only woman you see is in a glossy photo with staple marks in the middle."

Her lips twitched, but she managed to hold the smile to a bare acknowledgement. "No, I'm sure I can't. But I think you enjoyed your time at sea, Bennett. It showed in the way you spoke with the men and looked at the ship."

He said nothing for a moment, surprised and not displeased that she had understood that so quickly. "I was more of an officer and less of a prince then. I can't say I have the sea in my blood the way Captain Dumont does, but it isn't something I'll forget."

"What is it you remember best?" she asked before she caught herself.

"Watching the sun rise at sea or better, riding out a storm. God, we went through one off Crete. The waves were a fifty-foot wall. The wind was like the wrath of God, so loud, so enormous that you could shout in someone's ear and not be heard. No sky, only water, wall after wall of it. An experience like that changes you."

"How?"

"It makes you realize that no matter who you are, what you are, there's something bigger, greater. Nature's a powerful equalizer, Hannah. Look at her now." With one hand he gestured toward the sea as he negotiated another curve. "Calm, almost impossibly beautiful. A hurricane doesn't make her less beautiful, only more dangerous."

"It sounds as though you prefer the danger." She understood that, perhaps too well.

"At times. Danger's its own seduction."

She could say nothing to that. It was something she had learned herself years before.

With the briefest of signals to the car behind him, Bennett pulled over. "At the moment I prefer the calm." He got out of the convertible, ignoring the guard who stood anxiously by the hood of the trailing car. "Walk with me on the beach, Hannah." He opened her door and held out a hand. "I promised Marissa some shells."

"Your security doesn't look pleased." Nor was she when she noticed how open they were.

"They'd only be pleased if I were sitting in a bulletproof globe. Come now, Hannah, didn't you tell me sea air was good for the constitution?"

"Yes." She laid her hand in his. He was safe, after all, as long as she played her part and played it well. "You'll have to find shells big enough that they can't be swallowed. At Marissa's age, children tend to eat the oddest things."

"Always practical." With an easy laugh, he lifted her by the waist over the low seawall. He saw her gaze focus over his shoulder and knew a guard would be following at a discreet distance. "You should take your shoes off, Hannah. You'll only get sand in them."

It was the practical thing to do, of course. The logical thing. Hannah tried to tell herself she wasn't shedding part of her cover along with the pumps. "You must have some fascinating coral formations in these waters."

"Do you scuba?"

"No," she lied. "I'm not a very strong swimmer. I went to a marine exhibit in London a few years ago. Until then, I had no idea what an incredible variety of shells there were, or how valuable they can be."

"Lucky for me Marissa has simple tastes." With his hand on hers, he walked to the sea edge. "A couple of clam shells, and she'll be delighted."

"It's kind of you to think of her." He *was* kind, she thought. That itself was one of the most difficult things to overlook. "You seem to be a great favorite among your nieces and nephews."

"Oh, I suppose that's because I don't mind making a fool of myself now and then in a game. How about this one?" Bending, he picked up a long spiral that had broken off a larger shell and been worn smooth by the ebb and flow of the sea. At the top of the curve was a peaked cap that looked almost like a crown.

"Very suitable," Hannah commented when he handed it to her.

"Marissa doesn't care for suitable. She prefers pretty."

"It is pretty." With a smile, Hannah ran a finger along the curve that went from pale amber to polished pink. "She should have it in her windowsill where the sun would hit it. Oh look." Forgetting herself, she stepped into the surf and pried out an unbroken scallop shell. It was shaped like a fan, bone-white on one side, opalescent pink inside its shallow bowl. "You could tell her that fairies take their biscuits in it when they have tea."

"So Hannah believes in fairies," he murmured.

Caught up short, she handed him the shell. "No, but I think Marissa might."

Bennett slipped the shell into his pocket. "Your feet are wet."

"They'll dry quickly enough." She started to step back. He took her hand again, holding her in the shallow, foaming surf.

"Since we're here, we ought to try for a couple more." Without waiting for a response he began to walk along the shoreline.

The water was warm and soft on her feet and ankles, but no warmer, no softer, than the air that blew in over it. Through the crystal water she could see the bed of white sand and the glittering sparkles of shells that had been crushed by waves. The surf was quiet here, all sighs and whispers.

There was nothing romantic in it, Hannah warned herself. She couldn't allow there to be. The line she walked was thinner and sharper than any she'd walked before.

One misstep could mean tragedy at least, war at the worst. Determined to keep her place, she concentrated on the guards a few yards at their back.

"The ceremony today was lovely. I'm grateful you asked me to come."

"My reasons were purely selfish. I wanted your company."

Struggling not to be touched, she tried again. "In England there's often satire and criticism of the Royal Family, but beneath it all is a very real affection. I see that same kind of love and respect for your family here."

"My father would tell you that we serve as well as govern. He gives them solidity and confidence. Alex gives them the hope for the future. A continuation of tradition. In Brie they have glamour and intelligence as well as humanity."

"And in you?"

"Entertainment."

It annoyed her. She couldn't say why but his careless dismissal of himself made her stop and frown at him. "You underestimate yourself."

Surprised, Bennett cocked his head and studied her. It was there again, that something, that indefinable something in her eyes that had attracted him all along. "Not really. I'm well aware that I do my duty. My father raised all of us to understand that we didn't simply inherit a title or position. We had to earn it." He drew her back a bit so that the spray from the surf didn't dampen her skirt. "I won't rule. Thank God. That's for Alex and then for the son I continue to hope Eve gives us all this time around. Because I won't, I don't have to take myself as seriously as Alex, but that doesn't mean I take Cordina or my responsibilities to it lightly."

"I didn't mean to criticize."

"I didn't think you did. I only meant that above my official duties, my official position, I give the people something—someone to talk about over a glass of wine or an evening meal. I've been haunted by the title of Playboy Prince since I was in my teens." He grinned then and tucked a stray hair behind her ear. "I can't say I didn't do everything possible to earn it."

"I prefer literature to gossip," Hannah said primly as she started to walk on.

"Gossip has its place." Amused, Bennett stopped her.

"Apparently you enjoy it."

"No." His eyes darkened as he looked beyond her and out to sea. "I'm just accustomed to it. It's difficult, when you're twenty, to know that every time you look more than casually at a woman it's going to be splashed somewhere in bold print, pictures included. I like women." This time he smiled and looked back at her. "Since I didn't want to change that aspect of my personality, I decided to live with public speculation. If I've sinned, it was in lack of discretion."

"Some might say it was the quantity."

There was only the shortest of hesitations before he threw his head back and roared with laughter. "Oh, Hannah, what a gem you are. So you *have* whiled away some time with something besides Yeats."

"I may have skimmed a few headlines."

Laughing again, he swung her in a circle before she could prevent it. "Priceless. Absolutely priceless." His eyes were glowing as he set her back down. "I adore how you cut me down to size so skillfully."

Automatically, Hannah smoothed down her skirt. "I'm sure you've mistaken my intent."

"The devil I have. That's what delights me about you."

The frustrated look she gave him had nothing to do with the role she was playing. Delighting him had never been part of the plan. She was there to observe, to cement her position and to carry out a plan that was years in the making. Never before had the proper Lady Hannah had to worry about piquing a man's interest. Even as she calculated how to cancel it out again, he was reaching for her.

"Your hair's falling down." In a casual move he plucked a loose pin that was dangling near her shoulder. "My fault for not putting the top up."

"I must look as though I've been through a hurricane." She reached up to put the practical hairstyle back in place. Pins fell out in her hand, loosened by wind and weight. Even as she swore silently, her hair tumbled free, waterfalling past her shoulders to her waist.

"Mon Dieu." Before she could twist her hair back, Bennett had filled both hands with it. Twined around his fingers it was deep, honey blond and soft as silk. He stared, thunderstruck, by the transformation. It waved wild and free around her face, accenting the slash of cheekbones that only looked hard and angular without the framing. Her face no longer seemed thin and bony, but exotic. *"C'est magnifique. C'est la chevelure d'un ange."*

With her heart pounding, she tried to ignore what she saw in his eyes. It wasn't innocent delight or casual attraction now. Now there was desire, man for woman, basic, strong and as dangerous as the sea in a storm. She couldn't move back from him for his hands were buried in her hair. She couldn't deny the lunge of her own needs as he kept her close.

It wasn't supposed to happen. Even now she could tell

herself it couldn't happen. Yet she wanted to be held by him, to be comforted, to be, though the words sounded foolish in her mind, cherished. Desired, needed, loved. All of those things were against the rules, but she found it hard to pull back.

"Angel hair," Bennett repeated in a whisper. "Why does a woman bind beauty up and hide it?"

No, she couldn't deny what was happening inside her, but she could, as she'd been trained, deny herself. "It's more practical worn up." She lifted her hands to scoop it from his and met resistance.

Yes, he'd been right all along. There was more, much more to her than she allowed to show on the surface. Perhaps it was that which continued to draw him in, make him want, make him need in a way he never had before. If it had been possible, he would have pulled her to him then. It wasn't the guards that stopped him, but the trace of anxiety he saw in her eyes.

"If that was true, my most practical Hannah, why haven't you simply cut it off?"

How many times had she nearly done so then pulled back at the last minute? Drawing a deep breath she offered the simple truth because truth was often the best cover of all. "Even I have some vanity."

"It makes you beautiful." He dragged his hands through her hair again, hardly able to believe it had been hidden by a handful of pins.

"Only different." Her smile hid the tension that was pulling her in two directions.

"Any man would approve of such a difference." She was stiff beneath his hands. With reluctance he acknowledged it and released her. "But then, you don't look for a man's approval, do you?"

"I've never found it necessary." With a few expert twists, she had her hair at the base of her neck again. The pins were pushed in until it was secure. She could almost, just almost feel secure herself. "We should be getting back. Eve may need me."

With a nod, Bennett began to walk back to the car with her. There would be another time and another place. He found in himself something he experienced rarely, particularly when it had to do with a woman. Patience.

"You can pin it up, Hannah. But now that I know what it looks like down, I'll see it that way whenever I look at you." When they reached the seawall, he again lifted her over, but this time stood, his hands around her waist and the wall between them. "Knowing this one secret makes me wonder how many others you have, and how soon I'll find them."

Anxiety and desire were a powerful combination. She felt her heart thud with both. "I'm afraid you'll be disappointed, Bennett. I have no interesting secrets."

"We'll see," he said, before he vaulted easily over the seawall.

Chapter 5

It wasn't often Hannah yearned to be beautiful. Her work had given her a fine appreciation for the beauty of being unremarkable, even forgettable. Over the years, she'd experienced a twinge now and then, but only a twinge when she thought of soft colors and filmy dresses. It had always been possible to release the urge when she was off duty and out of the country. Then her appearance could be changed with a more discerning choice of color and cut and a few clever strokes with a makeup brush.

There could be no release now, and no yearning.

Hannah knew everyone would look wonderful for Eve's dinner party. An affair at the palace was meant to be elegant, even extravagant. Hannah had no doubt every woman who attended would strive to live up to the occasion. Every woman, of course, except her.

She'd already seen Eve's glittery black dress with its swirls of material from waist to ankle and its daring draping back. Gabriella would no doubt wear something delicate that would accent her fragile, feminine looks.

Then there was Chantel O'Hurley. Hannah was certain the actress would be stunning whether she chose silk or sackcloth. Remembering how Bennett had looked at her as he'd started down the stairs in the Center took no effort at all.

It shouldn't have mattered.

It mattered too much.

Lecturing herself, Hannah chose the best of the worst in a pale lavender gown with a fussy bodice that played down her curves. With her hair unpinned, it gave her the look of a wanton puritan. An image, she knew, that wouldn't go unnoticed. With only the smallest of sighs, she drew her hair back to begin the laborious job of braiding it into submission.

When it was neatly coiled at her neck, Hannah was satisfied that all traces of sexuality were tamed. She looked presentable, perfectly proper and sexless.

There could be no regrets, Hannah told herself as she slipped her pistol into her evening bag. Duty came above personal desire, and certainly far ahead of vanity.

He'd been waiting for her. The guests were being entertained in the Salle des Miroirs where they were served aperitifs by short-coated waiters. Both the cast and the crew of Eve's production had been invited so that conversation was a babble of noise underlaid with excitement.

Though impatient and distracted, Bennett performed his duty without a ripple. There were always polite questions to be asked, a hand to kiss and a joke to laugh at. Under usual circumstances, the party would have amused and entertained him, but...

Where was she? He found himself straining against the evening clothes he usually wore without a thought. All around him women glittered. Their scents mingled and mixed into one exotic fragrance that did nothing to tempt him. He wanted a moment alone with Hannah. He hadn't the least idea why it was so important, but he wanted it desperately.

He kept one eye on the doorway while he spoke with the wardrobe mistress. His gaze paused briefly on the ormolu clock while he listened to the director expound on the potential of Eve's play.

"Looking for me?" The sultry voice sounded in his ear just ahead of a cloud of scent.

"Chantel." Bennett kissed both her cheeks before drawing her back for a survey. "Stunning, as always."

"I do what I'm best at." Smiling, she accepted a glass from a passing waiter. Shimmering white left her shoulders bare, then dipped low enough to be tantalizing before it closely followed the subtle, feminine curves. "Your home is everything it's rumored to be." She lifted the wine to her lips as her gaze passed over the dozens of antique mirrors that graced the walls. "And how clever of you to choose such a room to entertain a group of narcissistic actors."

"We have our moments." He looked beyond her for a moment, but still saw no sign of Hannah. "I saw your last movie. You were extraordinary."

A woman who was accustomed to absorbing all of a man's attention knew instinctively when she had only a part of it. Still, Chantel only smiled and speculated. "I'm still waiting for you to come back to Hollywood."

"You seem to be keeping busy in the meantime." He reached in his pocket for a box of matches to light her cigarette. "How do you manage to divide your time among tennis stars, oilmen and producers?"

Chantel tilted her head as she blew out a thin stream of smoke. "Oh, much the same way I imagine you divide yours among countesses, marchesas and—was it a barmaid in Chelsea?"

Laughing, Bennett dropped the matches back in his pocket. "*Ma chère amie,* if either of us enjoyed all the incredible and innumerable affairs the press gifts us with, we'd be hospitalized."

With the true affection she felt for few men, Chantel touched a hand to his cheek. "To anyone else, I'd say speak for yourself. However, since we've never been lovers, regardless of the headlines to the contrary, I'll ask you how things are for you, romantically speaking."

"Confusing." At that moment, in the oval glass over Chantel's shoulder, he saw Hannah slip into the room. She looked like a dove lost in a group of peacocks. "Very confusing. Excuse me a moment, will you, love?"

"Of course." She'd seen which direction his attention had taken. "*Bonne chance,* Bennett."

A lifetime of experience allowed him to slip through the groups of people, exchanging a quick word, a smile or a murmured excuse without leaving any offense behind. Less than a minute after Hannah had settled into a corner, he was beside her.

"*Bonsoir,* Lady Hannah."

"Your Highness." She used his title and curtsied as protocol demanded. He caught her hands as she straightened, negating the formality.

"It's usual, when a woman is late, that she makes an entrance rather than slip into a corner."

Damn him for making her pulse skittish. Even as she

tried to calm it again, she noted that more than one head was turned in their direction. So much for going unnoticed. "I prefer watching to being watched, sir."

"I prefer watching you." He signaled a waiter, then took a glass from the tray for her himself. "You move well, Hannah, as though you wouldn't make a sound in an empty room."

That had as much to do with her training in tae kwon do as her childhood lessons in ballet. "I was raised not to make disturbances." She accepted the glass because it freed one of her hands. "Thank you. This is a lovely room." She said it casually, as casual as the glance she sent sweeping over the guests. Her reflection was thrown back at her a dozen times. Hers, and Bennett's, close together.

"I've always been partial to it." Now that she was here, he was content. He'd almost heard the click of things falling into their proper place when he'd taken her hand in his. "As it happens it was another Bennett, some generations back, who started the collection. It seems he was miserably vain without much cause and continued to buy mirrors in hopes one would tell him a different story."

She had to laugh. For a moment she felt almost as though she belonged there with the gowns and the glass and the glamour. "I'd say you made that up, but it sounds foolish enough to be true."

"You have the most alluring laugh," he murmured. "It's a laugh that reminds me how you look with your hair down and your eyes dark."

She couldn't allow this. Hannah told herself she was foolish to be moved when she knew how clever he was with women. She was more foolish to be caught off guard

when she knew what a dangerous game was being played.
This time her voice was cool and formal.

"Shouldn't you see to your guests?"

"I have been." He passed his thumb gently over her
knuckles. It was a small gesture and an intimate one that
made her wish once again she could have been lovely for
him. That she could, very simply, have been for him.
"While I was waiting for you." He stepped closer. Because she was already wedged into a corner, there was no
place to go. "You smell wonderful."

"Bennett, please." She almost lifted a hand to his chest
before she remembered eyes were on them. In defense she
lifted her glass instead.

"Hannah, I can't tell you how it pleases me to see you
become unnerved. The only time you become at all unsure
of yourself is when I'm just a bit too close."

It was true, and a bitter pill to swallow for a woman
who survived by being sure of herself. "People are watching."

"Then walk in the gardens with me later, when we can
be alone."

"I don't think that would be wise."

"Are you afraid I'd seduce you?"

There was both amusement and arrogance in his tone,
but when Hannah looked back at him, she saw desire as
well. She sipped again to moisten a throat that had gone
bone-dry. "Not afraid. Uncomfortable seems a better
word."

"It would give me great pleasure to make you uncomfortable, Hannah." His voice was low, a caress to accompany the brush of his lips over her knuckles. "I want to
make love with you in some dark, quiet place. Very
slowly and very gently."

The need sprinted inside of her until she had to fight off a shudder of anticipation. It could be like that, with him, it could be. If only...

There could be no "ifs" in her life. They meant uncertainty and uncertainty was lethal. Hannah, pulling herself steady by nerve ends, looked at him. He meant it. There was desire in his eyes—but more a kindness, a sweetness that was almost her undoing. She could marvel at the fact that he felt something real for her, that somehow, he'd looked beyond the surface and cared.

She could want it, but she couldn't accept it. There was only one way to stop what should never have started. She had to hurt him, and she had to do it now.

"I'm sure I should be flattered." Her voice was cool and calm again. "But if you'll forgive me, sir, I'm aware that your tastes are not very selective."

He stiffened his fingers on hers before he released her hand. She saw by his eyes that the arrow had hit its mark. "I'd appreciate an explanation for that, Hannah."

"The explanation seems obvious. Please let me pass, you'll cause a scene."

"I've caused one before." There was something new in his voice now. It was anger, certainly, but a reckless, heedless anger. Hannah knew that if she didn't play her game exactly right now, she'd find her name splashed in headlines for battling with Bennett in public.

"Very well." Setting her glass down on a nearby table, she folded her hands in her usual fashion. "I'm a woman, and therefore of some passing interest. To be blunt, the interest isn't returned."

"That's a lie."

"No." Firmer now, she cut him off. "Though it might be difficult for a man like you to understand, I'm a simple woman with simple values. As you told me yourself, your reputation precedes you.'' She paused just long enough to see him wince.

Oh, Bennett, I'm sorry. So sorry.

"I didn't come to Cordina to amuse you,'' she murmured as she took a step to the side.

He suddenly lifted his hand to stop her, and she waited. "You don't amuse me, Hannah."

"Then I must beg your pardon.'' Knowing it would be more insult than courtesy, she dipped into a curtsy. "If you'll excuse me now, sir, I'd like to speak with Eve.''

He held her another moment. Hannah could feel his fury sear through his fingertips and burn her flesh. Then, in an instant, there was ice. "I won't keep you. Enjoy the evening.''

"Thank you.''

Despising herself, Hannah moved into the crowd. The lights were so brilliant, she told herself. That was why her eyes hurt.

"Lady Hannah, good evening.'' Reeve stepped beside her and took her arm. "Would you care for some wine?''

"Yes, thank you.'' Falling into step beside him, she accepted the glass he held out.

"Have you seen this collection of mirrors? I've always found these three particularly impressive. Are you all right?'' he added in an undertone.

"Yes, they are lovely. I'm fine.''

He cupped his hand around the end of a cigarette, glancing around casually to be certain no one was within earshot. "It looked as though you were having some trouble with Bennett.''

"He's persistent.'' She sipped her wine, amazed that

her nerves had yet to calm. "Surely this is eighteenth-century."

"Hannah." He pointed out another glass as they walked, but his voice softened. "I worked with your father when I first got my feet wet with the ISS. That makes me feel almost like family. Are you all right?"

"I will be." She drew a deep breath and smiled as if he'd said something amusing. "I caused him pain just now. I didn't enjoy it."

Reeve brushed a hand over hers in the most casual of gestures. The touch was as reassuring as a hug. "It's rare to get through an assignment without hurting someone."

"Yes, I know—the end justifies the means. Don't worry, I'll do my job."

"I wasn't worried."

"It would help a great deal if you'd see that Bennett was kept busy over the next week or so. Things should be coming to a head and I don't need him…"

"Distracting you?"

"Interfering," Hannah corrected. She glanced in one of the mirrors and saw him across the room with Chantel. "Though I may very well have taken care of that myself. Excuse me."

He drove the horse hard, but still didn't find the level of release he'd been seeking. Swearing, Bennett plunged down the winding path, but neither joy nor excitement rode with him. Fury left little room.

He ached for her. He damned her to the devil and still ached for her. In the days that had passed since she'd turned him aside, the wanting hadn't eased. Now it was coated with self-derision and anger, but it hadn't eased.

He told himself she was a cold, insensitive prude with

no generosity or heart. He saw her as she had been on the beach, with a shell in her hand, her eyes rich with laughter as the wind pulled pins from her hair.

He told himself she was hard as stone and just as unfeeling. Then he remembered how soft, how sweet her lips had been when his own had tasted them.

So he cursed her and rode harder.

The skies threatened rain, but he ignored them. It was the first time in days he'd been able to get away from obligations long enough to take Dracula out for more than cursory exercise. The wind whistled in off the sea and set waves dancing high.

He wanted the storm. By God, he wanted the wind and the rain and the thunder.

He wanted Hannah.

Imbécile! Only a fool wanted a woman when there was nothing returned. Only a madman thought of ways to have what had already been denied. He'd told himself all this before, but still he caught himself dreaming of ways he could gather her up and take her somewhere until he found the right way to show her.... Show her what? Bennett asked himself. Show her that it was different with her?

What woman would believe it?

Dozens, he thought, and his own laughter echoed bitterly behind him. He could certainly attest to that. But now when it was true, when it mattered the most, this woman wouldn't believe.

Because he'd acted like an idiot. Drawing the stallion to a halt, he stopped at a precipice over the sea and looked out. He'd pushed, too hard, too fast. It was humbling to admit he might have done so because he'd never met with a great deal of resistance before.

Women were drawn to him—because of the title and position. He wasn't so vain or so foolish not to know it. But they were also drawn to him because he enjoyed them. He liked their softness, their humor, their vulnerabilities. It was also true that he hadn't been intimate with as many as his reputation allowed, but there'd been enough women in his life for him to understand and appreciate that romance was a two-way street.

Hannah was young, inexperienced, sheltered. The term "Lady" wasn't merely a title, but a way of life. As far as men were concerned, it was doubtful she'd taken herself away from her books long enough to form any strong relationships.

With another oath, Bennett dragged a hand through his wind-tossed hair. And what had he done? He'd tried to seduce her at a dinner party. How could he have expected a woman of her breeding and sensitivity to be anything less than insulted? It had been the clumsiest, and perhaps the crudest of propositions.

Dracula danced impatiently, but Bennett held him steady another moment as he watched the storm roll slowly from the horizon toward the shore.

He hadn't told her, had never attempted to tell her what it was she did to him inside, to his heart. Just talking with her, watching that solemn face and quiet manner excited him in a way the most exotic or flamboyant woman never had. It was something deeper, and so much richer. He'd never said that with her, he was on the edge of finding the love he hadn't been sure would ever be there for him.

He could hardly do all of that now that he'd alienated and insulted her. But he could do something else. His smile began as the first drops of water hit the sea. He could start at the beginning.

Bennett wheeled the horse around. As the first streak of lightning split the sky, they were racing for home.

Within an hour, in dry clothes and dripping hair, Bennett made his way up to the nursery. Bernadette barred him at the door.

"Your pardon, Your Highness, but it's Princess Marissa's nap time. Her Highness is resting with the baby."

"I'm looking for Lady Hannah." He leaned into the room, but Bernadette stood her ground.

"Lady Hannah isn't here, sir. I believe she went to the museum this afternoon."

"The museum." Bennett calculated a moment. "Thank you, Bernadette."

Before she could finish her curtsy, he was gone.

Le Musée d'Art was small and lovely as was the rest of Cordina. It was like a miniature palace itself with its marble floors and carved columns. In the main lobby was a high, domed ceiling of stained glass and a circling balcony that gave the illusion of space.

Rooms ran off this circular hub like spokes of a wheel. On the floor below was a moderately priced restaurant where diners could enjoy a view of the gardens through a wide glass wall.

Hannah had arrived early to take inventory of the entire building. Security was tight but people who rested on the benches near the exhibits were largely ignored. Groups of school children were led by, most of them more impressed with an afternoon away from classes than they were with the paintings and sculptures. Tourists, brochures in hands, muddled through with a weaving of French, Italian, British, and American accents.

On a rainy weekday afternoon, the museum was a

pleasant pastime. A healthy number of people flowed in and out. Hannah decided she couldn't have planned it better.

At the time she'd requested in her message, she strolled toward a Monet seascape. She loitered there long enough to read the plaque and study the brushwork. Whoever she was going to meet was probably there, making his own study of the building, and of her. In a leisurely pattern, she moved from painting to painting.

Then she saw the watercolor and both heart and mind raced back to the music room, and Bennett.

The plaque read Her Serene Highness, Princess Louisa de Cordina, but in small letters in the corner of the painting was the signature. Louisa Bisset.

She'd titled it simply *La Mer*. It was indeed the sea, but from a view Hannah had yet to see in Cordina. There was a jagged fall of cliffs that gave way to a sheer incline and ended in a jumble of rocks. From there, the beach spread white to the blue verge of water. But it wasn't peaceful. In this painting, the artist had looked for and captured the power and the danger. The spray rose high, and on the horizon a storm was brewing.

He found this stored in a trunk, Hannah thought and had to resist the urge to touch the frame as he might have done. He'd found it, she thought again, and perhaps had seen part of himself in it.

"An interesting subject."

The voice beside her was French, brusquely accented. Contact was made.

"Yes, the artist is very skillful." Hannah dropped her brochures. As she bent to pick them up she glanced around and was satisfied that no one was close enough to hear or even notice them. "I have information."

"You are to pass it through me."

She turned to smile at him as though they were exchanging a few pleasant remarks about the painting. He was of medium height, dark complexion with no scars. She gauged his age at fifty, though he might have been younger. Certain professions tend to age people quickly. He was not French by birth. The Germanic tone was faint, but she caught it and filed it away.

"There are certain aspects to some of my information that I feel must be given directly to the man who pays me."

"That is against the organization's policy."

"So I was told. However, I'm aware of what nearly happened six months ago because of policy. It wasn't looked on unfavorably when I used my own initiative and saved the organization, shall we say, certain embarrassments."

"*Mademoiselle*, I'm only here to receive your information."

"Then my information is this." Before speaking again, she moved toward another painting. Again, she took her time studying it. She lifted a hand as if to show her companion a certain combination of colors. "I have unlimited access to the palace. Neither my person nor my possessions are searched. I have already compiled the complete statistics on the security system both there, and at the Fine Arts Center."

"That will be most useful."

"And will be given to the man who pays me. That is *my* policy, *monsieur*."

"You are paid by the organization."

"And the organization is run by men. I know who I work for and why." She turned to him then, her smile very cool, very calm. They might have been discussing the weather. "I am not a fool. The...organization has certain goals. So do I. I am more than happy to have them merge to our mutual satisfaction. I will meet and speak with the highest authority. See that it's soon."

"Some people take a step and find themselves falling from a cliff."

"I'm surefooted. Pass this on, *s'il vous plaît*. What I know is worth a great deal. What I can find out is worth even more. You'll find enough to prove it in here." Hannah let her brochure fall to her feet, but this time she left it there. *"Bonjour, monsieur."*

She turned, knowing that such demands would either take her to the next stage, or end in her being summarily disposed of. Nerves tingling, she began to wander toward the exit. Her heart stopped when Bennett walked in.

A dozen thoughts ran through her mind in a matter of seconds. Had she been set up? Had they used her to get him out in the open at a certain time and place? Had he come for her because Deboque had already struck somewhere else?

It took her only seconds more to dismiss them all as irrational. It was simply coincidence and bad luck that he should show up now on the tail of her meeting.

"I hope you don't mind company," Bennett said before she could think of a plausible opening.

"Of course not." She didn't dare look behind her yet to see if her contact was still there. She smiled, not quite sure how to behave since both she and Bennett had done an excellent job of avoiding each other for days. "The museum is even more beautiful than I'd been told."

"Have you seen everything? I'd be glad to show you around." He took her hand in a casual, friendly way that she realized could only cement her position if Deboque's man was watching.

She let her fingers curl into his, hating herself for using Bennett's generosity against him. "I could spend days looking, but I'm a bit tired."

She saw him then. He'd moved into her peripheral vision. The brochure she'd passed him was in his hand, and though his back was to them, she knew he was listening.

Bennett didn't notice the man, but only her. "Let me give you coffee up in my office. I'd like to talk with you."

She felt the unexpected prick of tears. Everything he said, and the way he said it, only made her claims more plausible. "I'd love some coffee." Hannah let him take her arm and lead her out, knowing every detail would be reported back to Deboque.

With a silent and stone-faced bodyguard, they stepped into an elevator. Bennett used a key to send them up to the third floor.

They crossed pale gray carpet, past uniformed guards to a suite of rooms. Two secretaries, one manning a bank of phones, the other working on a state-of-the-art computer, rose as Bennett entered.

"Janine, could we have some coffee, please?"

"Yes, Your Highness. Right away."

With his hand still on Hannah's arm, Bennett opened a door. The moment it shut behind them, the whispers started. His Highness had never brought a woman to his office before.

It was a room that reflected a man who loved beautiful things. Grays and blues blended softly with ivory walls. Deep-cushioned chairs invited long stays and easy conversation while an ornamental lemon tree thrived in a corner. Glass shelves held small treasures, a china bowl, a

T'ang horse, a handful of shells she imagined he'd gathered himself and a chipped demitasse cup that might have been picked up in a flea market.

Though there was a very businesslike antique desk and chair, the essence of the room was relaxation. Hannah wondered if he came here when he needed to escape the palace and his title.

"Sit down, Hannah. If you've gone through the whole museum, you've been on your feet for hours."

"Yes, but I loved it." She chose a chair rather than the cozy lounge and folded her hands over each other on her lap. "I've always loved the Louvre, but this is so much more personal."

"The Board of Directors and the Chamber of Commerce will be delighted to hear it." He remained standing, his hands in his pockets, wondering just how to begin. "If you'd let me know you were coming today, I'd have enjoyed showing you through myself."

"I didn't want to disturb you. In any case, I rather liked just wandering."

Why, he's nervous, she realized. It might have pleased her in some secret place if she hadn't discovered she was nervous herself. It was the meeting, she told herself. No, it was Bennett. It was foolish to deny it.

"Do you work here often?"

"When necessary. It's often more convenient to work out of my office at home." He didn't want to talk about the museum. Bennett dug his hands deeper in his pockets. Since when had he had trouble talking to a woman? Since Hannah, he thought wryly, and tried again. "Hannah—"

The knock on the door had him biting off an oath. Bennett opened the door for Janine and the coffee tray.

The pot was silver, Hannah noted, while the cups were violet bone china edged in gold.

"Yes, just set it down there, Janine. I'll see to it."

"Yes, sir." She set it down on the table in front of the lounge then curtsied.

Aware he'd been terse, Bennett smiled at her. "Thank you, Janine. It smells wonderful."

"You're welcome, sir." The door closed behind her with a discreet click.

"Looks like we're in luck." Bennett lifted the pot and poured. "These little pastries are from the restaurant downstairs. They're wonderful. Cream?"

"Yes, thank you. No sugar." How polite we are, she thought as the tension began to spread from her neck to her shoulders. Like two strangers on a blind date.

"Will you come sit over here if I promise to behave?"

Though he said it lightly, Hannah heard the strain. She lowered her gaze to her hands. He couldn't know it was shame and not shyness. "Of course." Rising, she moved over and joined him on the lounge. She lifted her coffee while he left his alone.

"Hannah, I apologize for my behavior the other night. It's no wonder you were offended."

"Oh, please, don't." With a distress even her training couldn't smother, she set her cup down and started to rise. His hand reached for hers and held her still. "I don't want an apology." Fighting for control, she forced herself to look at him. "I wasn't offended, really. I was just—"

"Frightened then? That's just as inexcusable."

"No—yes." Which answer was the right one? In the end, she gave up. "Bennett, the truest thing I can say to you is that no one has ever confused me so well."

"Thank you."

"That wasn't a compliment, but a complaint."

"Hannah, thank God you're back." Laughing, he pulled both her hands to his lips. When she stiffened, he released them but continued to smile.

"Friends?"

Still wary, she nodded. "I'd like to be."

"Then friends it is." Satisfied the first hurdle was successfully negotiated, Bennett sat back. He would wait and be a great deal more cautious before attempting the second. "What did you like best about the museum?"

She didn't trust him. No, Hannah was far too good at game playing not to know when one was afoot. "The airy, unrestricted atmosphere, I think. Too often museums are solemn, serious places. Oh, I did see another of your ancestor's paintings. The one of the sea. It was stunning."

"One of my favorites." He was careful not to touch her again. "I was tempted to keep it locked in my room, all to myself, but..." With a shrug he picked up his cup. "It didn't seem fair."

"And you are fair," she murmured, knowing she'd used him.

"I try to be," he returned, knowing he would use fair means or foul to win her. "Hannah, you ride, don't you?"

"Yes."

"Ride with me tomorrow morning. It has to be early as the rest of my day is full, but it's been a long time since I had any company on a ride."

"I'm not sure I can. Eve—"

"Will be busy with Marissa until ten," Bennett finished.

How she would love a ride. An hour of freedom and movement. "Yes, but I've promised to go with her to the Center. She has appointments there at eleven."

"We'll be back by then if you're willing to start out early." He wasn't willing to lose the opportunity. In her eyes he saw hesitation and pressed his advantage. "Come, Cordina's at its best in the morning on horseback."

"All right then." It was impulse, she knew, but she could use an hour of relaxation.

In a matter of days, she would meet with Deboque. Hannah lifted her coffee again and sipped. Or she would be dead.

Chapter 6

He hadn't lied. Hannah had already thought Cordina beautiful, but in the early morning it was exquisite. With the dawn light, Cordina reminded Hannah of a young girl dressing for her first ball. The colors were soft, shimmering. Pinks and roses and misty blues still gathered to the east as they got mounted.

Settling into her own saddle, Hannah eyed Bennett's Dracula with a mixture of envy and anxiety. Her father's stables included some of the finest horseflesh in Britain, but he had nothing to compare with the black stallion. He looked fast and reckless and just a bit angry. Even as she imagined herself on his back, she could also picture Bennett being thrown.

"A mount like that would have a mind of his own," she commented when the old groom stepped back from the prince.

"Of course." Bennett steadied the stallion as he side-

stepped. Then, misunderstanding her, he smiled in reassurance. "Your Quixote's strong, but quite the gentleman.
Brie often rides him when she's here."

Hannah only lifted a brow, recognizing the soothing
words for what they were. "Thank you, sir. It eases my
mind to know you've given me a lady's mount."

He thought he caught a trace of sarcasm, but when he
looked at her he saw only calm eyes and a polite smile.
"I thought we'd ride to the sea."

"I'd like that."

With a nod, Bennett turned his horse and started off at
a gentle trot. "Are you comfortable?"

"Yes, thank you." As she settled into the easy rhythm,
Hannah tried not to yearn for a wild gallop. "It was kind
of you to invite me. I'm told your morning rides are sa-
cred."

He grinned at her, pleased that she sat the horse well
and confidently. "It's often true that I need an hour on
horseback before I can be civil. Still, there are times I
prefer company."

That hadn't been true lately. Since Deboque's release
he felt he could never stretch his arms out without bumping a guard. And still nothing. His eyes clouded, as much
with impatience as with anger. He wanted Deboque to
move. He relished the thought of being able to deal with
him personally, and finally. Instinctively he touched a
hand to his shoulder where a bullet had entered. Yes, he
would relish it.

The look in his eyes made her uneasy. There was something to watch for and defend against there. The man beside her was not the easygoing, easy loving prince she'd
come to expect. Whatever, whoever he thought of seemed
to communicate itself to his mount for Dracula shied ner-

vously. She saw how easily he controlled the stallion, only a flexing of muscle. He could be kind or harsh, gentle or rough. Her own palm grew damp on the reins.

"Is something wrong?"

"What?" He glanced over. For an instant the look was still there, hard and dark enough to make her tense. Then it was gone and he was smiling again. There was no Deboque this morning, Bennett told himself. He was sick of having every aspect of his life and his family's lives clouded by one name. "No, nothing. Tell me what you do at home, Hannah. I can't picture you there."

"We live quietly in London." It was partially the truth. She wondered why she thought of it as partially a lie. "I do a great deal of my work at home, which makes it convenient for me to keep house for my father."

"Your work," he repeated. "Your essays?" He was leading her along the easiest route, where the incline was gentle.

"Yes." Again, there was a twinge of discomfort. "I hope to have them ready for publication in a year or two."

"I'd like to read them."

She shot him a look of surprise, then almost immediately felt her muscles tighten. It had nothing to do with fear. Even if he'd demanded to see her work, she had enough that would satisfy him. No, it wasn't fear but a certainty that if she had to continue to lie to him much longer, she would be physically ill.

"You're welcome to, of course, but I don't think my writing would be of great interest to you."

"You're wrong. You're of great interest to me."

She looked down, but not in the shyness he thought he saw. Once again it was shame. "It's lovely here," she managed after a moment. "Do you ride this way often?"

She wouldn't allow him to get too close. Bennett fought back frustration and reminded himself he was in for the long haul. "No, actually I haven't been this way in quite a while." When they reached the top of a rise, he stopped. Her gelding was content to busy himself with the grass alongside the path. Beside her, Dracula nearly shivered with energy. She thought she felt the same impatience from Bennett.

"A little distance changes things," he murmured.

Following his gaze, she looked back at the palace. From here it looked like an exquisite child's toy, a magnificent dollhouse a pampered child might find near the tree on Christmas morning. To the east was the sea, still hidden from view by the cliffs and trees and barely heard. Like the palace, it hardly seemed real.

"Do you need to get away from it so badly?" Hannah asked him quietly.

"Sometimes." It no longer surprised him that she read his moods. With a hand firm on the reins, he controlled the stallion and continued to look at his home. "I had my time at Oxford, and at sea. When I was away, I missed Cordina so badly it was like an ache. In the past six months, past year, I've felt a restlessness, a waiting for something to happen."

They both thought of Deboque.

"Often in England, especially at this time of year, I'll complain about the cold and the damp." She shifted in the saddle then smiled as she thought of her home. "I'll look out the window and think I'd almost sell my soul for a week of warm, sunny days. Then, when I'm away, I begin to miss the fog and the mists and the smells of London."

They began to walk the horses again while she cast her

mind back to England. "There's a man who sells roasted chestnuts just around the corner from our house. You can buy a little bag and warm your hands on them and smell them, just smell them long before you ever eat them." Remembering made her smile again, but she had no idea how wistfully. "Sometimes I'd wonder how it could be Christmastime anywhere without roasted chestnuts."

"I didn't know you missed England so much."

Nor had she until that moment. "One always misses home. Our hearts are always there." And what she was, all that she had done, had always been for England first.

"I've often wondered how difficult it was for Reeve," Bennett said. The sounds of the sea became louder as they moved their way east. "Although he and Brie spend nearly six months every year at their farm in America. I know for Brie it's as much home as Cordina is."

"For many, real contentment comes with acclimation." Hadn't it been so for her, all of her adult life?

"It's a great deal harder for Eve. She has only a few weeks with her family in America."

"Some loves are greater than others. Some needs stronger." She was just beginning to truly understand it. "Eve would live anywhere as long as Alexander was with her. And I think the same is true for your brother-in-law."

Yes, it was true. Perhaps that was a part of the restlessness in him. Over the last few years he'd seen how beautiful, how strong, real commitment, real feelings could be. Somehow they always seemed so remote from him, so unattainable. Now there was Hannah.

"For love, could you turn your back on England?"

Hannah caught her first glimpse of the sea as they climbed higher. She concentrated on that, but saw, in her mind's eyes, the twisting charm of the Thames.

Could she? So much of her life, so much of her duty was bound with England. Even her current assignment had been as much to protect her country from Deboque as it had been to insure the safety of the Royal Family of Cordina.

"I don't know. You especially would understand how strong some ties can be."

The trees thinned. Those that remained were bent and battered from the wind that swept in from the sea. The path grew rougher so that Bennett put himself between the edge and Hannah. Her mouth twitched at the move, but she said nothing. He could hardly know that she was capable of riding down the path pell-mell without saddle or reins. Besides, she found herself savoring the unaccustomed feeling of being protected.

Without the trees to break its power, the wind swirled from the sea to the top of the rise, carrying traces of salt. Even Hannah's tightly pinned hair couldn't resist it completely. Wispy tendrils escaped to dance around her cheeks. As she watched, a gull caught the current and glided peacefully up on a stream of air. Another, far below, skimmed the water looking for food.

"It's breathtaking." She relaxed enough to sigh.

He saw what was always in her heart, but which showed so rarely in her eyes. Her love of adventure, of power and of risk. It made her beautiful, arousing, mysterious. The need to reach out for her was so strong, he had to tighten his fingers on the reins to keep them still.

"I wanted to bring you here, but I worried that the height might bother you."

"No, I love it." Her horse shied a bit and she controlled him with the ease of long experience. "There are so many beautiful places in the world, but so few special ones. This is a special one. I think I could..." She trailed off as the full impact struck her. "This is the scene from the painting. There's no storm brewing, but this is it, isn't it?"

"Yes." He had no idea that her recognition of it would mean so much. Nor did he know what to do with the sudden, inescapable realization that he was in love with her. Completely. Unalterably.

He tossed his head back as the wind blew his hair into his eyes. He wanted a clear look at her, at this, perhaps the most important moment in his life.

She sat straight in the saddle, her eyes dark with appreciation of the scene spread out before and below them. Her profile was sharp, sculpted. The plain brown riding shirt and pants did nothing to enhance her pale skin. But when he looked at her, he saw the most beautiful, the most precious thing he'd ever found. And for the first time in his life, he had no words to tell her.

"Hannah." He reached out a hand and waited.

She turned. He was the most magnificent man she'd ever seen. More breathtaking than the view, more dangerous than a plunge to the rocks below. He sat on the huge stallion, straight as a soldier, as heartbreaking as a poet. In his eyes she saw both passion and compassion, both need and generosity.

Her heart betrayed her and was lost to him even before she could tell herself it couldn't be. As duty warred with emotion, she let her hand join with his.

"I know what you think I am."

"Bennett—"

"No." His fingers tightened on hers. "You're not far wrong. I could lie to you and promise to change, but I won't lie or promise."

Before she could stop herself, she softened. Only for

this moment, she promised herself. There was magic, if only for the moment.

"Bennett, I don't want you to change."

"I meant what I said, though I said it badly the other night. I do want you, Hannah." Like her, he looked out to sea. "I also understand that it would be difficult for you to believe that I've never said that to another woman and meant it in the same way."

But she did believe him. It was thrilling, terrifying and forbidden, but she did. For one glorious moment, she let herself hope. Then she remembered who she was. Duty was first. Always.

"Please, believe me, if I could give you what you want, I would. It's just not possible." She drew her hand away because the contact was making her weak, making her dream.

"I've always believed anything is possible if you work hard enough for it."

"No, some things remain out of reach." She turned her horse away from the sea. "We should get back."

Before she could move, he'd backed up enough to cover the hands on her reins with his own. His arm brushed her arm, his leg, her leg. His face was close, too close, as their mounts stood in opposite directions.

"Tell me what you feel," he demanded. The patience was gone, dissolved in need and frustration. "Give me that much, dammit."

"Regret." As she spoke, the word shimmered with it.

He released her hands only to cup the back of her neck. "Tell me again how you feel," he murmured, then leaned toward her.

The kiss was like a whisper, soft, seductive, sultry. Hannah tightened her hands on the reins, then let them go limp as emotion swamped her. It wasn't supposed to be like this, so encompassing, so heady, so right. The wind ribboned around them. The sea crashed below. For a moment, just one moment, all rational thought fled, leaving only desires behind.

"Bennett." She only murmured his name as she started to draw away. He held her, firm, insistent.

"Another moment."

He needed it. He needed every scrap she would throw him. Never had he felt the desire to beg for what a woman could give or withhold. It wasn't just the passion he wanted; it was more than the physical. He wanted her heart with a desperation he'd never felt before.

It was that desperation that made him keep the kiss gentle, that made him draw back long before his craving for her was satisfied. If he wanted her heart, he would have to move slowly. His Hannah was delicate and shy.

"No regrets, Hannah," he said quietly, then smiled. "I won't hurt you, or push you further than you're ready for. Trust me. That's really all I want for now."

She wanted to weep. He was giving her a kindness, a sensitivity she didn't deserve. Lies were all she'd given him. Lies were all she would continue to give. To keep him alive, she reminded herself as the tears burned at the back of her eyes. To keep him and the people he loved safe and unharmed.

"No regrets," she told him, letting the words echo through her mind for herself. Tossing her head, she pressed her heels to the gelding's sides and took off in a gallop.

Bennett's first reaction was surprise. He hadn't expected her to ride so well or so forcefully. He took a moment to watch her race down the rise before he grinned

and let Dracula have his head. Though she'd taken a good
lead, Hannah heard them gaining ground behind her. Delighted, she bent lower over the gelding's neck as she
urged him on.

"We can't beat them head-to-head," she called to her
mount. "But we might outwit them."

The challenge was enough. Spurred by it, Hannah
swung off the track and into the trees. The path here was
narrow and rough, but what she sacrificed in speed, she
gained in maneuverability. Bennett was hard on her heels,
but she kept to the center giving him no room to pass.
She burst through the trees and onto a field less than two
lengths ahead. Instinct had her veering to the left and
pounding up another rise so that Bennett had to check his
momentum at the unexpected maneuver. Still, he continued to gain so that when the stables came into view they
were nearly neck and neck. Laughing, she veered left
again and headed for a hedge.

He felt an instant's panic as he imagined her flying off
her mount onto the ground. Then they were sailing over,
side by side. Heels down, knees snug, they thundered toward the stables.

Pipit stood with his hands on his hips. He'd watched
them since they'd barreled over the rise with the gelding
in the lead. Since they'd taken the jump, the stallion had
pulled ahead with smooth, easy strides. To be expected,
Pipit thought as he rubbed his hands on the thighs of his
pants. There wasn't another horse in Cordina—or in Europe as far as he was concerned—that could match the
stallion.

But he thought as he watched the woman keep the distance close that Prince Bennett had at last met his match.

Bennett reined in and slid from the horse's back with

excitement still drumming in his head. She was only seconds behind him. Her laughter was low and a bit breathless as she started to swing down. Bennett was there to take her by the waist and turn her to him before her feet hit the ground.

"How did you learn to ride like that?"

She lifted her hands to his chest, as much to keep the distance as her balance. "It's the one thing I excel at other than literature. I'd forgotten how much I've missed it these last few months."

He couldn't take his eyes off her. It was pure desire now, basic, vital. The ride they could have together would be as wild, as reckless as the ride they'd just completed. Somehow he knew it, could almost taste it. For reasons he couldn't name, he felt that he was holding two women. One calm, one passionate. He wasn't sure which one drew him more.

"Ride with me tomorrow."

Once had been a risk and a delight. Twice, Hannah knew, would be a foolish mistake. "I don't think that's possible. With Eve's play about to open, there's so much to be done at the theater."

He wouldn't push. He'd promised himself that he would give her the time to become accustomed to having him with her. From the moment on the rise when he'd realized just what that meant to him, he'd been more determined than ever to court her properly.

A first for the Royal Rake, he thought as he stepped back to kiss her hand.

"The stables are at your disposal whenever you find the time to use them."

"I appreciate that." She reached up a hand to her hair

to be certain her pins were in place. "I enjoyed this, Bennett, very much."

"So did I."

"Well, Eve will be waiting for me."

"Go ahead. Pipit and I will see to them."

"Thank you." She was stalling. The moment she realized it, Hannah drew herself in. "Goodbye, Bennett."

"Hannah." He nodded, then watched her walk back toward the palace. A smile tugged at his mouth as he patted his horse's neck. "I'm getting to her, *mon ami*," he murmured. "It's just going to take a bit of time."

Time moved so quickly. Locked in her room, Hannah held the letter from Sussex. Inside, she would find Deboque's answer to the demand she'd made only days before in the museum. Her hands were steady as she sat at her desk. With the ivory-handled letter opener provided her, she slit through the envelope. Inside was a casual, even uninspired letter from an acquaintance in England. It took Hannah less than fifteen minutes to decode it.

Request granted. December third, 23:30. Café du Dauphin. Alone. Contact will ask for the time, in English, then comment, in French, on the weather. Be certain your information warrants the exception to procedure.

Tonight. The next step would be taken tonight. Hannah folded the letter back into the envelope, but left it in plain view on her desk. Beside it was a single white rose Bennett had sent to her that morning. Hannah hesitated, then gave herself the pleasure of touching the petals.

If only life were as sweet and as simple.

Moments later, she was knocking on Prince Armand's office door.

It was opened by his secretary who bowed stiffly to her

before announcing her to the prince. Armand stood behind his desk as he gave permission to admit her.

"Your Highness." Hannah made a deep curtsy. "I apologize for disturbing you."

"Not at all, Hannah."

"But you're busy." She stood just inside of the door, hands folded. "I only wished to ask your advice on something. If it's convenient, I'll come back later."

"It's convenient now. Please come in and sit. Michel, if you would see to those few matters now, I'll have a private word with Lady Hannah."

"Of course, Your Highness." Michel bowed his way out of the room. When the door was closed, Hannah dropped her hands to her sides. Her stride firm, she walked to the desk. "We've gotten a break. You'll have to call Reeve immediately."

"I'm not easy about this," Armand said some time later when his son-in-law sat across from him. "How can we be sure Deboque will be fooled by the information Hannah will feed him?"

"Because it's so nearly the truth." Reeve downed his second cup of coffee. "Unless Hannah can give him something important, something he has no other way of getting, she'll never get close to him."

"But will he believe her?"

"It's my job to make sure he does," Hannah said quietly. "Your Highness, I know you've had objections to this operation all along, but up to this point it's worked exactly as we've wanted."

"To this point," Armand agreed, and rose. He gestured them both back into their seats so that he could pace in peace. "Now I'm in the position of asking a woman, a

woman who both my family and myself have become
very fond of, to go alone to meet a man who kills as much
for pleasure as for profit.''

"She won't be alone."

At Reeve's announcement, Hannah sat straight up. ''I
have to be. If Deboque or one of his men have the
slightest clue that I'm not, the whole operation goes up
in smoke. I won't have it.'' Now, she rose as well. ''I've
given this two years of my life.''

''And I intend to see that you live a bit longer,'' Reeve
said mildly. ''We suspect that Deboque has his headquarters in a small villa about five miles from here. We'll
have men watching it.''

''And they'll have Deboque's men watching them.''

''Leave that part to me, Hannah, and do your job. You
have the blueprints and the specs on the security systems?''

''Yes, of course.'' Annoyed, she sat again. ''And I
know I'm to give them to no one but Deboque.''

''You also know that at the first sign that things are
going wrong, you're to pull out.''

She nodded, though she had no intention of doing so.
''Yes.''

''There'll be two men stationed at the café.''

''Why don't you just send up a flare?'' Hannah tossed
back.

He understood her frustration, but merely poured a third
cup of coffee. ''It's a choice between that or wiring you.''

''The last agent who attempted to get a wire into Deboque's organization was sent back to the ISS in three
boxes.''

Reeve moved his shoulders. ''Your choice.''

Again, Hannah rose. ''I'm not used to being second-guessed, Reeve.'' When he said nothing, she set her teeth. ''I realize that you're my superior on this assignment, so I don't believe I have much of a choice.''

''As long as we understand each other.'' He rose then, and took her hand. ''Hannah, I'm aware of your reputation. Why don't we just say I don't want to take any chances on losing one of the best?'' Releasing her, he turned back to the prince. ''I have a few things to put into motion. I'll keep in touch.''

Armand waited until the door was closed again. ''Another moment, please,'' he said to Hannah. ''If you'd sit?''

She wanted to be alone, to plan each detail out carefully. There was only a matter of hours left. Breeding was as strong as training, so she sat. ''Would you like me to go over things with you again, sir?''

''No.'' His lips curved, just slightly. ''I believe I grasp the situation well enough. I have a personal question, Hannah, and I ask you beforehand not to be offended.'' He sat across from her, militarily straight. ''Am I mistaken, or has my son become fond of you?''

She linked her hands together immediately as her whole body went on alert. ''If you mean Prince Bennett, sir, he's been very kind.''

''Hannah, for my sake, please dispense with the evasions and the manners. Too often duty has interfered with the time I can spend with my family, but that doesn't mean I don't know my children and know them well. I believe Bennett is in love with you.''

She went pale instantly. ''No.'' She had to swallow, but the word came out a second time just as strongly. ''No, he's not. Perhaps he's a bit intrigued, but only because I'm not the kind of woman he's used to spending time with.''

"Hannah." Armand held up a hand before she could continue her rambling denial. "I don't ask in order to upset you. When I began to suspect this, it made me uncomfortable only because Bennett is unaware of your true purpose here."

"I understand."

"I'm not sure you do. Bennett is more like his mother than my other children. So…kindhearted. His temper has more of a lash, but his feelings are more easily reached. I only ask you this because if the answer to my next question is no, I must request that you tread softly. Do you love him, Hannah?"

Everything she felt was in her eyes. She knew it, and lowered her gaze quickly. "Whatever I feel for Bennett, for your family, won't interfere with my job."

"I know enough to recognize a person who will do what has to be done." He felt a stirring for her, a grave kind of pity that twined with empathy. "But you didn't answer me. Do you love my son?"

"I can't." This time her voice wasn't strong and there were tears chasing behind it. "I've lied to him since the first, and I'll go on doing so. You can't love and lie. Please excuse me, Your Highness."

Armand let her go. For a moment, he sat back in the chair and closed his eyes. For the next few hours, he could do nothing more than pray for her.

The café wasn't one of the pretty little tourist spots in Cordina. It was a local waterfront bar that catered to the crews from the fishing and cargo boats. Inside it was cramped with tables, many empty, and smoke and the smell of liquor. Not as rough as they came, Hannah thought as she slipped inside, but neither was it a place where a woman alone would wander unless she was looking for trouble.

Still, she didn't cause much of a stir as she came in. In her plain gray sweater and slacks, she nearly blended into the walls. The handful of women who were already there were more interesting fare. If she could get this over with quickly, she might not have to discourage any of the locals.

Hannah chose a bar stool and ordered a bourbon, neat. By the time it was served, she had sized up the room. If Reeve had indeed planted two agents here, they were certainly good ones. It was a rare thing when Hannah couldn't spot one of her own.

She'd been drinking silently for ten minutes when one of the men stood from a table and wandered in her direction. Hannah continued to drink while every muscle tensed. When he spoke, it was in French and thickened by whiskey.

"It's a sad thing for a woman to drink alone."

Hannah relaxed only enough to be annoyed. She used her primmest British tones. "It's a sadder thing for a woman not to remain alone when she chooses to."

"When one is so plain, she shouldn't be so picky," he grumbled, but moved away again. Hannah nearly smiled, then another man came through the doors.

He was dressed in seaman's clothes, with his cap pulled low. Beneath it his face was deeply tanned and gaunt. This time she tensed because she was certain.

Still, she idly lifted her drink as he moved to sit beside her at the bar.

"You have the time, *mademoiselle?*"

"Yes, it's quarter to twelve."

"Thank you." He signaled for a drink. Another minute passed as he toyed with it. *"Il fait chaud ce soir."*

"Oui, un peu."

They didn't speak again. Behind them a group began to sing a song, in French and off-key. The wine was flowing freely and the night was still young. He finished his drink and left the bar. Hannah waited only a moment, then got up to follow.

He waited for her at the edge of the dock. There was little lighting here so that he was more shadow than man. Hannah moved toward him, knowing it could be the beginning or the end for her.

"You have the information." Again he spoke in English. It was bland and unaccented, just as his French had been. Deboque chose well, she thought and only nodded.

"We go by boat." He indicated the small open runabout.

Hannah knew she had no choice. She could refuse, or she could go on. Though she knew she would have no backup on the sea, she never even considered the first. Deboque was the destination. That was the bottom line.

Without hesitation, she lowered herself into the boat and took a seat at the stern. In silence, her contact got in beside her, cast off, and started the engine. It sounded like thunder on the open water.

Hannah took a deep breath. She was on her way.

Chapter 7

Reeve would be furious. Hannah rested a hand on the seat for balance as the boat picked up speed. He could afford to be, she thought, but she had to keep her head.

So Deboque wasn't on land in the villa as they'd expected. He was, unless the boat made a sudden and dramatic change in direction, at sea. No, there would be no backup now. Hannah drew another deep breath and watched the water wake behind them. She preferred working alone in any case.

Tonight, she would meet Deboque. She could feel it. Her pulse was slow and steady, her breathing even. The spray the boat kicked up teased her skin as she kept her expression placid. Nerves, what there were of them, couldn't be allowed to show. Her midnight cruise across the Mediterranean was bringing her closer to the goal she'd worked toward for just over twenty-four months.

Excitement, not fear, was building inside of her. Even

that had to be controlled. Anything that made the pulse beat too fast or tempted the mind to swing too far ahead was dangerous. She couldn't make a mistake. Over the past two years she'd worked her way up in Deboque's organization, relying for the most part on her own skill. With the backing of the ISS she'd seen several jobs through to completion. Arms sold, diamonds liberated, drugs delivered.

The end justifies the means.

Rungs on the ladder, she thought. If she could continue to climb, it wouldn't be long before Deboque's kingdom of misery would come tumbling down on his own shoulders.

The trickiest rung had been making the well-placed Bouffe look incompetent. Deboque's senior lieutenant wasn't a fool and it'd taken a lot of guile and some risk to see that several of his assignments over the last few months had fallen through, without throwing suspicion back on herself. The biggest of these had been the arms deal with a terrorist group known for their lack of patience.

It had been sticky, but the timing had been perfect. Hannah had managed to make it seem as though Bouffe had nearly botched the deal before she had slipped in to make things right.

The terrorists had their arms—she had to leave the ISS to deal with that. And Deboque had his five million francs. It would be her pleasure to deal with that. And soon.

She saw the sleek white yacht anchored majestically in dark water. A thrill of anticipation moved through her. At the wheel, her contact signaled with an electric lantern. There was an answering flash from the ship. The engine was cut, throwing the night into silence as they drifted alongside the yacht.

Hannah reached out for the ladder and found the metal cool and hard. She knew she would be the same. Without a backward glance, she climbed up, and into the unknown.

"Lady Hannah."

There was a tall, dark-skinned man waiting for her. He took her hand and bowed over it. She recognized him from her last briefing, though she would have placed his accent as Jamaican in any case. He was Ricardo Batemen, a twenty-six-year-old islander, an ivy-league graduate with a degree in medicine. He still used a scalpel, but he preferred to wield it on the healthy and unanesthetized.

He had become a favorite of Deboque's.

"I'm Ricardo." His young, smooth face spread into a smile. "Welcome to the *Invincible*."

"Thank you, Ricardo." She gave a casual look around and counted five more men and one woman on deck. The men were dressed in dark suits and carried machine guns. The woman had a sarong draped over a bikini and looked bored. "Might I have a drink?"

"Of course." His eyes, she noted, were pale, an almost translucent green that never seemed to blink. His voice was like rich cream over hot coffee. "But first, you must excuse our precautions. Your bag, Lady Hannah."

She lifted a brow and met his eyes straight on. "I'll depend on you to see that everything in it is returned to me."

"You have my word." He bowed as she handed it to him. "Now, if you would go with Carmine. She will take you to your cabin. You may like to freshen up after she makes certain no one has planted any electronic devices on you."

A strip search, Hannah thought resignedly. "No one plants anything on me, Ricardo. But I admire a cautious man." Hannah crossed the deck to Carmine as though she was going to tea.

Moments later, Ricardo set Hannah's black alligator bag on a gleaming mahogany desk. "Carmine is seeing to her. She has a small-caliber pistol, her passport and identification and about three thousand francs along with a few cosmetics. There is an envelope, sealed."

"Thank you, Ricardo." The voice was deep and smoky with its traces of France. "You may bring her to me in ten minutes. Then we won't be disturbed."

"Oui, monsieur."

"Ricardo, your impressions?"

"Attractive enough, more so than her photograph. And cool, very cool. Her hand was dry and steady."

"Good." There was a trace of amusement in the voice now. "Ten minutes, Ricardo." He picked up the envelope and broke the seal.

A short time later, Hannah adjusted her sweater. She'd found the search more annoying than humiliating. Carmine had taken her stiletto, but she'd expected that. Ricardo had her pistol. For now, she was alone and unarmed in the middle of the sea. She still had her wits.

Hannah stood in the center of the cabin when Ricardo opened the door. "My apologies again for the inconvenience, Lady Hannah."

"A small annoyance, Ricardo." He hadn't brought back her bag, but she said nothing of it. "I hope there won't be too many more."

"None at all. If you'd just come with me."

Hannah followed him, walking easily as the boat swayed in the current. It was the size of a small hotel, she'd noted. And there were escape routes if it became necessary. The carpet they walked on was rich red. In the cabin where she'd been searched had been an antique mirror with beveled glass and a bedspread in velvet. There had also been a porthole big enough for a child, or a slender woman to work their way through.

Ricardo stopped by a glossy oak door and knocked twice. Without waiting for an answer, he turned the knob and gestured her inside. Hannah stepped through and heard the door click shut at her back.

It was opulent, elegant, even fanciful. Eighteenth-century France seemed to come alive. Now the carpet was the deep shimmering blue of kings and the paneled walls were polished to a mirrorlike gleam. Two delicate, glittering chandeliers sprinkled light over the antique wood and plush upholstery. Brocade had been used lavishly to drape over and around a bed fit for a king. All the colors were vivid, almost shocking.

There was a scent of something floral and something old that merged together into one strangely compelling and oddly uneasy fragrance. With the gentle sway of the ship, a collection of crystal animals shuddered with life.

It only took Hannah seconds to absorb this. As grand and extravagant as the room was, the man who sat behind the Louis XVI desk dominated. She didn't feel the evil she'd expected to. With the truly wicked, Hannah knew you often experienced a chill or a dread. What she saw was a slender and attractive man in his fifties, with steel-gray hair flowing back in a mane from a chiseled, aristocratic face. He wore black. It seemed to accent his almost poetically-pale skin. His eyes were black, too, like a raven's. They studied her now as his full, rather beautiful mouth curved into a smile.

She'd seen pictures of him, of course. She'd studied every scrap of information that had been gathered on him in the last twenty years. And yet... And yet she hadn't been prepared for the shock of sensuality which seemed to emanate from him.

He was a man women had died for. And now she understood it. He was a man who other men had killed for without question. She understood that, too, as she stood ten feet away and felt the power.

"Lady Hannah." He rose, slowly, gracefully. His body was trim, almost delicate. His hand, as he offered it to her, was narrow and beautiful with a trio of diamonds on long fingers.

She couldn't hesitate, though she felt if her hand touched his she would be pulled out of what she knew into something foreign and frightening.

Hannah smiled and stepped forward. "Monsieur Deboque." She was glad to see his slight surprise at her use of his name. "It's a pleasure."

"Please sit. Will you have brandy?"

"Yes, thank you." She chose a soft high-backed chair that faced the desk. There was music playing through hidden speakers. Chopin. She listened to the notes as Deboque crossed to an enameled cabinet and withdrew a decanter. "Your ship is exquisite, *monsieur*." There was a painting behind his desk. One of six she knew had been stolen from a private collection only the year before. She herself had helped execute the theft.

"I appreciate beauty." He offered the brandy, then instead of going behind the desk again, sat beside her. "To your health, *mademoiselle*."

"And yours." She smiled at him again before she sipped.

"Perhaps you will tell me how you became aware of my name."

"I make it a habit of knowing who I work for, Monsieur Deboque." She shook her head as he drew out a cigarette case and offered her one. "I must congratulate you on your security and your staff. Discovering who, shall we say, reigned, was hardly an easy matter."

He drew in the smoke slowly, as a man who appreciated fine tastes. "Most have found it impossible."

Her eyes were cool and amused on his. "I find little impossible."

"Others have found it fatal." When she only smiled, he let it pass. She was, as Ricardo had said, very cool. "My reports on you are very flattering, Lady Hannah."

"Of course."

It was his turn to smile. "I admire confidence."

"And I."

"It appears I'm in your debt for smoothing over an exchange with our Mediterranean neighbors a few months ago. I would have been, to say the least, annoyed to have lost that contract."

"It was my pleasure. It would seem, *monsieur*, that you have a few weak links in the chain."

"It would seem," he murmured. He'd already debated handing Bouffe over to Ricardo for disposal. A pity, Deboque thought. Bouffe had been a loyal and valued employee for over a decade. "You are enjoying your stay in Cordina?"

Her heart drummed lightly but she sipped again. "The palace is quite lovely." She moved her shoulders as she let her gaze roam around the room. "I, too, appreciate beauty. It helps compensate for the fact that the Bissets are a bit boring."

"You're not impressed with the Royal Family, Lady Hannah?"

"I'm not easily impressed. They are certainly very pretty people, but so...devoted." She tinted her voice with derision, lightly. "I prefer devoting myself to something more tangible than honor and duty."

"And loyalty, Lady Hannah?"

She turned to him again. He was looking deep, trying to see inside, trying to see beyond. "I can be loyal." She touched her tongue to the rim of her snifter. "As long as it's profitable."

It was a chance, she knew. Disloyalty in Deboque's organization was punishable by death. She waited, outwardly cool while a single line of sweat beaded down her back. He studied her a moment, then threw his lion's head back and laughed. Hannah felt each individual muscle in her body sing with relief.

"An honest woman. I admire that. Yes, I admire that a great deal more than sworn oaths." He drew in the rich French smoke then exhaled again. "It would seem to my advantage to continue to make it profitable for someone of your skills and ambitions."

"I was hoping you'd see it that way. I prefer the executive branch, if you comprehend, Monsieur Deboque, but I'm willing to work my way to it. Delegation, organization, is so much more rewarding than execution, don't you think?"

"Indeed, yes." He studied her again, considering. She appeared to be a mild, well-bred young woman of some means. He preferred a quiet, unassuming outer shell in a woman. He thought briefly of Janet Smithers who he'd used and discarded nearly a decade before. Lady Hannah, he thought, might prove to be a great deal more interesting, and more competent. "You've been with us two years now?"

"Yes."

"And in those two years, you've proven yourself to be very useful." He rose now and retrieved the envelope on his desk. "You brought this to me, I assume?"

"I did." She swirled her brandy. "Though I found the method with which it was delivered irksome."

"My apologies. This information is interesting, Lady Hannah, but I fear, incomplete."

She crossed her legs and relaxed back in the chair. "A woman who writes everything she knows on paper loses her value quickly. What isn't there, is in here." She laid a finger against her temple.

"I see." He admired an employee who knew her own worth, and guarded it. "If we say I'm interested in the security systems of the Royal Palace, the Fine Arts Center, the museum, for the purpose of emulating such systems for my own use, you would be able to fill in the blanks?"

"Of course."

"And if I asked how you came by such information?"

"This was the purpose of my visit to Cordina."

"One of them." Intrigued, he tapped the envelope on his palm. "It was fortunate that you were able to become close to Princess Eve."

"Fortunate, but not difficult. She was lonely for female companionship. I'm accommodating. I fuss over her daughter, listen to her fears and complaints. By easing some of her workload, I also earn the gratitude of Prince Alexander. He worries that his wife will tire herself while carrying his child."

"And you are trusted?"

"Implicitly. And why not?" she added. "My family is

well respected, my breeding without mark. Prince Armand sees me as a young cousin of his dead wife. Your pardon, *monsieur,* but aren't these the reasons you enlisted me to find a place at the palace?''

"Yes, they are." He sat back. She pleased him, but he was a long way from giving her his full confidence. "I have word that the young prince is interested in you."

Something inside her froze at that. "Your network of information is admirable." Hannah glanced at her empty snifter, then tilted it in question. Deboque rose immediately to refill her glass. It was just enough time to regain her composure.

"Bennett is, as I'm sure you're aware, invariably interested in the female closest at hand." She gave a low laugh and tried not to hate herself. "He's really only a boy, and spoiled at that. I've found the simplest way to handle him is to act disinterested."

Deboque nodded slowly. "Then he pursues."

"Such men are always more—accommodating under those circumstances."

"I beg your pardon if I seem to be getting too personal, my dear, but how accommodating?"

"He's a bit bored, a bit reckless. His weakness for women should have its uses. I believe with a certain— flair—information can be drawn out of him. It was he, you see, who took me through the Center, and through the naval base at Le Havre." She sipped again, lingering over it. Deboque would already know about her tête-à-tête with Bennett at the museum. So, she would use his knowledge and twist the truth.

"It was a simple matter to ask questions and express interest in how the museum guards its treasures. With that, I was shown the setup, alarms, monitors, sensors." She paused again to let it sink in. "The more a woman pretends ignorance, the more she learns."

Deboque warmed the brandy in his hands. "Hypothetically, you understand, can the security at the palace be broken?"

At last, she thought, they were homing in. "Hypothetically, any security can be broken. I will say that Reeve MacGee has designed an admirable system, but not an invincible one."

"Interesting." He picked up a small china figure of a hawk and began to study it. The room fell into silence long enough for her to be sure he was trying to unnerve her. "And do you have a theory on how this system can be undermined?"

"From inside." She sipped her brandy again. "It's always cleaner from the inside."

"And the Center?"

"Much the same."

"This play the princess wrote, it opens in a few days. It would be amusing to cause a small disturbance."

"Of what nature?"

He only smiled. "Oh, I'm just speaking in theory, you understand. It seems to me that the Royal Family would be uncomfortable if something disrupted the evening. I should hate to miss it. You'll be there?"

"I'm expected." She needed to push him, push him into something definite. "I prefer knowing which door to walk into, *monsieur*."

"Then you might be wise to remain in the audience. I wouldn't want to lose you now that we've become close."

She acknowledged this, but realizing he would demand the rest of the stats then dismiss her, Hannah changed gears. "As a matter of personal curiosity may I ask why you have such interest in the Royal Family? It intrigues me because I see you much as I see myself, as a person most interested in profit and personal gain.''

''Profit is always desirable.'' He set the hawk down. He had hands that might have played a violin or written sonnets. They rarely killed, only gestured for others to do so. ''Personal gain can have a multitude of variables, *n'est-ce pas?*''

''As long as it satisfies,'' she agreed. ''Using the kidnapping of the Princess Gabriella or the threats on the Bissets as a lever to gain your release from prison was one thing. You're no longer in prison.'' Again she looked with admiration around the room. ''I would think you would move on to more profitable waters.''

''All business needs a completion.'' She saw emotion for the first time as his fingers tightened around his glass. ''All debts require payment. The interest of ten years is dear, very dear. Do you agree?''

''Yes. Revenge, or retribution if you prefer. This I understand is as sweet as diamonds.'' And looking at him, she knew he would stop at nothing to collect. ''*Monsieur,* you have arranged for me to be in the palace. I intend to continue to remain there until you alter the order, but I prefer to do so with some direction.'' She gestured casually, palm up. ''The revenge, after all, is yours, not mine. I've never worked well blindfolded.''

''A man who puts all of his cards on the table loses his edge.''

''Agreed. So does a man who doesn't sharpen his tools and use them where they're best suited. I'm in, *monsieur.* Having a map of some sort would be useful.''

He intended to use her, and well. Sitting back again, Deboque steepled his hands. His diamonds shot out vio-

lent light. He had failed, twice before he had failed to use
the Bissets for his own purposes. He had failed to bring
Armand to his knees. Whatever had to be done, whomever
had to be used, he wouldn't fail this time. In Hannah, he
thought he'd found the instrument.

"Let me ask you this. If one man wishes to destroy
another, what does he do?"

"The simplest is to end his life."

Deboque smiled, and now Hannah saw the evil. It was
coated with class, pampered with elegance, but very real.
"I'm not a simple man. Death is so final, and even when
it is slow, it's soon over. To destroy a man, the soul, the
heart, requires more than a bullet in the brain."

He was speaking of Armand, she knew. It wasn't time
to demand he name names and reveal his plan. He would
tell her nothing and trust her less. Hannah set down her
glass and tried to think as he did. "To truly destroy, you
take away what is most valuable." Her heart began to
beat in the back of her throat, clogging a wave of nausea.
Still, when she spoke it was with cool admiration. "His
children?"

"You are intelligent as well as lovely." Leaning over
he placed his hand on hers. She felt it from him, the vile,
dark movement of death. "To make a man suffer, to destroy his soul, you deprive him of what he loves best and
leave him to live with it. His children and grandchildren
dead, his country in chaos, a man would have nothing left
but misery. And a country without an heir becomes un-
stable—and profitable—if one is shrewd."

"All of them," Hannah murmured. She thought of little
Marissa, so pretty and soft, and Dorian with his smudged
face and bright grin. Fear for them was suddenly so
strong, so vital, she thought it had to show in her eyes.

She kept them down, looking at his hand as it lay over hers and the cold, hard glint of the diamonds.

"All of them, *monsieur?*" When she thought she could trust herself again, she looked back at his face. He was smiling. In the fragile light of the chandeliers he looked wan as a ghost and infinitely more frightening. "Not an easy task, even for someone of your power."

"Nothing worthwhile is simple, my dear. But as you said, nothing is impossible—particularly when one is trusted and close."

Her brow lifted. She didn't shudder or draw away. Business, she told herself. Lady Hannah was all business. She was being offered a job, the most vital one Deboque had to offer.

"You were carefully chosen, Lady Hannah. For more than ten years, I've had one dream. I believe you are the instrument to see it to fruition."

She pursed her lips as if considering while her mind raced ahead. He was giving her a contract, a royal one. As she said nothing, his fingers played lightly over her knuckles. Like a spider, she thought, a handsome and very clever spider.

"Such a responsibility is weighty for someone in my position in your organization."

"That can be seen to. Bouffe is—retiring," he said softly. "I will be looking for a replacement."

She let her hand lie under his as she touched her tongue to her top lip. "A guarantee, *monsieur.*"

"My word."

She smiled a little. *"Monsieur."*

With a nod of acknowledgement, he rose and pressed a button on his desk. Within seconds Ricardo appeared.

"Lady Hannah will be replacing Bouffe. See to the arrangements, Ricardo. Discreetly."

"Of course." The pale green eyes half closed as if with pleasure.

Hannah waited for the door to shut again. A man's life was over. "The day may come when you decide to replace me as casually."

"Not if you continue to please me." He lifted her hand again and kissed it. "I have a feeling you will."

"I must tell you, *monsieur,* I have a distaste for killing children." His fingers tightened, very slightly on hers, but she didn't fidget. "I believe it will take five million American dollars to overcome this distaste."

She saw it in his eyes. He would break her fingers as easily as he would kiss them. Hannah kept her gaze steady on his and hoped she hadn't pushed her luck too far.

"Is it money that seduces you, *ma petite?*"

"Not seduces, pleases. I like to be pleased."

"You have two weeks to please me, Lady Hannah. Then I shall return the favor." He kept her hand in his as he drew her to her feet. "Now, as a show of faith, you will tell me what you failed to note down here."

Hannah walked over to the specs and prepared to lie to him.

She was exhausted. In a decade of assignments, nothing had left her feeling so empty and soiled. As she drove through the palace gates, she could only think about a long hot shower where she could scrub off whatever traces remained of Deboque's cologne. Reeve was standing a hundred feet beyond the gates. Hannah stopped the car and waited for him to slide in beside her.

"You were gone a long time." He gave her a long,

thorough study. "It wasn't in the plans for you to be out
of contact for over an hour."

"It was in the plans for me to get to Deboque."

"And you did?"

She rolled down her window a bit farther. "I met him
on a yacht, the *Invincible*. It's anchored about five miles
northwest. He has at least six armed guards, double that
by a guess. He has the information we wanted him to
have. I'm replacing Bouffe."

Reeve's brow lifted. "You must have impressed him."

"That was the idea." She wondered how soon she
could wash the taste of his brandy from her mouth. "He's
planning something for the opening of Eve's play." When
Reeve stiffened beside her, she went on. "I don't believe
it's going to be anything directly against the family. He
seemed to think it would be entertaining to confuse matters. He's very careful how he phrases things. Nothing too
direct. Even if I testified against him, it would be difficult
to actually convict him of conspiracy. He hypothesizes,
theorizes."

"Did he give you an idea where he intends to make
his move?"

She listened for a moment to a bird that was singing
its heart out. "He seemed most interested in the palace.
It's the biggest challenge. We have two weeks."

"He moves in two weeks?"

"That's how long he gave me to murder your family."
She turned to him then and saw his face was pale and set.
"All of you but Armand, Reeve. The children, everyone.
He wants to destroy Armand's soul and leave Cordina
without an heir. If you trust my judgment, he wants this
done as much for personal satisfaction as for the profit he
might make when Cordina is thrown into chaos."

Reeve drew out a cigarette but didn't light it. "I trust your judgment."

"We have two weeks to stop him, or to convince him that I've done what he wants."

It was his family, his heart, yet he knew he had to think as coolly as she did. "Is he setting you up?"

She thought for a moment, then shook her head. "I don't think so. It's certainly possible that he'd dispose of me after I've finished the job, but I think it's more likely he'd continue to use me. We did a good job of planting information about me, and over the past two years I've saved him a bit of trouble and money. If he believes I can give him this, he'll sit back and wait."

"Armand will have to be told."

"I know." But not Bennett. Armand and only Armand.

"For now, just go on as usual." He indicated that she should drive ahead. "We'll need some time."

"Eve's opening is in a few days."

"We'll handle it. You get some sleep. As soon as we have a direction, I'll let you know."

Hannah got out of the car, then as Reeve stood on the other side she stopped. "I want him. I want him for myself. I know it's unprofessional and stupid. But if I have the chance, if I find the way, I'm going to take him out myself."

Reeve said nothing as she walked up the steps. He'd already vowed the same thing.

Chapter 8

"I don't want you to go tonight."

"You know I have to." Eve stood, grim and stubborn, facing her husband. "It's my play, my troupe, my production. I don't have a choice, Alex."

"Excuses can be made." He looked at her, dressed in midnight blue that skimmed her shoulders and swirled to her ankles. Her hair was caught up in the back so that it fell over one shoulder like ebony. Even after all the years he'd known her, just looking at her made his pulse race. "You know how dangerous it could be. With the information we have now, we can be sure there'll be an incident tonight. I don't want you involved."

"I am involved." She was frightened. Ever since Reeve had told them that he'd received a tip that there would be trouble at the theater on opening night, her nerves had been stretched tight. Yes, she was frightened, but she was no less determined. She crossed to the beveled mirror above the bureau as if checking the arrangement of her hair was of some importance. "I wrote the play, I produced it, and more important than either of those," she continued before he could interrupt, "I belong at the theater tonight because I'm your wife."

The fact that her arguments were valid meant nothing. He wanted her in the palace, safe, untouchable. His heart would rest easy if he knew she was here, in the suite of rooms she'd decorated, tucked high in the palace that had been his family home for generations. Nothing could happen to her here. Anything could happen outside.

"My love, Reeve is rarely wrong. If he says there'll be trouble tonight, I want you well away from it. The fact that you're carrying a child is a very simple reason for you to be excused. I know the play is important to you, but—"

"Yes, it is," she interrupted. "But you're more important."

"Then do this for me, and stay home tonight."

She tilted her head, holding on to both her nerves and her temper. "Alexander, would you stay behind with me?"

"If it was possible, of course." Impatience had him dragging a hand through his hair. It was a ploy she'd used before, and one there was little argument against. "I can't close myself up every time there's a rumble from Deboque."

"For Cordina," she said quietly. "And Cordina is now my country, too."

"Eve." He thought he loved her as much as it was possible to love. Every day he learned there could be more. "You are the most precious thing in the world to me. I almost lost you once."

She crossed to him then, knowing the first step, the first touch should be hers. When both of his hands were in hers, she looked up into his eyes. "And I you, Alex. I'm going to sit in the Royal Box beside you, where I belong."

From outside the door, Hannah heard the conversation clearly enough. It was moments like this that made it difficult to think of what she was doing, what she had yet to do, as merely another assignment. There were people beyond the door who she'd come to care about. The Bissets were no longer names or symbols, but friends. After ten years of playing dangerous games, she knew how risky it could be to make friends.

She closed her eyes and drew her breath deep before she knocked.

"*Entrez.*" It was Alexander who answered, the impatience in his voice ripe. Hannah opened the door but didn't cross the threshold.

"I'm sorry. I'm disturbing you."

"Of course not." With the warmth that was so much a part of her, Eve smiled and gestured her inside. "I see you're ready for the evening." She felt a little twinge of regret at Hannah's severe beige dress and hairstyle. She'd hoped with a little time she could urge Hannah to soften her image. Tonight, however, there were more immediate matters of concern. "We were just about to come down ourselves."

Hannah saw Eve take Alexander's hand again. "I thought you might need some help."

"No, there's nothing." But the cloud of concern didn't leave Eve's eyes. "Hannah, I don't want you to feel obligated to go with the family. Knowing there's a possibility of an—incident," she began. "Well, it might be more comfortable for you here at home."

"Of course I'm going." With the hated secret tucked inside of her, she shifted the wrap on her arms. "And I really believe everything's going to be fine. If you don't need me then, I'll just go down."

"Please, let's not talk about it anymore," Eve said when Hannah shut the door behind her. "Let's go say good-night to Marissa before we leave."

"Eve." Alexander gathered her close. He could feel the slight swell where another child lay. "I love you."

"Talk's cheap," she murmured, and tried for a laugh. "Promise to show me later, after the play."

He let his cheek rest on her hair. "You have my word."

Bennett was already waiting in the main hall. Even with the distance separating them, Hannah could feel the impatience coming from him. Impatience, she thought, mixed with a recklessness that the elegant evening clothes couldn't disguise. He was looking for trouble, Hannah realized. More, he was hoping for it.

"There you are." Though he smiled up at her, his mind was already on the evening ahead. Instinctively he took her hand, holding it as she reached the bottom of the stairs. "You don't have to go tonight, Hannah. I'd be happier if you didn't."

Guilt came so quickly that she had squeezed his hand in reassurance before she could stop herself. "Now even you sound like Eve," she said lightly. "I want to be there. A vague tip from an anonymous source is a foolish reason to miss a night at the theater."

He touched the pearl cluster at her ear. "Is that what we call British pluck?"

"It's what we call common sense."

"Whatever it's called I want you to stay close. There'll be enough guards to smother us, but I prefer to keep an eye on you myself." Before she could stop him, he was leading her toward the doors.

"Eve and Alexander are nearly ready. I said I'd wait for them."

"Security feels better splitting us up." He acknowledged Claude with a brief nod. "You'll ride with me. Father will come along after Alexander and Eve."

"All right." She walked out into the star-studded night, calmly holding the .22 that lay within her beaded evening bag.

The theater was sold out. Long before the first curtain, the seats were filled so that the babble of conversation rose up to the Royal Box. There was thunderous applause when the Bissets entered. From the background as bows were made, Hannah held her breath and studied the sea of faces.

If Deboque had been there, she knew she would have found him.

"The Center's been swept twice," Reeve murmured in her ear. "There's nothing here."

She nodded and took her seat as the curtain rose.

The play was everything Eve had hoped for, though Hannah doubted anyone in the box had their full attention on the drama and pathos onstage. More than once, she cast a sidelong look at Bennett to find him studying the audience.

Deboque wasn't there. Hannah hadn't expected him. Whatever happened, whenever it happened, he would be far away with an alibi as solid as Cordinian rock.

So they would wait. And watch.

When the lights came up for intermission, Hannah could almost feel Eve relax. A false alarm? No. Though she preferred Eve believing it was so, Hannah knew better. There was an itch between her shoulder blades, vague but persistent. Some called it a hunch. Others called it instinct. Hannah had been in the game long enough to know when to wait and when to go with it.

"Would you like something to drink?"

She turned to Bennett, set to refuse. For personal reasons, she wanted him close at hand. "Yes," she heard herself saying, knowing this would be just one more deception. "I'd love something cool."

The moment he was through the doors behind them, Hannah leaned toward Reeve. "I'm going to look around."

"I'd stay close—I have a feeling." With him it was in the gut. He'd yet to let Gabriella move more than an arm's span away.

"I do too. Deboque said something about me staying in the audience. I want to take a walk backstage."

He started to object, but Gabriella took his hand and gave Hannah the few seconds she needed to slip out. She made her way toward the ladies' lounge until she was certain no one was watching. With the ease of long experience, she slipped into a stairway and began moving down. She had ten minutes, Hannah thought as she checked her watch, before anyone would miss her.

There were costume changes and stretched nerves backstage when Hannah crossed the corridor. Most of the actors were too wound up to spare her a glance. Nothing out of place. Nothing out of synch. And yet, the itch between her shoulder blades persisted.

Chantel's dressing room door was half-open. The actress caught a glimpse of Hannah, hesitated, then called out. "Lady Hannah."

Because she saw no choice, Hannah stopped at the doorway. "Miss O'Hurley. Her Highness wasn't able to come down, but you should know she's delighted with your performance."

"Thank you." Chantel set down the grease pencil she'd been using to touch up her eyes. "And what do you think of the play?"

"It's gripping. Your interpretation of Julia is breathtaking."

With a nod, Chantel moved toward her. The exaggerated stage makeup only made her look more exotic. "You know, I was born into show business. It's in the blood, if you get my drift. And I've always thought one inveterate actor easily recognizes another."

Very cool, almost smiling, Hannah met her eyes. "I suppose that's true."

"Perhaps that's why while I'm still not sure if I like you, I know I don't trust you." Chantel adjusted the cuff of the dress she'd wear in the next scene. "I've always been very fond of Bennett. A woman like myself has few men she can call real friends."

There was something strong, something honest in the woman who faced her. Hannah gave as much as she could. "I can tell you that Bennett is a special man, and one I care for very much."

Chantel was silent a moment, weighing, considering. "I'm not sure why, but I believe you." She shook her head. "I can't figure out why you're playing Jane Eyre, but I imagine you have your reasons."

"Places, Miss O'Hurley."

Chantel turned to give herself one last check in a full-length mirror. She lifted her chin to a different angle and became Julia. Her voice took on the slightest of drawls, an echo of the American South, as she turned back to walk past Hannah. "Darling," she said in character. "You must know beige is the worst possible color for you." Then she winked and walked to the wings.

Hannah let out a long breath. She'd seen nothing out of place, seen no one who didn't belong and had learned a lesson. Her cover wasn't as foolproof as she'd always thought.

She walked back down the corridor, turned into the stairway and started up. She heard the applause as the curtain came up. Then came the distant sound, the rumble and boom, of an explosion. The lights went out.

There were scattered screams as the theater plunged into darkness. From here, the warning rumble couldn't be heard. In the Royal Box, guards closed in like a wedge. Guns were drawn and held ready.

"Stay where you are," Reeve ordered. He gave Gabriella's hand a quick, reassuring squeeze. "Two of you come with me." He moved into the hallway with two guards. "We'll need a light." Swearing, he dug in his pocket for a lighter. "We'll need someone to go over the PA and keep the audience from panicking." Even as he flicked the lighter on, throwing dull and shadowy light off his face, Chantel's voice came cool and clear through the speakers.

"*Mesdames and messieurs,* if you would stay seated for a moment or two. We seem to be having some difficulties with the lights. If you'd like to take advantage of the opportunity by getting to know your neighbor better…"

"Good girl," Reeve murmured as he heard the nervous laughter. "Let's get down to the main breakers."

Hannah hadn't come back. The words kept echoing over in Bennett's mind as he heard Alexander murmuring reassurances to Eve. She was out there somewhere, alone in the dark. Without hesitation, he was moving toward the door.

"Your Highness." The looming figure of a guard inched toward him. "If you would please remain seated."

"Let me pass."

"Bennett." His father's voice cut through the dark. "Please sit. This should be over in moments."

"Hannah's not here."

There was the briefest of silences. "Reeve will handle things."

There was duty, and the honor he'd never questioned. Now there was love. Bennett shoved his way through the door and went to find her.

Hannah had the gun in her hand as she stood in the stairwell. She didn't move, barely breathed, as she debated whether to go up and check on the Bissets, or whether to go down and check the power. If there had been one bomb, there could all too easily be another.

Her head told her that the Bissets were well guarded and her job was to find the source of the trouble. Her heart wanted only to see if Bennett was well and safe. Following it, Hannah started up the stairs. She'd climbed no more than three when she heard the sound of a door closing on the landing below.

With her finger wrapped around the trigger, she pointed the barrel of the gun up and started down again. She saw the beam of the flashlight before she heard the footsteps.

Cautious ones. Quiet ones. Like a shadow, Hannah melted into a corner and waited.

She recognized him from the museum. He was dressed now in the dark blue uniform of the maintenance crew and carried a small toolbox. She almost nodded in approval. Anyone seeing him would simply assume he was assigned to fix whatever had gone wrong. The beam skimmed past the toes of her shoes before she stepped out and pressed the gun at his side.

"Be easy," she said in undertones. "I apologize for greeting you this way, but I didn't want a hole in my head before you recognized me."

"Mademoiselle." She heard the tightly controlled fury in his voice. No man liked to be caught unaware. "I was told you would remain out of the way this evening."

Hannah drew the gun back but kept it steady. "I prefer a firsthand look at what's going on. A dramatic distraction," she complimented him. "Are there other plans for tonight?" He was prepared to kill, she was certain. But was he armed? She knew if she detained him too long or pressed too hard, her cover would be in jeopardy.

"Only if the opportunity arises. You will excuse me?"

"Certainly." Her only thought now was to see him out of the theater and away before any opportunity arose. The theater was packed with people, the Royal Family was present. Now wasn't the time for a confrontation. "Can I assist you in making a discreet exit?"

"It's been seen to."

"Very well. Tell our employer that I won't be as dramatic, but I'll be effective." She turned toward the stairs when she heard the door above open.

"Hannah?"

At the sound of Bennett's voice her blood froze. Even

as the man beside her made a move, she clamped a hand over his arm. She knew without seeing that he reached for a weapon.

"Don't be a fool," she hissed. "In this light you could too easily miss and ruin everything. Turn off that beam and let me handle it." She felt his resistance, but turned quickly and started up the stairs. "Bennett." She didn't have to fake the fear in her voice. He was hardly more than a shadow at the doorway but she put her arms around him and let her body block his.

"What are you doing down here?" he began.

"I lost my way when the lights went off."

"For God's sake, Hannah. How did you manage to get all the way down here?"

"I—I'm not sure. Please, let's go back."

"You could've broken your neck on these stairs." When he gave her a slight shake and started to draw her back she shifted to block him more thoroughly.

"Kiss me," she ordered in a whisper.

Almost amused now that he'd found her safe, Bennett tilted up her chin. In the dim light he could only make out the vague outline of her face and the glint of her eyes. "If you insist."

Even as he closed his mouth over hers, she gripped the door handle behind him, prepared to shove him through.

Then his fingers spread over her face, gently. His lips coaxed and comforted and asked so little in return. On the handle her fingers tightened as much in response to him as in fear for him. One hand settled at the small of her back, again to soothe. Hannah felt her heart tear. She loved him, yet knew she couldn't. She wanted the kiss to be no more than what it was, a merging of lips, a symbol of caring. But what it was, what it had to be was a tool to give the man below them the time to escape.

Then Bennett would be safe. For seconds only, she put her heart into the kiss. He would be safe, and she could breathe again.

He felt the change and his heart thudded with it. He had imagined her lost in the dark, alone and in need of comfort and physical contact. So thinking, he had buried his own needs and had kissed her as a friend might, with affection and understanding. Her response was thunder and lightning. His fingers tightened on her face as he murmured her name.

The lights came on in a flash.

It happened very quickly then, but Bennett would remember, for a lifetime, each movement, each sound. There was no time for fear, only for surprise, then disillusionment.

When the lights went on, he stiffened. She knew in that moment that Deboque's man had not made his escape as she had hoped, but was waiting to take advantage of the opportunity that had presented itself. Without hesitation she whirled out of Bennett's arms and half shoved him through the door. The man's gun was drawn, but so was hers. And she was very fast.

Bennett had seen the man, and his weapon. He had pushed himself off the door to shield her even as she'd fired. For a moment, he simply stared, stunned at seeing the man fall and lay still. Then he saw the pistol in Hannah's hand. Surprise came and went. His face became very impassive. When he spoke, his voice was neutral.

"What game are you playing, and for whom?"

She'd never killed before. She'd been trained to, of course, but had never actually ended a life by her own hand. As she stood looking down, the gun felt foreign and slimy in her hand. Her face was very pale, her eyes very dark when she turned to Bennett. "I'll have to explain, but there isn't time." She heard the sound of running feet and struggled to pull herself together. "Please trust me."

"That's an interesting request at this point." He started to brush by her to go to the man below.

"Bennett, please." Grabbing his arm, she drew up beside him. "I'll tell you whatever I can later. You can verify it all with Reeve or your father."

She felt his muscles tense. "My father?"

"Please, for his sake, the sake of your family, play this out with me." She pushed the gun into his hand just as Reeve arrived with five guards on his heels. Now she let reaction set it. Again, truth was often the best cover.

"He tried to shoot the prince." Hannah let her voice shake and leaned heavily against Bennett. "He was going to kill him. If Bennett hadn't..." Trailing off, she buried her face against Bennett's shoulder.

He didn't move, though he didn't contradict her, there was no comforting hand now, no murmured reassurances. Reeve bent over the body, then lifted his gaze and met Bennett's. "It's fortunate you were quick—and accurate." The .45 lying beside the body hadn't been fired. His eyes shifted over briefly to rest on Hannah. "We'll handle this quietly."

Bennett's lips curved, but it wasn't a smile. "Of course."

"If you'll go back to your box." Reeve signaled two of the guards to accompany him. "We'll say nothing of this to the family until we can be private." With a pencil, he lifted the .45 automatic by the trigger guard. "The police will come in the back way."

Bennett brushed the guards aside with a gesture. It was the first time Hannah had seen him use true royal arrogance. "I want to talk to you. Alone. Now."

"All right." He'd seen too much, Reeve knew. It had to be handled quickly. "Eve's office then. If you'd give me a few minutes to deal with this first."

"You have ten," Bennett said, and turned his back on all of them.

"I'd like to go back to the palace." Hannah stood on the steps, alone now. Her hands, white at the knuckles, clutched her bag. "I'm not feeling well."

"See to a car and driver," Reeve ordered one of the guards. To another he gave the dead man's weapon before he climbed the stairs to slip an arm around Hannah. "I'll walk you out." The moment they were out of earshot, his voice became curt and professional. "What happened?"

Her knees were shaking, but she schooled her voice to the same tone. Briefly, she gave him her report. "The entire thing couldn't have taken more than five minutes." It had seemed like hours.

"It was just bad luck all around that Bennett found you. Still, the story will hold. He has a reputation for being an excellent shot. All I have to do is calm him down." Reeve let out a long breath at that. He knew his brother-in-law well, just as he knew all the Bissets. Once their temper was lost, it wasn't easily regained. "We'll go over this in the morning so that the story you pass on to Deboque is the most advantageous one."

"He'll never forgive me."

Reeve was intuitive enough to know she wasn't speaking of Deboque now. "Bennett is neither unjust nor hardhearted. He'll be angry at being kept in the dark, but he won't blame you."

"Won't he?" Hannah walked through the doors and into the night air without looking back.

She sat by the window looking out at the garden. An hour had passed, then two while she watched the moonlight. The palace was quiet. Perhaps the others had come back, but she wouldn't have heard because her rooms faced the back. Guests were always given the loveliest views and the quietest spots.

She could imagine all too well how Bennett would have reacted to Reeve's explanations. But it wouldn't be Reeve he would blame. Hannah knew the blame would be hers and had accepted it. In the morning he would probably demand to speak with her privately.

She wouldn't apologize. Hannah lifted her chin a fraction higher. She would accept his anger and his coldness, but she wouldn't apologize for being who and what she was.

She loved him. He would hardly believe her now if she had the right to tell him. She would have died for him tonight, not only for duty, not only for honor, but so much more for love. He would never understand or believe that now. Perhaps it was best. If her feelings for him had gotten beyond her control, it was wiser, and safer, if his for her had deadened.

She still had an assignment to complete and two years of work to finish.

Hannah laid her head on the windowsill and wished she were in London where the night would be cold and damp and smell of the river.

He didn't knock. The time for manners, formalities and small kindnesses had passed. She was curled on the window seat with her arms folded on the sill and her head resting on them. She'd loosened her hair so that it fell over the shoulders and down the back of a plain white robe. A man could almost believe she was a woman lost in the night. Bennett no longer believed what he saw and little that he felt. When he shut the door behind him, she was up and standing quickly.

She hadn't expected him that night. Looking at his face, Hannah saw that she should have. Because she knew the worst when she faced it, she braced.

"You spoke with Reeve?"

"Yes."

"And your father?"

His brow lifted. Though he had discarded his formal jacket, he could be very much the prince when he chose. "We talk tomorrow, though that doesn't concern you."

She acknowledged this with a slight nod. "Only inasmuch as it affects my position at the moment."

"Although you're obviously unaware of it, I'm not a fool. Your position remains." He took the small pistol from his pocket. After crossing to the stand beside her bed, he set it down. "Your property."

No, she would not be forgiven. She'd thought she'd been ready to accept it. She'd been wrong. "Thank you." As coolly as he, she walked to the stand, then placed the pistol in the drawer.

"You're an excellent shot, Lady Hannah."

The drawer shut again with the slightest of slams. "I've been well trained."

He caught her chin then, not gently. "Yes, by God, you have. What other talents do you have, I wonder? Deceit is certainly the sharpest. How many women can you be?"

"However many it takes to do my job. If you'd excuse me, I'm very tired."

"Oh, no." With his other hand, he gathered up her hair. He thought of what she'd put him through in one evening. Anxiety, outright terror and betrayal. "I'm afraid I won't fall for that again. With me, at any rate, the quiet, well-bred English lady is quite done. Cards on the table, Hannah."

It was fear, she realized, that had her stomach heaving. Not fear that he would hurt her physically, not fear that he would do something in temper that would jeopardize the operation, but fear, deadly and cold, that he would always look at her the way he was now.

"I doubt there's much I can tell you that Reeve hasn't. The operation was put in effect just over two years ago. The ISS needed an agent on the inside, so—"

"I've been apprised of the basic details." He let her go, dropping his hands to his sides. There, they balled into fists. "A bit late, but the information seems fairly complete. After establishing yourself with Deboque's organization, you pretended an affection for Eve so you could gain access to the palace." He saw the flicker of emotion cross her face at that but wasn't ready to interpret it. "In this way, Deboque would be deceived into believing he had one of his own on the inside. By playing both ends, you would be privy to his plans, and once he makes a move, the authorities would be able to close in and destroy his organization. I'm told I should be grateful you're so good at what you do."

"I don't need gratitude, just cooperation."

"Then perhaps you should have asked for it from the beginning."

She lifted her head. No, there would be no apologies. "I had orders, Bennett. You're no stranger to duty."

"No, but neither am I a stranger to honor. You played

me.'' Anger broke through the ice so that he held both of her arms. ''You used my feelings for you.''

''You weren't supposed to have any,'' she snapped back.

''We can't always choose what we feel. But there are other choices. Did you need to use how I felt for you, Hannah?''

''I had a job to do.'' Her voice wasn't steady now because she couldn't be sure if she'd done what she'd done coolly or because of her own needs. ''I tried to discourage you.''

''You knew I cared, that I wanted you.''

''I didn't want you to.''

''You still lie.''

''No.'' She yanked, but he held her firm. ''I did nothing to attract you. Then again, perhaps a woman only has to exist for you to be attracted.'' She saw the fury bloom but ignored it. ''Perhaps by refusing to sleep with you, I became more of a challenge. There are a lot of women who would gladly sleep with royalty.''

''Do you believe if all I had wanted was you in bed that you wouldn't have been there a half-a-dozen times already?''

''I go nowhere I don't take myself.'' She tossed her head back. His voice had been too low, too precise, but she was past caring. ''If you're angry because I'm not what you thought I was, it's because your ego's been bruised.''

The rest of her words and her breath were knocked away as she fell under him on the bed. Before she could counter the move, her arms were pinned at her sides. She'd been warned about his temper. There had even been some documentation of it in his dossier. But none of that was nearly as awesome as seeing it first hand.

"Ego?" He gritted out with his face only inches from hers. "So to you I'm still only what you've read, only what you've been told." It hurt, how it hurt. He could feel it shimmer inside of him until the only recourse was to turn it into anger. "I won't disappoint you then."

She scissored her legs and nearly succeeded in rocking him off. He shifted until her body was pressed flat against his. One hand rested dangerously on her throat. It gave him grim pleasure to feel her pulse flutter rapidly beneath his fingers.

"This won't prove anything." She managed to free one arm, but he caught it at the wrist. Her pulse beat there as well, fast, uneven. "You'll only demean both of us."

It didn't matter. He'd gone beyond right and wrong, truth and lies. "There was a time when I believed you to be shy and precious. That was a woman I only wanted to show tenderness to. For her I had such patience, such sweet feelings. But for you, we can dispense with such things, can't we?"

"Bennett, don't do this." She said it quietly, knowing it was already too late.

"Why not?" The recklessness was back, in full force, driven by betrayal. "It's a night for lies and passions."

She prepared to do battle, for herself and for him. "You won't rape me."

"No, I won't. But I will have you."

Chapter 9

It would be a battle of wits, a contest for control. Somehow it was easier for Hannah to think of that when Bennett's lips pressed down on hers. He didn't want to make love with her, but to punish, even to conquer. It was anger, not desire that had brought them here. She couldn't afford to forget it, not even for an instant.

Yet the kiss wasn't cruel. Hot and hard he moved his mouth over hers, more taunting than insistent. The hand on her throat didn't so much threaten as control. The callused fingers reminded her of the strength in his hands even as they stroked to arouse and seduce.

She made her body lie still and limp beneath his, waiting not just for a chance to fight back, but for a chance to fight and win.

But her blood was already beginning to stir.

He knew it. He was a man who understood passions, desires, vulnerabilities and how one would feed on the others. He'd used such things before, all in good humor, to give as much as to take. Now he would use them to wound as deeply as he had been wounded.

Women had frustrated him, amused him, baffled him and fascinated him. But no woman had ever hurt him before Hannah. That she'd done so not inadvertently, not in a fit of temper, but coolly, passionlessly, made the sin unforgivable. For the first time in his life he held a woman in his arms with the sole intention of bringing her pain.

Or so he told himself.

There was only flesh beneath the robe. He knew it before he drew the material down her bare shoulder. There was strength there. He'd felt it once before. Now he felt the softness as well. Both moved him, just as, he discovered, his touch moved her. As she began her first struggles, he shifted so that her loosened robe parted for him.

She knew better than to panic, but her heart and her needs betrayed her. The moment he'd stroked his palm down her bare skin the flare of pleasure had opened the door to fear. To excitement. To passion. Her struggles took them rolling over the bed, locked in combat. His lean build and easygoing manner made the steely strength she discovered both a surprise and an arousal. Muscles bunched under his shirt as he countered her moves and took her where he wanted her to go. Hannah found herself trapped beneath him again with her arms pinned by the robe that had slipped down her back.

Breathless, she stared up at him. She was beaten, but far from ready to submit. Moonlight slanted in over her face so that her skin was milky pale, her eyes dark and glowing. The fear in them had turned to condemnation. In a mass of confusion, her hair spread over the bed, making him think of mermaids and witches.

"I'll despise you."

Something ripped quietly inside him. His heart or perhaps his soul. He ignored it and fixed on the need to punish her for making him love an illusion.

He lowered his mouth again, but she turned her head away. A small defense, and an unwise one as his lips found the soft, vulnerable curve of her throat. Her breath caught, then expelled again on a moan. The sound had his heart drumming as he found her taste as unique and as dangerous as his feelings for her.

He wanted to love her, and to hate her. He needed to comfort and to punish. He sought to hurt and to give pleasure. In the midst of his confusion, he forgot everything but Hannah.

Hardened from work, gentle by nature, his hands moved over her. With the tip of his tongue, he traced patterns, tormenting, tempting patterns over her skin. He could feel it heat beneath him so that the flavor and the softness seemed to intensify. She twisted one way under him, then the other so that her agitated movements only served to arouse them both.

All at once her body became very still, almost as if even breathing had stopped. Then the trembling began.

She'd never been more aware of herself, more distanced from rational thought. She wanted to remember why he was with her, why it was wrong for both of them, but could only feel. Reasons no longer mattered, consequences were forgotten. He wanted. She wanted. Right and wrong were for the sane.

When he brought his mouth back to hers again, she was waiting. He didn't find pliancy or panic, but the passion she had ruthlessly strapped down most of her life. For him it was free, and she had a fleeting moment to realize it would never fully be disguised again.

Impatience. Desperation. Together they rolled over the bed again but in a far different kind of combat. Her robe was lost so that her arms were free to capture him. In a move that might have told him everything, she locked him to her.

Stay with me. Love me. Understand me.

Then even that was lost in a torrent of heat that left them both gasping.

Once before he'd sensed a volcano inside of her. Now as it erupted around him, he was rocked by the power, the dark violence of it. The breeze that fluttered the curtains was cool and temperate. In the center of the bed was a furnace each of them stoked higher and higher.

Frantic for more of him, Hannah pulled his shirt open, scattering buttons over the mattress and floor. When her laugh came, it was low and sultry as he'd heard it before, but now it had an edge of something that might have been triumph. Then it was a sigh as she ran her hands up his chest. Her kiss was hot and hungry on his as naked flesh met naked flesh.

Something snapped inside him. As a lover he'd always been clever, considerate, caring. Love had never been a game to him, nor had it been a contest. Always, it had been a result of affection, a natural culmination of needs.

But he'd never needed like this.

Tenderness was forgotten as completely as revenge as he dove his hands into her hair and dragged her against him. His teeth nipped into her lower lip, sending dizzying sparks of pleasure through her. Then he began to move swiftly, leaving her lips unsatisfied while his kisses tortured and tamed wherever they reached.

There was panic again, but so twined with excitement she could recognize neither. Afraid, aroused, she tried to draw him back when with a suddenness that left her gasping, he drove her up and over. Her body contracted, almost in defense, then filled with a rush of heat that had her blood burning. Release came on a flood, on a cry of his name, and with the knowledge that no one would ever take her there but him.

She was weak and shuddering. The hands that had clutched the bed clothes went lax. For a moment, she began to float. Then he fanned the flames again.

This is what he'd wanted for her, from her. Her skin was damp and soft under his hands. Her muscles were limber as she began to move with him again. In the moonlight, he saw her face, dazed with passion, flushed with pleasure. Cupping her hips in his hands, he started a lingering line of kisses up her body. He could feel the moment the strength poured back into her.

Still shuddering, still breathless, she tugged at his slacks. She'd had a sample, a taste, and wanted more. She wanted all. As she pulled his clothes from him, he skimmed his fingertips over her inner thighs, hampering her progress, arousing her unbearably. He watched her eyes fly open with the shock of the fresh climax as her body arched up and strained toward the power. Then even as her muscles went lax, his mouth was on hers again and urging her along the next journey.

He was a drug. Her arms felt like lead as she tried to lift them for him. Her head was spinning from the flood of sensations. The ripe scent of passion covered both of them so that their skin was slick and hot. She could hear her own breath come in sighs and moans as she struggled to focus on his face.

His eyes were tawny, like a cat's before it springs. She remembered how he'd looked on the stallion, daring, dangerous. She shuddered once, then surrendered. With her eyes open and her heart willing, she gathered him close.

She opened. He filled.

The ride was fast and rough. Locked together, they raced. Without slackening pace, they plunged headlong over the cliff.

Silence seemed to last forever. Hannah curled herself into it and waited for him to leave her. Though her mind wasn't cool, some sanity had returned. Covered by the dark, she could admit to herself that she would never be the same. He'd broken through that carefully polished veneer and had conquered the inner woman, the woman he hated. She couldn't tell him that she loved, that she already mourned the loss of what she never really had and would spend the rest of her life wishing for it.

He wanted to reach out to her, to gather her close and stroke her hair in the moonlight. It wouldn't be possible to touch her again. He'd taken in anger what he'd once dreamed of taking in tenderness. The guilt was there, real and ripe even as the sense of betrayal crept back.

The woman he'd fallen in love with didn't exist. She'd been a lie even more than an illusion. Now he'd done what even in his wildest moments he'd avoided. He'd made love with a stranger. And God help him, he'd fallen just as deeply in love with her.

Had he hurt her? He wanted to ask, but held himself back. He couldn't afford to feel remorse or he would end up making a fool of himself over this new Hannah as well. Pride followed honor. Since he'd sacrificed one to temper and pain, he would hold firm to the other.

As he rose, he dragged a hand through his hair. How could he love her when he didn't even know her? How could he still love the woman he knew had never existed?

He dressed in silence while Hannah lay still as a stone on the bed.

"Now it seems we've used each other," he murmured.

She opened her eyes then. There were no tears in them. Thank God she still had the strength for that much. He was standing by the bed, naked from the waist up with the ruined shirt balled in his hand. "We can consider ourselves even."

"Can we?" His fingers went white on his shirt. He'd nearly taken a step toward her before he made himself turn and leave her alone.

Hannah lay and listened to the silence until dawn.

"You have questions," Armand began as he faced his youngest son. The morning light was strong through the open windows and showed, all too clearly, the marks of a sleepless night on both faces. "I prefer it if you wait to ask them until after I've finished."

He'd been prepared to demand and to rage. The lines of strain and weariness made his father look suddenly old and much too vulnerable. Again, it was love rather than duty that guided him. "All right." Because he needed it, Bennett poured coffee and left it black.

"Will you sit?"

"No."

Armand's gaze sharpened at the tone. Then he, too, let love hold sway. "I shall." Once seated, he set his untouched coffee aside. "Two years ago, I sat in this office with Reeve and Malori. You and Alexander were also present. You remember?"

Bennett paced to the window and looked out. "Yes. We were speaking of Deboque and what could and should be done."

"Then you remember that Reeve, even then, had an operative in mind to infiltrate the organization."

"I remember, too, that it was decided that the name be kept from Alex and me." The trace of resentment he had felt then had grown to true bitterness in one night. "And that Malori was not completely satisfied with Reeve's choice."

"Malori has always been one of the most trusted members of the security staff in Cordina. But he's old-fashioned." Armand saw no need to add that he, too, had had his doubts. "He was concerned with using a woman."

Bennett downed half his coffee. "I felt then, as I feel now, that Alexander and I had a right to know what was being done. More, all of us had the right to know that the woman we accepted as friend was an ISS agent."

"I felt then as I feel now—" Armand's voice, though quiet, held the whip of authority "—that neither of you had a need to know. If I had become ill, Alex, of course, would have been apprised. However—"

"Do you think because I won't rule, Cordina is of less importance to me?" Bennett whirled on his father. The fury on his face was lethal. "All of my life I've been the younger brother. Alex was born to rule Cordina after you. He was molded for it, just as his son will be. Do you think because of that I cared less, loved less or would have offered less?"

Armand said nothing for a moment, knowing the words had to be chosen with care, even as they came from the heart. "Bennett, I've watched you grow from child to man and have waited for a sign, for a hint that you resented your position. You have been sometimes wild, always reckless and too often indiscreet, but never have I seen anything in you but love and devotion for your country and your family.''

"Then why, when something threatens both, do you keep your plans from me?"

There was a headache drumming behind Armand's temple. He closed his eyes a moment, but didn't lift a hand to soothe it. "Two years ago, Lady Hannah Rothchild was chosen out of a half dozen highly qualified operatives to infiltrate and destroy Deboque's organization. We were aware, as she was, of the risks involved, and the time and skill it would take to succeed."

"Why her?" Bennett found he didn't want to think beyond that for a moment. It was an answer he had to have before he could deal with the others.

"Reeve felt Hannah's talents were uniquely suited to the operation. She's been with the ISS for ten years."

"Ten years?" Bennett roamed the room again as he tried to take it in. "How is that possible? She's so young."

"She's second generation," Armand said mildly. "Her father trained her himself while she was still in school. Lord Rothchild, though semiretired now, is one of the most valued agents in the ISS. He had some part in Reeve's early training which was another reason Reeve leaned toward Hannah for this assignment."

"Ten years," Bennett repeated. How many women had she been? How many lies had she told?

"Apparently she had a natural aptitude for this kind of work." He saw his son's jaw set, but went on. "After reading Reeve's report on her, I had to agree that she was best suited for what we had in mind."

"Deboque often uses women," Bennett murmured.

"He feels they can be more cunning, even more cruel, than men." Armand remembered Janet Smithers and the bullet that had been dug out of his son's flesh. "His preference runs to a certain type, quiet, well-bred, spotless pedigrees."

"Hannah."

"Yes. It was those qualities in her which weighed the decision in her favor. With the cooperation of the ISS a deep background was created for her. The credentials she was given made it possible for her to slip into Deboque's company. In two years, she's moved from messenger to the top of the organization."

"The top?" The fear started then, like something foul in the back of his throat. "What do you mean?"

"She's met with Deboque himself, and by managing to discredit one of his top men, is now filling that position herself. Reeve explained to you that as far as Deboque knows, she's here at the palace as his instrument."

Bitterness was more palatable than fear. He concentrated on it. "She plays the game very well."

"An agent in her position plays the game well or loses her life. You know firsthand that Deboque doesn't hesitate to kill. Her name and the operation itself were kept in strictest confidence not to protect you or the rest of the family, Bennett, but to protect her."

Bennett set his cup down and stopped pacing. "In what way?"

"Three other agents have been killed trying to do what Hannah has nearly succeeded in doing. The last was butchered." He watched Bennett's face pale. He would have spared his son this, as a father. Now, as prince, he could spare him nothing. "By bringing her here in this way, letting you, all of you, believe what Deboque wanted you to believe, Hannah had the only protection we could offer. If she's discovered, even the ISS can't protect her. Now that you know all that you know, her risk is greater than ever.''

In silence, Bennett crossed the room to sit across from his father. Though the turmoil was building all too quickly inside, his face was calm. ''I'm in love with her.''

''Yes.'' Armand sat back. ''I was afraid you were.''

''I will not stand still and watch Deboque hurt someone else I love.''

''Bennett, there are times, too many times, when our personal feelings can't influence our actions.''

''For you.'' Bennett's voice was still calm, but slightly colder. ''Perhaps for Alex as well, but not for me. I prefer to kill him myself.''

Armand felt a ripple of fear, a tingle of pride and controlled both. ''If you do anything to interfere with the operation at this point, you could be responsible for Hannah's death, not Deboque's.''

Pushed to his limit, Bennett leaned forward. ''Do you understand, I'm in love with her? If you were in my position, could you do nothing?''

Armand studied his son's face and remembered the only woman he'd ever loved. ''I can only say that I would do whatever was necessary to keep her safe. Even if that meant doing nothing.'' He rose and went to his desk. ''Read these.'' He lifted a small stack of files that carried the stamp of highest security. ''These contain background information on Hannah, some of her own reports concerning certain assignments and most recently, her progress with Deboque. I'll leave you so that you can read them here. They mustn't leave this room.''

Bennett rose to accept the files. "Where is she now?"

He had hoped the question wouldn't be asked. "She received a message early this morning. She's gone to Deboque."

She had to play this one very carefully. Hannah sat with her hands folded on her lap in the elegant salon of Deboque's rented villa. Though the meeting was on land this time, she knew if her cover hadn't held up, she was just as much alone as she had been on the yacht.

If he had a hint of the part she'd played in the events of the evening before, her throat would be slit before she could voice a denial. A risk every agent takes, she reminded herself. To test herself, she lifted the small china pot on the table in front of her and poured coffee. Her hand was steady.

It was imperative that her mind stay sharp and focused on the assignment.

Every other thought in her mind was of Bennett.

"Lady Hannah." Deboque walked into the salon then shut the double doors at his back. "How delightful to see you again."

She added a careful dollop of cream. "The message I received this morning left little option."

"Ah, I was brusque." He crossed to her, taking her hand and brushing his lips over it. "My apologies. The events of last night caused me some distress."

"And me." She drew her hand away. Instinct told her annoyance was the wisest course. "I find myself wondering if I've chosen wisely."

Deboque chose the seat beside hers, then taking his time, chose a cigarette from a crystal holder. He wore emeralds today. "Meaning?"

"Only months ago, I found myself in the position of having to clean up for another of your employees." She sipped coffee. It was hot and Turkish. "Last night, another of them nearly ruined every carefully laid step I've taken toward the Bissets."

"May I remind you, *mademoiselle,* you were advised to stay out of the way?"

"I'll remind you, *monsieur,* that I haven't reached my current position by not looking toward my own interests. If I hadn't followed Bennett, you and I might even now be sitting in less agreeable quarters."

Deboque blew out smoke. "Explain."

"Bennett was a bit bored with the play and thought to wait in the American actress's dressing room until the curtain. Because I was aware that there were plans of some sort in the works, I decided it best to keep close. When the lights went out, I had to decide whether to go back or keep Bennett within reach. If I'd gone back, *monsieur,* the prince might indeed be dead."

"And for that you wish my gratitude?"

"He might be dead," Hannah repeated, "and a member of your organization would even now be in custody. Shall I pour you some coffee?"

"Merci." He waited patiently while she filled a second cup. At his nod, she added cream.

Hannah sat back again and folded her ringless hands. "MacGee and the guards were already on their way. I spotted your man." She made a look of disgust. "He was bumbling his way around with a flashlight. I managed to distract Bennett by playing the hysterical female, but the idiot didn't take the opportunity to make good his escape. The lights came up again. Bennett saw him and his weapon. You should be flattered that since your release the prince has carried a small-caliber pistol with him. He used it, and for personal reasons, I'm grateful he used it well. Dead men can't name names." Playing up the role, she rose. "I ask you now, was the man under orders to kill one of the Bissets? Do you or do you not trust me to complete the contract?"

Say it! she ordered silently. Say it out loud, say it plainly so that this can be over.

Smoke curled up in a column toward the ceiling as he tapped the cigarette into an ashtray. "Please, my dear, be calm. The man you speak of may have been told to use initiative, but was never given a specific request. I have confidence in you, of course."

"We agreed. I would dispose of the Bissets in return for five million dollars."

He smiled, like a generous uncle. "We agreed that if such a thing were to happen, there would be some compensation."

"I'm tired of playing games." As if to prove it, Hannah picked up her bag. "If you won't speak frankly, if you won't honor our arrangement, there's no reason to go on with this."

"Sit." The order came sharp and clear as she walked to the door. Hannah stopped, turned, but didn't walk back. "You forget yourself. No one who works for me leaves until they are dismissed."

She knew there would be men outside the door, to detain or dispose of her at Deboque's whim. She gambled that he would respect audacity. "Perhaps it's best if I find other employment then. I'm not accustomed to being dealt only half the cards."

"Remember that I hold them. I ask you again, sit."

This time she obeyed. She let the impatience shimmer, but only enough to let him see her control. "Very well."

"Tell me how the Bissets cope this morning."

"With dignity, of course." She pretended to be amused. "Bennett's pleased with himself. Armand is worried. Eve is confined to bed for the day. Gabriella stays with her. MacGee is closeted with Malori—you know the name?"

"Yes."

"I would guess that they are trying to see what purpose the disturbance last night had. Your man did an excellent job on the main power, though I think the explosive was a bit overstated." She shrugged as though it had been a hat with one too many feathers. "In any case, they ran on auxiliary for the rest of the evening and have a crew in the Center this morning for repairs. It's their belief that the power was blown so that the assassin could break his way into the Royal Box."

"A natural assumption," Deboque said as he went back to his coffee. And exactly the one he'd hoped for. "Though such a move would have been messy and unstylish. And you, my dear? How do you cope after witnessing a killing?"

"I've chosen to be shocked and weakened by the events. But brave, naturally. We British are, you know."

"I've always admired the quality." He smiled at her again. "I have to congratulate you on the depth of your skill. You look as though you didn't close your eyes all night."

It was a mistake to remember, to think even for an instant, of Bennett. "I drank enough coffee to keep me awake until dawn," she said easily as her stomach tied itself in knots. "At the moment I'm supposedly out for a walk to clear my head.'' To take his attention from that, she added the last of what she and Reeve had discussed. ''Are you aware that the entire Royal Family will gather at the palace for the Christmas Ball?''

''So is tradition.''

''With Eve being a bit delicate, the Princess Gabriella brings her family to stay for several days during the preparations. The MacGees share a wing with Alexander and Eve so that they can be close to the children.''

''Interesting.''

''And obliging. I'll require the makings for three plastic explosives.''

Deboque only nodded. ''The younger prince doesn't reside in the same wing.''

''The younger prince will be fatally injured while trying to save the rest of his family. Leave it to me. Just make sure the five million is waiting.'' She rose again, then inclined her head as if waiting for his permission to leave. Deboque stood as well, then surprised her by taking both of her hands.

''I had thought that some time after the holiday I would take a long vacation. I have an urge to sail, to be in the sun. Vacations can be very dull without companionship.''

Her stomach turned over. She prayed the revulsion wouldn't show, even for an instant. ''I've always been fond of the sun.'' She didn't object when he stepped closer, but smiled. ''You have a reputation for discarding women as easily as you collect them.''

''When they bore me.'' He cupped a hand around her neck. His fingers were light, smooth, and still made her think of spiders. ''I have a feeling you won't. I'm not attracted to looks, but brains and ambitions. Together, I believe we could be very comfortable.''

If his lips touched hers, she would retch. Knowing it, Hannah tilted her head back just an inch. "Perhaps—after our business is completed."

The fingers on her neck tightened, then released. The marks they had left wouldn't fade for several minutes. "You're a cautious woman, Hannah."

"Cautious enough to want the five million before I sleep with you. Now if you'll excuse me, I should get back before I cause any concern."

"Of course."

She walked to the door. "I'll need those supplies by the end of the week."

"Expect a Christmas present from your aunt in Brighton."

With a nod, she swung easily through the door.

Deboque took his chair again and decided he'd become quite fond of her. It was a shame she'd have to die.

Chapter 10

It was midafternoon before Bennett went to find her. He'd read every word in the files Armand had given him. Though some had fascinated him, some had frightened him and some had angered him, he still wasn't sure he knew the woman.

Now he, too, was part of the deception, he thought as he made his way up to Eve's rooms. Nothing he'd read, nothing he'd been told could be confided to his brother. He couldn't comfort his sister or Eve with the fact that every move Deboque made was being monitored. He had, as he was coming to understand Hannah had, no choice but to play the game through. So he went to find her, knowing it was long past time they talked calmly.

He found Eve and Gabriella together at a table with piles of lists and a pot of tea.

"Bennett." Gabriella reached a hand out. "Just in time. We need a man's viewpoint on the Christmas Ball."

"Make sure there's plenty of wine." He bent to kiss both of her cheeks. Though she'd smiled at him, he'd recognized the signs of strain, just as he recognized them in Eve. "Hannah's not with you?"

"No." Eve set her pencil down as she lifted her face for Bennett's kiss. "I told her I wanted her to rest today. Last night…" She tightened her fingers on his. "Last night must have been dreadful for her. And you."

He shrugged, remembering too clearly the way he'd left her—curled into a silent ball on the bed. "It wasn't a dull evening in any case."

"Don't joke, Ben. You could have been killed. All I can think is that it's the second time in the theater. The second time one of my plays—"

Keeping Eve's hand in his, he crouched down. "I wasn't hurt, and I don't want you letting that fertile imagination go. I'd be very annoyed if my nephew were born with worry lines. Where's Marissa?"

"Napping."

He rubbed a thumb under her eyes. "You should do the same."

Annoyance replaced the strain, as he'd hoped. "Now you sound like Alex."

"God forbid. Where is he, anyway?"

"Meetings." She nervously traced her fingers over the papers. "Most of the day. Everything's been switched to his offices here because of—because security prefers it."

"Then you should relax." He covered her hand with his. "You should know by now the Bissets are indestructible. At the least you should be grateful he's tied up for a while, otherwise he'd be in here hovering over you."

She managed to smile. "You do have a point."

Rising, he grinned down at Gabriella. "I suppose we

can trust you to keep her in line—though you're not looking your best, either.''

"Chivalry is never dead with you around."

"What are brothers for?" He wanted to gather them
both close and tell them that nothing and no one would
ever hurt them again. Instead, he gave his sister's hair a
tug. "Now I'll let you two get back to what I'm sure is
fascinating work." He'd gotten no farther than the head
of the stairs when Gabriella caught up with him. "Ben."

He turned, and though he was ready with a smile, her
expression stopped it.

Gabriella looked back over her shoulder to be certain
they were far enough away from Eve's office, then laid a
hand over his on the banister. "Reeve tells me little about
certain matters." A trace of temper came into her eyes,
then was dismissed. "That's something I have to live
with. But particularly since I once lost everything, I have
very good instincts when it comes to my family."

"I know you're worried," he began. "All of us are."

"It's more than that, though everything comes back to
Deboque and his obsession with destroying us. I still have
dreams, even after all these years." She could remember
a cabin, and the dark, and the fear.

"Brie." He laid a hand on her cheek. "Nothing like
that is ever going to happen again."

She closed her fingers lightly over his wrist. "And I
remember seeing you shot and bleeding on the terrace
floor. I remember sitting in the hospital while Eve hung
between life and death. Deboque." Her face was very
pale, but there was strength in it and in the hand that lay
on his. "It's all been Deboque. And he isn't finished."

"He will be." Something dangerous came into his
voice, into his eyes. "That I promise you."

"I want you to be careful, Bennett."

He smiled, so that the look vanished. "How can I be otherwise with a dozen guards smothering me?"

"Very careful," she repeated. "I've never known you to carry a pistol to the theater."

She knew it was a lie. He didn't have to hear her say it, only to look in her eyes. She knew, but didn't understand. And because she was Gabriella, she wouldn't stop until she did.

"Leave it for now."

"So Reeve told me," she said with an impatient gesture. "It's my family. How can I?"

"I only know it's going to be over soon. In the meantime we have to stand together. Something's being done, Brie. Hold on to that."

"I have been." She knew it was unfair to push, so released him. "I want you to promise you won't do anything rash."

"What is this reputation I carry with me?"

"Ben, please."

"All right, you have it." He kissed her again. "I adore you, even if you did bring Dorian into the world to pester me." He gave her hand a final pat before he started down the stairs. *"A bientôt."*

She watched him go, but the worry stayed with her. *"A bientôt."*

Hannah wasn't in her rooms. Bennett found himself frustrated yet again when he entered and found them empty. Had she gone out again? he wondered. Was she even now putting herself in danger to protect his family?

He hated it. The thought of her risking her life, of blocking his body with her own as she had done last night was impossible to accept. Whether it was family, friend or country, he protected. How could he do less for the woman he loved?

Wandering in her rooms, he moved to her dresser. There was a small enameled box with a peacock on the lid. He ran a finger over it, wondering where she had come by it. A gift? From whom? A purchase in some little shop in London? He needed to know even those inconsequential details about her. Couldn't she understand that in order to resolve his feelings he had to know the woman he'd given them to?

He looked up, and reflected in the mirror was the bed where they'd fought, and loved, the night before. If he stood very still, he could almost feel the echoes of passion and discovery in the air. Would she hate him for that? Even though the loving had been as intense and as stunning for her as for him, would she forgive him for forcing her to set the barriers aside?

He'd been rough.... Bennett looked down at his own hands, turning them over, spreading his fingers. And he hadn't cared. All of his life he'd taken such pains never to hurt a woman. Now, when he'd found the only woman, he'd set out to do just so.

Walking to the window he stared out and tried to sort out his feelings. He still resented her. No matter what his brain told him, his heart was still bruised by the deception. More, he couldn't shake off the feeling that he'd fallen in love with two women and could trust neither.

Then he saw her in the gardens below.

She needed some time, Hannah told herself. Just an hour alone to clear her mind and calm her nerves. She knew she'd handled Deboque as smoothly as possible that morning. If nothing went wrong, they would close the trap on him in a week. Then she would have succeeded. In her file would go another favorable report. A two-year assignment successfully tied up could very well mean a promotion. She was, she knew, only inches away from a captaincy. Why didn't it excite her as it once had?

Time, Hannah told herself again. She just needed some time.

She would take a much needed and well earned vacation. Perhaps at last she would go to America—New York, San Francisco. Wouldn't it be possible to lose herself in such places for a while?

Or perhaps she would go back to England. She could spend time in Cornwall walking the moors or riding by the sea. In England she couldn't lose herself, but perhaps she could find herself again.

Wherever she went, she would be leaving Cordina. And Bennett.

Wisteria rose up in an arch, sheltering a bench and inviting long, lazy contemplations. She sat, and closing her eyes, tried to bring her troubled mind to rest.

Who was she? For the first time in years she was forced to ask herself and admit she didn't know the answer. A part of her was the quiet woman who enjoyed a long afternoon with a book, who liked to talk of literature and art. A part of her was the woman who kept a weapon within reach and listened to footsteps behind her.

The fact that she could be both had always been a benefit before, never, as it was now, a painful puzzle to solve. She wished she could talk with her father, even for an hour. He understood what it was to live two lives and find contentment and challenge in each.

But she couldn't risk even that. In this, as in the assignment that had brought her here, she was alone.

He detested her. It was Bennett who had caused the ache and the doubts. It was Bennett who had forced her to question what she'd always taken for granted. Last night he'd taken her mind and heart and body, only because he'd wanted to humiliate her. And he had. No one, no one had ever shown her how much there could be, how much she could give. No one had ever left her so empty and alone.

He wouldn't know how much he'd hurt her. He couldn't know, she thought as the tears she'd held off throughout the night began to fall. Because he would never know how strong her feelings were for him, and how hopeless.

She had chosen her path, Hannah reminded herself, and she would live with it. In a matter of days it would no longer cross his.

He would be safe. His family would be safe. And she would be gone.

He found her sitting on the bench, her hands folded neatly in her lap, her eyes closed and her face wet with tears. So many feelings tumbled into him that he couldn't separate them. Regret, confusion, love, guilt.

She'd want to be left alone. He thought he understood her that well. There was still enough bitterness in him to want to leave her alone. He could no more have left her there than he could have left a wounded dog on the side of the road.

As he went closer, Hannah sprang up from the bench. He saw the shock and humiliation run across her face. For a moment, he thought she would turn and run. But she held her ground.

"I thought I was alone." Her voice was cold as she fought anger and embarrassment.

He took out a handkerchief and offered it. At the moment it was the only comfort he could give, or she accept. "I'm sorry I disturbed you." His voice was as stiff as hers. "I think we need to talk."

"Haven't we?" She dried her face then crumpled the linen in her hands.

"Would you like to sit?"

"No, thank you."

He slipped his hands into his pockets. She hadn't slept, he thought as he saw the shadows under her eyes. Neither had he. So perhaps there they were even. "I spoke with my father this morning. You've met with Deboque already today."

She started to cut him off, but relented. The garden was as secure as the palace—for the moment. "I don't report to you on those matters, Your Highness."

Temper narrowed his eyes and balled his hands into fists, but he spoke evenly. "No, but I'm now fully aware of the situation. I read your files."

Her breath came out on a huff of air. Was nothing she was or had done hers alone any longer? "Very well then, your questions have been answered, your curiosity satisfied. You know everything there is to know about me—I hope you were entertained."

"I didn't read it to be entertained," he tossed back. "Dammit, Hannah, I have a right to know."

"You have no rights where I'm concerned. I'm neither servant or subject."

"You're the woman I took to bed last night."

"That's best forgotten. Don't." Her body went rigid as he started forward. "Don't you ever touch me again."

"Very well." He stiffened even as she did. "But we both know certain things can't be forgotten."

"Mistakes can," she countered. "I'm here as an agent of the ISS to protect you and your family, to stop Deboque's plans to ruin Cordina and avoid the repercussions in Europe. Whatever has to be done to assure that, I'll do, but I will *not* let you humiliate me again." The tears started again, blinding her. "Oh, damn you, can't you leave me alone? Wasn't last night enough retribution for you?"

That snapped the very tenuous control he had on his own temper. He grabbed her arm, closing his fingers over the firm muscle. "Is that all it meant to you? Retribution? Can you stand here now and tell me you felt nothing, feel nothing? How accomplished a liar are you?"

"It doesn't matter what I felt. You wanted to punish me, and you did."

"I wanted to love you, and I did."

"Stop." That hurt, more than she was able to stand. She pushed him away only to be caught closer. The movement sent wisteria blossoms raining. "Do you think I couldn't see how much you hated me? You looked at me and made me feel vile. For ten years I've been proud of what I do, and you took even that away from me."

"And what of you?" He kept his voice low, but the anger was just as potent. "Can you tell me you didn't know I was in love with you?" She started to shake her head in denial, but he tightened his fingers. "You knew I was in love with a woman who didn't even exist. A quiet, shy and honest woman to whom I only wanted to show tenderness and patience. For the first time in my life there was a woman I could give my heart and my trust to, and she was nothing but a mirage."

"I don't believe you." But she wanted to and her heart

began to race. "You were restless, even bored. I entertained you."

"I loved you." He lifted his hand and held her face very still, very close. She saw his eyes as she had the night before, tawny with passion. "You'll have to live with that."

"Bennett—"

"And when I came to your room last night, I found another woman, one who had lied and used me." He dragged the hand up, raking through her hair so that pins scattered. "One who looked like a witch," he murmured as her hair fell heavily over his hands. "And I wanted her just as badly, but without those tender, those sweet feelings. God help me, I still want her."

When his mouth came down on hers, she didn't protest. She'd also seen the truth in his eyes. He had loved her. Or he had loved the pretense of her. If desire was all he could give her now, she would take it. For duty she had sacrificed love, but even for duty, she wouldn't sacrifice the crumbs she had left.

She wrapped her arms around him. Perhaps if she could give him the passion, some day he would forgive her the rest.

How easily he could lose himself in her. The passion was edgy and achy but it didn't seem to matter. Her mouth was warm, her body slender and straining. If it wasn't love she felt for him, at least there was need. He'd settled for no more than that before.

"Tell me you want me," he demanded as he moved his mouth desperately over her face.

"Yes, I want you." She hadn't known it possible to feel triumph and defeat at the same time.

"Come with me now."

"Bennett, I have no right to this." She turned her face into his throat, wanting to draw just a little more of him into her. "I'm here only because—"

With his hands on her shoulders he drew her away before she could finish the denial. "For today, for one day, we'll put your duty and mine aside."

"And tomorrow?"

"Tomorrow comes whether we want it to or not. Give me a few hours, Hannah."

She would have given him her life, and somehow knew that would be easier than what he was asking now. Still, she put her hand in his.

They went on horseback. As Hannah cantered beside him, she could see that Bennett knew the route to their destination well. They turned into the woods where they'd raced once before, and he took the lead. Each time doubts rose up to plague her, she beat them back. She would take the few hours she was being offered.

She heard the stream before she saw it. It was a simple, musical sound that suited the leafy shade and towering trees. When Bennett came to it, he turned his horse south. For a quarter of a mile they rode along the bank in silence.

The stream curved and twisted, then widened at a point where a trio of willows draped over it. Bennett stopped there and swung from the saddle.

"What a lovely spot." Hannah reined in, but found herself not quite courageous enough to dismount. "Every time I think I've seen the most beautiful place in Cordina, I find another. Do you often come here?"

"Not often enough." He'd secured his horse and now walked to her. Saying nothing, he held up a hand.

Here was the choice he'd refused to give her the night before. Perhaps he gave it to her now because he knew the decision had already been made. Hannah curled her fingers into his, held a moment, then dismounted. The silence continued while she tethered her horse beside his.

"I came here when my mother died." He didn't know why it seemed important that he tell her. "Not to grieve really, but because she always loved places like this. See the little white flowers along the bank?" His hand was on hers again as they moved closer to the stream. "She called them angel wings. They're sure to have a complicated Latin name, but angel wings seemed right."

Bending, he plucked one. It was no bigger than his thumb with thin petals cupped around a tiny blue center. "Every summer, before I'd have to go back to Oxford, I'd come here. For some reason it made leaving easier." He tucked the flower into her hair. "When I was a child, I thought the fairies lived here. I used to look for them in the clover and under toadstools."

She smiled and touched a hand to his cheek. "Did you ever find one?"

"No." With his hand on her wrist, he turned his head to press his lips to her palm. "But I think they're still here. That's why this place is magic. That's why I want to make love with you here."

Their lips were still an inch apart as they lowered to the grass. They remained a breath apart as they began to undress each other. Kneeling, gazes locked, they unfastened buttons. Sunlight dappled over skin as material was pushed aside. Their lips brushed, then clung.

He couldn't stop the rush of power, the flood of need. In seconds they were rolling over the grass. He caressed her everywhere, seeking, finding, exploiting until her moans shuddered into his mouth. The need to take her quickly, fiercely, couldn't be fought down, especially when her fingers were already tugging at the clasp of his jeans.

They waited only until all barriers were removed, then joined in a rocketing, furious journey that left them both sated.

Naked, with the grass tickling her back, Hannah looked up at the sunlight filtering through the leaves overhead. It had been moonlight before and she'd experienced a range of feelings from anger, shame, ecstasy and back to shame again. Today, in the sunlight, she no longer felt the shame.

What was between them could be, for this short time, between the man and the woman. Tomorrow they would be prince and agent again.

"What are you thinking?"

She was able to smile and turn her head toward him. "That this is a beautiful spot."

He'd wanted to bring her there before. He'd imagined it. How he would slowly, patiently, show her the pleasures of loving. Shaking off the mood, he drew her closer. This was a different day, and a different woman. "Are you warm enough?"

"Hmmm. But I..." she trailed off, knowing she'd sound foolish.

"But?"

"Well, I've never—" How to phrase it? "I've never lain naked in the grass under the sun before."

He laughed, not even realizing that the tone and the feeling behind it had come from the woman he'd first known. "Life should always include new experiences."

"I'm sure you've found yourself naked in all manner of unusual places."

The dry voice delighted him. Rolling over, he pressed a kiss to her mouth then drew back just to look at her.

Her hair was fanned out over the dark grass. The tiny white flower was tangled in it as though it had grown there. Bruising shadows under her eyes made her look both wanton and delicate, as though she were a virgin who'd just spent a night being initiated into womanhood.

This was how he had once imagined her, how he had once wanted, how he had once loved.

"You're so beautiful."

She smiled, relaxed enough to be amused. "Now *that* I've never been."

He traced a fingertip along her cheekbone. "How unobservant of you, Hannah. Or how foolish. Making yourself look less attractive doesn't change the truth. Flawless skin." He traced his lips over it as if to taste. "These elegant bones that make a man wonder if you're made of flesh and bone or glass. Those calm, intelligent eyes that drove me mad wondering how they might darken and cloud if I could find the right way to touch you. And this." He rubbed a finger over her lips. "So soft, so generous." He lowered his head but only traced the shape with his tongue. "Do you remember the first time I kissed you?"

Her breath was already shaking, her eyes already closing. "Yes. I remember."

"I wondered how it was that such a quiet woman could make my knees weak with just a taste."

"Kiss me now," she demanded and drew him down to her.

It wasn't what she expected. There was tenderness instead of passion, patience rather than urgency. She murmured against his mouth in confusion. Bennett only stroked his fingers over her face and waited for her to relax. More, he waited for her to accept. Even when he deepened the kiss it remained gentle. The fire was there but smoldering rather than blazing.

He was making love to the Hannah he'd understood, she realized and wanted to weep. There was lust for one, affection for the other. How could she fight another woman when the woman was herself?

On a trembling sigh, she let her mind empty. She would give him whatever it was he needed today.

He felt the change—the slow, almost fluid surrender. With a murmured approval, he pressed his lips to her throat. He wanted to show her there could be more than flash and speed. If they only had a few hours, then he would use them to give her whatever sweetness she would accept from him.

Lightly he stroked the smoothness of her body. What he'd demanded from her the night before, he now requested, coaxed, offered. He took the time to watch her arousal grow as the sun filtered down on her face and the stream rushed by beside them. He murmured to her as he kissed her throat. There were promises, endearments, reassurances. She answered him in words so fragile they almost dissolved in the air.

She'd never been loved like this before—as though she was precious, as though she was special. Even with her mind fogging over she could hear the gentle hiss of water running over rock. She could smell the grass and the wild sweet flowers scattered through it. With her eyes half-opened, the sunlight seemed gold and bountiful over her lover's skin. She ran her hand over it, finding it smooth and taut and warm.

Her lover. Hannah brought his mouth back to hers and gave him everything that was in her heart. If the place was magic, then so was the moment. Dreams hadn't been a part of her life for too long to remember, but she opened herself to them now.

She was so giving, so pliant. He'd wanted too badly to feel this kind of emotion from her. It went far beyond heat, far above desire. She touched him as though she'd been waiting for him all of her life. She kissed him as though he were her first and only lover. The more she gave, the more he found in himself to give back. The shadows shifted and lengthened over them as they stroked and offered and discovered.

Even when he slipped into her, it was slow and easy. The passion that had built was still harnessed by stronger emotions. They moved together in a harmony that seemed almost painful in its perfection while she framed his face with her hands and his lips met hers.

They glided over the top and settled softly.

"You wanted to see me, Monsieur Deboque?"

"Yes, Ricardo." Deboque lifted his teapot and poured. He admired the British habit of tea in the late afternoon. It was so civilized. "I have a little shopping list for you." With one hand he gestured toward the desk by the window. "I'd like you to supervise it personally."

"Of course." Always pleased to be given trust, Ricardo picked up the list written on heavy cream-colored paper. His brow lifted only a fraction. "Shall I requisition this from within the company?"

"Please." Deboque added cream to his tea. "I prefer to keep this at home, so to speak. The delivery should be set up with Lady Hannah on…Thursday, I'd say. It's no use passing the merchandise along to her too soon."

"She risks much, smuggling such a—volatile package into the palace."

"I have implicit trust in our British friend, Ricardo."
He remembered the way she'd sat across from him that
morning. Trim, tidy and cultured. It gave his plans such
a pleasant touch when they were carried out by delicate
hands. "She has a certain style, wouldn't you say?"

"Class, even when so quietly cloaked, is still class,
monsieur."

"Precisely." Deboque smiled and sipped at his tea. "I
have no doubt she will carry out her objective with class."
He sipped his tea again and sighed. "I do admire the
British, Ricardo. So traditional, so resilient. Not as passionate as the French, but so wonderfully pragmatic. In
any case, see that the merchandise is shipped from the
address on that list. I don't wish it to come through my
hands."

"Of course."

"I'm preparing an itinerary, Ricardo. We'll be sailing
the end of next week. I'll see Lady Hannah once more.
You'll see to the details?"

"As you wish."

"Thank you, Ricardo. Oh, by the way, did you see that
a wreath was sent to Bouffe's funeral?"

"Roses as you requested, *monsieur.*"

"Excellent." Deboque chose one of the little sugared
biscuits from the Wedgwood plate. "You're very depend-
able."

"I try, *monsieur.*"

"Have a pleasant evening then, Ricardo. Do let me
know if we get any further word on the accident at the
theater. I'm very uncomfortable with the current report."

"I will. Good evening, *monsieur.*"

Deboque sat back, nibbling on the cookie. Ricardo continued to please him a great deal. An intelligent man with

sociopathic tendencies was an excellent addition to his staff. Deboque was certain Ricardo would be very grateful to have the assignment of dealing with Hannah when her job was completed. It was tempting, but Deboque discarded it.

He would deal with Hannah himself. After all, the least he could do after she'd given him his fondest wish was to see she died as painlessly as possible.

Chapter 11

Hannah appeared very calm as she sipped tea in the library. She listened to Reeve give an updated report to Malori, filling in occasionally when requested to, then lapsing back into silence.

Bennett had started to show her the library once. Then they'd detoured into the music room. And he'd kissed her. Was that when her life had really begun to change? she wondered. Had it been then, or the day on the beach when he'd given her a shell? Perhaps it had been that first night in the gardens.

"Do you agree, Hannah?"

She snapped back, cursing herself for letting her mind wander at such a crucial time. They had only thirty minutes for the briefing, half of which was already gone. Even within the walls of the palace it was dangerous for them to meet.

"I'm sorry. Could you repeat that?"

Armand had been watching her, wondering if her shoulders were strong enough to hold the fate of so much. "The last few days have been a strain." There wasn't criticism in his voice but concern. Hannah would have preferred the first.

"The last two years have been a strain, Your Highness." Then she lifted her shoulders in a gesture that was more acceptance than dismissal.

"If you're beginning to wear under it," Malori said in his clipped, no-nonsense voice, "it's best we know now."

"I don't wear." Her eyes met his without wavering. "I believe my record shows that."

Before Malori could speak again, Reeve cut in. She was wearing, he knew, but he had to gamble she'd hold out for a few more days. "If we could backtrack? We can assume that Deboque has already ordered the supplies you requested. An educated guess on where he'd procure them?"

"Athens," she said immediately. "I feel strongly that he'd draw from within his own organization. He feels totally secure, invulnerable if it comes to that. He wouldn't want to risk ordering from outside sources. From my other reports, we know that he keeps a warehouse in Athens. He has others, of course, but I think he'd go there because of its proximity to Cordina."

"We'll check our contact there and see if there's news of any explosives being moved." Malori noted it down. "With luck we'll close down his Athens branch once we have him here."

"The ISS won't move on Athens, Paris, London or Bonn until we have an airtight case on Deboque here." Hannah set down her tea. "That's a button I push, *monsieur.*"

"Bien." Malori obviously didn't like it, but nodded.

"Will the case be strong enough when Hannah receives the explosives?" Armand glanced at Hannah, then at Reeve. "Hannah has taken the contract, requested the supplies. Once they are delivered, can that be the end of it?"

Hannah started to speak, then subsided. She would let Reeve explain. He was family. "We would have enough for an arrest, possibly for an arraignment. Even with the supplies being traced back to Athens or another of Deboque's companies, it wouldn't be enough for a conspiracy conviction. He's careful enough to divorce himself from business dealings of this kind."

Business dealings, Armand thought as he drummed his fingers on the arm of the chair. "And his request that Hannah assassinate my family?"

"His hypothetical theory of what might happen if such a thing occurred," Reeve corrected. "Your Highness, I'm aware, very aware, of the frustration of not being able to close in on the evidence we have now. We had him once for over a decade, and it didn't stop him. If we want to crush Deboque once and for all, sever all these strings and hack away his control in Europe, we have to have solid and indisputable evidence of murder and conspiracy. Hannah will give us that in a matter of days."

Armand drew out a cigarette and shifted his gaze to Hannah. "How?"

"The payoff." She felt herself on solid ground again. It helped to have Malori there, sharp-eyed and just a bit disapproving. "When Deboque is convinced I've completed the job, he'll pay me off. As soon as money changes hands, we've got him."

"He's not a fool. You agree?"

"No, Your Highness, he's not a fool."

"But you will convince him you have murdered my family."

"Yes. If you would look at this diagram, sir?" She rose and waited for him to accompany her to a table. With Reeve's help, she stretched out a long roll of paper. "The blueprints I smuggled to Deboque show this wing as occupied by Prince Alexander and his family. I gave Deboque the information that Princess Gabriella and her family would also be staying here during the days before the Christmas Ball."

"I see. In truth, my son's family's wing is here." He skimmed his finger to the opposite side of the drawing.

"The night before the ball, I'll set some charges here, and here." She laid a fingertip on the areas. "They'll be much smaller than what Deboque assumes, but with Reeve's special effects added, it should be quite a show. There will be some damage, sir, but it will appear much worse, particularly from the outside, than it really is. You'll need to do some replastering and painting."

He lifted a brow, but she couldn't tell if he was amused. "There are areas of the palace that could do with some redecorating."

"It will be imperative, of course, to clear this wing. Discreetly."

"Of course."

"Ten minutes before the explosion, I will leave to meet with Deboque or his agent. The payment will be made after he considers the job done."

"Have you considered that he would want to have the deaths verified before he pays you?"

"Yes." Hannah straightened away from the diagram. "To some extent we'll use the press. In addition, I'm making it clear that payment must be made that night, as

well as arrangements for my passage out of the country.
Deboque has invited me to sail with him. I shall accept."
She pressed her lips together as Malori grumbled. "The
money will change hands because he'll believe I'll be
easily accessible if anything has gone wrong."

"And will you be?"

"I'll be with him."

"The ISS will be covering both Deboque's villa and
his yacht," Reeve cut in. "The moment we have Hannah's signal, we move."

"There is no other way?"

Again there was concern. This time Hannah found herself laying a hand on the prince's arm. On the arm of
Bennett's father. "We could perhaps tie him to other
crimes. With the information I've been able to dig up in
the last two years, we would have something, but it would
take months, even years and we would have no guarantee.
This is the only way, Your Highness, to stop him once
and for all."

With a nod, the prince looked over at Reeve. "You
agree?"

"Yes."

"Malori?"

"It is more dramatic, and certainly more risky than one
would like, but yes, Your Highness."

"Then I will presume that you two will see to whatever
details have yet to be seen to. I will expect reports every
four hours."

Recognizing dismissal Malori bowed. Even as Reeve
rolled up the diagram again, Hannah was preparing to
curtsy.

"Hannah, I'd like another moment, please."

"Yes, Your Highness." She stood by the table, stiff

and tense as the two other men left them alone. He would know of her feelings for Bennett, Hannah thought. Even in the brief time she'd been in Cordina, she'd learned that Armand was both astute and observant. He didn't merely rule from a throne, but behind a desk and in boardrooms. If his country was at peace and prosperous, it was largely because he knew how to govern, how to make choices and how to remain objective.

Yes, he would know, she thought again. And he would not approve. She was European. She was an aristocrat. But she was by choice and by profession a spy.

"You're uncomfortable," Armand began. "Sit, please."

In silence she took a seat and waited.

She looked like a dove, he thought. A small gray dove who expected and accepted the fact that she was about to be mauled by a fox. Studying her, he had difficulty believing she would be the one to end the turmoil that had haunted his family for more than a decade.

"Reeve has confidence in you."

"I can promise it's not misplaced, Your Highness." She nearly relaxed. It wasn't about Bennett, but Deboque.

"Why did you agree to take this assignment?"

Her brow lifted because it seemed such a simple question with such a simple answer. "I was asked."

"And had the right to refuse?"

"Yes, sir. In such matters an agent always has a choice."

A prince didn't. He understood the difference, yet still didn't envy her. "You took the assignment because your superiors requested it."

"Yes, and because what Deboque does here has affected and could continue to affect my country and the rest of Europe. A terrorist, in whatever garb he chooses, remains a terrorist. England wants Deboque's hands tied, tightly."

"Your first consideration is country."

"It always has been."

He nodded again, knowing this could bring both joy and misery. "Did you choose your profession because you looked for adventure?"

Now she relaxed completely and laughed. The moment she did, Armand saw what had captivated his son. "Pardon, sir, I realize that the word 'spy' conjures up all sorts of glamorous images: foggy docks, Parisian alleyways, nickel-plated revolvers and fast cars. In truth, it's often tedious. In the past two years, I've done more work on telephones and computers than the average secretary."

"You wouldn't deny the danger involved."

"No." She sighed a little. "No. But for every hour of danger, there's a year of legwork and preparation. As for Deboque—Reeve, Malori, the ISS, have taken this plan step-by-step."

"Still, in the end, you'll be alone."

"That's my job. I'm good at it."

"Of that I have no doubt. Under normal circumstances, I would worry less."

"Your Highness, I assure you everything that can be done is being done."

He was aware of the truth of it and that, for the moment, his hands were tied. "And if a mistake is made, how will I comfort my son?"

She locked her fingers together. "I know, I promise you whatever happens, Deboque will be punished. If you—"

"I'm not speaking of Deboque now, but of you, and of Bennett." He held up a hand before she could speak again. "It is a rare thing for me to be able to speak as only a father. I ask you to allow me that luxury now, here in this room."

She drew in a breath and tried to be clear. "I realize Bennett is angry and upset because he wasn't told the reasons for my being here. I believe he feels a certain responsibility toward me because I'm here to protect his family."

"He's in love with you."

"No." The panic set in again, along with the shame and the desperate desire for it to be true. "That is, he thought, before when he believed me to be... At one time he began to feel a certain affection, but when he learned who—what I was, that changed."

Armand settled his hands on the arms of his chair. The ring of his office glinted in the lamplight. "My dear, are you any more clear on your feelings for him?"

She looked up. The dark eyes that watched her were kinder than they had been. Hard yes, he could be hard. But she could see now why his family and his country loved and trusted him. "Your confidence, sir?"

"You have it, of course."

"I love him more than I've ever loved anything or anyone. If I could change things, if I could go back and be what he thought I was, and only that, I swear to you I would." There were no tears. She had shed them once and had sworn not to do so again. Instead she looked down at her hands. "Of course, I can't."

"No, we can't change what we are. When we love, and love deeply, we can accept a great deal. Bennett's heart is very generous."

"I know. I promise you, I won't hurt him again."

His lips curved. She was so young, so valiant. "I have

no fear of that. When this is done, I ask that you remain in Cordina for a few more days."

"Your Highness, I think it would be best if I returned to England immediately."

"We wish you to remain," he said again, and he no longer spoke as a father. He rose then, extending a hand. "You may want to rest before dinner."

Left without a choice, Hannah stood and curtsied. "Thank you, Your Highness."

Dinner was long and formal. Hannah was introduced to the Minister of State and his wife, as well as a German businessman who had interests in shipping and an ancient Frenchwoman who was some vague connection of the Bissets' and was visiting Cordina for the holidays. The Frenchwoman spoke in a husky grumble that kept Hannah straining to hear enough to make polite answers. The German spoke in short, loud blasts and was obviously delighted to have an invitation to the Royal Palace. Hannah was grateful that he was across the table so that she could avoid direct conversation with him.

Bennett wasn't there at all. A late board meeting at the museum had edged into a dinner for the Equestrian Society. Hannah tried to remember that Claude had been joined by two more guards who would keep Bennett annoyed and protected throughout the evening.

As the Frenchwoman hissed in her ear again, Hannah could only think Bennett the fortunate one.

Across the table, Eve sipped sparkling water and listened with apparent fascination as the German regaled her with stories of his business. Only when she turned to pick up her dessert spoon did her eyes meet Hannah's long enough for the humor to come through. Answering a question in low, polite tones, she rolled her eyes once, quickly, in a gesture that said everything. Then she was smiling at the German again and making him feel fascinating.

Hannah had to lift her glass to hide the grin. The royal were human after all. Not the same, not ordinary, but human. The child Eve carried might one day rule, but he would also laugh and cry and feel and dream.

She herself had loved a prince. Hannah picked up her spoon and began to toy with the elegant chocolate and cream concoction in front of her. She'd given her heart to a man who was second in line to one of the few remaining thrones in Europe. In a few days, she could very likely give her life for him.

For that was the truth of the matter, she thought as the woman beside her droned on. It might have started as duty, to her country and to the organization she had chosen, but when it ended, what she did would be for Bennett.

It would never be possible to tell him, just as it hadn't been possible to say as much to his father earlier that evening. If she admitted what she felt to a superior, even with all the planning, all the time lost, she could very well be pulled out.

So she would say nothing, but she would feel. And feeling as she did, she would see Deboque finished, if she lived.... And then, Hannah admitted, it would be a choice between her captaincy and retirement. Fieldwork would be all but out of the question now. She didn't believe that she could ever maintain the pose of quiet, unassuming Lady Hannah again. Not now that she had loved and been loved by a prince.

It was nearly midnight before escape could be politely made. Hannah deliberated over a hot bath or quick oblivion in bed as she stepped into her room. Eve was insistent about returning to the Center the next day, so she would have no choice but to go along. Would the message come the next day, or would Deboque take her right down to the wire?

She'd walked into the center of the bedroom when the warning signals began to throb at the base of her neck. There was no one in the room. A quick glance showed her nothing had been disturbed. But...

Hannah took a cautious step back and opened the drawer of the bedside table. She took out her weapon. The light was low and at her back as she began to move toward the adjoining room. The door was slightly ajar, but that could have been done by one of the maids. Her feet were silent on the carpet as she crossed to it. With one hand she pressed on the panel so that it opened slowly and without sound.

There was nothing in the room beyond—nothing except the neat sitting room that smelled of the gardenias that lay moist and lovely in a bowl.

So it had been a maid, she thought, relaxing gradually. One of them had set fresh flowers in the sitting room, and—

It was then she heard a sound, material against material, and tensed again. Keeping the gun secure in her hand, she slid against the wall and into the room.

The little settee faced away from the door so she didn't see him until she was fully inside. Bennett lay sprawled on it, his tie unknotted and hanging, his shoes off and his face buried in a blue velvet pillow.

Hannah swore, but softly, as she lowered the pistol. He looked exhausted, and very much at home, she thought as she lifted a brow. Her first instinct was to tuck a cover around him, but there was still enough of the proper Lady Hannah in her to know that it would never do for Bennett of Cordina to be found snoozing in her sitting room. She started to bend down to him, then remembered the gun in her hand.

Almost curiously, she turned it over in her hand. It looked like a toy, but had already proven itself lethal. A part of her job, she thought. A part of her life. Yet she knew it was a part Bennett would find unpalatable. Moving back into her bedroom she secured it. She had to wake him and send him on his way, but she didn't have to keep a physical reminder of their differences close at hand.

She went back to him, and kneeling by the settee put a hand to his shoulder. "Bennett." She shook gently and received a mumbled response. Her lips curved. She had to resist the urge to brush at the hair tumbling over his forehead. In sleep, the energy, the amusement and the temper were put to rest. He looked as though he would be perfectly content to cuddle there, half on, half off the little sofa for days. Hannah bent closer and raising her voice gave him a quick, brisk shove. "Bennett, wake up."

He half opened his eyes, but Hannah noted that they focused quickly. Reaching up, he grabbed her earlobe. "Haven't you any respect for a dead man?"

"Ow!" She grabbed his wrist in defense, but she was already several inches closer. "If it's respect you want, I'll call a couple of the servants and have them carry you out, in state. Meanwhile, let go or I'll have to show you how easy it is to cause unconsciousness by applying pressure to certain nerves."

"Hannah, you've got to learn not to be so flighty and romantic."

"It's in the blood." She sat back on her heels to massage her ear. "Bennett, why are you sleeping on my settee instead of in your own bed?"

"I don't know who designed this thing. Another foot longer and a man could be comfortable." He dragged himself up a bit so that his feet dangled over the arm. "I wanted to talk to you." He rubbed both hands over his face. "When I got in, I saw that we still had guests. I took the coward's way and used the back stairs."

"I see. And Madame Beaulieu spoke so highly of you."

"Madame Beaulieu doesn't speak, she hisses."

"I know. I sat next to her at dinner."

"Better you than me."

"How gallant."

"You want gallant?" With one swing, he had her off the floor and stretched on top of him. He cupped the back of her neck with his hand, pressing as his mouth took hers quickly, completely.

"What does that have to do with gallantry?" she managed after a moment.

He smiled and ran a finger down her nose. "All the other women I've known have been impressed by it."

Hannah drew back another inch. Smiling, she ran a finger down his throat, then up again. "About those nerves I mentioned."

He caught one wrist, then the other. "All right then, tomorrow I'll look for a puddle to toss a cape over."

"A safe enough promise since it hasn't rained in days." She started to shift, but he brought her close again.

"Stay. I haven't seen you at all today." His lips were warm and coaxing against her cheek. "Do you know, Hannah, a man has to have you in his arms, has to have his lips against your skin before he catches your scent. Do you do that on purpose?''

She wore no perfume. It had to do with leaving no traces behind. "You said you..." He moved his lips to her ear. "You wanted to talk to me."

"I lied." His teeth closed gently over her earlobe. "I wanted to make love with you. In fact, I had a devil of a time keeping my mind off that thought throughout a long and frustrating board meeting and a noisy dinner." He drew down the zipper at the back of her dress. "I had to give a speech." He found silk, thin, fragile silk, beneath the linen. "It was difficult not to babble when I kept imagining myself here, with you."

"I don't want to interfere with your official duties." With her eyes closed, she pressed her lips to his neck and let herself enjoy the gentle stroking of his hands.

"But you do, *ma mie*. I sat listening to the huffing and puffing of ten stuffy men who are more interested in paintings than people, and I imagined you sitting there with your hands neatly folded and your eyes solemn. And you were wearing nothing but your hair."

She'd slipped off his tie, but paused now on the third button of his shirt. "In the boardroom?"

"In the boardroom." Would he ever stop being fascinated by that dry, serious tone and those dark eyes? "You can see why I had such a problem concentrating." He didn't tell her he'd also dealt with unexpected tingles of fear as he'd pictured her with Deboque, at his mercy, helpless, alone. It was an image he hadn't been able to drown out in innumerable cups of coffee or glasses of wine. "So I came in here to wait for you."

"And fell asleep."

"I'd hoped you'd see the irony and reverse the fairy

tale. Wake the sleeping prince with a kiss. Instead I got a shove.''

With her hands framing his face, she drew his head up. "Let me make up for it now then."

She touched her lips to his, brushed, retreated, teased then touched again. She felt him tense his fingers at her back as she toyed with his mouth. Her tongue traced, her teeth nipped as heat built to a flash point. She didn't object when he pressed her head closer, when his mouth closed hungrily over hers. If he had longed for her through the day, his need had been no sharper than her own. They would take the night hours together.

She had his shirt unbuttoned and open. Her dress had slipped down, revealing the shimmer of honey-colored lace beneath. Bennett let his fingertips play over it while he absorbed the contrasts and delights that were his Hannah. He drew the pins out of her hair so that it flowed over her shoulders and his. The scent of it was as light and elusive as the scent of her skin. What witchery she had was an innate part of her rather than something that came from bottles and pots.

Fresh, real, his. Delirious from her, he tugged the dress down her body and let it fall to the rug.

And his fingers slid over the stiletto strapped to her thigh.

She stiffened, remembering the weapon the instant he discovered it. Passion cooled so swiftly, she shivered. When she drew away he didn't stop her.

"Bennett, I'm sorry." She'd forgotten there could be no apologies, no regret. His eyes were on hers, blank and flat, as he sat up. Because there was nothing for her to say, no way for her to remove the barrier, she lapsed into silence.

Her hair was a riot of honey-toned waves that fell over her shoulders and the silk that echoed the color. Her eyes, darkly, richly green, were solemn now as she waited for him to speak. Or to leave.

Fighting the first stirrings of anger, he let his gaze pass over her, the milk-pale skin, the slender curves, the delicate silk. She was what she'd convinced herself she was not—beautiful, stunning, desirable. On one long slim thigh strapped by thin strong leather, was a knife associated with dark alleys and smoky bars. Saying nothing, Bennett reached for it. She automatically caught his wrist.

"Bennett—"

"Be quiet." His voice was as flat and cool as his eyes. Hannah let her fingers fall away. Slowly, he drew the weapon from its sheath. It was warmed from her skin, small enough to fit into the palm of his hand. Until he pushed the button and the thin blade slid silently, lethally out. It caught the lamplight and glistened silver.

She wore it intimately, he thought. He wanted to ask her if she'd used it, but a part of him knew it was best to keep the question to himself for now. It weighed nothing, but sat heavy as lead in his hand.

"Why do you need this in the palace?"

She pushed a strap back onto her shoulder, then rubbed the skin there that was growing colder and colder. "I'm expecting word from Deboque. I can't be sure when or where it will come from. Because I may have to respond to it immediately, it's best to be prepared."

"What kind of word?"

"I think you should ask—"

"I'm asking you." His voice carried a lash he used rarely, but effectively. "What kind of word, Hannah?"

Hannah drew her knees up to her chest, wrapped her

arms around them and told him everything. There could be no objection now, she reminded herself. He already knew too much.

"So we sacrifice a part of the east wing. Camouflage." He twisted the blade under the light. He knew, without doubt, he could have plunged it into Deboque's heart.

"The more genuine things seem, the more easily Deboque will be convinced. He won't part with five million dollars until he's sure Cordina is left without an heir."

"He would kill the children," Bennett murmured. "Even Alexander's unborn child. All for what? Revenge, power, money?"

"For all three. He would have his revenge on your father, his own power would grow from the chaos, and money would follow. It's his greed that will topple him this time, Bennett. I promise you."

It was the passion in her voice that had him looking at her again. Her eyes were wide and dry, but the emotion almost leapt from them. To protect his family, he thought as he tightened his hand on the handle of the stiletto. To protect herself. As suddenly as he'd fallen in love, he realized the full truth. Whatever she did, whatever she used didn't matter, as long as she kept herself safe.

He pressed the release and sent the blade back home. And he would see to that himself. After setting the knife aside, he reached over to unsnap the strap from her thigh. Her skin had gone cold, he discovered, though the room was warm. It stirred something in him that he recognized again as a need to protect. She didn't move, didn't speak and flinched only slightly when he rose. She was waiting for him to reject her, to dismiss her, to leave her.

He felt both her surprise and her doubt as he gathered

her up into his arms. "You should trust me more, Hannah," he said quietly.

When she relaxed against him, when she let her head rest on his shoulder, he carried her to bed.

Chapter 12

The package was delivered in the most pedestrian of ways. It was carried by Dartmouth Shippers, one of Deboque's less profitable but most useful tentacles. It was marked with the return address of Hannah's aunt in England and stamped FRAGILE.

The only difficulty came from the fact that Eve was present when it was delivered.

"Oh, what fun!" Eve hovered around the package. "It's a Christmas present, isn't it? Why don't you open it?"

"It isn't Christmas," Hannah said mildly, and set the package on the shelf in her closet. She would turn it over to Reeve at the first opportunity.

"Hannah, how can you be so casual about it?" With nerves just below the surface, Eve poked around the room. "Didn't you ever search under beds and in closets for packages at this time of year?"

"No." Hannah smiled and went back to arranging the flowers Eve had brought her. "I never wanted to spoil Christmas morning."

"It doesn't spoil it, it only adds to the excitement." Eve glanced back at the closet. "Couldn't we just peek?"

"Absolutely not, though I can tell you the package probably contains five dozen homemade cookies—as hard as bricks. Aunt Honoria is nothing if not predictable."

"It doesn't feel like Christmas." Moody, Eve wandered to the window. She laid one hand protectively over the swell of her belly and fidgeted nervously at the curtain with the other. "The ballroom's being scrubbed and polished for the holiday, the tree's already trimmed. If I walk by the kitchens there are the most glorious scents, but it just doesn't feel like Christmas."

"Are you homesick, Eve?"

"Homesick?" Puzzled for a moment, she turned around, then smiled. "Oh, no. Alex and Marissa are here. I do hope my sister manages to get away from her art gallery for a week or two, but I don't miss the States really. It's just that everyone tries to pamper me, protect me by hiding things." Sighing, she moved to Hannah's dresser to toy with the little enameled box Bennett had admired. "I know how tense and worried Alex is, no matter how hard he tries to pretend everything's fine. Even when I talk to Bennett, his mind only seems to be half with me. It has to stop, Hannah. I can't bear to see the people I love torn apart this way."

She too would pamper, and protect by hiding things, but it was the only comfort Hannah could allow herself to give. "It's this Deboque, isn't it?"

Eve set the box down again. "How can one man bear so much hate? How can one man cause so much pain? I know, though after years I still can't really understand, I know that he won't be satisfied until he's destroyed us.''

"It isn't possible for most of us to understand real evil," Hannah began, though she could and did understand it. "But I think we only add to it when we let our lives be affected so strongly."

"You're right, of course." Eve held out both hands. "Do you know how grateful I am that you're here? Without you I'm afraid I'd be moody and brooding all of the time. Brie's coming later today with all the children. We still have florists and musicians to deal with." She squeezed Hannah's hands as she drew a deep breath. "I hate being helpless. What I'd like to do is to go up and spit in Deboque's eye, but if all I can do is make things easier here, then I'll have to be content with that."

Hannah vowed, at the first opportunity, to spit in Deboque's eye for her. "Why don't you take me up to the ballroom and show me what's been done? I'd like to help." She wanted to help—and she wanted Eve away from the package that sat on the shelf in the closet.

"All right, but I want you to come to my room first. I have a present for you."

"Presents are for Christmas," Hannah reminded her as they walked to the door.

"This one can't wait." She had to get her mind off the undercurrents that were pressing on them all. Dr. Franco had already warned her that her tension could affect the child. "Pregnant princesses must be indulged."

"How clever of you to use that to your advantage when it suits you." They climbed a short flight of stairs and crossed to the next wing. "You said Gabriella would be here soon. Is the whole family coming today?"

"In force, this afternoon."

Hannah relaxed a little. It would be easy to transfer the package to Reeve and continue on with the plan. "Has Bennett put his treasure in the vault?"

"Treasure? Oh, his yo-yo." With her first easy laugh of the day, Eve entered her bedroom. "He adores that child, you know. I've never known anyone quite as good with children as Bennett. He puts an enormous amount of time into the Aid for Handicapped Children even though it takes away from his free days with his horses." She walked into the adjoining dressing room as she spoke. "Another reason I suppose I've been moody is that I know Bennett should be on top of the world right now, and he looks as though he rarely closes his eyes."

"On top of the world?"

"It's taken him six months and a lot of frustration to get approval for the children's wing in the museum. He finally pushed it over the top at the board meeting the other night, but not without a lot of work and fast talking. He didn't mention it to you?"

"No," she said slowly. "No, he didn't mention it."

"It's been his pet project for a couple of years. It took him months to find the right architect, one who'd mesh practicality with the essence of what Bennett wanted to do. Then, because the board wouldn't give an inch, he had the plans drawn up at his own expense. They're wonderful." Eve came back into the room carrying a long box. "You should ask him to see them sometime. He wanted it open, lots of windows so that the kids wouldn't feel closed in. The board mumbled and grumbled when he talked of sculptures the children could make contact with and illustrations from storybooks instead of Rubenses and Renoirs and Rodins under glass."

"I didn't realize he was so...involved."

"Whatever Bennett does he does with total involvement. His idea was to introduce children to art through media they could understand and enjoy. Then there's a section that's reserved for paintings and models the children make themselves."

Eve set the box on the bed and smiled. "I'm surprised he didn't tell you about it. Usually no one's safe. It's taken him two years of planning and six months of fighting to get this project off the ground."

"It sounds lovely." She felt her heart twist and expand and fill with more love. "One often thinks of him as a man only interested in horses and the next party."

"He enjoys the image, but there's more to Bennett than that. I thought that the two of you had gotten quite close."

"Bennett's very kind."

"Hannah, don't disappoint me." A little tired, Eve sat on the edge of the bed. "He watches you walk of a room and waits for you to come into one."

"He does?"

"Yes." Now she grinned. "He does. With all the anxiety and all the tension of the last weeks, at least I've had the pleasure of seeing Bennett fall in love. You do care, don't you?"

"Yes." It was almost over. Some deceptions were no longer necessary. "I've never known anyone like him."

"There isn't anyone like him."

"Eve, I don't want you to think, or to hope, for something that isn't going to happen."

"I'm entitled to think and hope as I choose." She lay a hand on the box beside her and patted the lid. "But for now, open your present."

"Is this a royal command or a request?"

"Whatever it takes to get you to open it. Please, I'm dying to see if you like it."

"Well, it's against my principles to open a present before Christmas, but..." Giving in, Hannah lifted the lid. She pushed aside the layers of tissue paper, then stood staring.

It glittered like a jewel and shimmered like fire. The dress was the rich, luscious green of emeralds with thousands and thousands of tiny beads that caught the afternoon light.

"Take it out," Eve insisted, then too impatient for Hannah, drew it out of the box herself.

The silk swayed, whispered and settled. It was cut straight, with a high neck that glistened with its beaded band at the throat. The arms would be bare well onto the shoulders as would the back before the material draped again and followed a long line to the floor. It was a dress made to glitter under chandeliers and shimmer under moonlight.

"Tell me you like it. I've driven the dressmaker crazy for a month."

"It's beautiful." Tentatively Hannah reached out. The dress shivered with life at the barest touch. "Eve, it's the most beautiful thing I've ever seen. I don't know what to say."

"Say you'll wear it to the Christmas Ball." Delighted with herself Eve turned Hannah toward the mirror and held the dress in front of her. "Look what it does to your eyes! I knew it." Laughing, she pushed the dress into Hannah's hands so she could step back and take it in. "Yes, I was sure of it. With that skin of yours... Oh yes," she said as she tapped a finger to her lips. "Bennett's going to take one look and babble like an idiot. I can't wait to see it."

"I don't think I should—"

"Of course you should, and you will because I refuse to take no for an answer." She stepped forward, eyes narrowed to pull free a lock of Hannah's hair. "My hairdresser's going to have a whack at you, too."

"That sounds a little ominous." As much as she longed to, she couldn't let herself go. The plain and proper Lady Hannah Rothchild wouldn't have had the nerve to wear such a dress. "Eve, it's lovely, you're lovely, but I don't think I'm made for a dress like this."

"I'm never wrong." Eve brushed off denials with a careless flick of her wrist. She may have been a princess for only two years, but she'd always been determined. "I've spent too long in the theater not to know what suits and what doesn't. Trust me, and if that's too much, do me a favor as a friend."

They *had* become friends, no matter what the initial reasons were or the ultimate goal. What harm would it do to accept? It was very possible that she wouldn't even be in Cordina for the ball. "I'll feel like Cinderella," she murmured, and wished it could be so.

"Good. And you should remember the clock doesn't always strike twelve."

But it did. Hannah remembered Eve's words as she and Reeve moved silently through the palace. The game was almost up, and so was her time.

The package had contained the explosives she'd requested and a coded message. She was to make her move that night and meet Deboque's agent at the docks at one a.m. The payoff would come then.

"This has to work," Hannah muttered as she carefully set the first charge. The equipment she used now was ISS-approved. The package she'd received was already being traced. Deboque would soon lose Athens and very much more.

"From outside the walls, it'll look as though the fire's burning out of control," Reeve said, working as quickly and competently as she. "The blasts are rigged for more noise than power. We'll blow out a few windows and put on a hell of a show while Malori and his men will remain here to bank it if necessary."

"Is the prince with them now?"

"Yes, Armand is filling the rest of the family in. Malori objects, but I think you're right. No harm can come from them knowing what's under way at this point, and a lot of anxiety can be relieved." He thought of Gabriella. After tonight, perhaps even the nightmares would fade.

"I couldn't bear to think of Eve waking up to the explosion and thinking it Deboque's doing. And Bennett? He's safe in the family wing?"

"Bennett's safe," he said, and left it at that. "I'm giving you ten minutes. That's enough time for you to get off the grounds. The dock's secure, so that if anything goes down there, we'll be on top of you. I'll be on the boat that has Deboque's yacht under surveillance. We'll move in the moment we have your signal. Hannah, I know the wire's risky. If you're searched—"

"If I'm searched, I'll deal with it." The mike was an ISS masterpiece that resembled an intricately worked locket that rested inches below the pulse in Hannah's throat.

"If he sees through this, he'll move fast."

"I'll move faster." She laid a hand on his when he

started to speak again. "Reeve, I have a stake in this too. I don't want to die."

He looked at her for a moment as a woman. "I have a reputation for keeping my partners alive."

She was grateful he could make her smile. "I'm counting on it. But if something goes wrong, would you give Bennett a message for me?"

"Of course."

"Tell him…" She hesitated, unused to trusting her feelings to anyone. The clock struck the hour, midnight, and she prayed the magic would hold. "Tell him I loved him, both parts of me loved him. And there are no regrets."

She left through the main door and drove slowly toward the gates. In minutes, the guards who'd not been informed of the camouflage would react in precisely the way it was expected. Anyone watching the palace would see the shock and the action. For now, she passed through the gates with only the briefest of checks.

She kept an eye on her watch as she drove, hearing the minutes tick off and thinking of Bennett. He would be safe now. Whatever happened that night, he and his family would be safe. If Deboque paid her, he would be arrested for conspiracy. If he killed her, he would be arrested for the murder of an ISS agent. The end justified the means.

Hannah stopped the car, waited and heard the explosion. Malori had promised loud, and had delivered. She opened the door and stood beside the car a moment. The palace was a dim white blur against the night sky, but the east wing was lit like day. The fire was impressive from here, and knowing that none of Deboque's men could get much closer, she was satisfied. Within twenty minutes one of Malori's men would leak word that the Royal Family, save Armand, had perished in the explosion.

By the time she arrived, the docks were deserted. Word of trouble had already spread this far. Hannah parked her car in the shadows, then left it behind to wait in the light. She made an excellent target.

The boat anchored off the coast appeared to be a small, expensive pleasure yacht. Several times during the day, a dark-haired woman had appeared on deck, to sun, to read. From time to time, she'd been joined by a man, bare chested, young, bronzed. They'd sipped wine, cuddled, slept. The watch on the *Invincible* had kept it under surveillance, and had taken bets as to whether the two lovers would have sex under the sun. They'd been disappointed.

Belowdeck, the ISS had everything from television monitors to grenade launchers. Eight men and three women crowded into the hulled-out cabin and waited.

Bennett had been confined to the cabin since an hour after dawn. For the past three hours, he'd swallowed nothing but coffee and impatience. He'd watched the monitor until his eyes had blurred. Not once had Deboque appeared in the focus of the long-range camera. He wanted to see him. By God, he wanted to look into his eyes as the trap snapped shut. But more, so much more, he wanted to hear over the transmitter that it was done, and Hannah was safe.

"MacGee's boarding." The man with the headphones spoke, and continued to smoke. Seconds later, Reeve slipped into the already crowded cabin. He was dressed in black from head to foot. Even his face and hands were smeared with it. He took off his sailor's cap and tossed it aside.

"First stage is finished." He nodded toward Bennett. "From beyond the gates, it looks as though the east wing is devastated. The ISS is theatrical."

"The family?" Bennett asked as he looked back to the monitor.

"Safe."

He reached for the bitter, cooling coffee beside him. "Hannah?"

"Word should be coming in within minutes. Some of our best men are on the docks as backup."

Bennett shot him a look that held for a long moment. He'd wanted to be at the docks, as close by as possible. He'd run into the stone wall of his father, Reeve and Malori on that, and eventually had had to concede. If he'd been spotted, the entire operation would have been put in jeopardy.

Now it was only Hannah, he thought, only Hannah who risked it all.

"Deboque hasn't been seen all day."

"He's there." Reeve lit a cigarette and prepared to wait. "He wouldn't want to be too far away tonight."

"Contact." An agent on the port side of the cabin lifted a hand to his headphones. "She's made contact."

The breeze off the water was cool and the night was clear. Hannah recognized the man who approached her as the one who had come into the smoky little bar. He came alone and empty-handed.

"Mademoiselle."

"My part of the bargain is met, *monsieur*. You have the compensation?"

"It's a nice night for a ride on the water."

The yacht. She felt a ripple that was both unease and

excitement. "You understand I'm no longer in a position to return to Cordina?"

"This is understood." He gestured toward a small motorboat. "Your needs will be seen to."

As before, she had a choice. She could draw her weapon now and take him in. If luck was with them, he would trade his own freedom for Deboque's. She couldn't risk Bennett's safety to luck. Without a word, she stepped into the boat and sat.

Her life was in her own hands now, Hannah thought, and folded them. However the night turned out, Deboque would be ruined.

Her contact didn't speak again, but his gaze shifted back and forth over the dark water. They were all waiting and watching now. Because the night was clear, Deboque's yacht stood out white and stark on the sea. She could see three men on deck, Ricardo and two others. It was Ricardo who assisted her onto the yacht.

"Lady Hannah, it's a pleasure to see you again."

There was something in his eyes, something smirking and self-satisfied. She knew then, as surely as if he'd held a knife to her throat, that she wasn't meant to leave the *Invincible.* Her voice was cool and calm when she spoke, and she hoped, clearly received across the span of water.

"Thank you, Ricardo. I hope this won't take long. I'm forced to admit I'm uneasy in Cordinian waters."

"We sail in an hour."

"For?"

"A more comfortable climate. The radio has announced the tragic deaths of several members of the Royal Family. Prince Armand is grieving in seclusion."

"Of course. Cordina is left without its heart, and without its heir. Monsieur Deboque has been informed?"

"He waits for you in his cabin." Ricardo reached out a hand for Hannah's bag.

"Are employees always searched, Ricardo?"

"We can dispense with that, Lady Hannah, if you will allow me to hold your weapons." He drew out her pistol and pocketed it. "And your knife?"

With a shrug, Hannah lifted her skirt to her thigh. She watched Ricardo's gaze dip and hold there as she drew out the knife. She pushed the release. On either side of her guns clicked.

"An admirable weapon," she said mildly as she held the blade up to the light. "Quiet, stylish, utilitarian." She smiled and sent the blade sliding back into place. "And one I would hardly use on the man who is about to give me five million American dollars." She dropped the knife into Ricardo's palm, knowing she had only her wits as defense now. "Shall we go? I enjoy the smell of money when it's still warm."

He took her arm in his surgeon's hand and with considerable panache, led her belowdeck to Deboque's cabin.

"Lady Hannah." The cabin was lit with a dozen candles. It was a Beethoven sonata this time that poured gently through the speakers. He wore a burgundy jacket and rubies. Blood colors. A magnum of champagne sat nestled in a silver bucket. "How prompt you are. You may leave us, Ricardo."

Hannah heard the door shut behind her. She didn't have to be told Ricardo would be stationed outside it.

"A pleasant ambience," she stated. "Most business isn't transacted in candlelight."

"There's no need for formalities between us now, Hannah." He was smiling as he moved to the champagne. "The announcements from Cordina are a bit hysterical and tragic." The cork rushed out. Wine bubbled to the lip. "I felt a small, tasteful celebration was in order."

"I rarely refuse champagne, *monsieur,* but its taste goes down so much more smoothly when I have money in my hand."

"Patience, my dear." He filled two tulip glasses and offered one. His face was marble pale in the dim light, his eyes almost black and full of pleasure. "To a job well done and a rich, rich future."

She touched her glass to his then sipped. "An excellent vintage."

"I've come to understand you prefer the excellent, and the expensive."

"Precisely. *Monsieur,* I hope you won't be offended if I say while I appreciate the wine and soft light, I would appreciate them more after our business is completed."

"So mercenary." He ran his fingers down her cheek. The candlelight flattered her, he thought. In time she would bloom under his hands. A pity he couldn't take the risk and keep her with him for a few months. He had only an hour for her. But much could be accomplished in an hour. "You'll forgive me, but my mood is very light. I find myself wanting to celebrate your success, our success."

His hand roamed down her throat, within inches of the microphone. She caught it at the wrist and smiled. "You set the mood, *monsieur,* first by taking my weapons. Do you prefer defenseless women?"

"I prefer amenable women." He lifted his hand to her hair, digging his fingers into its richness. Hannah steeled herself for the kiss. She could show resistance, but not revulsion. "You're strong," he murmured and brought his mouth to hers again. "I prefer that as well. When I take you to bed, you'll give me a fight."

"I'll give you more than that. After I've seen the money."

He tightened his fingers, bringing pain quickly enough so that she gasped. Then they relaxed with his laugh. "Very well, *mon amie cupide.* You will see your money, and then you'll give me something in return."

When he turned his back to reveal a hidden safe, Hannah scrubbed her lips with the back of her hand. "I've already given payment for payment."

"The lives of the Royal Family." He spun the dial as Hannah's heart began to drum. "Five million dollars to assassinate the Bissets. Five million dollars to give me a full plate of revenge and the sweet dessert of power. Do you think it so much?" His eyes glittered as he turned back to her with a large case. "My dear child, you could have asked ten times as much. For over ten years I've plotted, and twice very nearly succeeded in killing a member of the Royal Family. Now, for the paltry sum of five million dollars, you have disposed of them all for me."

"That's it," Reeve announced as Deboque's voice came over the receiver. "Move in. Slowly."

Bennett's hand closed over his brother-in-law's. "I board with you."

"It's out of the question."

"I board with you," Bennett repeated in a hard, icy voice. Moment by moment, he had listened and sweated as Hannah stood alone with Deboque. As Deboque put his hands on her. As Deboque prepared to pay her for the murder of everything and everyone he loved. "Give me a weapon, Reeve, or I go unarmed."

"My orders are to keep you here."

"If it were Brie?" Bennett's eyes were hot and reckless. "If it were Brie, would you stay behind and let others protect her?"

Reeve looked down at the hand closed over his. It was strong and capable. And young. Then he looked into the eyes that were darker than his wife's but that held the same passions. Rising, he took a .45 automatic from the arsenal.

They would move now, Hannah thought and struggled to keep her voice impassive. "Do you tell me this now so I can regret?" She laughed and walked to the desk. "Five million will do me nicely. I plan to invest and to live quietly in Rio for the next few years."

He kept his eyes on hers as he unlocked the case. The money was there, but would be for his own uses. "You have no desire to continue in my employment?"

"Unfortunately, that would be risky for both of us after the events of tonight."

"Yes." His thoughts exactly. But he opened the lid so that she would at least have the pleasure of seeing the money before he killed her.

"Lovely." Clinging to the role, Hannah stepped forward and lifted a thick stack of crisp hundreds. "Do you know how sensual new money smells?" She fanned the stack.

"Indeed." He slid the top drawer of his desk open. Inside was an elegant pearl-handled revolver. He thought it just to kill her with style. He closed his fingers over it when the first shots were heard from above.

Hannah swung toward the door, hoping he would take excitement for alarm. "What game is this?" she demanded. She slammed the lid on the case, and taking the money headed for the door. Her hand closed over the knob.

"Remain still." Deboque warned. The gun was in his hand now and pointed at her heart. A fine film of sweat pearled over his brow as the sound of running feet pounded over their heads. He held the trigger lightly, but didn't press home. Whatever trouble was on deck, he didn't want to draw it down to him. "The case, Hannah."

"A double cross?" Her eyes narrowed as she calculated how much time she dared stall him. "Yes, you would easily have paid me ten times this if you never intended to pay me at all."

"The case." He started toward her, slowly. Fear was blossoming inside him, not of death, not of defeat, but of prison. He would never survive behind bars again.

Hannah waited until he was two feet away, then with both hands on the handle, swung the heavy case at his gun arm.

Deboque's men, whether in loyalty or fear, fought madly. Gunfire exploded back and forth from the two boats. A spray of bullets from a machine gun smashed in the wood above Bennett's head and sent splinters raining down his back. He watched a man fall over the rail of the yacht and into the water below.

Already the firing from Deboque's side was coming more sporadically, but time was speeding by. And Hannah was still with Deboque. Alive, Bennett told himself as he aimed and fired. She was alive. He'd know if it was otherwise because his heart would have stopped. But there was an urgency churning in him, more than the wild night and the scent of blood. Moving with it, he worked his way to stern and slipped into the water.

The night was rent with shooting and the shouts of men. He saw a man dive from Deboque's yacht and swim frantically toward a shore that was ten miles off. His hand brushed a body that floated facedown. ISS or the enemy, he didn't know. While the fighting raged, he swam silently around the yacht.

Because it was nearly over, Reeve signaled for his men to close in. It was then he noticed that Bennett was no longer beside him.

"The prince." His throat went dry with panic. "Where is Prince Bennett?"

"There." One of the men spotted Bennett just before he disappeared around the stern of Deboque's yacht.

"In the name of God," Reeve breathed. "Move in fast. Prepare to board."

There was no one on the starboard side as Bennett dragged himself on deck. There was the occasional blast and rip of bullets, but the shouting had died. He'd spent an hour during that long, endless day belowdeck studying Hannah's diagram of Deboque's yacht. He went to find her.

She'd managed to knock the gun across the room, but he was faster and stronger than he appeared. Even as she dove after it, Deboque was on top of her. One hand closed over her throat, shutting off her air. Hannah freed one arm and brought her fist into his windpipe. Then both of them were gasping. She reached forward and her fingers scrabbled over the handle of the gun. She swore in both pain and fury as he dragged her back by the hair. For thirty grim and exhausting seconds, they struggled on the cabin floor. Her blouse tore at the seam. Beneath, bruises were already forming. She bloodied his mouth but was frustrated, unable to land a disabling injury.

Wrapped like lovers they rolled toward the gun again. She reached again, nearly grasping it. Out of the corner of her eye, she saw the fist coming and dodged. The blow was glancing, but strong enough to send her reeling. Then she was looking into the barrel of his gun.

She'd prepared herself to die. Struggling for breath, she braced. If she could do nothing else, she could fulfill her vow to spit in his eyes. "I'm an ISS agent. The Bissets are safe, and you've nowhere to run."

She saw the fury come into his eyes. She smiled at him and waited for the bullet.

When Bennett broke into the room, he saw Deboque crouched over Hannah, pointing a gun at her head. It happened in flashes, so quick that immediately afterward he couldn't be sure who had fired first.

Deboque's head swung around. Their eyes met. As the gun swiveled from Hannah's head toward Bennett's, she screamed and swung out. Two triggers were pressed. Two bullets exploded.

Bennett felt one whiz by him, so close that his skin shuddered and heated from it. He saw the blood bloom on Deboque's chest an instant before he crumpled onto Hannah.

She started shaking then. All the years of training dissolved as she lay trembling under the dead man. She'd prepared for her own death. That was duty. But she'd seen the bullet smash into the wood less than an inch from Bennett's face.

Even when he came to her, pushing what had been Deboque aside and gathering her close, the trembling didn't pass. "It's over, Hannah." He cradled her, rocked her, pressed kisses to her hair. "It's over now." Instead of the satisfaction, even the glory he'd expected to feel there was only relief. She was safe. And he was going to see that she stayed that way.

"You might have been killed. Damn you, Bennett, you were supposed to be home."

"Yes." He glanced up as Reeve rushed into the room. "We'll both go there soon."

There were tears on her cheeks. Brushing them aside, Hannah struggled to stand. She faced Reeve, but had to draw several breaths. "I'm ready to make my report."

"The hell with that." Bennett swept her into his arms. "I'm taking her home."

Epilogue

She'd slept around the clock. It wasn't until over twenty-four hours had passed that Hannah realized that Dr. Franco, the Bissets' personal physician, had given her a sedative.

She'd woken rested and resentful. And though she'd hated to admit it, aching.

The doctor had fussed for another full day, murmuring over her bumps and bruises in his kind but implacable tones. Because his orders to keep her in bed had come from His Royal Highness, neither doctor nor patient had a choice but to obey.

She complained. Even though visitors came often, she fidgeted at the inactivity. Word was delivered through Reeve from ISS headquarters, word that should have delighted her. Deboque's operation had crumbled. She'd been given her promotion. Hannah sulked in bed and wished for escape.

It was Eve who ultimately provided it on the night of the Christmas Ball.

"You're awake. Wonderful."

"Of course I'm awake." Cranky from two days in bed, Hannah shifted. The fact that her ribs were still sore to the touch only made it worse. "I'm going crazy."

"I'm sure you are." Smiling, Eve sat on the edge of the bed. "And I'm not going to embarrass you by going on again about how grateful we all are for everything you did. What I'm going to do is give you Dr. Franco's latest orders."

"Oh, spare me."

"Which are, to get up, get dressed and dance until dawn."

"What?" Hannah pushed herself up, wincing only a little. "I can get up? Do you mean it?"

"Absolutely. Now here." Rising, she lifted Hannah's robe. "Put this on. My hairdresser's expected any minute and she's going to do her magic on you first."

"Magic." With a sigh, Hannah lifted a hand to her hair. "More like a miracle at this point. Eve, as much as I want to get up and be doing, I don't think the ball is the best idea."

"It's the perfect idea." After helping Hannah into her robe, she leaned over to smell the clutch of gardenias by the bedside. "From Bennett?"

"Yes." Hannah gave in enough to touch the waxy leaves with her fingertips. "He brought them this morning. I haven't seen a great deal of him." Shaking off the mood, she tied the belt of the robe. "I know how busy you've all been, with the press conferences and public statements to clear up the entire mess."

Eve lifted a brow. She decided against telling Hannah

that Bennett hadn't moved from her bedside throughout the first night. There was enough romance in her for her to want them to discover each other for themselves.

"Speaking of messes, you should see the east wing. Mostly glass. It'll take the maids weeks to get it all. Hannah." On a long breath, Eve took both her shoulders. "I'm going to embarrass you. I know it was an assignment, but whatever reasons brought you to us, you've given us peace. There's nothing I can say or do that can repay that. My child…" She smiled a little. "Marissa and this one are safe. I know what Deboque had planned to do."

"It's over now, Eve."

"Yes." Solemn, Eve kissed both of Hannah's cheeks. "I owe you my life, and the lives of all of my loved ones. If there's anything I can ever do, and I speak as your friend and as the wife of the heir of Cordina, you have only to ask."

"Put it behind you, and me. Eve, I've never been able to make and keep friends. I'd like to feel that's changed."

Eve studied the woman she was just beginning to know. "I have two sisters, the one I was born with and the one I was given by Alexander." She held out a hand. "I'd like to have three."

"Your Highness." One of the young maids hovered at the doorway. "I beg your pardon, but Madame Frissoutte is here."

"Wonderful." Eve hooked her arm through Hannah's. "Prepare to be transformed."

It was a transformation, Hannah thought as she studied herself in the glass. Her hair, curled wild as a gypsy's down her back, was caught away from her face with two glittering combs. The dress sparkled and shimmered as it draped from her throat to her ankles. She was clever enough with makeup to have covered the bruises on her arms and face.

All she needed were glass slippers, she thought with a half laugh. More illusion. But if this was to be her last night with Bennett, she would take it. There would be no regret when the clock struck twelve.

There was already music in the ballroom. Hannah slipped in, as was her habit, and absorbed the brilliance. Mirrors were polished to reflect the glitter and glamour of gowns and jewels. Chandeliers shone like stars. It was all shimmering silver and icy blue with draping garlands and shiny balls. On a tree that towered to twenty feet were a thousand crystal angels that caught the light.

He'd been watching for her. Waiting. When he saw her the breath simply left his body. The couple he'd been chatting with fell silent, brows lifting as he walked away without a word.

He caught both her hands even as she dipped into a curtsy. "My God, Hannah." For the first time in his life his tongue tied itself into knots. "You're exquisite."

"It's Eve's doing." He wore dress whites, with the insignia of his rank and a sword at his side. However many ways she remembered him, and she knew there would be many, she would never forget how he looked just now. "Everything is so beautiful."

"It is now." His hand slipped around her waist as he swirled her into the waltz.

It was magic, she thought. The music, the lights, the mirrors. For hours they danced together, spinning around and around the room, leaving the food and the wine for others. When he circled her out to the terrace, she didn't object. There were still a few minutes until midnight.

Drawing away, she went to the rail to look out at Cordina. Lights glowed in festive colors for the holiday. The breeze held a springtime warmth and scent.

"Do you ever tire of looking at it?"

"No." He stood beside her. "I think it means even more now."

She understood, but wanted to keep even Deboque's ghost at bay. "In England, it would be cold, sleeting. There might be snow by morning, or we'd have gray, heavy skies. All the fires would be lit and the rum warmed. The cooks would have all the puddings and turkeys cooking so that you'd smell Christmas everywhere."

"We can't give you snow." He lifted her hand and kissed it. "But we could offer the fire and warm rum."

"It doesn't matter." She drew a deep breath. "When I'm home, I'll remember standing here with Christmas almost upon us. I'll remember it smelled like roses and jasmine."

"Would you wait here a moment?"

"All right."

"Just here," he said, and kissed her hand again. "I'll only be a minute."

When he was gone, she turned back to look out again at the lights and the sea. She would be home in a few days, and in time, perhaps Cordina would seem like a dream. Cordina, she thought, but never Bennett. She lifted her face to a star but didn't dare wish.

"I have something for you."

With a half smile, she turned, then caught the scent. "Oh, chestnuts!" With a laugh, she took the bag he offered. "And they're warm."

"I wanted to give you something from home."

She looked up. There was so much to say, and nothing that could be said. Instead, she rose on her toes to kiss him. "Thank you."

He brushed his fingers over her cheek. "I'd thought you'd share."

Hannah opened the bag and with her eyes closed, drew in the scent. "Isn't it wonderful? Now it feels like Christmas."

"If Cordina can be enough like home, perhaps you'll stay."

She opened her eyes, then lowered them quickly to the bag. "I have orders to return at the end of the week."

"Orders." He started to reach for her, but held himself back. "Your position in the ISS is important to you." He couldn't prevent the trace of resentment. "I'm told you received a promotion."

"A captaincy." She bit her bottom lip. "I'll be working behind a desk for a good while. Giving orders." She managed to smile.

"Have you ever considered giving it up?"

"Giving it up?"

It was the blank, puzzled look that worried him. Was it possible she could think of nothing else but her duty to her organization? "If you had something to replace it. Is it the excitement that pulls you?" He cupped her face in his hand, turning it toward the light so that the bruise Deboque had put there showed in a shadow.

"It's simply what I do." She drew a breath. "Bennett, we never talked about what happened on the yacht. I never thanked you for saving my life. I suppose it's because I've been used to taking care of myself."

"I would have killed him for this alone," he murmured

as he traced the bruise on her cheek. She started to step back, but a look from him stopped her. "Don't back away from me. I haven't spoken before this because Franco was concerned with keeping you quiet and undisturbed. But dammit, I'll speak of it now."

He stepped closer so she could feel it, the recklessness, the barely controlled fury. "I had to sit and wait and listen to you deal with that man. I had to stay where I was, helpless while you were alone with him. And when I broke into that cabin and saw him holding a gun at your head, I had one hideous flash of what life would be like if you weren't in it. So don't back away from me now, Hannah."

"I won't." She steadied her breathing then lay a calming hand on his. "It's over, Bennett. The best thing for everyone is to put it aside. Cordina is safe. Your family is safe. And so am I."

"I won't accept your risking your life again for anyone."

"Bennett—"

"I won't." He caught her hair in his hands and kissed her, but this time with a force and power that left her breathless. He dragged himself away, reminding himself he had a plan and meant to see it through. "Are you going to try those chestnuts or just stand there smelling them?"

"What?" She had the bag locked in a viselike grip. She swallowed and opened it again. "I'm sure they're wonderful," she began, knowing she was going to babble. "It was so thoughtful of you to…" She broke off when she reached in and touched a small box. Puzzled, she drew it out.

"There's an American tradition. A box of candied pop-corn with a prize in it. I had an urge to give you your Christmas present early."

"I've always been very strict about waiting until Christmas morning."

"I could make it a command, Hannah." He touched her cheek again. "I'd rather not."

"Well, since it *is* the Christmas Ball." She opened the lid and for the first time in her life felt faint.

"It was my grandmother's. I had it reset but it meant more to me to give you this than to choose another from a jeweler." He touched her hair, just the ends of it with his fingertips. "She was British, like you."

It was an emerald, fiery, stunning, made only more brilliant by the symphony of diamonds that circled it. Just looking at it made her light-headed. "Bennett, I couldn't take something like this. It belongs in your family."

"Don't be thick-headed." He took the bag from her to set it on the wall. The scent of chestnuts mixed with the summer fragrance of roses. "You know very well I'm asking you to marry me."

"You—you're carried away," she began, and this time did step back from him. "It's everything that's happened. You're not thinking clearly."

"My mind's never been more clear." He took the box from her, slipped the ring out and tossed the container aside. "We'll do it my way then." Taking her hand, he pushed the ring on. "Now, I can drag you back inside and announce our engagement—or we can talk about it reasonably first."

"Reasonably." How was it she needed to laugh and cry at the same time? "Bennett, you're being anything but reasonable."

"I love you—unreasonably then." He pulled her into

his arms and covered her mouth with his. He could feel her heart thud, hear her breath shudder, taste both need and fear. "I'm not letting you go, Hannah, not now, not tomorrow, not ever. You'll have to exchange captain for princess. Believe me, it can be every bit as wearing."

Was it magic, or was it a dream come true? Her head was still spinning as she tried to get a grip on common sense. "You know I'm not the woman you cared for. Please, Bennett, listen to me."

"Do you think I'm a fool?" He spoke so mildly she was deceived into thinking him calm.

"Of course I don't. I only mean that—"

"Shut up." He caught her face in his hands, and she saw by his eyes he was anything but calm. "I thought the woman I first fell in love with was an illusion." He gentled as he brushed his lips over her cheeks. "I was wrong, because she's right here. There was another woman who made my mouth dry every time I looked." His kisses were more urgent now, more possessive. "She's here as well. It's not every man who can love two women and have them both. And I will have you, Hannah."

"You already have me." She was almost ready to believe it could be real, and true and lasting. "But even you can't command a marriage."

He lifted his brow, arrogant, confident. "Don't be too sure. You told me once you wanted me. Was it a lie?"

"No." She steadied herself with two hands on his chest. She was crossing a line in her life, one that allowed for no deceptions. He was offering her a chance to be herself, to love openly and honestly. "No, it wasn't a lie."

"I ask you now if you love me."

She couldn't speak. From deep within the palace the clock began to strike. Midnight. She counted off the gongs and waited for the illusion to fade. Then there was silence and she was still in his arms. Looking down, she saw the ring glow against her finger. A promise. A lifetime.

"I love you, and nothing's ever been more true."

"Share my home." He caught her ring hand in his and pressed his lips to the palm.

"Yes."

"And my family."

She twined her fingers with his. "Yes."

"And my duty."

"From this moment."

She wrapped her arms around him. She lifted her face for his kiss. Below and as far as eyes could see, Cordina spread out before them and prepared to sleep.

* * * * *

CORDINA'S
CROWN JEWEL

To all the new princes and princesses in my family. May all grow up strong and live happily ever after.

Prologue

She was a princess. Born, bred and meticulously trained. Her deportment was flawless, her speech impeccable and her manners unimpeachable. The image she presented was one of youth, confidence and grace all wrapped up in a lovely and carefully polished package.

Such things, she knew, were expected of a member of Cordina's royal family—at least in the public arena. The charity gala in Washington, D.C. was a very public arena. So she did her duty, greeting guests who had paid handsomely for the opportunity to rub elbows with royalty.

She watched her mother, Her Serene Highness Gabriella de Cordina, glide effortlessly through the process. At least her mother made it seem effortless, though she had worked as brutally hard as her daughter on this event.

She saw her father—so wonderfully handsome and steady—and her eldest brother who was serving as her escort for the evening, mingle smoothly with the crowd.

A crowd that included politicians, celebrities and the very wealthy.

When it was time, Her Royal Highness Camilla de Cordina took her seat for the first portion of the evening's entertainment. Her hair was dressed in a complicated twist that left her slender neck bare, but for the glitter of emeralds. Her dress was an elegant black that was designed to accent her willowy frame. A frame both she and her dressmaker knew was in danger of slipping to downright thin.

Her appetite was not what it had been.

Her face was composed, her posture perfect. A headache raged like a firestorm behind her eyes.

She was a princess, but she was also a woman on the edge.

She applauded. She smiled. She laughed.

It was nearly midnight—eighteen hours into her official day—when her mother managed a private word by sliding an arm around Camilla's waist and dipping her head close.

"Darling, you don't look well." It took a mother's sharp eyes to see the exhaustion, and Gabriella's eyes were sharp indeed.

"I'm a bit tired, that's all."

"Go. Go back to the hotel. Don't argue," she murmured. "You've been working too hard, much too hard. I should have insisted you take a few weeks at the farm."

"There's been so much to do."

"And you've done enough. I've already told Marian to alert security and see to your car. Your father and I will be leaving within the hour ourselves." Gabriella glanced over, noted her son was entertaining—and being entertained by—a popular American singer. "Do you want Kristian with you?"

"No." It was a sign of her fatigue that she didn't argue. "No, he's enjoying himself. Wiser to slip out separately anyway." And quietly, she hoped.

"The Americans love you, perhaps a little too much." With a smile, Gabriella kissed her daughter's cheek. "Go, get some rest. We'll talk in the morning."

But it was not to be a quiet escape. Despite the decoy car, the security precautions, the tedium of winding through the building to a side entrance, the press had scented her.

She had no more than stepped out into the night when she was blinded by the flash of cameras. The shouts rained over her, pounded in her head. She sensed the surge of movement, felt the tug of hands and was appalled to feel her legs tremble as her body-guards rushed her to the waiting limo.

Unable to see, to think, she fought to maintain her composure as she was swept through the stampede, body-guards pressed on either side of her rushing her forward.

It was so horribly hot, so horribly close. Surely that was why she felt ill. Ill and weak and stupidly frightened. She wasn't sure if she fell, was pushed or simply dived in to the car.

As the door slammed behind her, and the shouts were like the roar of the sea outside the steel and glass, she shivered, her teeth almost chattering in the sudden wash of cool air-conditioned air. Closed her eyes.

"Your Highness, are you all right?"

She heard, dimly, the concerned voice of one of her guards. "Yes. Thank you, yes. I'm fine."

But she knew she wasn't.

Chapter 1

Whatever might, and undoubtedly would be said, it hadn't been an impulsive decision. Her Royal Highness Camilla de Cordina was not an impulsive woman.

She was, however, a desperate one.

Desperation, she was forced to admit, had been building in her for months. On this hot, sticky, endless June night, it had reached, despite her efforts to deny it, a fever pitch.

The wild hive of paparazzi that had swarmed after her when she'd tried to slip out of the charity gala that evening had been the final straw.

Even as security had worked to block them, as she'd managed to slide into her limo with some remnants of dignity, her mind had been screaming.

Let me breathe. For pity's sake, give me some space.

Now, two hours later, temper, excitement, nerves and frustration continued to swirl around her as she paced the floor of the sumptuous suite high over Washington, D.C.

Less than three hours to the south was the farm where she'd spent part of her childhood. Several thousand miles east across the ocean was the tiny country where she'd spent the other part. Her life had been divided between those two worlds. Though she loved both equally, she wondered if she would ever find her own place in either.

It was time, past time, she found it somewhere.

To do that, she had to find herself first. And how could she do that when she was forever surrounded. Worse, she thought, when she was beginning to feel continually hounded. Perhaps if she hadn't been the eldest of the three young women of the new generation of Cordinian princesses—and for the past few years the most accessible due to her American father and time spent in the States— it would have been different.

But she was, so it wasn't. Just now, it seemed her entire existence was bound up in politics, protocol and press. Requests, demands, appointments, obligations. She'd completed her duty as co-chair for the Aid To Children with Disabilities benefit—a task she'd shared with her mother.

She believed in what she was doing, knew the duty was required, important. But did the price have to be so high?

It had taken weeks of organizing and effort, and the pleasure of seeing all that work bear fruit had been spoiled by her own bone-deep weariness.

How they crowded her, she thought. All those cameras, all those faces.

Even her family, God love them, seemed to crowd her too much these days. Trying to explain her feelings to her personal assistant seemed disloyal, ungrateful and impossible. But the assistant was also her oldest and dearest friend.

"I'm sick of seeing my face on the cover of magazines, of reading about my supposed romances inside them. Marian, I'm just so tired of having other people define me."

"Royalty, beauty and sex sell magazines. Combine the three and you can't print them fast enough." Marian Breen was a practical woman, and her tone reflected that. As she'd known Camilla since childhood it also reflected more amusement than respect. "I know tonight was horrid, and I don't blame you for being shaken by it. If we find out who leaked your exit route—"

"It's done. What does it matter who?"

"They were like a pack of hounds," Marian muttered. "Still, you're a princess of Cordina—a place that makes Americans in particular think of fairy tales. You look like your mother, which means you're stunning. And you attract men like an out of business sale attracts bargain hunters. The press, particularly the more aggressive element, feed on that."

"The royalty is a product of birth, as are my looks. As for the men—" Camilla dismissed the entire gender with an imperious flick of the wrist. "None of them are attracted to *me* but to the package—the same one that sells the idiotic magazines in the first place."

"Catch-22." Since Camilla was keeping her up, Marian nibbled on the grapes from the impressive fruit bowl that had been sent up by the hotel management. Outwardly calm, inwardly she was worried. Her friend was far too pale. And she looked like she'd lost weight.

It was nothing, she assured herself, that a few quiet days in Virginia wouldn't put right. The farm was as secure as the palace in Cordina. Camilla's father had made certain of it.

"I know it's a pain to have bodyguards and paparazzi surrounding you every time you take a step in public," she continued. "But what're you going to do? Run away from home?"

"Yes."

Chuckling, Marian plucked another grape. Then it spurted out of her fingers as she caught the steely gleam in Camilla's tawny eyes. "Obviously you had too much champagne at the benefit."

"I had one glass," Camilla said evenly. "And I didn't even finish it."

"It must've been some glass. Listen, I'm going back to my room like a good girl, and I'm going to let you sleep off this mood."

"I've been thinking about it for weeks." Toying with the idea, she admitted. Fantasizing about it. Tonight, she was going to make it happen. "I need your help, Marian."

"Non, non, c'est impossible. C'est completement fou!"

Marian rarely slid into French. She was, at the core, American as apple pie. Her parents had settled in Cordina when she'd been ten—and she and Camilla had been fast friends ever since. A small woman with her honey-brown hair still upswept from the evening, she responded in the language of her adopted country as she began to panic. Her eyes, a warm, soft blue, were wide with alarm.

She knew the look on her friend's face. And feared it.

"It's neither impossible nor crazy," Camilla responded easily. "It's both possible and sane. I need time, a few weeks. And I'm going to take them. As Camilla MacGee, not as Camilla de Cordina. I've lived with the title almost without rest since Grandpère…"

She trailed off. It hurt, still. Nearly four years since his death and it still grieved inside her.

"He was our rock," she continued, drawing together her composure. "Even though he'd passed so much of the control already to his son, to Uncle Alex, he still ruled. Since his death, the family's had to contribute more—to pull together. I wouldn't have wanted it otherwise. I've been happy to do more in an official capacity."

"But?" Resigned now, Marian lowered herself to perch on the arm of the sofa.

"I need to get away from the hunt. That's how I feel," Camilla said, pressing a hand to her heart. "Hunted. I can't step out on the street without photographers dogging me. I'm losing myself in it. I don't know what I am anymore. There are times, too many times now, I can't *feel* me anymore."

"You need a rest. You need a break."

"Yes, but it's more. It's more complicated than that. Marian, I don't know what I want, for me. For myself. Look at Adrienne," she continued, speaking of her younger sister. "Married at twenty-one. She set eyes on Phillipe when she was six, and that was that. She knew what she wanted—to marry him, to raise pretty babies in Cordina. My brothers are like two halves of my father. One the farmer, one the security expert. I have no direction, Marian. No skills."

"That's not true. You were brilliant in school. Your mind's like a damn computer when you find something that sparks it. You're a spectacular hostess, you work tirelessly for worthwhile causes."

"Duties," Camilla murmured. "I excel at them. And for pleasure? I can play piano, sing a little. Paint a little, fence a little. Where's my passion?" She crossed her hands between her breasts. "I'm going to find it—or at least spend a few weeks without the bodyguards, without the protocol, without the damn press—*trying* to find it. If I don't get away from the press," she said quietly. "I'm afraid—very afraid—I'll just break into pieces."

"Talk to your parents, Cam. They'd understand."

"Mama would. I'm not sure about Daddy." But she smiled as she said it. "Adrienne's been married three years, and he still hasn't gotten over losing his baby. And Mama…she was my age when she married. Another one who knew what she wanted. But before that…"

She shook her head as she began to pace again. "The kidnapping, and the assassination attempts on my family. Passages in history books now, but still very real and immediate for us. I can't blame my parents for sheltering their children. I'd have done the same. But I'm not a child anymore, and I need…something of my own."

"A holiday then."

"No, a quest." She moved to Marian, took her hands. "You rented a car."

"Yes, I needed to—oh. Oh, Camilla."

"Give me the keys. You can call the agency and extend the rental."

"You can't just drive out of Washington."

"I'm a very good driver."

"Think! You drop out of sight, your family will go mad. And the press."

"I'd never let my family worry. I'll call my parents first thing in the morning. And the press will be told I'm taking that holiday—in an undisclosed location. You'll leak Europe, so they'll hardly be hunting around for me in the U.S."

"Shall I point out that what started this madness was you being annoyed by having your face splashed all over magazines?" Marian plucked one from the coffee table, held it up. "You have one of the most famous images in the world, Cam. You don't blend."

"I will." Though she knew it was foolish, Camilla's stomach jumped as she walked to the desk, pulled open a drawer. And removed a pair of scissors. "Princess Camilla." She shook her waist-length fall of dark red hair, and sucked in her breath. "Is about it get a whole new look."

Horror, so huge it would've been comical if Camilla hadn't felt an echo of it inside herself, spread over Marian's face. "You don't mean it! Camilla, you can't just— just whack off your hair. Your beautiful hair."

"You're right." Camilla held out the scissors. "You do it."

"Me? Oh no—absolutely not." Instantly Marian whipped her hands behind her back. "What we're going to do is sit down, have a nice glass of wine and wait for this insanity to pass. You'll feel better tomorrow."

Camilla was afraid of that. Afraid it would pass and she'd go on just as she was. Doing her duty, fulfilling her obligations, sliding back into the bright lights and the undeniable comfort of her life. The unbearable fleeing from the media.

If she didn't do something—*something*—now, would she ever? Or would she, as the media continued to predict, marry one of the glossy men deemed suitable for someone in her position and rank and just...go on.

She set her jaw, lifted it in a way that made her friend gasp. And taking a long lock of hair, snipped it off.

"Oh, God!" Weak at the knees, Marian folded herself into a chair. "Oh, Camilla."

"It's just hair." But her hand trembled a little. Her hair had become so much a part of her image, of her life, that one snip was like cutting off a hand. She stared at the long length of gilded red that dangled from her fingers. "I'm going in the bathroom to do the rest. I could use some help with the back."

In the end, Marian came through, as friends do. By the time they were finished, the floor was littered with hanks of hair and Camilla's vision of herself with long flowing hair had to be completely adjusted. A snip here, a snip there. A glass of wine for fortification. Another snip to even things up. And she'd ended up with a cap short as a boy's, with long spiky bangs to balance it out.

"It's awfully—well...different," Camilla managed to say.

"I'm going to cry."

"No, you're not." And neither, Camilla vowed, was she. "I need to change, and pack some things. I'm already behind schedule."

She packed what she felt were essentials and was both surprised and a bit ashamed that they filled a suitcase and a enormous tote to bursting. She put on jeans, boots, a sweater and topped them all with a long black coat.

She considered sunglasses and a hat, but decided the addition would make her *look* like she was in disguise rather than letting her pass unnoticed.

"How do I look?" she demanded.

"Not like you." Marian shook her head and walked two slow circles around Camilla.

The short hair was a dramatic change, and to Marian's surprise an intriguing one. It made Camilla's golden-brown eyes seem bigger and somehow more vulnerable. The bangs concealed the regal forehead and added a youthful edge. Without makeup, her face was rose and cream, maybe a bit paler than it should be. The high cheekbones stood out, and the long mouth seemed fuller.

Rather than cool, aloof and elegant, she looked young, careless and just a little reckless.

"Not like you at all," Marian said again. "I'd recognize you, but it would take me a minute, and a second look."

"That's good enough." She checked her watch. "If I leave now I can be well away before morning."

"Camilla, where are you going to go?"

"Anywhere." She took her friend by the shoulders, kissed both Marian's cheeks. "Don't worry about me. I'll keep in touch. I promise. Even a princess is entitled to a little adventure." Her long mouth bowed up in a smile. "Maybe *especially* a princess. Promise me you won't say anything to anyone before eight in the morning—and then only to my family."

"I don't like it, but I promise."

"Thanks." She hefted the tote then walked over to pick up the suitcase.

"Wait. Don't walk like that."

Baffled, Camilla turned back. "Like what?"

"Like a princess. Slouch a little, swing your hips a little. I don't know, Cam, walk like a girl. Don't glide."

"Oh." Adjusting the strap of the tote, she practiced. "Like this?"

"Better." Marian tapped a finger on her lips. "Try taking the steel rod out of your backbone."

She worked on it a bit, trying for a looser, easier gait. "I'll practice," she promised. "But I have to go now. I'll call in the morning."

Marian rushed after her as Camilla headed for the bedroom door. "Oh, God. Be careful. Don't talk to strangers.

Lock the car doors. Um... Do you have money, your phone? Have you—"

"Don't worry." At the door, Camilla turned, shot out one brilliant smile. "I have everything I need. *A bientôt.*"

But when the door shut behind her, Marian wrung her hands. "Oh boy. *Bonne chance, m'amie.*"

After ten days, Camilla sang along with the radio. She *loved* American music. She loved driving. She loved doing and going exactly what and where she wanted. Not that the interlude had been without its snags. She knew her parents were concerned. Especially her father, she mused.

There was too much cop in him, she supposed, for him not to imagine every possible pitfall and disaster that could befall a young woman alone. Especially when the young woman was his daughter.

He'd insisted she call every day. She'd been firm on offering a once-a-week check-in. And her mother—as always the balance—had negotiated between the two for every three days.

She loved them so much. Loved what they were to her, to each other. What they were to the world. But it was so much to live up to. And, she knew, they would be appalled that she felt so strongly she had to live up to anything, anyone, but herself.

Other snags were more practical than emotional. It had struck her the first time she'd checked into a motel—and what an experience that had been—that she couldn't risk using a credit card. If any clever clerk tagged the name Camilla MacGee and realized who she was, with one call to the local papers she would be—as her brother Dorian would say—busted.

As a result, her cash was dwindling quickly. Pride, stubbornness and sheer annoyance at her own lack of foresight prevented her from asking her parents to front her the means to continue with her journey.

It would, after all, negate one of the purposes. A few precious weeks of total independence.

She wondered how one went about pawning an item. Her watch was worth several thousand dollars. That would be more than enough to see her through. Perhaps she'd look into it at her next stop.

But for now it was glorious to simply drive. She'd headed north and west from Washington, and had enjoyed exploring parts of West Virginia and Pennsylvania.

She'd eaten in fast-food restaurants, slept in lumpy beds in highway motels. She'd strolled the streets of small towns and larger cities, had been jostled rudely in crowds. And once had been ignored, then snapped at by a convenience store clerk when she'd stopped for a soft drink.

It had been marvelous.

No one—absolutely no one—had taken her picture.

When she'd wandered through a little park in upstate New York, she'd seen two old men playing chess. She stopped to watch, and found herself being drawn in to their discussion of world politics. It had been both fascinating and delightful.

She'd loved watching summer burst over New England. It was all so different from her homes in Cordina and Virginia. It was all so...liberating to simply drift where no one knew her, where no one expected anything of her, or caught her between the crosshairs of a camera lens.

She found herself doing something she did only with family, and the most intimate of friends. Relaxing.

Each night, for her own pleasure, she recounted the day's events and her observations in a journal.

Very tired now, but pleasantly so, she'd written last. *Tomorrow I'll cross into Vermont. From there I must decide whether to continue east to the coast, or turn. America is so big. None of the books, the lessons, none of the trips I've taken with family or on official business had really shown me the size, the diversity, the extraordinary beauty of the country itself, or the people in it.*

I'm half American, have always found pride in that part of my heritage. Oddly, the longer I'm on my own here, the more foreign I feel. I have, I see, neglected this part of my blood. But no more.

I'm in a small motel off the interstate, in the Adirondack Mountains. They are spectacular. I can't apply the same description to my room. It's clean, but very cramped. Amenities run to a cake of soap the size of a U.S. quarter and two towels rough as sandpaper. But there's a soft drink machine just outside my door should I want one.

I'd love a good glass of wine, but my budget doesn't run to such luxuries just now.

I called home this evening. Mama and Daddy are in Virginia at the farm, as are Kristian and Dorian. I miss them, the comfort and reliability they represent. But I'm so happy I'm finding out who I am and that I can be alone.

I believe I'm fairly self-sufficient, and more daring than I'd imagined. I have a good eye for detail, an excellent sense of direction and am easier in my own company than I thought I might be.

I have no idea what any of this means in the grand scheme, but it's all very nice to know.

Perhaps, if the bottom drops out of the princess market, I could get work as a trail guide.

*   *   *

She adored Vermont. She loved the high green mountains, the many lakes, the winding rivers. Rather than cut through toward Maine, or turn west, back into New York state, she took a rambling route through the state, leaving the interstate for roads through tidy New England towns, through forest and farmland.

She forgot about trying to sell her watch and put off scouting out a motel. She had the windows open to the warm summer air, the radio up, and munched on the fast-food fries in the bag tucked in her lap.

It didn't concern her when the sky clouded over. It added such an interesting light to the tall trees lining the road, and gave the air blowing in her windows a faint electric edge.

She didn't particularly mind when rain began to splatter the windshield, though it meant winding up the windows or getting soaked. And when lightning slashed over the sky, she enjoyed the show.

But when the rain began to pound, the wind to howl and those lights in the sky became blinding, she decided it was time to make her way back to the interstate and find shelter.

Ten minutes later, she was cursing herself and struggling to see the road through the curtain of rain the windshield wipers washed rapidly from side to side.

Her own fault, she thought grimly. She was now driving into the teeth of the storm rather than away from it. And she was afraid in the dark, in the driving rain, she'd missed—or would miss her turn.

She could see nothing but the dark gleam of asphalt, pierced by her own headlights, the thick wall of trees on either side. Thunder blasted, and the wind rocked the car under her.

She considered pulling over waiting it out. But the stubborn streak—the one her brothers loved to tease her about—pushed her on. Just a couple more miles, she told herself. She'd be back on the main road. Then she'd find a motel and be inside, safe and dry, and be able to enjoy the storm.

Something streaked out of the trees and leaped in front of the car. She had an instant to see the deer's eyes gleam in her headlights, another to jerk the wheel.

The car fishtailed, spun in a complete circle on the slick road, and ended up—with a jolt and an ominous squeal of metal—front-first in a ditch.

For the next few minutes, there was no sound but the hard drum of rain and her own ragged breathing. Then a flash of lightning slapped her clear of shock.

She drew in breath slowly, released it again. Repeating this three times usually served to calm her. But this time that third breath came out with an oath. She slapped the wheel, gritted her teeth, then slammed the car in reverse.

When she hit the gas, her wheels spun and dug their way deeper. She tried rocking the car—forward, reverse, forward, reverse. For every inch she gained, she lost two.

Giving up, muttering insults at herself, she climbed out in the pouring rain to take stock.

She couldn't see any body damage beyond a scraped fender—but it was dark. Darker yet, she noted, as one of her headlights was smashed. The car was not only half on, half off the road, but the front tires were sunk deep.

Shivering now as the rain soaked through her shirt, she climbed back into the car and dug out her cell phone. She'd need to call a tow truck, and hadn't a clue how to go about it. But she imagined the operator would be able to connect her.

Camilla turned on the phone, then stared at the display. *No Service.*

Perfect, she thought in disgust. Just perfect. I drive into the middle of nowhere because the trees are pretty, sing my way into a vicious summer storm, and end up getting run off the road and into a ditch by an idiotic deer in the one place in the world where there's no damn mobile phone service.

It appeared the next part of her adventure would be to spend the night, soaking wet, in her car.

After ten minutes, the discomfort sent her back into the rain and around to the trunk for her suitcase.

Next adventure: changing into dry clothes in a car on the side of the road.

As she started to drag the case out, she caught the faint gleam of headlights piercing through the rain. She didn't hesitate, but rushed back around to the driver's side, reached in and blasted the horn three times. She slipped, nearly ended up facedown in the ditch, then scrambled back up to the road where she waved her arms frantically.

No white charger had ever looked as magnificent as the battered truck that rumbled up, and eased to a stop beside her. No knight in shining armor had ever looked as heroic as the dark figure who rolled down the window and stared out at her.

She couldn't see the color of his eyes, or even gauge his age in the poor light and drenching rain. She saw only the vague shape of his face, a tousled head of hair as she ran over.

"I had some trouble," she began.

"No kidding."

She saw his eyes now—they were green as glass, and sharply annoyed under dark brows that were knitted together in a scowl. They passed over her as if she were a minor inconvenience—a fact that had her hackles rising even as she struggled to be grateful—and studied the car.

"You should've pulled *onto* the shoulder during a storm like this," he shouted over the wind, "not driven your car off it."

"That's certainly helpful advice." Her tone went frigid, and horribly polite—a skill that had goaded her brothers into dubbing her Princess Prissy.

His eyes flicked back to her with a gleam that might have been humor. Or temper. "I'd very much appreciate it if you'd help me get it back on the road."

"Bet you would." His voice was deep, rough and just a little weary. "But since I left my super power suit on Krypton, I'm afraid you're out of luck."

She sent him one long stare. He had a strong face, she could see that now. It was raw boned and shadowed by what seemed to be two or three days' worth of beard. His mouth was hard and set in stern lines. Professorial lines, she thought. The kind that might just lecture.

She was hardly in the mood.

She fought off a shudder from the chill, fought to maintain her dignity. "There must be something that can be done."

"Yeah." His sigh told her he wasn't too happy about it. "Get in. We'll go to my place, call for a tow."

In the car? With him?

Don't talk to strangers.

Marian's warning echoed in her ears. Of course, she'd ignored that advice a dozen times over the last week and a half. But get into the car with one, on a deserted road?

Still, if he'd meant her harm, he didn't need her to get

into the car. He could simply climb out, bash her on the head and be done with it.

So, faced with spending hours in her disabled car or taking a chance on him and finding a dry spot and—God willing—hot coffee, she nodded. "My bags are in the trunk," she told him.

"Fine. Go get them."

At this, she blinked. Then, when he simply continued to scowl at her, set her teeth.

Shining knight her butt, she fumed as she trudged through the rain to retrieve her bags. He was a rude, miserable, ill-mannered boor.

But if he had a telephone and a coffeepot, she could overlook it.

She heaved her bags in the back then climbed in beside him.

It was then she saw that his right arm was in a sling strapped close to his body. Immediately guilt swamped her.

Naturally he couldn't help with the car, or her bags, if he was injured. And he was likely impolite due to discomfort. To make up for her hard thoughts, she sent him a brilliant smile.

"Thanks so much for helping me. I was afraid I'd have to spend the night in the car—soaking wet."

"Wouldn't be wet if you'd stayed in the car."

Something wanted to hiss out between her teeth, but she swallowed it. Diplomacy, even when it wasn't deserved, was part of her training. "True. Still, I appreciate you stopping, Mr...."

"Caine. Delaney Caine."

"Mr. Caine." She pushed at her wet hair as he drove through the storm. "I'm Camilla—" She broke off, the briefest of hesitations when she realized she'd been about to say MacGee. The episode had rattled her more than she'd realized. "Breen," she finished, giving Marian's last name as her own. "How did you hurt your arm?"

"Look, let's just ditch the small talk." He was driving, one handed, through a wailing bitch of a storm, and the woman wanted to chat. Amazing. "We both just want to get out of the rain, and put you back on the road to wherever the hell you're going."

Make that ill-mannered swine, she decided. "Very well." She turned her head and stared out the side window.

One advantage, she decided. The man hadn't looked at her twice—had barely managed once. She wouldn't have to worry about him identifying the damsel in distress as a princess.

Chapter 2

Oh, he'd looked at her all right.

It might have been dark, she might have been wet and spitting mad. But that kind of beauty managed to punch through every obstacle.

He'd seen a long, slender, soaked woman in shirt and jeans that had clung to every subtle curve. He'd seen a pale oval face dominated by gold eyes and a wide, mobile mouth and crowned by a sleek cap of hair that was dark fire with rain.

He'd heard a voice that hinted of the South and of France simultaneously. It was a classy, cultured combination that whispered upper crust.

He'd noticed the slight hesitation over her name, and had known she lied. He just didn't happen to give a damn about that, or any of the rest of it.

She was, at the moment, no more than a nuisance. He wanted to get home. To be alone. To pop some of the medication that would ease the throbbing of his shoulder and ribs. The damp and the rain were killing him.

He had work to do, damn it, and dealing with her was likely to cut a good hour out of his evening schedule.

On top of it all, she'd actually wanted to chatter at him. What was it with people and their constant need to hear voices? Particularly their own.

The one benefit of having to leave the dig in Florida and recover at home was being home. Alone. No amateurs trying to horn in on the site, no students battering him with questions, no press wheedling for an interview.

Of course, the downside was he hadn't realized how problematic it would be to try to deal with paperwork, with cataloging, with every damn thing essentially one-handed.

But he was managing.

Mostly.

It was just an hour or so, he reminded himself. He couldn't have left the woman stranded on the side of the road in the middle of a storm. Okay, he'd considered it—but only for a couple seconds. A minute, max.

Brooding, he didn't notice her shivering on the seat beside him. But he did notice when she huffed irritably and leaned over to turn up the heat.

He only grunted and kept driving.

Baboon, Camilla thought. Delany Caine was rapidly descending the evolutionary chain in her mind. When he turned into a narrow, rain-rutted, bone-jarring lane that had her bouncing on the seat, she decided he didn't deserve whole mammal status and regulated him to horse's ass.

Cold, miserable, fuming, she tried to make out the shape of the structure ahead of them. It was nestled in the woods, and looked to be some sort of cabin. She assumed it was wood—it was certainly dark. She caught a glimpse of an overgrown lawn and a sagging front porch as he muscled the truck around what was hardly more than a mud-packed path to the back of the building.

There, a yellow, unshielded lightbulb was burning beside a door.

"You...live here?"

"Sometimes." He shoved open his door. "Grab what you need, leave the rest." And with that, he stomped through the rain toward the back door.

Since she needed, more than breath, to change into dry, warm clothes, Camilla dragged her cases out and lugged them toward the cabin. She had to maneuver to open the door, as he hadn't bothered to wait for her or hold it open as any Neanderthal with even half a pea for a brain would have.

Out of breath, she shoved through into a tiny mudroom that lived up to its name. It was, in a word, filthy—as was everything in it. Boots, coats, hats, gloves, buckets, small shovels. Under a heap of pails, trowels and laundry were, she assumed, a small washer and dryer unit.

Cochon, she thought. The man was a complete pig.

The opinion wasn't swayed when she walked through and into the kitchen. The sink was full of dishes, the small table covered with more. Along with papers, a pair of glasses, an open bag of cookies and several pencil stubs.

Her feet stuck to the floor and made little sucking sounds as she walked.

"I see soap and water are rare commodities in Vermont."

She said it sweetly with a polite smile. He only

shrugged. "I fired the cleaning lady. Wouldn't leave my stuff alone."

"How, I wonder, could she find it under the dirt?"

"Tow truck," he muttered, and dug out an ancient phone book.

At least he seemed to be fairly clean, Camilla mused. That was something at least. He was roughly dressed, and his boots were scarred, but his hands and hair—though it was long, wet and unkempt—were clean. She thought his face might even be handsome—of a type—under that untidy beard.

It was a hard face, and somewhat remote, but the eyes were striking. And looked fairly intelligent.

She waited, with admirable patience, she thought, while he found the number. Then he picked up the phone, started to punch in a button. Swore.

"Phone's out."

No, she thought, fate couldn't be so cruel. "Are you sure?"

"On this planet, no dial tone equals no phone."

They stared at each other with equal levels of dismay and annoyance. Her teeth wanted to chatter.

"Perhaps you could drive me to the nearest inn, or motel."

He glanced toward the window as the next blast of lightning lit the glass. "Twenty miles in this—flash flooding, high winds." He rubbed his aching shoulder absently. Two good arms, he might have tried it, just to get rid of her. But with one, it wasn't worth it. "I don't think so."

"What would you suggest?"

"I'd suggest you get on some dry clothes before you end up sick—which would just cap things for me here.

Then we'll see if we can find something to eat in this
place, and make the best of it.''

"Mr. Caine, that is incredibly gracious of you. But I
wouldn't want to—'' She sneezed, three times in rapid
succession.

"Down the hall,'' he told her, pointing. "Up the stairs.
Bathroom's all the way at the end. I'll make coffee.''

Too chilled to argue or think of an alternative, she
picked up her suitcases again, struggled with them down
the short hall and up the stairs. Like a horse with blinders
heading toward the finish line, she kept her gaze straight
ahead and closed herself in the bathroom.

Locked the door.

There were towels on the floor, toothpaste—sans cap—
on the counter on a small white sink that, while not gleaming, at least appeared to have been rinsed sometime within
the last six months.

There was also, she soon discovered, hot water.

The minute she stepped into the shower, the glory of it
wiped out every other sensation. She let it beat on her,
flood over her head. She very nearly danced in it. When
the warmth reached her bones, she simply closed her eyes
and sighed.

It was with some regret that she turned off the taps,
stepped out. Locating a reasonably clean-looking towel on
the rack, she wrapped herself in it as she dug out a shirt
and trousers.

She was standing in her underwear when the lights
went out.

She screamed. She couldn't help it, and ended up ram-
ming her hip sharply against the sink before she controlled
herself.

Her hands shook and her temper spiked as she fought to dress herself in the dark.

"Mr. Caine!" she shouted for him as she inched out of the bath. The place was pitch-black.

"Yeah, yeah, don't blow a gasket."

She heard him tromping up the stairs, saw the narrow beam of light bobbing with him. "Power's out," he told her.

"I never would've guessed."

"Perfect time for sarcasm," he muttered. "Just stay put." He and the light disappeared into another room. He came back with the flashlight, and offered her a flickering candle. "You done in there?" he gestured with his head toward the bathroom.

"Yes, thank you."

"Fine." He started back down, and the next boom of thunder had her hurrying after him.

"What do we do now?"

"We build a fire, drink coffee, heat up some soup and wish you were someplace else."

"I don't see any reason to be rude. It's hardly my fault there's a storm." She tripped over a pair of shoes and rapped into his back.

"Damn it!" The jar had his shoulder singing. "Watch it, will you?"

"I beg your pardon. If you didn't live like a pig, I wouldn't trip over your mess."

"Look, just go in there." He pointed to the front room of the cabin. "Sit down. Stay out of the way."

"Gladly." She sailed into the room, then spoiled the effect by letting out a muffled shriek. "Are those..." She lifted a hand weakly toward what her light had picked out on a littered table. "Bones?"

Del shined the flashlight over the bones sealed in air-tight plastic. "Yeah. Human, mostly." He said it matter-of-factly as he headed toward the fireplace. "Don't worry." He crouched and set kindling. "I didn't kill any-one."

"Oh, really." She was edging back, wondering what she might use for a weapon.

"The original owner died about seven thousand years ago—but not in the fall that fractured a number of those bones. Anyway, she doesn't miss them." He set the kindling to light.

"Why do you have them?"

"I found them—on a dig in Florida."

He set logs to blaze and stood. The fire snapped at his back, shooting light around him. "You...dig graves?" she managed to ask, the horror only a hint in her voice.

For the first time, he smiled. It was a flash as bright as the lightning that shot across the sky. "In a manner of speaking. Relax...what was your name?"

She moistened her lips. "Camilla."

"Right, well relax, Camilla. I'm an archaeologist, not a mad scientist. I'm going for the coffee. Don't touch my bones—or anything else for that matter."

"I wouldn't dream of it." She also wouldn't dream of staying alone in the dark room on a storm ravaged night with a pile of human bones. No matter how carefully packaged or old they might be. "I'll give you a hand." Because she wanted to cover her unease, she smiled. "You look like you could use one."

"Yeah, I guess." The injury still irritated him, in more ways than one. "Look, there's a spare room upstairs. You might as well figure on bunking there. We'll deal with your car in the morning."

"Thanks." She was warm, she was dry and the coffee smelled wonderful. Things might've been a great deal worse. "I really do appreciate it, Mr. Caine."

"Caine, just Caine, or Del." When he walked straight back to the mudroom, she followed him.

"Where are you going?"

"What?" He paused in the act of struggling into a slicker. He just wasn't used to explaining his moves. "We're going to need water. Rain, water, bucket," he said, picking up one. "And there's a generator in the shed. I might be able to get it going. Don't mess with my stuff," he added, and walked back into the storm.

"Not without a tetanus shot, believe me," she muttered as the door slammed behind him.

Afraid of what she might find, she eased open a cupboard. Then another, and another. As the first three were empty, she found what she assumed were the only clean dishes in the cabin in the last one.

She poured coffee into a chipped mug, and took the first wary sip. She was delighted and stunned that the man made superior coffee.

Braced by it, she took stock of the kitchen. She couldn't just stand around in this sty and do nothing. If they were going to eat, she was going to have to figure out how to cook under these conditions.

There were plenty of cans in the pantry, among them two cans of condensed tomato soup. It was something. Cheered, she cracked open the refrigerator.

While it wasn't filthy, perhaps worse, it was very nearly empty. She frowned over three eggs, a hunk of very old cheese, a six-pack of beer—minus two—and to her delight, a bottle of excellent pinot noir.

Things were looking up.

There was a quart of milk which—after a testing sniff—proved to be fresh, and a half gallon of bottled water.

Rolling up her sleeves, Princess Camilla got to work.

Fifteen minutes later, armed with a pail of her own, she stepped outside. She could barely make out the shed through the rain. But over its drumming, she heard plenty of cursing and crashing. Deciding Del would be busy for a while yet, she switched his half-filled pail with her own, and hauled the water back inside.

If he'd had some damn light, Del thought as he kicked the little generator again, he could see to fix the stupid son of a bitch. The problem was, to get some damn light he needed to fix it.

Which meant he wasn't going to get it up and running before morning. Which meant, he thought sourly, he'd wasted the best part of an hour fumbling around in a cramped shed, and had bumped his miserable shoulder countless times.

Every inch of his body hurt in one way or the other. And he was still wet, cold and in the dark.

If it had been just himself, he wouldn't have bothered with the generator in the first place. He'd have opened a can, eaten a cold dinner and worked a bit by candlelight.

But there was the woman to think about. He hated having to think of a woman under the best of circumstances—and these were far from the best.

"Fancy piece, too," he muttered, shining the flashlight around the shed to see if there was anything he could use in the cabin. "On the run from something. Probably a rich husband who didn't buy her enough sparkles to suit her."

None of his business, he reminded himself. She'd be

out of his hair the next day, and he could get back to work without interruptions.

He turned, caught his shin on the generator, jerked. And literally saw stars as he aggravated his broken collarbone. Sweat slicked over his face so that he had to slap his good hand against the wall and wait for the dizzy sickness to pass.

His injuries were the reason he wasn't still on site at the Florida dig—one that had been his baby since the beginning three seasons before. He could handle that. Someone had to do the written reports, the journals, the cataloging and lab work.

He preferred that someone be himself.

But he hated the damn inconvenience of the injuries. And the weakness that dogged him behind the pain. He could barely dress himself without jarring the broken bone, the dislocated shoulder, the bruised ribs.

He couldn't even tie his own damn shoes.

It was a hell of a situation.

Steady enough to brood over his unsteadiness, he picked up the flashlight he'd dropped and made his way back to the cabin. He stopped to pick up the pail of rain-water and swore viciously as even that weight strained his resources.

In the mudroom he set down the bucket, ditched the slicker, then headed straight for a mug in the kitchen.

When he reached for the coffeepot, he saw it wasn't there.

It took him a minute. Del didn't notice details unless he meant to notice them. Not only was the coffee missing, but so were all the dishes that had been piled in the sink, over the table and counters.

He didn't remember washing them. It wasn't a chore

he bothered with until all options were exhausted. Baffled, he opened a cupboard and studied the pile of clean dishes.

The counters were clean, and the table. He snarled reflexively when he saw his notes and papers tidily stacked.

But even as he marched through the cabin, prepared to skin some of that soft, rosy skin off his unwelcome visitor, the scent of coffee—and food—hit him, and hit hard. It reminded him he hadn't eaten in hours, and buried the leading edge of his temper under appetite.

There she was, stirring a saucepot over the fire. He noted she'd jury-rigged a grill—probably one of the oven racks—bracing the ends of it with stacks of bricks.

He recalled the bricks had been piled on the front porch, but had no idea why.

Resourceful, he admitted—grudgingly—and noted that for a skinny woman, she had an excellent backside.

"I told you not to touch my stuff."

She didn't jolt. He clumped through the cabin like a herd of elephants. She'd known he was there.

"I'm hungry. I refuse to cook or to eat in a sty. The papers in the kitchen are relatively undisturbed. It's the filth I dispensed with."

And the papers, she thought, were fascinating. What she could read of his handwriting, in any case.

"I knew where everything was."

"Well." She straightened, turned to face him. "Now you'll have to find where it all is now. Which is in two ordered stacks. I have no idea how you—" She broke off as she saw the blood dripping from his hand. "Oh! What have you done?"

He glanced down, noticed the shallow slice in the back of his good hand, and sighed. "Hell. What's one more?"

But she was rushing to him, taking the wounded hand

and clucking over the cut like a mother hen over a chick. "Back in the kitchen," she ordered. "You're bleeding all over the place."

It was hardly a major wound. No one had ever fussed over his cuts and scrapes—not even his mother. He supposed that was due to the fact she'd always had plenty of her own. Taken off guard, he let himself be pulled back into the kitchen where she stuck his bleeding hand into the sink.

"Stay," she ordered.

As she might have said, he mused, to a pet. Or worse— a servant.

She unearthed a rag, dumped it in the pail of water and proceeded to wash off his hand. "What did you cut it on?"

"I don't know. It was dark."

She clucked again, as she examined the cleaned cut. "Do you have a first-aid kit? Antiseptic?"

"It's just a scratch," he began, but gave up and rolled his eyes at her fulminating stare. "Back there." He gestured vaguely.

She went into the mudroom, and he heard her slamming cabinet doors—and muttering.

"Vous êtes un espece de cochon, et gauche aussi."

"If you're going to curse at me, do it in English."

"I said you're a pig of a man, and clumsy as well." She sailed back in with a first-aid kit, busied herself digging out antiseptic.

He started to tell her he knew what she'd called him, then stopped himself. Why ruin what small amount of amusement he might unearth during this ordeal? "I'm not clumsy."

"Hah. That explains why your arm's in a sling and your hand is bleeding."

"This is a work-related injury," he began, but as she turned to doctor his hand, he sneezed. That basic bodily reaction to a dousing in a rainstorm had his vision wavering. He swayed, fighting for breath as his ribs screamed, and his stomach pitched.

She looked up, saw the pain turn his eyes glassy, his cheeks sheet pale.

"What is it?" Without thinking, she slid her arms around his waist to support him as his body shuddered. "You should sit."

"Just—" Trying to steady himself, he nudged her back. His vision was still gray at the edges, and he willed it to clear. "Some bruised ribs," he managed to say when he got his breath back. At her expression of guilt and horror, he bared his teeth. "Dislocated shoulder, broken clavicle—work-related."

"Oh, you poor man." Sympathy overwhelmed everything else. "Come, I'll help you upstairs. You need dry clothes. I'm making soup, so you'll have a hot meal. You should've told me you were seriously hurt."

"I'm not..." He trailed off again. She smelled fabulous—and she was cooking. And feeling sorry for him. Why be an idiot? "It's not so bad."

"Men are so foolish about admitting they're hurt. We'll need the flashlight."

"In my back pocket."

"Ah." She managed to brace him, shift her body. He didn't mind, not really, when her nice, firm breast nestled against his good side. Or when her long, narrow fingers slid over his butt to pull the flashlight out of his jean's pocket.

He really couldn't say he minded. And it took his mind off the pain.

He let her help him upstairs where he eased down to sit on the side of his unmade bed. From there he could watch her bustling around, finding more candles to light.

"Dry clothes," she said and started going through his dresser. He opened his mouth to object, but she turned with jeans and a sweatshirt in her arms and looked at him with a bolstering smile.

"Do you need me to help you...um, change?"

He thought about it. He knew he shouldn't—it was one step too far. But he figured if a man didn't at least think of being undressed by a beautiful woman he might as well be shot in the head and end it all.

"...No, thanks. I can manage it."

"All right then. I'm going down to see to the soup. Just call if you need help."

She hurried downstairs again, to stir the soup and berate herself.

She'd called him a pig. The poor man couldn't possibly do for himself when he was hurt and in pain. It shamed her, how impatient, how unsympathetic and ungrateful she'd been. At least she could make him as comfortable as possible now, give him a hot bowl of soup.

She went over to plump the sprung cushions of the sofa—and coughed violently at the dust that plumed up. It made her scowl again. Really, she thought, the entire place needed to be turned upside down and shaken out.

He'd said he'd fired his cleaning service because they—she—had touched his things. She didn't doubt that for a minute. The man had an obviously prickly temperament. But she also imagined finances could be a problem. Being an archaeologist, he probably subsisted on grants and that sort of thing.

She'd have to find a way to send him payment for the night's lodging—after she sold her watch.

When he came back down, she had bowls and cups and folded paper towels in lieu of napkins on the scarred coffee table. There was candlelight, and the glow from the fire, and the good scent of hot soup.

She smiled—then stared for just a moment. His hair was dry now, and she could see it wasn't brown. Or not merely brown as she'd assumed. It was all shot through with lighter streaks bleached out, she imagined, from the sun. It curled a bit, a deep and streaky oak tone, over the neck of the sweatshirt.

A gorgeous head of hair, she could admit, with a rough and tumbled style that somehow suited those bottle-green eyes.

"You'll feel better when you eat."

He was already feeling marginally better after swallowing one of his pain pills. The throbbing was down to an irritating ache. He was counting on the hot food smoothing that away.

He'd have killed for a hot shower, but a man couldn't have everything.

"What's for dinner?"

"*Potage.*" She gave it a deliberately elegant sound. "*Crème de tomate avec pomme de terre.*" Laughing, she tapped her spoon against the pot. "You had plenty of cans, so I mixed the soup with canned potatoes and used some of your milk. It'd be a great deal better with some herbs, but your pantry didn't run to them. Sit down. Relax. I'll serve."

Under normal circumstances, he didn't care to be pampered. At least he didn't think so. He couldn't actually remember ever having *been* pampered. Regardless, it wasn't what anyone could call a normal evening, and he might as well enjoy it.

"You don't look like the type who'd cook—more like the type who has a cook."

That made her frown. She thought she looked like a very normal, very average woman. "I'm a very good cook." She spooned up soup. Because it had interested her, she'd taken private lessons with a cordon bleu chef. "Though this is my first attempt over an open fire."

"Looks like you managed. Smells like it, too." It was his idea of praise—as his anticipatory grunt was his idea of thanks when she handed him his bowl.

"I wasn't sure what you'd like to drink. Coffee, or the milk? There's beer…and wine."

"Coffee. I took some meds, so I'd better back off the alcohol." He was already applying himself to the soup. When she simply stood in front of him, waiting, he spared her a glance. "What?"

She bit back a sigh. Since the man didn't have the courtesy to offer, she'd have to ask. "I'd enjoy a glass of wine, if you wouldn't mind."

"I don't care."

"Thank you." Keeping her teeth gritted, she poured his coffee, then headed to the kitchen. How, she wondered, did a man get through life with no manners whatsoever? She opened the wine, and after a brief hesitation, brought the bottle back with her.

She'd have two glasses, she decided, and send him the cost of the bottle along with the money for lodging.

Since he'd already scraped down to the bottom of the

bowl, she served him a second, took one for herself, then settled down.

She had suffered through countless tedious dinner parties, official events and functions. Surely she could get through a single stormy evening with Delaney Caine.

"So, you must travel considerably in your work."

"That's part of it."

"You enjoy it?"

"It'd be stupid to do it otherwise, wouldn't it?"

She pasted on her diplomat's expression and sipped her wine. "Some have little choice in certain areas of their lives. Their work, where they live. How they live. I'm afraid I know little about your field. You study...bones?"

"Sometimes." He shrugged slightly when she lifted an eyebrow. Chitchat, he thought. He'd never seen the point of it. "Civilizations, architecture, habits, traditions, religions, culture. Lapping over into anthropology. And bones because they're part of what's left of those civilizations."

"What're you looking for in your studies?"

"Answers."

She nodded at that. She always wanted answers. "To what questions?"

"All of them."

She rose to pour him another mug of coffee. "You're ambitious."

"No. Curious."

When her lips curved this time it wasn't her polite smile. It was generous and warm and slid beautifully over her face, into her eyes. And made his stomach tighten. "That's much better than ambition."

"You think?"

"Absolutely. Ambition can be—usually is—narrow. Curiosity is broad and liberated and open to possibilities.

What do your bones tell you?'' She laughed again, then gestured to the cluttered side table before she sat again. ''Those bones.''

What the hell, he thought. He had to write it up anyway. It wouldn't hurt to talk it through—in a limited fashion.

''That she was about forty-five years old when she died,'' he began.

''She?''

''That's right. Native American female. She'd had several fractures—leg and arm, probably from that fall—several years before she died. Which indicates that her culture was less nomadic than previously thought, and that the sick and injured were tended, treated.''

''Well, of course, they would tend to her.''

''There's no 'of course' about it. In some cultures, injuries of that type, the type that would incapacitate and prevent the wounded from pulling her weight in the tribe, would have resulted in abandonment.''

''Ah well. Cruelty is nothing new,'' she murmured.

''No, and neither is efficiency, or survival of the fittest. But in this case, the tribe cared for the sick and injured, and buried their dead with respect and ceremony. Probably buried within a day. She, and others unearthed in the project, were wrapped in a kind of yarn made from native plants. Complex weave,'' he continued, thinking aloud now rather than talking to Camilla. ''Had to have a loom, had to take considerable time. Couldn't have moved nomadically. Semipermanent site. Plenty of game there—and seeds, nuts, roots, wood for fires and huts. Seafood.''

''You know all this from a few bones?''

''What?''

She saw, actually saw him click back to her. The way

his eyes focused again, clouded with vague annoyance. "You learned this from a few bones?" she repeated.

It was barely the surface of what he'd learned—and theorized. "We got more than a few, and findings other than bones."

"The more you learn, the more you understand how they lived, why they did things. What came from their lives, and what was lost. You look for—is this right—how they built their homes, cooked their food. How they raised their children, buried their dead. What deities they worshiped, and battles they fought. And in the end, how we evolved from that."

It was, he admitted, a nice summary for a layman. There was a brain inside the classy package. "That's close enough."

"Perhaps the women cooked soup over an open fire."

The glint of humor caught him, had him nearly smiling back. "Women have been copping kitchen duty since the start. You've got to figure there's a reason for that."

"Oh, I do. Men are more inclined to beat their chests and pick fights than see to the more basic, and less heroic tasks."

"There you go." He rose. Despite the coffee, he was dragging. It was the main reason he skipped the pain pills as often as possible. "I'm going up. Spare bed's in the first room, left of the stairs."

Without a thank-you, a good-night or even one of his occasional grunts, he left Camilla alone in front of the fire.

Chapter 3

I don't know what to make of my host, Camilla wrote. It was late now, and she'd opted to huddle on the miserable sofa in front of the fire as the spare room upstairs had been chilly and damp—and dark.

She hadn't heard a sound out of Del, and though she'd tried both the lights and the phone, she'd gotten nothing out of them, either.

I've decided to attribute his lack of social skills to the fact that his line of work puts him more in company with the long dead than the living. And to season this with some sympathy over his injuries. But I suspect he's every bit as brusque and unpardonably rude when in full, robust health.

In any case, he's interesting—and spending time with people who will treat me as they treat anyone is part of this experiment.

As a lovely side benefit of his, apparently, hermit life-

style, there is no television in the cabin. Imagine that, an American home without a single television set. I saw no current newspapers or magazines, either. Though some may very well be buried in the refuse heap he lives in.

The chances of such a man recognizing me, even under these oddly intimate conditions, are slim to none. It's very reassuring.

Despite his odd choice of living arrangements when not actively working on a dig, he's obviously intelligent. When he spoke of his work—however briefly—there was a spark there. A sense of curiosity, of seeking answers, that appeals to me very much. Perhaps because I'm seeking something myself. Within myself.

Though I know it was not entirely appropriate behavior, I read through more of his papers when I was certain he was in his room upstairs. It's the most fascinating work! As I understand from the scribbles, he's part of a team which has discovered a site in south-central Florida. Deep in the black peat that was being dug for a pond in a development, the bones from an ancient people—tests show seven thousand years ancient—were unearthed.

His notes and papers are so disordered, I'm unable to follow the exact procedure, but The Bardville Research Project began from this discovery, and Delaney has worked on it for three years.

Their discoveries are amazing to me. A toddler buried with her toys, artifacts of bone, antler and wood, some of them inscribed with patterns. A strong sense of ritual and appreciation of beauty. There are sketches—I wonder if he did them himself. Quite intricate and well-done sketches.

There are so many notes and papers and pieces. Honestly, they're spread willy-nilly over the cabin. I would love to organize them all and read about the entire project from its inception through to the present. But it's impossible given the state of things, not to mention my departure in the morning.

For myself, I'm progressing. I'm sleeping better, night by night. My appetite's returned, and I've indulged it perhaps a little more than I should. Today, after a long drive, and a minor accident, I spent a considerable amount of time on elemental domestic chores. Fairly physical. Less than two weeks ago the most mundane task seemed to sap all my energy—physically, emotionally, mentally. Yet after this day, I feel strong, almost energized.

This time, this freedom to simply be, was exactly the remedy I needed.

I'm taking more, a few weeks more, before Camilla MacGee blends back into Camilla de Cordina again.

In the morning, the bright, bold sunlight slanted directly across Del's eyes. He shifted, seeking the dark and the rather amazing dream involving a lanky redhead with a sexy voice and gilded eyes. And rolled on his bad side.

He woke cursing.

When his mind cleared, he remembered the lanky redhead was real. The fact that she was real, and sleeping under the same roof, made him a little uneasy about the dream. He also remembered the reason the classy dish was in the spare bed was that her car was in a ditch, and the power and phones were out.

That meant, rather than a hot shower, he was going to take a dip in a cold pond. He gathered what he needed, and started downstairs. He stopped when he heard her singing.

The pretty voice with its faintly exotic accent seemed

out of place in his cabin. But he couldn't fault the aroma of fresh coffee.

The coffee was heating on the fire, and she was in the kitchen, rooting around in the pantry.

He saw that the floor had been washed. He had no idea it had any shine left in it, but she'd managed to draw it out. There were wildflowers stuck in a tumbler on the kitchen table.

She had opened the kitchen window, the door to the mudroom and the door beyond that so the fresh and balmy air circled through.

She stepped back, a small can of mushrooms in her hand—and muffled a short scream when she saw him behind her.

He hadn't clomped this time. He was barefoot and barechested, clad only in a ragged pair of sweatpants and his sling.

His shoulders were broad, and his skin—apparently all of it—was tanned a dusky gold. The sweatpants hung loose over narrow hips, revealing a hard, defined abdomen. There were fascinating ropy muscles on his uninjured arm.

She felt the instinctive female approval purr through her an instant before she saw the sunburst of bruises over his right rib cage.

"My God." She wanted to touch, to soothe, and barely stopped herself. "That must be very painful."

"It's not so bad. What're you doing?"

"Planning breakfast. I've been up a couple of hours, so I'm ready for it."

"Why?"

"Because I'm hungry."

"No." He turned away to find a mug. If he didn't have

caffeine immediately, he was going to disintegrate. "Why have you been up a couple of hours?"

"Habit."

She knew most people's fantasies of a princess, and the reality of the life were dramatically different. In official mode, it was rare for her to sleep beyond 6:00 a.m. Not that Delaney Caine knew she had an official mode.

"Bad habit," he muttered and strode back to the coffeepot.

She got her own mug and went back with him. "I took a walk earlier," she began. "It's a gorgeous day and a beautiful spot. The forest is lovely, simply lovely. And there's a pond. I saw deer watering, and there's foxglove and wild columbine in bloom. It answered the question for me why anyone would live here. Now I wonder how you can bear to leave it."

"It's still here whenever I get back." He drank the first mug of coffee the way a man wandering in the desert drank water. Then closing his eyes, he breathed again. "Thank you, God."

"The power's still out. We have three eggs—which we'll have scrambled with cheese and mushrooms."

"Whatever. I've got to wash up." He picked up his travel kit again, then just stopped and stared at her.

"What is it?"

Del shook his head. "You've got some looks, sister. Some looks," he repeated with a mutter and strode out.

It hadn't sounded like a compliment, she thought. Regardless her stomach fluttered, and kept fluttering when she went back to the kitchen to mix the eggs.

He ate the eggs with a single-mindedness that made her wonder why she'd worried about flavor.

The fact was, he was in serious heaven eating something he hadn't thrown together himself. Something that actually tasted like food. Happy enough that he didn't mention he'd noticed that his papers in the living room had been shuffled into tidy piles.

She earned extra points by not chattering at him. He hated having someone yammering away before he'd gotten started on the day.

If her looks hadn't been such a distraction he might have offered her a temporary job cleaning the cabin, cooking a few meals. But when a woman looked like that—and managed to sneak into your dreams only hours after you'd laid eyes on her—she was trouble.

The sooner she was out and gone, the better all around.

As if she'd read his mind, she got to her feet and began to clear the table. She spoke for the first time since they'd sat down.

"I know I've been an inconvenience, and I appreciate your help and hospitality, but I'll need to ask another favor, I'm afraid. Could you possibly drive me to the nearest phone, or town or garage? Whichever is simpler for you."

He glanced up. Camilla, whatever the rest of her real name was, had class as well as looks. He didn't like the fact that her easy grace made him feel nasty for wanting to boot her along.

"Sure. No problem." Even as he spoke, he heard the sound of a car bumping down his lane. Rising, he went out to see who the hell else was going to bother him.

Camilla walked to the window. The instant she saw the car marked Sheriff, she backed up again. Police, she thought uneasily, were trained observers. She preferred avoiding direct contact.

Del caught her quick move out of the corner of his eye, frowned over it, then stepped outside.

"Hey there, Del." Sheriff Larry Risener was middle-aged, athletic and soft-spoken. Del had known him since he'd been a boy.

"Sheriff."

"Just doing a check. Whopping storm last night. Power and phones are out for most of the county."

"Including here. Any word when we'll have it back?"

"Well." Risener smiled, scratched his cheek. "You know."

"Yeah. I know."

"Saw a compact sedan in a ditch a few miles down the road here. Rental car. Looks like somebody had some trouble in the storm."

"That's right." Del leaned on the doorjamb of the mudroom. "I came along just after it happened. Couldn't call for a tow. Driver bunked here last night. I was about to drive down to Carl's, see what he can do about it."

"All right then. Didn't want to think some tourist was wandering around in the woods somewhere. I can radio Carl's place, give him the location. Save you a trip that way, and he can swing by and let you know what's what."

"I'd appreciate that."

"Okay then. How're you doing? The shoulder and all."

"It's better. Only hurts like a bitch about half the time now."

"Bet. You hear from your folks?"

"Not in about a week."

"You give them my regards when you do," Risener said as he strolled back to his cruiser. "My youngest still prizes those fossils your mother gave him."

"I'll do that." Del waited until the cruiser eased down the lane and out of sight. Then he simply turned, aware Camilla had stepped into the mudroom behind him. "Are you in trouble with the law?"

"No." Surprise at the question had her voice jumping, just a little. "No, of course not," she added firmly.

When he turned those green eyes were sharp, fully focused on her face. "Don't string me along."

She folded her hands, calmed herself. "I haven't broken any laws. I'm not in trouble with or wanted by any authorities. I'm simply traveling, that's all, and prefer not to explain to the police that I don't have any particular destination."

Her voice was steady now, and her gaze clear and level. If she was a liar, Del thought, she was a champ. At the moment it was easier to take her word.

"All right. It'll take Carl a good hour to get to your car and swing by here. Find something to do. I've got work."

"Delaney." She knew she should thank him for taking her word, but part of her was still insulted he'd questioned it. Still, she owed him for what he'd done—and she always paid her debts. "I imagine it's difficult for you to compile your notes and papers one-handed. I have two, and I'd be happy to lend them out for an hour."

He didn't want her underfoot. That was number one. But the fact was, he wasn't getting a hell of a lot done on his own. And if he had his eye on her, she couldn't go around tidying up his papers behind his back. "Can you use a keyboard?"

"Yes."

He frowned at her hands. Soft, he thought. The kind that were accustomed to weekly manicures. He doubted they'd do him much good, but it was frustrating to try to transcribe with only five working fingers.

"All right, just...sit down or something. And don't touch anything," he added as he walked out of the room.

He came back with a laptop computer. "Battery's good for a couple of hours. I've got backups, but we won't need them." He set it down, started to fight to open it.

"I can do it." She brushed him away.

"Don't do anything else," he ordered and walked out again. He came back struggling a bit with a box. He simply snarled when she popped up to take it from him. "I've got it. Damn it."

She inclined her head—regally, he thought. "It's frustrating, I'm sure, to be physically hampered. But stop snapping at me."

When she sat again, folding her hands coolly, he dug into the box and muttered. "You're just going to type, that's it. I don't need any comments, questions or lectures." He dumped a pile of loose papers, clippings, photos and notebooks on the table, pawed through them briefly. "Need to open the document."

She simply sat there, hands folded, mouth firmly shut.

"I thought you could use a keyboard."

"I can. But as you've just ordered me not to ask questions, I'm unable to ask which document you might like me to open, out of which program."

He snarled again, then leaning over her and started hitting keys himself. His nose ended up nearly buried in her hair—which annoyed him. It was soft, shiny, fragrant. Female enough to have the juices churning instinctively. He beetled his eyebrows and concentrated on bringing up the document he wanted.

Without thinking, she turned her head. Her mouth all

but brushed his, shocking them both into jerking back. He shot her a fulminating, frustrated glare and stuck his good hand into his pocket.

"That's the one. There."

"Oh." She had to swallow, hard, and fight the urge to clear her throat. She took quiet, calming breaths instead. His eyes were so *green,* she thought.

"You have to page down to the end." He'd nearly stepped forward again to do it himself before he remembered he'd be on top of her again. "I need to pick it up there."

She did so with a casual efficiency that satisfied him. Cautious now, he circled around her for his reading glasses, then plucked from the disordered pile the precise notes he needed.

His eyes, she thought, looked even more green, even more intense, when he wore those horn-rims.

"Interred with the remains are plant materials," he began, then scowled at her. "Are you going to sit there or hit the damn keys?"

She bit back an angry remark—she would *not* sink to his level, and started to type.

"It's probable the plants, such as the intact prickly pear pad which was retrieved, were food offerings buried with the dead. A number of seeds were found in the stomach areas of articulated skeletons."

She typed quickly, falling into the rhythm of his voice. A very nice voice, she thought, when it wasn't snarling and snapping. Almost melodious. He spoke of gourds recovered in another burial, theorizing that the plant specimen may have been grown locally from seeds brought from Central or South America.

He made her see it, she realized. That was his gift. She

began to form a picture in her mind of these people who had traveled to the riverbank and made a home. Tended their children, cared for their sick and buried their dead with respect and ceremony in the rich peaty soil.

"Chestnut trees?" She stopped, turned to him, breaking his rhythm with her enthusiasm. "You can tell from pollen samples that there were chestnut trees there nine thousand years ago? But how can you—"

"Look, I'm not teaching a class here." He saw the spark in her eyes wink out, turning them cool and blank. And felt like a total jerk. "Jeez. Okay, there's a good twelve feet of peat, it took eleven thousand years since the last ice age to build up to that point."

He dug through his papers again and came up with photos and sketches. "You take samples—different depths, different samples, and you run tests. It shows the types of plants in the area. Changes in climate."

"How does it show changes in climate?"

"By the types of plants. Cold, warm, cold, warm." He tapped the sketches. "We're talking eons here, so we're talking a lot of climatic variations. Leaves, seeds, pollen fall into the pond, the peat preserves them—it creates an anaerobic atmosphere—shuts out the oxygen," he explained. "No oxygen, no bacterial or fungi growth, slows decay."

"Why would they have buried their dead in a pond?"

"Could've been a religious thing. There's swamp gas, and it'd cause the pond to glow at night. Methane bubbles up, it gives the illusion—if you're into that stuff—that the water breathes. Death stops breath."

Poetic, she thought. "So they might have chosen it to bring breath back to their dead. That's lovely."

"Yeah, or it could've been because without shovels for digging, it was easier to plug a hole in the muck."

"I like the first explanation better." And she smiled at him, beautifully.

"Yeah, well." Since her smile tended to make his throat go dry, he turned away to pour coffee. And was momentarily baffled not to see the pot.

"It's in the other room," she said, reading his expression perfectly. "Would you like me to put on a fresh pot?"

"Yeah, great, fine." He looked down at his watch, then remembered he wasn't wearing one. "What's the time?"

"It's just after eleven."

Alone, he paced the kitchen, then stopped to glance over what had been transcribed. He was forced to admit it was more—a great deal more—than he'd have managed on his own with his injuries.

A couple of weeks at this pace and he could have the articles done—the most irritating of his tasks—while still giving an adequate amount of attention to organizing lab reports and cataloging.

A couple of weeks, he thought, giving his shoulder a testing roll. The doctors had said it would take a couple more weeks for him to have his mobility back. The fact was, they'd said it would be more like four weeks before he'd be able to really pull his own weight again. But in his opinion doctors were always pessimistic.

He should hire a temp typist or something. Probably should. But jeez, he hated having some stranger in his hair. Better to invest in a voice-activated computer. He wondered how long it would take him to get one, set it up and get used to it.

"Coffee'll take a few minutes." Camilla sat back

down, placed her fingers over the keys. "Where were we?"

Staring out the kitchen window, he picked up precisely where he left off. Within minutes, he'd forgotten she was there. The quiet click of the keys barely registered as he talked of cabbage palms and cattail roots.

He'd segued into fish and game when the sound of tires interrupted. Puzzled, he pulled off his glasses and frowned at the red tow truck that drove up his lane.

What the hell was Carl doing here?

"Is that the garage?"

He blinked, turned. His mind shifted back, and with it a vague irritation. "Right. Yeah."

Carl was fat as a hippo and wheezed as he levered himself out of the cab of the wrecker. He took off his cap, scratched his widening bald spot, nodded as Del came outside.

"Del."

"Carl."

"How's the folks?"

"Good, last I heard."

"Good." Carl's eyes squinted behind the lenses of amber lensed sunglasses when he spotted Camilla. "That your car down the road a piece, miss?"

"Yes. Were you able to get it out?"

"Not as yet. Took a look at it for you. Got a busted headlight. Wrecked your oil pan. Left front tire's flat as a pancake. Looks to me like you bent the wheel some, too. Gonna have to replace all that before you're back on the road."

"I see. Will you be able to fix it?"

"Yep. Send for the parts once I get it in the shop. Shouldn't take more'n a couple days."

A couple of days! She readjusted her plans to drive on by evening. "Oh. All right."

"Towing, parts, labor, gonna run you about three hundred."

Distress flickered over her face before she could stop it, though she did manage to swallow the sound of it that rose up in her throat. Three hundred was twenty more than she had left in cash.

The interlude, she realized as she gnawed over it, was going to leave her flat broke. She couldn't call the car rental company as she wasn't on their records and that left her no option but to call home for funds. The idea of it made her feel like a failure.

Her silence, and the worried look in her eyes had Carl shifting his feet. "Ah…I can do with a hundred down. You can pay the balance when the work's done."

"I'll just go get the money."

She'd work something out, Camilla promised herself as she went back inside, and upstairs for her wallet. There had to be a way she could sell the watch—or something— within the next day or two. She had enough for a motel, for food until the car was repaired. As long as she was careful.

She'd figure something out in the meantime. She was good at solving problems.

But her stomach was busy sinking as she counted out the hundred dollars. It was, she discovered, lowering to need money. An experience she'd never had before—and, she acknowledged, likely one that was good for her.

A hundred-eighty and some change left, she mused, tucked into a wallet that had cost more than twice that. Let that be a lesson to you, she ordered herself, and went back downstairs.

Del was in the kitchen again, going through more notes.

"I thought I'd ask the tow-truck operator to give me a lift into town."

"He's gone."

"Gone?" She rushed to the window, stared out. "Where?"

"To deal with your car."

"But I haven't paid him yet."

"He put it on my account. Are you going to get that coffee?"

"On your account." Embarrassed pride stiffened her spine. "No. I have the money."

"Good, you can pay me when your car's up and running. I want some damn coffee."

He grabbed a mug and strode off. She marched right after him. "Here, take this."

He ignored her and the money she held out, instead going through the process of taking the pot off the fire, carrying it to the table so he could pour it into the mug, carrying it back again, then picking up the mug.

The woman was quivering with temper, he noted. Which was pretty interesting. He gave her points for being pissed. She wasn't used to being obligated, he decided. Or being in financial straights. There was money somewhere—she was wearing a few grand in that slim, Swiss efficiency on her wrist. But, at the moment, it wasn't in her wallet.

That was a puzzle, but he wasn't going to make it his business to solve it.

He'd felt sorry for her—not a usual reaction in him—when he'd seen all that worry cross her face. And he'd admired her quick control of it. She hadn't fluttered or whined, or used her looks to soften Carl up and cut a better deal.

She'd sucked it up. That he respected.

And it had occurred to him he could give her a hand, and solve one of his own problems without making either of them feel uptight about it.

"I figure you earned about twenty this morning," he told her. "Figuring ten bucks an hour for the work. I'll give you that for the keyboarding, and you can earn off the bed and meals by cleaning this place up, doing the cooking. If Carl says a couple days, you figure four. In four days, you'll have a place to stay and pay off the repair bill."

She stared at him, let it sink in. "You want me to work for you. To…do your housekeeping?"

"Been doing it anyway, haven't you? You get a bunk for four days, I don't lose time with my work, and we part square at the end of it."

She turned away, in what he assumed was embarrassment. He'd have been surprised, and confused, to see she had a huge grin and was fighting off laughter.

Oh, what the media would do with it, Camilla thought as she bit back chuckles. Camilla of Cordina paying for a roof over her head by scrubbing floors, heating up cans of soup and typing up notes on bones and elderberry seeds.

"How the princess spent her summer vacation." She could see the headline now.

She had to squeeze her eyes shut and bite her lip to keep the laughter from tumbling out.

She should refuse, of course. Give him the hundred dollars, beg a ride to town where she could contact her parents for a small loan or pawn the watch.

But, Lord, it was so *delicious.* And so wonderfully out of character. Wasn't that precisely the purpose of this quest?

No televisions, no newspapers with her image on them. Interesting work in a beautiful part of the country she'd never spent time in. Learning things she found far more compelling than anything she'd studied in school and knowing she was making a positive impact solely on her own skills. Not because of who she was, or any obligations or favors—but most importantly because it was her choice.

No, she couldn't possibly walk away from the opportunity that had just fallen into her lap.

"I'm very grateful." Her voice trembled a bit with suppressed humor—which he mistook for the onset of tears.

Nothing could have frightened him more.

"It's a fair deal, that's all. Don't get all sloppy about it."

"A very fair deal." She turned back, eyes shining, and struggled to keep her tone casual and brisk. "Accepted," she added, and held out a hand.

He ignored the hand because he'd added a personal stipulation to the deal. He would not, in any way, shape or form, touch her.

"I'm going to get the generator started, in case we don't get the power back. Clean something up. Just don't touch my stuff."

Camilla waited until she heard the rear doors slam behind him before she sat down and let the gales of laughter roll.

Chapter 4

An hour later, thoroughly appalled with the state of the cabin now that she had given it a thorough assessment, Camilla sailed into the shed. She was armed with a long list.

"You need supplies."

"Hand me that damn wrench."

She picked up the tool and considered herself beyond civilized for not simply bashing him over the head with it. "Your home is an abomination. I'll require cleaning supplies—preferably industrial strength. And if you want a decent meal, I'll need some food to stock the kitchen. You have to go into town."

He battled the bolt into submission, shoved the switch on. And got nothing but a wheezy chuckle out of the generator. "I don't have time to go into town."

"If you want food for your belly and clean sheets on which to sleep, you'll make time."

He used the wrench to beat viciously at the generator, then gave it three solid kicks. Much too accustomed to the male response to irritating inanimate objects to be surprised, Camilla simply stood where she was, list in hand.

When he'd finished cursing, she angled her head. "I've always wondered why men refer to uncooperative machines with crude female euphemisms."

"Because they fit like a glove." He leaned over, slapped on the switch and grunted with satisfaction as the generator let out a loud belch and began to run.

"Now that you've accomplished that amazing feat, you'll want to clean up before you go fill this list."

Eyes narrowed on her face, he picked up the wrench again, weighed it consideringly in his hand.

The implication wasn't lost on her. She simply stuck out her chin.

He tossed the wrench aside, snatched the list and smeared it with the motor oil on his fingers. "I hate bossy women."

"I can't stand crude men. We'll both just have to live with it, since I'm currently washing your underwear."

The faintest glint of humor flicked into his eyes. "You've got plenty of starch. Just don't use any on my shorts."

They started for the door at the same time, and ended up jammed together. Her hand went automatically to his chest where she felt the surprised kick of his heart match hers.

"You're going to have to keep out of my way," he told her.

"You'll have to watch where you're going, then." She saw, with reluctant excitement, his gaze lower, and linger on her mouth. In response, her lips parted on one quiet and catchy breath.

"You got that right, sister," he muttered, and squeezed out of the door.

"Well." She breathed out, rubbing her finger experimentally over lips that felt just a little too warm. "Well, well."

She was angry, exhausted and energized—in a way she hadn't been in a very long time. Alive, whole, healthy and, she realized, interested. It was something to think about.

Del discovered, very quickly, he didn't care to be an errand boy. Shopping cut deeply into his day, and half the items on her list had him scratching his head in frustration.

What the hell was chervil, and why did it have to be fresh?

What the devil did she need with *two* dozen eggs?

And three gallons of bleach.

Maybe she was going to poison him with it, he mused as he drove back to the cabin. She'd looked mad enough to, behind that cool, queen-to-peasant stare she tended to aim at him.

That was some face she had, he reflected. The kind that kicked a man right in the gut. Then you added on the voice, those legs that seemed to go straight up to her ears, and you had one dangerous female.

He was starting to regret that he'd felt sorry for her.

Still, he knew how to be careful around dangerous packages. And she was, after all, no more than a handy tool for the next few days. So he'd give her a wide berth when they weren't actively working, keep his hands to himself at all times and do his best to think of her as a nonsexual entity.

Then when he pulled up behind the cabin and she came running out, his heart all but stopped. Nonsexual? A tool? The woman was a weapon—and a lethal one at that, he decided.

She was laughing, her face flushed with it as she pulled open the door and began to haul out grocery bags. "The power came back on. I never thought I'd be so delighted with something as basic as a working light switch. Still no phone service, but I'm sure that's next."

He snagged a bag and followed her inside. She walked across the dirt and gravel, he thought, as if she were gliding across the polished marble floor of a ballroom. He decided it had something to do with all that leg. Which he wasn't, of course, paying any attention to. Whatsoever.

"How many people are you planning to feed for the next few days?"

"Oh, don't be cranky." She waved him off and began to unload supplies. "I'll make you a sandwich as soon as these are put away."

She knew how to make a sandwich, he had to give her that. He ate, and ate well, in his now spotless kitchen, his mood improving as he scanned the next batch of notes. His ribs ached a bit, but the discomfort had eased to tolerable with just aspirin.

When he was done, he dictated for another three hours while she transcribed. She interrupted now and then, but her questions didn't bother him as much.

The fact was, they were good questions, the kind that made him think. He did classroom duty from time to time, though it was never his first choice. He was forced to admit that the majority of students professing a desire to make a career in the field didn't have as quick an understanding of the *point* as she did.

He caught himself studying the long line of her neck. The graceful curve and arch of it. Mortified, he turned away, pushed himself back into his notes and forgot her.

She knew he'd been staring, just as she knew he'd switched her off again as easily as a finger flicked a light from on to off.

She found she liked it—all the aspects. His interest, his annoyance with it and the focus that allowed him to dismiss it.

His interest had nothing to do with her family, her blood or her rank. It was the first time in her life she'd been utterly sure of that, and the response inside her was quick and pleased. As to the annoyance she could sense him feeling, that was purely satisfying.

He saw her as a woman, first and last. Not an image, not a title. And that made her feel like a woman. He was attracted to her and didn't want to be. That gave her a lovely edge of control—an essential female control that wasn't weighed down with royal command.

And his focus, well, that attracted *her*. It was a kind of skill she respected, and stemmed from willpower, intellect and passion for his work.

It also challenged her. Though she knew it would be wise to resist that challenge. She was, after all, essentially alone with him—a man she knew little about—and flirting with that focus, trying to undermine it for her own curiosity and satisfaction might have…consequences.

Then again, what was a quest without consequences?

When he paused long enough, she rolled her stiff shoulders, smiled over at him. "Would you mind if we took a break?"

She watched him come back to the present, back to the room, back to her. Felt his gaze, sexy and scholarly behind his reading glasses, slide over her as she rose to stretch.

"I'm not finished," he told her.

"We can pick it up again after dinner, if you like." She kept her smile easy. "I could use a walk before I start cooking. Do you ever walk in the woods, Del?"

There was the faintest hum of invitation in her voice. He was sure—damn sure—it was deliberate. It packed a hell of a punch. He hated to think what she could do if she took a good, solid shot at a man.

"Go ahead, I've got stuff to do." He picked up more notes, dismissing her. He waited until she'd passed into the mudroom before he called out, "Watch out for snakes."

The hesitation in her stride, the faintest gasp, gave him a great deal of satisfaction.

He woke in the middle of the night with his ribs aching and his mind blurry.

He'd been dreaming of her again, damn it. This time they'd been in the kitchen working on his notes. She'd sat at the keyboard, stupendously naked.

The fantasy was juvenile enough to embarrass him.

The problem with women was they could get to you just by breathing.

He lay there a moment, willing his ribs to settle and his blood to cool.

He'd gotten through the day and the evening, hadn't he, holding on to his stipulation. He'd never touched her, not once. It would've been easy to. A finger trailed down that pretty nape while she'd typed. A brush of his hand when she'd passed him the salt over dinner.

Easy, as easy as grabbing her one-handed, diving in and finding out what that long, mobile mouth tasted like.

But he hadn't. Points for him.

Still, it made him a little nervous that he kept *thinking* about doing it.

And she was flirting with him. He'd ignored, evaded or moved in on flirtations often enough to recognize one. Especially when the woman wasn't being particularly subtle.

He'd had students—or the occasional groupie who hung around digs—put moves on him. Mostly, in his estimation, because they'd dreamed up some romantic image about the field. He put the blame squarely on Indiana Jones for that. Though those movies had been so damned entertaining he couldn't be sore about it.

He dismissed the flirtations, or fell in with them, depending on the timing, the woman and his mood. But as far as serious relationships went, he'd managed to avoid that boggy complication. The redhead had complication written all over her, so fun and games were out of the question.

He should get her a room in town. Pay for it. Move her out.

Then he thought of the pile of neatly typed pages, and the intensity of his annoyance went way down. She was a miracle worker. Not only did her help mean he didn't need to fight his way through the material on his own, but her questions, her interest and her organizational ability was actually getting him to deliver the best material he'd ever done. Not that he was going to mention that.

He thought of the meal she'd put on the table. He hadn't a clue what she'd done to that humble chicken, but she'd turned it into a feast.

He began to revise his notion that she had a rich, irritated husband or lover stashed somewhere. She was too efficient, too clever in the kitchen to be somebody's spoiled and pampered tootsie.

Which was a good thing as fantasizing about another man's woman was too close to fooling around with another man's woman. And that was on his short list of unbreakable rules.

If he moved her out, he'd be back to square one. If he moved her out, he'd be admitting he couldn't keep his hands off her. If he admitted that, well, where was he?

Giving up, he rose—remembered at the last minute to tug on sweats—and went down the hall to the bathroom. He didn't notice the sparkling tiles and neatly hung fresh towels any more than he'd have noticed soap scum and damp heaps. But the scent caught him, because it was hers.

And it tightened every muscle in his body.

He yanked his pain medication from the cabinet, then shoved it back again. Damn pills made him stupid. He'd rather toss back a handful of over-the-counter stuff and a short, neat whiskey.

He didn't allow himself to so much as glance at her bedroom door, to think—even for an instant—of her lying in bed behind it. A minute later, he realized that fantasy would've been wasted because she wasn't in bed.

He heard her voice, the quiet murmur of it coming from the kitchen. Eyes narrowed, he paused, listened. He couldn't quite make out the words, but the tone was soft, full of affection. It set his teeth on edge.

Who the hell was she talking to? He moved forward and caught the end of her conversation.

"Je t'aime aussi. Bonne nuit."

The quiet click of the phone on the receiver came an instant before he hit the lights.

She stumbled back, bit off a scream and slapped both hands to her mouth. *"Mon Dieu! Vous m'avez fait peur!"* She let out a shaky breath, shook the French out of her head. "You frightened me."

"What are you doing down here in the dark?"

She'd crept down to check the phone, and finding it working, had called home to reassure her family. She kept the lights off and her voice low to avoid exactly what was happening now. Explanations.

"The phone's back on."

"Yeah. Answer the question."

Her shoulders went back, her chin went up. "I didn't realize I was meant to stay in my room like a child after bedtime," she tossed back. "I'm repaying you for the lodging, and assumed I was free to make use of the house."

"I don't give a damn if you dance a tango in the moonlight. I want to know why you're sneaking around and whispering on the phone in the dark."

She gave him the truth, and coated it with ice. "I couldn't sleep. I came down for a drink and checked the phone. When I discovered it was in order, I made a call. Don't worry, I reversed the charges. If my mobile worked in this…backwater, I wouldn't have presumed to use yours. And having the courtesy to be quiet when another person in the house was, *presumably,* sleeping isn't sneaking."

It was reasonable. It rang true. So he nodded, slowly.

"Fine. You want to check in with your husband or boy-friend, go ahead. But don't prowl around like a thief."

Her color bloomed, her eyes went burning gold. "I was not prowling, and I don't have a husband. If you must know, I spoke with my mother to reassure her I was well. Is this inquisition over?"

He hated feeling stupid so he said nothing and stepped to the cabinet for aspirin.

"I should've known." With an impatient huff, she took down a glass to fill it with water. "You're only more impossible when you're in pain. Here."

"I don't want water." He moved around her to root at the bottle of whiskey from the pantry.

"Have the water first, you'll spoil the taste of the whis-key otherwise." She got down another glass, took the bottle from him and poured a tidy three fingers. "I imag-ine it should help the discomfort. Is it your shoulder or your ribs?"

"Ribs mostly."

"I suppose they hurt more as they heal. Why don't you sit and I'll make you an ice pack for them."

"I don't need a nurse."

"Stop being such a hardhead." She filled a small plas-tic bag with ice, then wrapped it in a thin dishcloth. "Sit, drink your whiskey. Tell me about one of your other digs. Something foreign and exotic."

It amused her, pleased her, to hear her mother in her voice, the brisk indulgence of it, the tone she'd used to soothe and distract her children during illness.

"Go away." The order didn't have much punch behind it, and he sat down.

"When I was cleaning I noticed some correspondence to Dr. Caine. I was impressed." She sat, holding the cloth to her cheek and waiting for it to cool. "Where did you study?"

She was wearing a robe, the color of copper. He figured it had to be silk, and from the way it clung, shifted, that she had little to nothing on under it. In defense he closed his eyes and let the whiskey slide down his throat.

"Oxford."

"Now I'm more impressed. Delaney Caine, a doctorate degree from Oxford. How did you know you were an archaeologist?"

It was an odd way to phrase it, he thought. Not how did you become, or when did you decide, but how did you know. And it was exactly right. "I always wanted to know how and why and when. And who. Whenever I'd go on a dig with my parents—"

"Ah, they're archaeologists, too."

"Paleontologists. Dinosaurs." He kept his eyes closed, knowing between will and whiskey the ache would ease. "I liked the digs, but it seemed more exciting to me when they'd dig up something human. Pieces of pottery or tools or weapons. Something that said man walked there."

He hissed a bit through his teeth when the cooled cloth made contact with his ribs.

Poor thing, she thought sympathetically. So angry at the pain. "My brothers went through a fascination with dinosaurs. I think all boys do." She saw the strain go out of his face as the ice numbed the ache. "Were they disappointed, your parents, that you didn't go into their field?"

"Why would they be?" He let himself relax, inch by inch. An owl hooted, long, slow calls from the woods beyond the cabin. Her scent drifted over him like a gentle stroke of hands.

"Oh, tradition, I suppose. It's comforting, isn't it, to have parents who understand—at least try to understand—when you have to test yourself, try your own direction? Some of us wait too long to do so, fearing disapproval or failure."

He was relaxed, she thought, drifting toward sleep. Odd, he looked no less formidable now than he did when he was alert. Maybe it was the bones of his face, or that prickly shadow of beard. Whatever it was, it had a snake of arousal twining through her to look at him, really look at him when he was unaware.

Then his eyes opened, and that interesting face was very close to hers. She nearly eased back with instinctive courtesy, but there was a wariness in those deep green depths. An intriguing awareness that nudged her to test her power.

She stayed close, very close, and lifted a hand to give the rough stubble on his face a testing, and flirtatious, rub. "You need a shave, Dr. Caine."

He could smell her, all fresh and dewy despite the lateness of the hour. Her breath fanned lightly over his skin. And made his mouth water. "Cut it out."

"It'd be tricky to shave one-handed." She trailed a fingertip along his jaw. Down his throat. "I could do it for you in the morning."

"I don't want a shave, and I don't like you touching me."

"Oh, you like me touching you." Surely this lust that was curling around in her belly wasn't all one-sided. "You're just afraid of it. And annoyed that I'm not afraid of you."

He grabbed her wrist with his good hand, and his fingers tightened warningly. "If you're not afraid, you're stupid.'' Deliberately he raked his gaze over her, an insulting pass down her body and back up again. ''We're alone out here, and you've got no place to hide. I may have only one good arm, but if I decided to help myself, you couldn't stop me.''

Anger danced up her spine, but there was no fear in it. No one had ever laid hands on her unless she'd allowed it. She didn't intend for that to change. ''You're wrong about that. I don't hide, I confront. I'm not weak or helpless.''

He tightened his grip on her wrist, fully aware his fingers would likely leave marks. He hoped they did, and she remembered it. For both their sakes. ''You're a woman, and I outweigh you by close to a hundred pounds. A lot of men would use that advantage to take a sample of you. Whether you were to their taste or not. I'm more particular, and, sister, you don't appeal to me.''

''Really?'' Her anger was full-blown now, a state she worked to avoid. When she was angry, overcome with anger, she knew she could be incredibly rash. She did her best to cool down, to take the reins of her temper in hand. ''That's fortunate for both of us then.''

She eased back, tugged her arm free when his grip on her loosened. She saw something flicker in his eyes— relief or disdain, she wasn't sure. But either way, it fanned the flames again.

''But it's a lie.''

She was angry, rash—and, she supposed, incredibly stupid. But the reins of temper slipped, and she fisted both hands in his hair and crushed her mouth to his.

Her first reaction was satisfaction, pure and simple, when she heard his quick, indrawn breath. She went with it, using her lips and tongue to get a good taste of him.

And as that taste filled her, pumped inside her with an unexpected wave of heat, it led to her second reaction.

A slow and slippery meltdown.

She hadn't been prepared for it, not for need to burn through anger, every layer of it, and pull the hair trigger of her own passion. She made a little sound, both surprise and pleasure, and slid into him.

His mouth was hard, his face rough and his hair as thick and soft as mink pelt. She could feel the jackhammer of his heart, and the grip of his hand—this time vised on her nape. His teeth, then his tongue met hers. All she could think was: Give me more.

His reflexes were sluggish. It was the only excuse he could give for not shoving her away before she slid into him. And he was only human. That was the only reason he could find for his hand lifting—not to push her off, but to clamp over her neck, to keep her just where she was.

All over him.

The soft, greedy sounds she made had his blood surging, drove him to fight to deepen the kiss even as it reached depths he wasn't sure he could stand.

He wanted to swallow her whole—one wild, voracious bite. He wanted it, wanted her, more than he wanted his next breath.

He shifted, struggling to wrap his other arm around her, drag her onto his lap. The sudden careless move had bright, blinding pain smothering passion.

She jerked back. She'd felt his body go rigid, heard him fight to catch his breath, knew she'd hurt him. Concern, apologies nearly fell off her tongue before his vicious glare stopped them.

"Stay the hell away from me." He couldn't pull in any air, and his head swam. He cursed because he knew it had every bit as much to do with his body's reaction to her as it did to the pain.

"Let me help—"

"I said stay the hell away." His chair crashed to the floor as he pushed himself upright. When his vision blurred he nearly swayed, and the weakness only added to his fury. "You want a quick roll, go somewhere else. I'm not in the market."

He strode out of the house, the two doors slamming like bullets at his back.

She was thoroughly ashamed of herself, and had barely slept all night for cringing every time she replayed the scene in her head.

She'd pushed herself on him. All but *forced* herself on him. It meant nothing that she'd been angry and insulted and aroused all at once. Why if a man had behaved as she had, Camilla would have been first in line to condemn him as a brute and a barbarian.

She'd made him kiss her, taking advantage of the situation and her physical advantage. That was unconscionable.

She would have to apologize, and accept whatever payment he wanted for the offense. If that meant booting her out of the house on her ear, he had a perfect right to do so.

She hoped it wouldn't come to that.

It might have been an embarrassingly female cliché, but she stationed herself in the kitchen, only an hour after dawn, and prepared to fix him a lovely breakfast to soften him up.

Of course, she might have to adjust that to lunch, as he hadn't come back into the house until after three in the morning. When she heard him come in, she hadn't started breathing again for ten minutes, half expecting him to burst into her room, haul her out of bed and pitch her out of the window then and there.

Not that he hadn't responded to her advance, she reminded herself as shame continued to prick. He'd all but devoured her like a man starving. And if he hadn't tried to drag her closer and caused himself pain...

Well, she supposed it was best not to think of that.

She had coffee brewed, juice chilling. She'd made batter and filling for apple-cinnamon crêpes from scratch and had a generous slice of country ham waiting. Now if the bear would only lumber out of his cave.

Minutes later she heard the creak overhead that told her he was up and about. She had to wipe suddenly damp palms on her slacks before she turned to heat the griddle for his breakfast.

Because Del was also replaying the scene in his head, he was in the foulest of moods as he showered. Part of him was furious with the woman for putting him in such an impossible position. The other stood back in amazed disgust at his reaction.

He'd had a beautiful woman come on to him in a staggeringly open and avid way. A gorgeous, sexy, unattached woman had grabbed him in the middle of the night and kissed his brains out.

And he'd stormed out of the house in a huff.

What was he, crazy?

Careful, he corrected, annoyed with the internal debate. He had no problem with casual, healthy sex between consenting adults. But if there was a casual bone in Camilla's body, he'd dance a jig naked in the middle of the road to town.

The woman breathed complications.

Besides the fact, he reminded himself as he dressed, he didn't have time for fun and games. He had work to do. And when he did have time, *he* made the damn moves.

Not that it hadn't been...interesting to have that step taken out of his hands, momentarily.

The woman had a mouth like a goddess, he thought. Hot, persuasive and potent.

Better not to think about it. Much better to decide what the hell to do about it. As far as he could see, there were two choices. He could pretend it never happened, or he could fire her, drive her into town and dump her.

The latter, it seemed to him, was the safest bet all around.

He was halfway down the stairs when he smelled coffee. The siren's scent of it weakened his resolve. He could count on the fingers of one hand the number of times in his adult life he'd woken to the aroma of fresh coffee.

Then he caught the scent of grilling meat.

Plays dirty, he noted. Just like a female.

The minute he stepped into the kitchen, she turned, coffee mug in hand. Rather than hand it to him, she set it on the table. She didn't smile, but her eyes met his and stayed level.

"I want to apologize for my behavior."

The tone, judge-sober, threw him off stride. He figured the best move was to keep his mouth shut—and drink the coffee.

"It was," she continued, "completely indefensible. I took advantage of the situation and abused your hospitality. I couldn't be more sorry for it. You'd be perfectly justified in throwing me out. I hope you won't, but I won't argue if that's what you've decided to do.''

Did he think she played dirty? he mused, eyeing her over the rim of his cup as she stood, solemn and patient with ham sizzling at her back. A heavyweight champ wouldn't last a full round with her.

"Let's just forget it."

Relief trickled through her, but she couldn't relax until she'd finished. "That's very generous of you." She shifted to pick up the kitchen fork and turn the meat. "I'd like to tell you I've never done anything like that before."

He thought of the kiss, the smoldering punch of it. "Like what before?"

"Pushed myself on a man." The memory of it had hot color washing into her cheeks, but she continued to cook with a steady hand. "It occurred to me afterward that if the situation had been reversed—if you had pushed yourself on me, particularly when I was incapacitated—"

"I'm not incapacitated." Irritated, he swallowed coffee, then went for more.

"Well…in any case, it occurred to me that it would've been contemptible, perhaps even criminal, so—"

"We locked lips. Beginning and end," he snapped out, growing more and more uncomfortable. "It's not a big damn deal."

She slid her gaze toward him, then away again. The deal, big or otherwise, had kept him out of his own house most of the night. So she *would* finish groveling. "A sexual act of any kind must be mutual or it's harassment. Worst, molestation."

"The day some skinny-assed woman can molest me is the day pigs go into orbit."

"I'm not skinny, assed or otherwise, but to finish. I

was angry and I'm attracted to you—God knows why—
and both those reactions, as well as the simple curiosity I
felt, are my responsibility to control. I appreciate your
acceptance of my apology. Now if you'd like to sit down,
I'm going to make crêpes.''

She stabbed the ham, dumped it on a plate. Before she
could turn to the crêpe batter, he spun her around,
clamped his hand over her throat. And lifting her to her
toes closed his mouth over hers.

The fork she still held clattered to the counter. Her arms
fell helplessly to her sides. It was an assault, a glorious
one that made her weak-kneed, light-headed and hot-
blooded all at once. Even as she started to sway toward
him, he gave her a light shove. Stepped back.

''There, that clears the slate,'' he said, then picking up
his coffee again, sat. ''What kind of crêpes?''

Chapter 5

The beard irritated him. So did the woman. His ribs were a constant dull ache. As was his libido.

Work helped such nagging and unwelcome distractions. He'd always been able to lose himself in work—in fact he figured anyone who couldn't just wasn't in the right field.

He had to admit she didn't annoy him when she was helping transcribe and organize his notes. The fact was, she was such an enormous help he wondered how the devil he would get anything done when she was gone.

He considered playing on her gratitude and wheedling another couple of weeks out of her.

Then he'd be distracted by something as ridiculous as the way the light hit her hair as she sat at the keyboard. Or the way her eyes took on a glint when she looked over at him with a question or comment.

Then he'd start thinking about her. Who she was, where

she was from. Why the hell she was sitting in his kitchen in the first place. She spoke French like a native, cooked like a gift from God. And over it all was a glossy sheen of class.

He hated asking people questions about themselves. Because they invariably answered them, at length. But he had a lot of questions about Camilla.

He began to calculate how he could get some information without seeming to ask the questions.

She was smart, too, he thought as she painstakingly filed and labeled on-site photographs while he pretended to study more notes. Not just educated, but there was plenty of that. If he had to guess, he'd say private schools all the way—and with that whiff of France in her voice, he'd put money on some kind of Swiss finishing school.

In any case, wherever she'd been educated, she was smart enough to let the whole matter of that little sexual snap drop.

She'd simply nodded when he'd said they were even, and had made her fancy breakfast crêpes.

He admired that, the way she'd accepted the tit for tat and had gone back to business as usual.

There was money—or there had been money. Pricey Swiss watch, silk robe. And it had been silk. He could still feel the way it had floated and slithered over his bare skin when she'd wrapped herself around him.

Damn it.

Still, she was no stranger to work. She actually seemed to *like* cooking. It was almost beyond his comprehension. Plus she'd sit at the keyboard for hours without complaint. Her typing was neat and quick, her posture perfect. And her hands as elegant as a queen's.

Breeding, he thought. The woman had breeding. The kind that gave you spine as well as a sense of fair play.

And she had the most incredible mouth.

So how did it all add up?

He caught himself scratching at the beard again, and was struck with inspiration.

"Could use a shave."

He said it casually, waited for her to glance his way.

"I'm sorry?"

"A shave," he repeated. "I could use one."

Because she considered it a friendly overture, she smiled. "Can you manage it, or do you want help?"

He frowned a little, to show he was reluctant. "You ever shave a man?"

"No." She pursed her lips, angled her head. "But I've seen my father and my brothers shave. How hard can it be?"

"Brothers?"

"Yes, two." Thoughtful, she stepped to him, bending a bit to study the terrain of his face. A lot of angles, she mused. Dips and planes. There certainly wasn't anything smooth or simple about it, but that only made it challenging. "I don't see why I couldn't do it."

"It's my flesh and blood on the line, sister." Still he lifted a hand, rubbed irritably. "Let's do it."

She took the job seriously. After some debate, she decided the best spot for the event was the front porch. They'd get a little fresh air, and she'd be able to maneuver a full three hundred and sixty degrees around his chair as she couldn't in the tiny upstairs bathroom.

She dragged out a small table, and set up her tools. The

wide, shallow bowl filled with hot water. The can of shaving cream, the towels, the razor.

Part of her wished it was a straight rather than a safety razor. It would've been fun to strop it sharp.

When he sat, she tied a towel around his neck. "I could trim your hair while I'm at it."

"Leave the hair alone."

She couldn't blame him. It was a marvelous head of hair, wonderfully streaky and tumbled. In any case her one attempt at cutting hair—her own—had proved she had no hidden talent for it.

"All right, just relax." She covered his face with a warm, damp towel. "I've seen this in movies. I believe it softens the beard."

When he gave a muffled grunt and relaxed, she looked out at the woods. They were so green, so thick, dappled with light and shadows. She could hear birdsong, and caught the quick flash of a cardinal—a red bullet into a green target.

No one was huddled in those shadows waiting for her to make some move that would earn them a fee for a new photograph. There were no stoic guards standing by to protect her.

The peace of it was like a balm.

"It's beautiful out today." Absently she laid a hand on his shoulder. She wanted to share this lovely feeling of freedom with someone. "All blue and green with summer. Hot, but not oppressive. In Virginia, we'd be drenched in humidity by now."

Aha! He knew he'd tagged a touch of the South in her voice. "What's in Virginia?"

"Oh, my family." Some of them, she thought. "Our farm."

As she took the towel away, his eyes—sharp and full of doubt—met hers. "You're telling me you're a farmer's daughter? Give me a break."

"We have a farm." Vaguely irritated, she picked up the shaving cream. Two farms, she thought. One in each of her countries. "My father grows soy beans, corn and so on. And raises both cattle and horses."

"You never hoed a row with those hands, kid."

She lifted a brow as she smoothed on the shaving cream. "There's been a marvelous new invention called a tractor. And yes, I can drive one," she added with some asperity.

"Hard to picture you out on the back forty."

"I don't spend much time with the crops, but I know a turnip from a potato." Brows knitted, she lifted his chin and took the first careful swipe with the razor. "My parents expected their children to be productive and useful, to make a contribution to the world. My sister works with underprivileged children."

"You said you had brothers."

"One sister, two brothers. We are four." She rinsed the razor in the bowl, meticulously scraped off more cream and stubble.

"What do you do, back on the farm?"

"A great many things," she muttered, calculating the angle from jaw to throat.

"Is that what you're running away from? Hey!"

As the nick welled blood, she dabbed at it. "It's just a scratch—which I wouldn't have made if you'd just stop talking. You say nothing for hours at a time, and now you don't shut up."

Amused, and intrigued that he'd apparently hit a nerve—he shrugged his shoulder. "Maybe I'm nervous.

I've never had a woman come at me with a sharp implement.''

"That is surprising, considering your personality.''

"Tagging you as Rebecca of Sunnybrook Farm's surprising, considering yours. If you grew up in Virginia, where's the French pastry part come from?''

Her brows lifted above eyes lit with humor. "French pastry, is it? My mother,'' she said, ignoring the little twist of guilt that came from not being completely honest. Because of it, she gave him more truth—if not specifics. "We spend part of our time in Europe—and have a small farm there as well. Do this.'' She drew her top lip over her teeth.

He couldn't stop the grin. "Show me how to do that again?''

"Now he's full of jokes.'' But she laughed, then stepped between his legs, bent down and slowly shaved the area between his nose and mouth.

He wanted to touch her, to run his hand over some part of her. Any part of her. He wanted, he realized, to kiss her again. Whoever the hell she was.

Her thumb brushed his mouth, held his lip in place, then slid away. But her gaze lingered there before it tracked up to his.

And she saw desire, the dangerous burn of it in his eyes. Felt it stab inside her like the fired edge of a blade.

"Why is this, do you think?'' she murmured.

He didn't pretend to misunderstand. He didn't believe in pretense. "I haven't got a clue—other than you being a tasty treat for the eyes.''

She nearly smiled at that, and turned to rinse the razor again. "Even attraction should have more. I'm not sure we even like each other very much.''

"I don't have anything against you, particularly."

"Why, Delaney, you're so smooth." She laughed because it eased some of the tension inside her. "A woman hasn't a prayer against such poetry, such charm."

"You want poetry, read a book."

"I think I do like you." She considered as she came back to finish the shave. "On some odd level, I enjoy your irascibility."

"Old men are irascible. I'm young yet, so I'm just rude."

"Precisely. But you also have an interesting mind, and I find it attractive. I'm intrigued by your work." She turned his face to the side, eased in close again. "And your passion for it. I came looking for passion—not the sexual sort, but for some emotional—some intellectual passion. How strange that I should find it here, and in old bones and broken pots."

"My field takes more than passion and intellect."

"Yes. Hard work, sacrifice, sweat, perhaps some blood." She angled her head. "If you think I'm a stranger to such things, you're wrong."

"You're not a slacker."

She smiled again. "There now, you've flattered me. My heart pounds."

"And you've got a smart mouth, sister. Maybe, on some odd level, I enjoy your sarcasm."

"That's handy. Why don't you ever use my name?" She stepped back to pick up a fresh towel and wipe the smears of shaving cream left on his face. "It is my name," she said quietly. "Camilla. My mother enjoys flowers, and there were camellias on my father's farm when he took her there for the first time."

"So, you only lied about the last name."

"Yes." Testingly she ran her fingers over his cheeks. "I think I did a fine job, and you have a nice, if complicated face. Better, by far, without the scraggly beard."

She walked to the table, wiped her hands. "I only want a few weeks for myself," she murmured. "A few weeks to *be* myself without restrictions, responsibilities, demands, expectations. Haven't you ever just needed to breathe?"

"Yeah." And something in her tone, something in her eyes—both haunted—told him that, at least, was perfect truth. "Well, there's plenty of air around here." He touched his face, rubbed a hand over his freshly shaved chin. "Your car'll be ready in a couple days. Probably. You can take off then, or you can stay a week or two, and we'll keep things the way they are."

Tears stung her eyes, though she had no idea why. "Maybe a few days longer. Thank you. I'd like to know more about your project. I'd like to know more about you."

"Let's just keep things the way they are. Until they change. Nice shave…Camilla."

She smiled to herself as the screen door slammed behind him.

To demonstrate her gratitude, Camilla did her best not to annoy him. For an entire day and a half. She had the cabin scrubbed to a gleam, his photographs and sketches labeled and filed. The neatly typed pages from his notes and dictation now comprised two thick stacks.

It was time, she decided, for a change in routine.

"You need fresh supplies," she told him.

"I just bought supplies."

"Days ago, and the key word is fresh. You're out of

fruit, low on vegetables. And I want lemons. I'll make lemonade. You drink entirely too much coffee.''

''Without coffee: coma.''

''And you're nearly out of that as well, so unless you'd like to be comatose, we have to go into town for supplies.''

For the first time, he spared her a look, taking off his reading glasses to frown at her. ''We?''

''Yes. I can check on the status of my car as your Carl only makes mumbling noises over the phone when I call to ask about it.'' She was already checking the contents of her purse, taking out her sunglasses. ''So. We'll go to town.''

''I want to finish this section.''

''We can finish when we get back. I'm happy to drive if your shoulder's troubling you too much.''

In point of fact, his shoulder barely troubled him at all now. He'd put the hours he spent restless and awake in his room at night to good use by carefully exercising it. His ribs were still miserable, but he was about ready to ditch the sling.

''Sure, I'll just let you behind the wheel of my truck since you've proven what a good driver you are.''

''I'm a perfectly good driver. If the deer hadn't—''

''Yeah, yeah, well you can forget driving my truck, kid.'' Since he knew her well enough now to be sure she'd nag and push for the next hour, he decided to save time and aggravation and just go. ''I'll drive—but you do the grocery thing.''

When he simply stood, frowning, she angled her head. ''If you're trying to remember where you put your keys, they're in the ignition of your precious truck, where you left them.''

"I knew that," he muttered and started out. "Are we going or not?"

As pleased as if she'd been offered a night on the town, she hurried after him. "Is there a department store? I could use some—"

"Hold it." He stopped short at the back door so that she bumped solidly into him. "No, there's not, and don't get the idea we're going on some spree. You want lemons, we'll get some damn lemons, but you're not dragging me off on some girl safari looking for shoes and earrings and God knows."

She had a small—and perfectly harmless—weakness for earrings. Her mouth moved into something perilously close to a pout. "I merely want some eye cream."

He tugged her sunglasses down her nose, gave her eyes a hard look. "They're fine."

She rolled them at his back as he continued toward the truck, but she decided not to push the issue. Until they were in town. Now, it was better to distract him.

"I wonder," she began as she hitched herself into the cab of the truck, "if you could tell me how radio-carbon dating works."

"You want a workshop—"

"Yes, yes, take a course. But just a thumbnail explanation. I do better with the transcribing if I have a picture in my head."

His sigh was long-suffering as the truck bumped along the lane toward the main road. "Carbon's in the atmosphere. You got trillions of atoms of carbon to every one atom of radioactive Carbon 14. Plants absorb Carbon 14, animals absorb it by—"

"Eating the plants," she finished, pleased with herself.

He shot her a look. "And other animals. Absorbed, it

starts to disintegrate. It gets replenished from the atmosphere or from food. Until whatever's absorbed, it dies. Anyway, in a plant or an animal it gives off about fifteen disintegration rays every minute, and they can be detected by a Geiger counter. The rest is just math. The dead source loses radioactivity at a rate... Why am I talking to myself?''

"What?" She dragged her attention back. "I'm sorry. It's just so beautiful. I missed so much in the storm. It's so green and gorgeous. A bit like Ireland, really, with all those hills."

She caught the glint that could only be sun flashing off water. "And a lake, all the lovely trees. It's all so still and quiet."

"That's why most people live in this part of Vermont. We don't like crowds and noise. You want those, you don't come to the NEK, you go west to Lake Champlain."

"The NEK?"

"Northeast Kingdom."

The name made her smile. So, she thought, she'd slipped away from a principality for a time, and landed in a kingdom. "Have you always lived here?"

"Off and on."

She gave a little cry of delight as they approached a covered bridge. "Oh, it's charming!"

"It gets you over the stream," Del said, but her pleasure was infectious. Sometimes he forgot to look around, to take satisfaction in the pretty piece of the world where he often made his home.

They rattled over the bridge toward the white church spires that rose over the trees. She thought it was like a book, some brilliant and deeply American story. The green roll of hills, the white churches and tidy houses with their tidy lawns. And the town itself was laid out as neatly as a game board with straight streets, a small park and weathered brick buildings tucked in with faded clapboard.

She wanted to stroll those streets, wander the shops, watch the people as they went about their day. Perhaps have lunch in one of the little restaurants. Or better, she thought, stroll about with an ice-cream cone.

Del pulled into a parking lot. "Grocery store," he informed her as he dragged out his wallet. He pushed several bills into her hand. "Get what you need. I'll go check on your car. You've got thirty minutes."

"Oh, but couldn't we—"

"And get some cookies or something," he added along with a meaningful shove.

Eyes narrowed behind her shaded glasses, she climbed down, then stood with her hands on her hips as he pulled out of the lot again. The man was a complete blockhead. Ordering her, pushing her, cutting her off before she completed a sentence. She'd never been treated so rudely, so carelessly in her life.

It was beyond her comprehension why she enjoyed it.

Regardless, she'd be damned if she wouldn't see something of the town before he hauled her back to the cave for another week. Squaring her shoulders, she headed off to explore.

The pristine and practical New England village didn't run to pawnshops, but she did find a lovely jewelry store with a fine selection of estate pieces. And the earrings *were* tempting. Still, she controlled herself and earmarked the shop as a possibility for selling her watch should it become necessary.

She wandered into a drugstore. Though the choices of eye cream didn't include her usual brand, she settled for what she could get. She also picked up some very nice scented candles, a few bags of potpourri.

An antique store proved a treasure trove. It pained her to have to pass up the crystal-and-silver inkwell. It would've made a lovely gift for her uncle Alex—but was beyond her current budget unless she risked the credit card.

Still, she found some interesting old bottles for a reasonable price, and snapped them up. They'd be perfect for wildflowers and twigs, and would perk up the cabin considerably.

The clerk was a woman about Camilla's age, with dark blond hair worn in a sleek ponytail and sharp blue eyes that had noted her customer lingering over the inkwell. She smiled as she wrapped the bottles in protective paper.

"That inkwell's nineteenth century. It's a nice piece for a collector—at a good price."

"Yes, it's lovely. You have a very nice shop."

"We take a lot of pride in it. Visiting the area?"

"Yes."

"If you're staying at one of the registered B&B's, we offer a ten percent discount on purchases over a hundred dollars."

"Oh, well. No…no, I'm not." She glanced back to the desk where the inkwell was displayed. Her uncle's birthday was only three months away. "I wonder, would you take a small deposit to hold it for me?"

The clerk considered, giving Camilla a careful measure. "You could put twenty down. I'll hold it for you for two weeks."

"Thanks." Camilla took the bill from her dwindling supply.

"No problem." The clerk began to write out a receipt for the deposit. "Your name?"

"My...Breen."

"I'll put a hold tag on it for you, Miss Breen. You can come in anytime within the next two weeks with the balance."

Camilla fingered her watch, and a glance at it widened her eyes. "I'm late. Delaney's going to be furious."

"Delaney? Caine?"

"Yes. I was supposed to meet him five minutes ago." Camilla gathered her bags and rushed toward the door.

"Miss! Wait!" The clerk bolted after her. "Your receipt."

"Oh, sorry. He's just so easily annoyed."

"Yes, I know." The woman's eyes danced with a combination of laughter and curiosity. "We went out once or twice."

"Oh. I'm not sure if I should congratulate you or offer my sympathies." So she offered a smile. "I'm working for him, temporarily."

"In the cabin? Then I'll offer you *my* sympathies. Tell him Sarah Lattimer sends her best."

"I will. I have to run or I'll be hiking back to the cabin."

You got that right, Sarah mused as she watched Camilla dash away. Del wasn't a man known for his patience. Still, she sighed a little, remembering how she'd nearly convinced herself she could change him—tame him—when she'd been twenty.

She shook her head at the idea as she walked back to put the hold tag on the inkwell. She wished the pretty redhead plenty of luck. Funny, she thought now, the woman had looked familiar somehow. Like a movie star or celebrity or something.

Sarah shrugged. It would nag at her until she figured out just who Del's new assistant resembled. But she'd get it eventually.

Juggling bags, Camilla made it to the parking lot at a full run. She grimaced when she spotted the truck, then just wrenched open the door and shoved her purchases inside. "Have to pick up a few things," she said gaily. "I'll just be another minute."

Before he could open his mouth—to snarl, she was sure—she was rushing inside the market.

Snagging a cart, she set off toward produce at a smart pace. But the process of selecting fresh fruits and vegetables simply could not be rushed. She bagged lemons, delicately squeezed tomatoes, pursed her lips over the endive.

The supermarket was such a novelty for her, she lingered longer than she intended over fresh seafood, over the baked items. She liked the colors, the scents, the textures. The big bold signs announcing specials, and truly horrible canned music numbers playing over the loud speaker, interrupted only by voices calling for price checks and cleanups.

She shivered in frozen foods, deciding the chances of talking Del into an ice-cream cone now were nil. So she bought the makings for them. Delighted with the variety of choices, she loaded the cart, then wheeled it to checkout.

If she were a housewife, she thought, she would do this every week. It probably wouldn't be nearly as much fun. Just another obligation, she thought, and that was a shame.

She came back to reality with a thud when she moved up in line and saw her own face staring out from the cover of a tabloid.

Princess Camilla's Heartbreak

Why, they had her in grieving seclusion, Camilla saw with growing irritation. Over an aborted romance with a French actor. One she'd never even met! *Imbéciles! Menteurs!* What right did they have to tell lies about her personal life? Wasn't it enough to report every move she made, to use their telephoto lenses to snap pictures of her night and day?

She started to reach for the paper, for the sheer pleasure of ripping it to pieces.

"What the hell are you *doing* in here?" Del demanded.

She jumped like a thief, and instinctively whirled around to block the paper with her body. Fury, which she'd considered a healthy reaction, became a sick trembling in her stomach.

If she was unmasked here, now, it would all be over. People would crowd around her, gawking. The media would be on her scent like hounds on a rabbit.

"I'm...waiting in line to pay."

"What is all this stuff?"

"Food." She worked up a smile as a cold sweat slid down her back.

"For what army?"

She glanced at the cart, winced. "I may have gotten a little carried away. I can put some of it back. Why don't you go outside and—"

"Just get through the damn line." He stepped forward, and certain he'd see the tabloid, she dug in her heels.

"Don't push me again."

"I'm not pushing you, I'm pushing the stupid cart."

When he moved past the newspaper rack without a glance, Camilla nearly went limp.

"Hey, Del, didn't expect to see you back in here so soon." The cashier began ringing up the things Del began pulling out of the cart and dumping on the conveyer belt.

"Neither did I."

The woman, a plump brunette whose name tag identified her as Joyce, winked at Camilla. "Don't let him scare you, honey. Bark's worse than his bite."

"Not so far," Camilla muttered, but was relieved that he was at the wrong angle now to see the grainy photograph of her. Still, she put her sunglasses back on before turning her face toward the cashier. "But he doesn't scare me."

"Glad to hear it. This one's always needed a woman with plenty of spine and sass to stand up to him. Nice to see you finally found one, Del."

"She just works for me."

"Uh-huh." Joyce winked at Camilla again. "You hear from your mom lately?"

"Couple weeks back. She's fine."

"You tell her I said hi—and that I'm keeping my eye on her boy." She rang up the total and had Camilla wincing again.

"I think I might need a little more money."

"Damn expensive lemons." Resigned, Del took what he'd given her, added more bills.

She helped him load the bags into the truck, then sat with her hands folded in her lap. She'd overreacted to the tabloid, she told herself. Still her initial spurt of anger had been liberating. Regardless, she'd recovered well, and a

342 _Cordina's Crown Jewel_

lot more quickly than she might have done just a week or two before.

That meant she was stronger, steadier. Didn't that serve to prove she was doing the right thing?

Now it was time to put that issue away again, and deal with the moment.

"I'm sorry I took so long, but I don't think it's unreasonable for me to want to see something of the town."

"Your car should be ready tomorrow. Maybe the next day seeing as Carl's claiming to be backed-up and overworked. Next time you want to play tourist, do it on your own time."

"Be sure I will. Sarah Lattimer at the antique store said to give you her best. I wonder that anyone so well-spoken and courteous could have ever gone out with you."

"She was young and stupid at the time."

"How fortunate for her that she matured and wised-up."

"You got that right." He caught her soft chuckle. "What's so funny?"

"It's hard to insult you when you agree with me." It was hard to brood about a silly photograph in a trashy newspaper when he was so much more interesting. "I like you."

"That makes you young and stupid, doesn't it?"

She grinned, then amused at both of them leaned over and kissed his cheek. "Apparently."

Chapter 6

I'm having the most wonderful time. It wasn't the plan to stay in one place so long, or to do one thing for any length of time. But it's such a beautiful place, and such an exciting thing to do.

Archaeology is truly fascinating. So much more interesting and layered to me than the history I enjoyed and was taught in school, or the sociology classes I took. More fascinating, I find, than anything I've studied or explored.

Who, where and why? How people lived, married, raised their children, treated their elderly. What they ate, how they cooked it. Their ceremonies and rituals. Oh, so much more. And all of it, society after society, tribe by tribe speaks, doesn't it, to our own?

He knows so much, and so much of what he knows is almost casual to him, in the way a true scholar can be. Not that knowledge itself is casual to him. He seeks it, every day. He wants to know.

I find that passion admirable, enviable. And I find it alluring.

I'm attracted to his mind, to all those complex angles. Working with—all right, for—him is hard and demanding, sometimes physically exhausting. Despite his injuries, the man has astounding stamina. It's impressive the way he can lose himself, hours at a go, in his work.

It's also an absolute thrill for me to do so as well. I've studied bone fragments that are centuries old. Sealed, of course, in plastic.

I wonder how they might feel in my hands. If anyone had told me I'd actually want to handle human bones, even two weeks ago, I'd have thought them mad.

How I wish I could go to the dig—or wet archeological site—and actually see the work being done there. Though Delaney paints a very clear picture when he speaks of it, it's not the same as seeing it for myself.

This is something I want to see, and do, for myself. I intend to look into classes, and what Delaney somewhat disdainfully refers to as knap-ins (a kind of camping session on sites for amateurs and students) when I'm home again.

I believe I've found an avocation that could become a vocation.

On a personal level, he's not as annoyed by me as he pretends to me. At least not half the time. It's odd and very educational to have someone treat me as he would anyone else—without that filter of manners and respect demanded by rank. Not that I appreciate rudeness, of course, but once you get to know the man, you can see beneath the rough exterior.

He's a genius. And though courtesy is never out of place, the brilliant among us are often less polished.

I find him so attractive. In my life I've never been so physically drawn to a man. It's exciting on one level, terribly frustrating on another. I was raised in a loving family, one which taught me that sex is not a game, but a joy—and a responsibility—to be shared with someone you care for. Someone you respect, and who affords you those same emotions. My position in the world adds another, complex and cautious layer, to that basic belief. I cannot risk taking a lover casually.

But I want him for a lover. I want to know what it's like to have that fire inside him burn through me. I want to know if mine can match it.

The tabloid in the supermarket reminded me of what I'd nearly let myself forget. What it's like to be watched, constantly. Pursued for an image on newsprint. Speculated about. The fatigue of that, the unease, the discomfort. Gauging how I feel now against how I felt the night I left Washington, I understand I was very close to breaking down in some way. I can look back and remember that hunted feeling, feel the nerves that had begun to dance, always, so very close to the surface.

Much of that is my own fault, I see now, for not giving myself more personal time to—well, decompress, I suppose—since Grandpère died, and everything else.

I'm doing so now, and none too soon.

My time here is, well, out of time, I suppose. I feel it's been well spent. I feel—perhaps renewed is an exaggeration. Refreshed then, and more energized than I have felt in so many months.

Before I leave and take up my duties again, I'll learn all I can about the science of archeology. Enough that I might, in some way, pursue it myself. I'll learn all I can about Camilla MacGee—separate from Camilla de Cordina.

And I might consider seducing the temperamental Dr. Delaney Caine.

The cabin smelled like a woodland meadow. Since it was a nice change from the musty gym sock aroma he'd gotten used to before Camilla, it was tough to complain.

And he wasn't running out of socks anymore. Or having to scavenge in the kitchen for a can of something for his dinner. His papers—after a few rounds of shouts and threats—were always exactly as he left them. A good third of his notes were typed, and the articles needed for the trade journals and the site's Web page were nearly finished. And they were good.

The coffee was always fresh, and so were the towels. And so, he thought with some admiration, was Camilla.

Not just the way she looked, or the pithy remarks that she aimed regularly in his direction, but her brain. He hadn't considered just how much a fresh mind could add to his outlook and his angle on the project.

He liked the way she sang in the mornings when she cooked breakfast. And how rosy she looked when she came out of the woods after one of her breaks. Breaks, he recalled, they'd negotiated with some bitterness.

He couldn't say he objected to the candles and bowls of smelly stuff she'd set around the place. He didn't really mind the fancy soaps she'd put out in the bathroom, or coming across her little tubes and pots of creams in his medicine cabinet.

He'd only opened them for a sniff out of curiosity.

He even liked the way she curled up on the sofa in the

evening with a glass of wine and grilled him about his work until he gave in and talked about it.

Alone in the kitchen, he did slow curls with a two-pound can of baked beans with his weak arm. It was coming back, he decided. And he was burning that damn sling. His muscles tended to throb at odd times, but he could live with that. Mostly it just felt so good to *move* his arm again. The ribs would take longer—the doctors had warned him about that. And the collarbone would probably trouble him for some time yet.

But he didn't feel so frustratingly helpless now.

Maybe he'd see if Camilla could give him a neck and shoulder massage, just to loosen things up. She had small hands, but they were capable. Besides, it was a good way to get them back on him again. She'd taken his orders to back off just a little more seriously than he discovered he'd wanted.

He paused, set down the can with a little thump. God, he was getting used to her, he realized with some horror. Getting used to having her around, and worse to *wanting* her around.

And that, he was sure, was the beginning of the end.

A man started wanting a woman around, then she expected him to be around. No more coming and going as you pleased, no more heading off to some dig for months on end without a concern about what you left back home.

Scowling, he looked around the kitchen again. Bottles of wildflowers, a bowl of fresh fruit, scrubbed counters and cookies in a glass jar.

The woman had snuck around and made the cabin a home instead of a place. You left a place whenever the hell you wanted. But home—when you left home it was always with a wrench.

When you left a woman, it was with a careless kiss and a wave. When you left *the* woman, he suspected it would rip you to pieces.

She came out of the woods as he thought of her, her face glowing, white wildflowers in her hand. How the devil had she come so close to becoming *the* woman? he asked himself with a spurt of panic.

They hadn't known each other for long. Had they? He ran a hand through his hair as he realized he'd lost track of time. What the hell day was it? How long had she been there? What in God's name was he going to do with himself when she left?

She came in, full of smiles. Well, he could fix that.

"You're late," he snapped at her.

Calmly she glanced at her watch. "No, I'm not. I am, in fact, two minutes early. I had a lovely walk, and fed the ducks who live on the pond." She moved over to the bottle, working her new flowers in with the old. "But it's clouding up. I think it's going to rain."

"I want to finish the section on brain tissue. I can't do if you're out feeding a bunch of ducks."

"Then we'll get started as soon as I pour us some lemonade."

"Don't placate me, sister."

"That would be beyond even my masterly capabilities. What's wrong, Del? Are you hurting?" She turned, the pitcher in her hand, and nearly bobbled it when she focused on him. "Your arm. You've taken off the sling." Quickly she set the pitcher aside and went to him, to run a hand along his arm.

He said nothing because, God help him, he wanted her to touch him.

"I suppose I expected it to be thin and wan. It's not."

Her lips pursed as she tested the muscle. "A bit paler than the rest of you, and I imagine it feels odd and weak."

"It's all right. It just needs—ow!" The jolt made his eyes water when she pressed down firmly on his shoulder. "Hey, watch it, Miss de Sade."

"I'm sorry. Still tender?" More gently, she kneaded it. "You're all knotted up."

"So would you be if you'd had one arm strapped against you for the best part of two weeks."

"You're right, of course. Maybe some linament," she considered. "My mother would rub some on my father when he overdid. And I've helped treat some of the horses that way. I saw some witch hazel upstairs. After dinner, I can put some on your shoulder. Then you'll get a good night's sleep."

He had a feeling having her rub him—anywhere— wasn't going to insure quiet dreams. But he figured it was a good trade-off.

"Laboratory tests proved that the substance found inside the recovered skull was, indeed, human brain tissue. In total, during the three six-month field studies, preserved brain tissue was found in ninety-five of the recovered skulls. Twenty-eight contained complete brains, albeit shrunken to approximately a third of their normal size. The find is completely unique, with significant scientific impact and potential. This will give scientists a never-before possible opportunity to study brain matter which is more than seven thousand years old, with its hemispheres and convolutions intact. The DNA, the basic human building block, can be cloned from tissue older than any previously available."

"Cloned." Camilla's fingers stopped. "You want to clone one of the tribe."

"We can get into a debate on cloning later. But no, the purpose would be to study—disease, life expectancy, physical and intellectual potential. You can go back to your science fiction novel after we're done."

"They've cloned sheep," Camilla muttered.

He gave her a mild look behind the lenses of his reading glasses. "That's not my field. DNA research isn't my area. I'm just outlining the potential and import of the find. We have intact human brains, seven millenniums old. People thought with them, reacted with them. Developed language and motor skills. They used those brains to build their village, to hunt their food and prepare it. They used these minds to interact, to raise their children, to find a mate and for survival."

"What about their hearts?"

"What about them?"

"Didn't their hearts tell them how to tend their children—how to make those children in the first place?"

"One doesn't happen without the other, does it?" He took off the dark-framed glasses and tossed them aside. "These people cared for their young and had interpersonal relationships. But procreation is also an instinct—one of the most basic. Without young, there would be no one to care for the old, no replacement for the dead. There'd be no tribe. Man mates for the same reason he eats. He has to."

"That certainly takes the romance out of it."

"Romance is an invention, a tool, like..." He picked up the scarred head of an old, crudely fashioned hammer. "Like this."

"Romance is a human need, like companionship, like music."

"Those are luxuries. To survive we need food, water, shelter. And to insure continued survival, we need to procreate. Man—being man—came up with tools and means to make meeting those needs easier. And often more pleasant. And being man, he devised ways to make a profit from those needs, to compete for them, to steal for them. Even to kill for them."

She enjoyed him like this—enjoyed the casually lecturing mode when he discussed ideas with her as he might with a bright student. Or perhaps an associate. "That doesn't say much about man," she commented.

"On the contrary." He touched the jaw of a old, bleached-out skull. "It says man himself is a complex, ingenious and constantly evolving invention. He builds and destroys with nearly the same skill and enthusiasm. And is constantly remaking himself."

"So what have you made yourself?" she asked him.

He turned the hammer head over in his hand, then set it down again. "Hungry. When are we going to eat?"

She wasn't giving up on the discussion, but she didn't mind taking the time to think about it while she finished fixing dinner. She slid pasta into boiling water, tossed the salad. Sprinkled herbs on oil for the thick slices of bread.

She poured wine. Lighted candles.

And looking at the cozy kitchen, hearing the rain patter gently on the roof, she realized she had—unwittingly—employed a tool tonight. The scene she'd created was, unquestionably, a romantic one. She'd simply intended to make it attractive and comfortable. Instinct must have kicked in, she decided. Maybe for a certain type of person, particularly when that person was sexually attracted to another—creating romance was instinctive.

She found she liked knowing that about herself. Romance—to her thinking—was warm and generous. It took the other party's comfort and pleasure into account.

It was not, she decided as she drained the pasta, a damn hammer.

"A hammer," she declared to Del when he stepped in, "implies force or a threat."

"What?"

"A hammer," she said again, testily now. "Romance is not a hammer."

"Okay." He reached for a piece of bread and had his hand slapped aside for his trouble.

"Sit down first. Prove you've evolved into a civilized human being. And don't say okay just because you're bored with the subject and want to stuff your face."

"Getting pretty strict around here," he muttered.

"I'm saying that your tribe demonstrated human emotions. Compassion, love—hate certainly, as you did find remains that showed evidence of violent injury or death. Emotions make us human, don't they?" she demanded as she served the salad. "If it was only instinct that drove us, we wouldn't have art, music, even science. We wouldn't have progressed far enough that we'd build a village near a pond, create rituals to share and love enough that we'd bury our child with her toys."

"Okay. I mean okay," he insisted when she narrowed her eyes. He wanted the food in his belly and not dumped on his head. "It's a good point—and you could do an interesting paper on it, I imagine."

She blinked at him. "Really?"

"The field isn't cut-and-dried. It isn't only about facts

and artifacts. There has to be room for speculations, for theory. For wonder. Edge over into anthropology and you're dealing with cultures. Out of cultures you get traditions. Traditions stem from necessity, superstition or some facet of emotion.''

"Take our tribe." Mollified, she offered him the basket of bread. "How do you know a man didn't woo a woman by bringing her wildflowers, or a cup of fresh elderberries?''

"I don't. But I don't know that he did, either. No evidence either way.''

"But don't you think there was a ritual of some sort? Isn't there always? Even with animals there's a mating dance, *oui?* So surely there had to be some courtship procedure.''

"Sure." He dipped the bread, grinned at her. "Sometimes it just meant picking up a really big rock and beating some other sap over the head with it. Loser gets the concussion. Winner gets the girl.''

"Only because she either had no choice, or more likely, she understood that the man strong enough, passionate enough to smash his rival over the head to win her would protect her and the children they made together from harm.''

"Exactly." Pleased with the tidy logic of her mind, he wagged a chunk of bread at her. "Sexual urge to procreation. Procreation to survival.''

"In its own very primitive way, that's romantic. However, the remains you've studied to date don't show a high enough percentage of violent injury to support the theory that head bashing was this tribe's usual courtship ritual.''

"That's good." Admiring the way she'd spun his example back to prove her point, he gestured with his fork. "And you're right."

"Del, do you think, eventually, there might be a way for me to visit the site?"

He frowned, thoughtfully now, as she served the pasta. "Why?"

"I'd like to see it firsthand."

"Well, you've got six months."

"What do you mean?"

"In six months if the articles and reports I'm putting together don't beat the right drum and shake out a couple million in grants, the site closes."

"Closes? You mean you'd be finished with the dig?"

"Finished?" He scooped up pasta. "Not by a long shot. But the state can't—or won't—allocate more funds. Bureaucrats," he muttered. "Not enough media attention after three seasons to keep them smiling for the cameras and handing over grants. The university's tapped out. There's enough private money for another six months. After that, we're shut down and that's it."

The idea of the site closing was so appalling she couldn't get her mind around it. "That can't be it if you're not done."

"Money talks, sister." And he'd sunk all he could afford of his own into that dark peat.

"Then you'll get more. Anyone who reads your work will want to keep the project going. If not from the incredible archaeological significance of such amazingly rich findings, then for the completely unique scientific opportunities. I could—" She broke off. She was an expert fund-raiser. People paid, and dearly, to see Princess Camilla at a charity function.

Media attention? That was never a problem.

More, she had connections. Her thoughts went instantly to her godmother, the former Christine Hamilton, now the wife of a United States senator from Texas. Both were avid supporters of arts and science.

"You got an extra million or so weighing you down, just pass it my way." Del reached for the wine bottle, stretching his healing shoulder a little too far, a little too fast. And cursed.

She snapped back to the moment. "Be careful, you don't want to overtax yourself. I'm afraid I don't have a million on me." She smiled as she topped off his wineglass. "But I have ideas. I'm very good with ideas. I'll think of something."

"You do that."

She let it go, and he forgot about it.

When dinner was finished, he vanished. It was a talent of his to disappear when dishes were involved. Camilla was forced to admire it. She couldn't claim the washing up pleased her nearly so much as making the mess in the first place.

Cooking was a kind of art. Washing dishes a mindless chore she'd have been happy to pass along to someone else.

In the cabin, however, she was the someone else.

In any case, she knew he wouldn't come near the back of the house until they were done. It gave her the opportunity to call home.

She kept one eye and one ear on the doorway while the connection to Virginia went through. Her youngest brother, Dorian, answered, and though normally she'd have been delighted to chat, to catch up on family news, to just hear his voice, she was pressed for time.

"I really need to talk to Mama."

"You take off like a gypsy, and now you can't give me the time of day."

"When I get back, I'll bore your ears off with everything I've done. I miss you, Dorian." She laughed quietly. "I never thought I'd actually say that, but I do. I miss all of you."

"But you're having a great time. I can hear it in your voice."

"I am."

"So you're not pining away for the French guy."

She huffed out a breath. Dorian considered teasing a royal duty. "I take back that I miss you. Where's Mama?"

"I'll get her. But I'd better warn you, she's got her hands full keeping Dad from sending out a search-and-rescue. You're going to have to dance double-time to smooth things out with him."

"I know it. I'm sorry, but I'm not a child."

"That's what Mama said. And he said—at the top of his lungs—that you were *his* child. Keep that in mind. Hang on."

She knew he might tease, but Dorian was good as gold. He'd find a way to get their mother on the line without letting her father know.

Where would Mama be now? she wondered, and brought the image of the big, sprawling house in Virginia into her mind. In her sitting room perhaps. No, more likely out in the gardens, enjoying the evening.

Was it raining there, too?

Maybe she was entertaining. But no, Dorian would have said so.

As the silence on the line grew lengthy, Camilla began to fret.

Then she heard her mother's voice. "Camilla, I'm so glad you called. We were just talking about you."

"Is Daddy still very upset?"

"He's…adjusting. Slowly."

"I'm sorry, Mama. I just had to—"

"You don't have to explain to me. I remember what it's like. We just want to know you're safe, and happy."

"I'm both. I told you about the cabin, about Delaney. His work is so important, so interesting to me. Mama…" She reverted to French as English seemed too ordinary to explain her excitement in the project.

"You sound like a scientist," Gabriella laughed.

"I feel like a student. One who can't learn enough fast enough. Tonight I learned something distressing."

She explained about the project deadline as quickly as possible.

"That's difficult. Your professor must be very concerned."

"I'd like to help. I thought perhaps you could use your connections to find out what can be done, how much is needed. I was thinking—could you contact Aunt Christine? I'm good at raising money for causes, but she's even better. Finally I've found something that's really interesting—something that's personally important to me. I just need an idea of the right wallets to open."

"I can make some inquiries. Florida, is it? The Bardville Research Project, Dr. Delaney Caine. Give me a few days."

"Thanks. Thank you, Mama. You will be discreet? I'd just as soon he didn't know right now that Her Serene Highness Gabriella de Cordina had taken an interest in his work. It's so nice just being Camilla, I don't want to take a chance on anyone making the connection. Not just yet.''

"Don't worry. The family's leaving for Cordina in a few days, Camilla. I'd hoped you might be ready to go with us.''

"Another few weeks. Please. I'll contact you there and make arrangements to fly directly over when I...when I leave here.''

"Take care of my baby. We love her.''

"She loves you, too. I'll see you soon, Mama. I have so much to tell you.''

After she hung up, Camilla hummed as she set the kitchen to rights. In so short a time, she thought, she'd accomplished much of what she'd set out to do. She was content with herself—and that had been something missing the past several months. She'd done ordinary things— too many of which had slipped away from her since adulthood.

And she realized much of that had been her own doing.

When she'd been a child, her parents had made certain she had a normal life, or as normal as possible. They'd done everything they could to keep her and her siblings out of the spotlight. But there had been duties, a gradual escalation of them as she'd grown.

Then the media had focused on her. Cordina's crown jewel, they'd dubbed her. And normality had begun to erode around the edges until the fabric of it was frayed. It had been flattering at first, exciting, even amusing. Then mildly annoying. After nearly a decade of constant attention, of speculative and outright fabricated articles, of being seen as a commodity, never as a human being, it had become smothering.

But now she could breathe again. And she knew she

would go back to her life stronger, more capable and less vulnerable to the barrage.

She'd found a passion, and would now find a way to embrace it. This was the balance she'd seen and envied in her mother, in her aunts. Duty was never shirked, but each pursued a life full of interests and richness as a woman. So could she.

So *would* she.

One day she'd go on a dig and be part of a team that *discovered*. That sought knowledge and celebrated it. Let the media come, she thought as she prepared fresh coffee. The attention, while it lasted, would only generate interest in the field. And that meant funding.

It was unthinkable to allow their project to come to a premature end because of money. And it was their project now, she thought with a dreamy sigh. Hers and Delaney's. They shared it as they did the cabin, with each bringing their own stamp, their own mind, their own talents to the whole.

It was…marvelous.

Her excitement and passion might even be responsible for sparking the imagination of a generation of young women, bringing archaeology, the study of past peoples, cultures and customs into fashion.

She stopped, laughing at herself. Never satisfied with little steps, she thought. She always wanted more.

She filled two mugs and carried them into the living area. There he was, sitting on the horrible little sofa, his eyes intense behind his reading glasses, papers scattered over his lap and across the sprung cushions.

What leaped inside her was a wild and wonderful mixture of lust and longing, and, she discovered with a slow, warm sigh, love.

Why she was in love with him, she thought with surprise. Wasn't that…fascinating. Somewhere during this complicated and problematic interlude, she'd slid headlong into love with a bad-tempered, irritable, rough-mannered scientist who was more likely to snarl at her than smile.

He was rude, demanding, easily annoyed, impatient. And brilliant, passionate, reluctantly kind. It was a captivating mix that made him uniquely himself. She wouldn't change a single thing about him.

More, she thought, leaning against the wall to watch him. He had one of the most essential traits she wanted in a friend, and in a lover. He had honor.

They were alone here, yet he'd never tried to take advantage of that. In fact, he rarely touched her even in the most casual way. Though he was attracted—she knew she wasn't wrong about that—his personal code wouldn't allow him to exploit the situation.

Her lips twitched in a smile. That made him, under it all, a gentleman. How he would hate to be termed so.

So, she was in love with an ill-tempered gentleman who wouldn't allow himself to seduce his temporary assistant. That meant it was going to be up to her to seduce him.

The idea, only an interesting fantasy until now, became more intriguing, more exciting now her heart was engaged. Love, she thought, gave her a marvelous advantage.

You're going to have to deal with me now, she decided. And you, Dr. Delaney Caine, don't have a prayer.

She nearly went back to the kitchen to exchange the coffee for wine. But she reasoned the caffeine would be more…stimulating.

The plan of attack should be simple. And subtle.

She walked to him, held out the coffee. "Which area has you snagged?"

"Huh?"

"Which area," she repeated, gesturing toward the scattered papers, "has you snagged?"

"I just need to think it through. Get this damn paperwork done. I need to get back to the site." He rolled his shoulder, testing it. "Into the lab."

She felt the quick hitch in her throat. If he was starting to think about going back, she couldn't afford to be subtle for long.

Because when he went back, she intended to go with him. As his student, his associate. As his lover.

"The work you're doing here is just as important, just as essential. Though I'm sure it's not as rewarding for you."

"I'm not an administrator." He said it as though it were something foul, which made her smile.

"You'll soon be back in the field. You just need a little more time to finish here, and to heal."

He shifted, experimenting by stretching his torso. His ribs sang. An hour on the dig would have him crawling like a baby, he thought in disgust. But the lab...

"Let's get some of this down," he began, and rose too quickly. He had to grit his teeth as his body objected.

"Tell you what." Gently she took the coffee out of his hand. "I'll give you that rubdown first. It should help. You're always more uncomfortable first thing in the morning and after a long day. Let's loosen you up again. Then if you still want to work tonight, we'll work."

"I'm fine."

"You're not. And if you don't take care of yourself, you'll just delay your recovery and your return to the dig." Keeping her voice brisk, she started toward the stairs carrying both mugs. "Come on, we'll just consider it physical therapy."

He hurt, and that irritated him. He could take a pill— which would end up putting him to sleep and wasting work hours. He could put the damn sling back on, which would irritate him more. Or he could give the lubricant a try.

All he had to do was handle her rubbing her hands over him. And a man ought to have enough willpower to deal with that.

Besides, she had the coffee. He *had* to follow her upstairs.

"We can do it down here."

"Easier up here," she called back, smirking. "The sofa's a torture board, and too small in any case. No point in being uncomfortable. Just sit down on your bed. Take your shirt off."

Words, he thought, most men dreamed of hearing.

He wasn't going to think along those lines, he reminded himself. He was going to consider the entire experience a kind of therapeutic medicine.

Chapter 7

She made a quick detour into her own bedroom and dabbed on perfume. Undid another two buttons of her shirt. If the man thought of romance as a tool, she was going in fully equipped.

She gathered the witch hazel, some fresh towels and some of the scented candles.

It was conniving, she admitted, but surely a woman in love was allowed some ploys. Just as, she thought as she stepped into his bedroom and saw every available light blazing, a wary man was allowed to try for some defense.

She found his safety precautions wonderfully sweet. And easily foiled.

"Let's have a look." She circled around the bed where he sat, then instantly lost her calculation in her sympathy. "Oh, Del, you really did a job on yourself, didn't you?"

"It's better."

"I'm sure, but..." The shoulder which had been hidden

behind shirt or sling up till now was visibly swollen still.
The bruising was a sickly yellow and green pattern that
matched the clouds that ran along his ribs.

She wanted, more than anything else now, to simply
nurse him, to ease his hurts.

"I didn't think about the swelling," she murmured,
gently touching his shoulder.

"It's nearly gone." He moved his shoulder, as much
to test it as to dislodge her hand. He wasn't, he realized,
quite ready to have her touch him.

"Regardless. We should've been icing this down." Re-
calling what had happened before when she'd tried that
particularly kind of medical attention had her pulse dancing.

She wanted to nurse him, and soothe. But that wasn't
all she wanted, for either of them.

"Well, just relax, and we'll see what we can do about
making you more…comfortable."

She turned away, started to arrange and to light the
candles.

"What're you doing with those?"

The wariness in his voice had her lips curving.
"Haven't you ever heard of aromatherapy? Just get as
comfortable as you can, and we'll start on the shoulder
first. You never told me how you were hurt."

"I was stupid enough to let some idiot kid drive from
the lab. Some people just can't handle a wet road," he
added with a bland stare. "He flipped the Jeep."

"Flipped?" Horror for him replaced any need to defend
her own driving skills. "My God, you're lucky you
weren't killed."

"He walked away with a couple scratches," Del said

bitterly. "He's lucky I didn't snap his neck like a twig. This has put me on the DL over three weeks already."

She walked over to turn off lights. "DL?"

"No baseball in your world, sister? Disabled list." He'd just think about baseball—sports were good—or work, or world politics. Anything but the way she looked in candlelight.

"How're you going to see if you turn off the lights?"

"I can see perfectly well. You won't relax with lights shining in your eyes." She wished he had a radio, a stereo system. Something. But they'd just have to cope without it.

She climbed onto the bed behind him, knelt.

The give of the mattress had his stomach muscles fumbling into knots—and his body bracing as if for battle.

"Now don't be stoic," she said. "Tell me if I hurt you. I'd say you're healing remarkably well if it's only been three weeks. And that you've carved through an impressive amount of work while you've been here."

She rubbed the lubricant in her hands to warm it, then began to gently stroke it over the bruises. "I think we can all use a change of routine now and again, to step away from what we've become steeped in so that we can have a clearer vision of the whole picture."

"Maybe." It was true enough that since he'd come back to the cabin he'd been able to look at the project from angles he'd missed or ignored when he'd been in the middle of it. Such as the money problem.

"Don't tense up," she murmured. "Just close your eyes." Her fingers stroked, gently kneaded. "Let your mind drift. Did you play in the woods here as a boy?"

"Sure." Baseball, he was going to think about baseball.

How was he supposed to keep a box score in his head when she kept talking in that exotic, sexy voice.

"Swim in the pond? Fish?"

"My mother likes to fish."

"Really?"

Because the image of her, wearing one of her ugly hats, stout boots, ragged shirt and trousers with a pole in her hand made him smile, he closed his eyes.

Surely thinking of your mother was as good a way to control your glands as sports. Probably better.

"She never could get me or my father into it. Bores both of us crazy."

"I'm afraid I have the clichéd girl response to fishing," Camilla confessed. "Fish are slimy and they wriggle. I prefer them sautéed in a nice herbed butter. You don't have brothers, sisters?"

"No."

"Feel this knot here." She discovered one at the base of his neck. "You carry too much worry. That's why you're so irritable."

"I'm not irritable."

"No, you've a sunny disposition. Candy sweet."

"Ow."

"Sorry."

Oh, the man had a back, she thought with sheer delight. Broad and tanned with intriguing scars marring any hope of perfection. A warrior's back, she thought. Strong and male. She wanted, badly, to slide her lips down the length of it, nibble her way along the ridges. But it wasn't quite the time to abandon subtlety.

In any case, she wanted to help, wanted to ease his discomfort. Then jump him.

Distractions, she decided. As much for herself as for

him. "The book there, the mystery novel? I've read that author before, but not that book. Is it good?"

"Yeah, it's not bad."

"You have a small selection of books here, but it's quite eclectic."

Okay, they'd talk literature, he decided. Talking was fine. Books instead of baseball. Same thing. "Novels can relax the mind, or stimulate it."

At the moment, he couldn't decide which she was doing to him. Her hands were like heaven. Soft and strong, soothing and arousing. His blood warmed despite his efforts to control it. Yet at the same time the aches and stiffness eased, bit by bit.

The scent of candles, the scent of her, the sound of her voice—low and soft as she spoke of books—relaxed him until his mind, as she'd ordered, began to drift.

He felt the bed give as she changed position, then that smooth glide of her fingers, her palm, on the front of his shoulder. Her breast brushed against his back, pressed cozily against him as she worked.

He wondered, dreamily now, how it would feel in his hand. Firm, small, smooth. How it would taste in his mouth. Warm and sweet and essentially female.

Her free hand moved to his other shoulder, kneading until tension melted away.

The rain pattered quietly on the roof, and the candle-light flickered, warm and red against his closed lids.

"Lie down." It was a murmur in his ear.

"Hmm?"

Her lips curved. Maybe he was a little too relaxed, she thought. She didn't want him nodding off on her. The more she touched him, the more she looked at him, the more she wanted. Desire was a tightening ball in her belly.

"Lie down," she repeated, and resisted—barely—the urge to nip at his earlobe. She'd never in her life craved the taste of flesh so much. "So I can reach."

His eyes blinked open, his mind tried to focus. Lying down wasn't a good idea. He started to say so, but she was already nudging him back. And it felt so good, so damn good to ease down.

"Your ribs are still a mess, aren't they? We'll get to them. I suppose it's lucky you didn't break any."

"Yeah, it was my lucky day." He started to tell her she'd done enough—God, he was so stirred up he could barely keep two thoughts together—but when she leaned over him, stretching out for the bottle she'd set on the bedside table, those pretty breasts blocked his vision. And then even those thoughts scattered like ants.

"It would have been worse." She poured more lubricant into her palms, her eyes on his as she rubbed it warm. "But you're in such good shape. You have a strong, healthy body." She laid her palms on his bruised ribs.

She was counting on the healthy part.

"How old are you, Delaney?"

"Thirty. No, thirty-one." How the hell was he supposed to remember when she was smiling down at him?

"Young. Strong. Healthy. Mmm." She sighed, and it wasn't all calculation as she carefully straddled him. "That's why you've made such a quick recovery."

He didn't feel recovered. He felt weak and stupid. Tension, of a much different sort, was pumping through him. She had her weight on her knees and was, slowly, rhythmically moving in a way that made him imagine her naked, made him imagine himself inside her.

He curled his fingers into fists before he reached up and

just grabbed that tight, sexy bottom. "That's enough." His voice was a croak, a thin one. God help him.

She just kept her eyes on his. His had gone dark, gone hot. And his breath had quickened. "I haven't finished." She trailed fingers down to the waistband of his jeans, up again. And felt his stomach quiver. "There's a lot of you, isn't there? All hard and...tough."

He swore, but he couldn't work any venom into it. "Get off. You're killing me."

"Am I?" She only shifted. It was a very satisfying thing to hear the first time she set out, deliberately, to seduce a man. "I'll just kiss it, make it better."

Her gaze was a gold gleam under her lashes as she lowered her head, hesitated, then slowly rubbed her lips over his chest. She felt his heart kick like a stallion.

"Better?" She trailed her lips up his throat, over his jaw, then drew back, inches only when she heard him bite off a moan.

"This is nuts," he managed to say. "How long do you expect me to keep my hands off you when you're climbing all over me?"

"Who said I expect you to keep them off me?" She closed her teeth lightly over his chin. "Who said I want you to? I think..." She brushed her lips teasingly at the corner of his mouth. "I'm making it very clear what I expect. What I want."

"You're making a mistake."

"Maybe." She felt his hand grip her calf, then run firmly up to her thigh. And triumph lit her eyes. "So what?"

He couldn't come up with an answer, not when his system was screaming for her. He slid his hand over her hip until he could mold that lovely bottom. "You're taking advantage of me."

"I certainly am." She brought her mouth a breath closer. "Do you want me to stop? Now? Or do you want…" She nipped her teeth teasingly into his lower lip, chewed gently, released. "More?"

Either way, it was probably going to kill him. But if he was going to die, he'd damn well die happy. "All or nothing."

"All then," she agreed and closed her mouth over his.

The first flash of heat stole his breath. It bolted through him, a lightning strike of power and electricity. He'd have sworn he felt every circuit in his brain fry.

The hand on her dug in reflexively, then clawed up to her back and fisted in her shirt. Impatient, nearly desperate, he yanked. And the jolt of pain had him swearing.

"No, no, let me. Just let me." She all but crooned it, running her lips over his face, his throat, bringing them back to his for a deep and drowning kiss. "I'm mad for your body."

His groan had nothing to do with pain as she ranged hot kisses over his chest, down to his belly and back again. Her low, humming sounds of approval seemed to vibrate from her and into him until he was trapped somewhere between pleasure and pain.

Aching to touch her he worked his hands between their bodies to find her breasts.

Breath unsteady, she sat back, shivered once. Then that slow female smile spread over her face. Watching him watching her, she reached for the buttons of her shirt, flipping them open one, by one, by one.

"I'm in charge this time," she told him and slowly

peeled off the shirt. "You'll just have to lie there and take it."

"You got me up here for this, didn't you?"

She tilted her head, reached behind to unclasp her bra. "Yes. So?"

As the bra fell away and those lovely white breasts spilled out, he let out a long breath. "So. I appreciate it."

"Good. Touch me. I've spent hours at night wanting you to touch me."

He skimmed his fingers over her, saw her eyes cloud. "I wasn't going to let this happen."

"I wasn't going to give you any choice. Oh, *mon dieu, tes mains.*" His hands, his wonderful hands, big and strong and rough with calluses.

She was rose-petal soft, just as he'd imagined. He wanted to be gentle, careful with her. But he couldn't stop himself. And when she leaned over, bracing her weight on her arms, to mate her mouth with his again, his hands took more, took greedily.

He shifted, swore again as he fought against the protest of his ribs. "I need...I want..." His weight on her, his mouth on her. And though his side throbbed at the move, he managed to roll over.

"Wait. You'll hurt yourself."

"Shut up, shut up, shut up." Half mad for her, he scraped his teeth over the curve of her shoulder, breathed in her skin like a wolf scenting its mate. And had them both moaning when his mouth roamed down to her breast.

So hot, she thought as sensations battered her. His mouth, his skin, so hot against hers. As if they both raged with fever. His heartbeat was a gallop, and so was hers, as they raced to take more of each other. The weight of him was glorious, sinking her into the thin mattress and making her think of swimming beneath thunderous clouds.

To want and be wanted like this, for only herself, made her giddy and strong. And so very sure.

The thrill of it had her hands combing restlessly through his hair, digging urgently into his back as his muscles bunched.

Beneath them the bed creaked, overhead the rain drummed incessantly on the roof. Candlelight danced in the damp breeze that whispered through the open window.

And denim strained against denim as she arched beneath him. This time she quivered as he fought with the button of her jeans.

So soft, so tasty. And so ready, he thought, breathless as he fought her zipper down. She was already moving against him, those sexy little whimpers sounding in her throat. His mind was full of her, the scent, the shape, the flavor.

And he wanted more.

His fingers slid down, over the thin barrier of cotton, under it to the heat. Her whimpers became moans, and moans became quick, mindless gasps. When she erupted beneath him, he pressed his face to her belly and shuddered with her.

When his mouth roamed lower, she gripped the bedspread and prepared for the next onslaught on her senses. Her mind was hazed, her body a churning mass of needs and pleasures as sensations tumbled over and through her. It was staggering to *feel* so much, and still crave more.

He tugged the jeans over her hips, greedy for the next flash of flesh. And his bad shoulder gave out from under him. She let out a yelp of surprise when he collapsed on her. And while he cursed, violently, she began to laugh.

"It's all right, it's all right. *Merde!* My head's spinning. Let me help. Let me do it."

"Just a damn minute."

"I can't wait a minute." Still laughing, she wriggled, writhed and managed to drag herself free. Half naked and vibrating, she shoved and pulled until he rolled on his back again.

His face was fierce with frustration and temper, and only made her laugh harder.

"When I get my breath back, I'm going to whallop you."

"Yes, yes, I'm terrified." She scooted around on the bed, then had saliva pooling in his mouth as she wiggled out of the jeans. Temper, he admitted as she slipped off her panties, seemed a waste of time. Under the circumstances.

"Come back here."

"I intend to. But now." She reached over, unbuttoned his jeans. "Let's just get these out of the way. My hands are trembling," she said with a half laugh holding them out. "It's yours that have made them unsteady. I love the way they feel on me."

She yanked and tugged, pulling off jeans and shorts at the same time. Then her gaze roamed over him. Lingered.

"Oh. My." She drew in, then let out, a long breath. "Well, I did say there was a lot of you." Her eyes glinted with a combination of amusement and desire as she slid her body over his. "Put your hands on me again. Del, kiss me again."

"Bossy, aren't you?" But he cupped a hand at her nape and brought her mouth down to his.

She wallowed in the kiss, and it went slow and soft and deep. And when his hands moved over her, she felt the kiss edge over to urgent. "Tell me you want me," she murmured. "Say my name. Say my name and that you want me."

"Camilla." Her name echoed again and again in his head. "I want you."

She shifted, rose over him. And with her pulse pounding, took him inside her.

The first jolt of awareness had her bowing back. Holding, holding to absorb every drop of sensation until her system felt it might burst from the glory of it. His hands slid up her, closed over her breasts. Pressing her hands to his, she began to move. To rock. To push them both toward madness.

She was beautiful. He didn't know how to tell her. Slim and white with that bloom of rose under the milk of her skin. Her hair was like a sleek cap of gold-shot fire. And the candlelight flickered, gold on gold, in eyes blurred with pleasure.

He couldn't breathe without breathing her.

He watched, unspeakably aroused, as she crested to another peak. And that long, lovely body pressed against his sparking sensation after sensation.

He wanted his arms around her, wanted to wrap them around her like chains. But he was pinned by his own injuries and the relentless demands of her body.

He fought to cling to reason another minute. Then one more. But his system screamed for the grand insanity of release. And his body plunged toward it, through it, as her head fell back on a low cry of triumph.

A cat, licking the last drop of a quart of cream from her whiskers, could not have felt more self-satisfied. That was Camilla's thought as she basked in the afterglow of lovemaking.

Everything about him, she decided, was completely delicious.

She wished she could stretch her body over his and just wallow. But he was lying so still, he might have been a dead man but for the regular sound of his breath.

She settled for slithering over to his good side and pressing a kiss on his shoulder. "Did I hurt you?"

He hurt, literally, everywhere. His bruises were throbbing like a nest of demons dancing under his skin. At the moment, pain and gratification were so mixed, he wasn't certain he'd ever be able to tell the difference. But he only grunted.

Arching eyebrows, she lifted herself on an elbow and stared down at his face. She should've helped him shave again, she mused. Though there'd been something oddly erotic about having that stubble rub over her naked skin.

He opened his eyes. "What?"

"You're trying to be annoyed this happened. It won't work."

Later, he decided, he'd think about if he were amused or uneasy that the woman read him so well. "Why not? I'm good at being annoyed."

"Yes, you should get an award. But you're going to want me again as soon as you've recovered, so you won't be able to be annoyed about it. Defeats the purpose."

"Awfully damn sure of yourself, aren't you?"

"About some things." She leaned down and kissed him. "About this."

"Well, it so happens, you're wrong, smart mouth." Because she was frowning at him, she didn't see the direction of his hand until it closed, possessively, over her

breast. "I already want you again, and I might never recover from round one."

"I think you will. But I'm sorry you're hurting. I think
I'll go down and make you an ice pack."

"I think you should settle down and be quiet for five
minutes." To help her out, he pushed her elbow out from
under her so her head bounced on his good shoulder.

"You have a body like a rock," she muttered.

"Don't try to get me going again, sister. I'm going to
sleep for a half hour."

"Just let me—"

"Shh!" This time he solved the problem by wrapping
an arm around her, and clamping a hand over her mouth.

She narrowed her eyes, considered biting. Before she
could decide, his fingers went lax, his breathing evened
out. She saw, to her astonishment, that he was as good as
his word. He was, in ten seconds flat, sound asleep.

Thirty minutes later, shortly after she'd drifted from
consternation into sleep herself, he woke her with a mind-
numbing kiss. She shot to the surface, floundered there,
then was dragged under again.

Later, when she lay sprawled on the bed, feeling dazed
and used and gloriously ravished, he rolled over onto his
good side, muttered something about blowing out the
damn candles, and went instantly back to sleep.

For a long time after, Camilla stared up at the ceiling,
grinning foolishly. She'd found another passion, she realized, and his name was Delaney Caine. The man she
was going to marry, whether he liked it or not.

She was, as always, up before him in the morning. Rou-
tinely she brewed coffee, then decided to take the first cup

with her on a walk to the pond. She felt Del deserved to sleep in.

They would, of course, have to juggle their time between Vermont, digs, Virginia and Cordina. It was going to make for a full, busy and, she thought, very rich life.

He'd like her family, and they him. After they got to know each other, she thought, nibbling on her lip.

She didn't suppose he'd care for the protocol and formality demanded by her duties to Cordina as a princess and niece to the king. But surely he could adjust there. Marriage was, after all, give and take.

Naturally she was going to have to convince him he wanted to marry her first. And before that she'd have to convince him he was in love with her.

He *had* to be in love with her. She couldn't have all this feeling inside her for someone who didn't return at least a part of it.

She wandered through the woods, watching the early sun slant quivering rays through the boughs. For now, she reminded herself, she would simply appreciate the moment. This time with him, and with herself, without a past or future. Time to enjoy the discoveries, the courtship and romance.

Just because she'd fallen in love quickly didn't obligate him to rush. And it didn't mean she couldn't drift a bit and savor the sensation of being a woman in love.

When she reached the pond, she sat on a stump. She'd have to see that they found a nice, weathered old bench to put here, she thought. And maybe she'd sink some containers of water lilies along the edge of the water.

Small changes, subtle ones, she mused. Nothing major. Just as she didn't intend to try to change anything vital and elemental where Del was concerned.

She'd put her mark on the cabin, hadn't she, while respecting its basic personality and charm. She would hardly afford the man less respect than she did his home.

No, she liked him the way he was. Her lips curved as she lifted the coffee cup. Just exactly as he was.

When they were both more accustomed to this new stage of their relationship, she'd find a way to tell him about her birthright. In another week, she decided. Surely she was entitled to one more week.

She'd have to find the right way to present things. She could start with her father, she mused. Casually mentioning that he'd once been a cop, and had gone into private security, buying the land in Virginia because he'd wanted to farm. How her paternal and maternal grandfathers had been friends. That was why, when her mother was in trouble, her grandfather had reached out to the son of his old friend for help.

A bit confusing, Camilla supposed, but it was a good start. Then she could say something like—oh, did I mention my mother's from Cordina?

That should, hopefully, open the door a bit wider. With any luck Del would comment, or have some minor question, so she could slide into a casual mention that her uncle, her mother's brother, was His Royal Highness Alexander de Cordina.

He'd probably laugh at that, say something like: *Sure, sister, and you're the queen of the May.*

She could laugh back, treating it all very lightly. *No, no, just a mere princess on a short, stolen holiday.*

And that, she decided, would never work.

She cursed in frustration, and in French, and propped her chin on her fist.

"You come all the way out here to swear at the ducks."

She yelped, spilling coffee onto the back of her hand. She sprang up and whirled to face Del. "I like it better when you clumped around like an elephant."

And he'd liked it better when he hadn't kept thinking how very beautiful she was.

He'd woken reaching for her. It seemed to him if the woman was going to slip into his bed, the least she could do was stay there. Then he'd panicked because she hadn't been in the house. The thought of her gone had sent him out in a rib-jarring run until he'd calmed himself down.

Now it was worse, a hundred times worse, because she wasn't gone. She was standing there, the sun and water at her back, looking like something out of a storybook.

The light played over that sleek cap of hair like jewels in a crown. Her eyes were more gold than brown, and seemed impossibly rich against the cool, clear skin. She had a half smile on her mouth—that long, lovely mouth.

He wanted, as he'd wanted the night before, to wrap his arms around her. To hold her exactly as she was.

And that was crazy.

"I didn't smell any breakfast."

"Because I haven't started it yet. I thought you'd sleep awhile longer."

"We said we'd start early today."

"So we did." Now she smiled fully. "I wasn't sure that still held, after last night." Since he wasn't coming to her, she stepped to him. Lifted a hand to brush at his hair. "How do you feel?"

"I'm okay. Listen, about last night…"

"Yes?" She rose on her toes, touched her lips lightly to his. And wound his stomach muscles into knots.

"We didn't lay out any of the… Look, there are no strings here."

A little bubble of temper rose to her throat, but she swallowed it. "Did I try to tie any on you while you slept?"

"I'm not saying—" He hated being made to feel defensive. "I just want us to be clear, since we didn't get into any of it last night. We enjoy each other, we'll keep it simple, and when it's over it's done."

"That's very clear." It would be undignified to strike him, and she didn't believe in resorting to physical violence. Particularly against the mentally deficient. Instead she smiled easily. "Then there's nothing to worry about, is there?"

With her expression pleasant, even patient, she ran her hands up his chest, lightly over his shoulders and into his hair. And fixed her mouth on his in a long, smoldering kiss.

She waited for his hand to fist in the back of her shirt, then nimbly stepped away and left him vibrating. "I'll fix omelets, then we'll get to work."

Her eyes sparked with temper and challenge as she started up the path. And smiled in the friendliest of manners as she turned, held out her hand.

Baboon, she thought—with some affection—as he took her hand to walk back to the cabin. You're in for one hell of a fight.

Chapter 8

They had a week of relative peace. Camilla decided peace would always be relative when Delaney was involved. His grumpiness was just one of the things about him she'd come to count on. In fact, it was part of his charm.

She raided his books on archaeology. Though he muttered about her messing with his things, she knew he was pleased she had a sincere interest in the field.

When she asked questions, he answered them—and in more and more detail. It became routine for them to discuss what she had read. Even for him to suggest, offhandedly, another book or section she might want to study.

When he gave her a small Acheulean hand ax from his collection, she treasured the crude, ancient tool more than diamonds.

It was more than a gift, she thought. Much more than a token. It was, to her mind, a symbol.

He hardly complained at all about driving her back into town to pick up her car. And he took it for granted that whatever her plans had been before, mobile or not, she was staying awhile.

They were, Camilla thought, making progress.

She'd managed to peel a layer or two away as well. She learned his father was English, also Oxford educated, and had met his mother, an American, on a dig the senior Dr. Caine had headed in Montana.

So he'd spent some of his childhood in England, some in Vermont, and the bulk of it in trailers and tents on various sites all over the world.

The hand ax he'd given her was from Kent, and one he'd unearthed when he'd been a boy. It made the gift doubly precious to her.

He could read Sanskrit and Greek, and had once been bitten by a coral snake.

The scar just beneath his left shoulder blade was from a knife wielded by a drunk in a bar in Cairo.

However foolish it was, Camilla found all of this fabulously romantic.

She drove into town to mail off the first of his reports and correspondence. *Their* reports, she corrected, smugly. She'd contributed more than typing skills and he'd managed to indicate just that with a few approving grunts when she'd suggested a change or another angle of approach.

They made a good team.

When they made love, it seemed there was nothing and no one in the world but the two of them. Past, future were distant and irrelevant in that intense and eager present. She knew by the way he looked at her when they joined, the way his eyes would stay so vivid on hers, that it was the same for him.

None of the men who had touched her life had brought this kind of impact. To her heart, her body, her mind. She hoped—needed to know—that she brought the same to him.

No strings, she thought with a quick snort. Typical. If he wanted no strings why had he begun to take walks with her in the woods? Why did he answer patiently—well, patiently for him—when she asked questions?

Why did she sometimes catch him looking at her the way he did? So intense and direct, as if she were a puzzle he was trying to figure out?

And why did he, at the oddest moments, simply lean over and capture her mouth in a kiss that sizzled her brain?

The man was in love with her, and that was that. He was just too boneheaded to realize it. Or at least to admit it.

She'd give him a little more time, then she'd tell him she was in love with him. When he got used to the idea, she'd explain about the other part of her life.

It all seemed so reasonable as she ran her errands. Her mood was mellow when she strolled into the antique shop. She would try Sarah first regarding the watch, she decided. It was mortifying to be so low on cash, and have Del hand her money every time something was needed for the cabin.

Besides, if she could pay her way a bit more, she could fairly demand that he pull more weight on domestic chores. It was time he washed a few dishes.

"Good morning." She beamed a smile at Sarah as she wound her way through the antiques.

Sarah turned over the magazine she'd been paging through. "Good morning, ah...Miss Breen."

"I noticed you have a selection of secondhand jewelry and watches."

"Yes." Sarah answered cautiously as she studied Camilla's face.

"I wonder if you'd be interested in this." Camilla took off her watch, held it out.

"It's lovely. Um..." Hesitantly Sarah turned the watch over. She ran her fingers over the smooth gold, watched the tiny diamonds wink. "It's not the sort of thing we usually..."

She trailed off, then simply stared at Camilla.

"It's all right. I thought I'd see if you might be interested in buying it. I'll try the jeweler."

"You are her." Sarah barely breathed it, her eyes wide and dazzled.

There was a hard clutching in Camilla's throat, but her face remained perfectly calm. "I beg your pardon?"

"I thought...when you were in the other day...I knew you looked like somebody."

"Everyone looks like someone." With a steady hand, Camilla reached for her watch. "Thank you anyway."

"Princess Camilla." Sarah pressed her fingertips to her lips. "I can't believe it. Princess Camilla, in my shop. You're right here. And, and here!" Triumphantly now, she flipped the magazine over.

And there, Camilla saw with a sinking heart, was her own face being touted as one of the most beautiful in the world.

"You cut your hair. All that fabulous hair."

"Yes, well." Resigned, Camilla sighed. "It was time for a change."

"You look wonderful. Even better than—" Catching herself, Sarah paled. "Oh. Excuse me. Um. Your Highness." She dipped in a quick curtsy that had her blond tail of hair bouncing.

"Don't. Please." Struggling to smile, Camilla glanced toward the door and prayed no other customers would come in. "I'm traveling very quietly at the moment. I'd really prefer keeping it that way."

"I taped that documentary on the royal family. After you were in last week, I kept thinking and thinking, and then it hit me. I watched it again. But I thought I had to be wrong. Cordina's Crown Jewel doesn't just drop in to my store for old bottles. But here you are."

"Yes, here I am. Sarah—"

"That Del." Overwhelmed Sarah babbled on. "I know you have to pry news out of him with a crowbar, but this is taking it too far. He's got royalty staying at his cabin, and he doesn't say a word."

"He doesn't know. And I'd prefer to keep things that way as well, at least until... Oh, Sarah."

Having a princess in her shop was one thing, having one who looked so miserably distressed was another. "Golly." Biting her lip, Sarah hurried around the counter, but stopped short of taking Camilla's arm. She didn't think it was done. "Would you like something to drink, Your Highness?"

"Yes. Yes, thank you, I would."

"I've got, jeez, I'm so flustered. I have some iced tea in my office."

"That's very kind of you."

"It's nothing. Just let me, boy...I'll put the Closed sign on."

She hurried to the door and back again, then wrung her

hands and couldn't stop herself from doing another curtsy
"Behind the counter. It's not much."

"I'd love something cool." She followed Sarah int(
the little office and took a seat on a swivel chair whil(
Sarah fumbled with the door of a small refrigerator
"Please don't be nervous. I'm no different than I was th(
first time I came in."

"I beg your pardon, Your Highness, but you are. O
course you are."

"You needn't address me by my title," Camilla sai(
wearily. "Madam or ma'am is sufficient, and in this case
I'd prefer you just use my name."

"I don't think I can. You see I've read about you an(
your family since I was a kid. We're almost the same age
and I used to imagine myself living in a palace, wearin(
all those beautiful clothes. Being a princess. I guess mos
little girls do."

She turned back to Camilla, eyes shining. "Is it won
derful?"

"It can be. Sarah, I have a great favor to ask you."

"Anything. Anything at all."

"Would you not tell anyone?"

Sarah blinked. "Anyone? At all?"

"Just for a little while. Please. Sarah, it can be won
derful being a princess, but there were times, you see
when I was a little girl, that I dreamed of being just that
Just an ordinary girl. I want time now to live that dream.'

"Really?" It sounded beautifully romantic. "I gues:
we always want what we don't have." She handed Ca
milla a glass of iced tea. "I won't tell anyone. It'll kil
me," she admitted with a wry laugh. "But I won't. Coul(
you, would you mind, ah, madam, signing my maga
zine?"

"I'd be happy to. Thank you very much."

"You're nicer than I thought you'd be. I always imagined princesses would be, well, snobby."

"Oh, we can be." Camilla smiled, sipped. "Depending."

"Maybe, but, excuse me, but you seem so...normal."

The smile warmed, as did her eyes. "That's the nicest thing you could say to me."

"Classier of course. I noticed that right off, too, but..." Sarah's eyes popped wide again. "Del doesn't *know?*"

Guilt circled, nibbled at the back of her neck. "It hasn't come up."

"It's just like him. Oblivious." Sarah threw up her hands. "The man's oblivious. When we were dating, I think he forgot my name half the time. And forget noticing the color of my eyes. Used to make me so mad. Then he'd smile at me, or say something to make me laugh, and I wouldn't mind so much."

"I know what you mean."

"He's so smart about some things, and so lame about others." She picked up her own glass, then nearly bobbled it when she caught the dreamy expression on Camilla's face. "Holy cow. Are you in love with him?"

"Yes, I am. And I need a little more time to convince him he likes the idea."

It was just like a movie, Sarah thought. "That's nice. Really nice. And it's perfect, really, when you think about it."

"It is for me." Camilla admitted, then rose. "I'm in your debt, Sarah, and I won't forget it." When she held out a hand, Sarah quickly wiped her own on her slacks before taking it.

"I'm glad to help."

"I'll come in and see you again before I leave," Camilla promised as she started back into the shop.

When she picked up her watch from the counter, Sarah bit her lip again. "Your Highness, ma'am, do you really want to sell that watch?"

"Yes, actually. I'm embarrassingly short of liquid funds, just now."

"I can't give you what it's worth, not even close. But I could...I could lend you five hundred. And, well, you could have the inkwell you liked so much."

Camilla looked over at her. The woman, she thought, was nervous, intimidated and confused. But it didn't stop her from wanting to help. Another gift, Camilla thought, she would treasure.

"When I started out on this quest of mine, I wanted to discover... To find parts of myself as well as see...I'm not sure what now—maybe just things from a different perspective. It's such a wonderful bonus to have found a friend. Take the watch. We'll consider it a trade, between friends."

Del walked out on the front porch and stared at the rutted lane. Again. How long did it take to run a few errands? That was the trouble with women. They turned a couple errands into some sort of pilgrimage.

He wanted his lunch, and a fresh pot of coffee, and to answer the half-dozen e-mails that had come through his laptop that morning.

All of which, he was forced to admit he could handle for himself. Had always handled for himself.

What he wanted, damn it, was her.

His life, he thought jamming his hands into his pockets,

was completely screwed. She'd messed everything up, scattered his focus, ruined his routine.

He should've left her stranded in the rain that night. Then everything would be the way it had been before. He wouldn't have some woman cluttering up his space. Cluttering up his mind.

Who the hell was she? There were secrets tucked inside that sharp, complicated brain of hers. If she was in trouble, why didn't she just tell him, so he could deal with it?

He needed for her to tell him, to confide in him, to depend on him to help her.

And when the hell had he started seeing himself as some knight on a white charger? It was ridiculous, totally out of character.

But he wanted to fix whatever was wrong. More, he realized, much more, he needed her to trust him enough to tell him. Trust him enough to fix it.

Because he'd tripped over his own unspoken rule and fallen flat on his face in love with her.

And he didn't much care for the way it felt, he mused, rubbing a hand over his heart. It was a lot more uncomfortable than a few bruised ribs. And, he feared, a lot more permanent.

He'd had to go and say no strings, hadn't he? Of course, she'd had no problem with that, he thought now. Bitterly. That was just fine and dandy with her.

Well, if he was going to have to adjust, then so was she.

Besides, no strings didn't mean no faith, did it? If she didn't believe in him enough to even tell him her full name, where were they?

He paced into the house, then back out again.

Maybe he should go check on her. She'd been gone

nearly two hours. She'd already had one accident, which meant she could easily have another. She might be sprawled over the wheel of her car, bleeding. Or...

Just as he was working himself into a fine state of agitation, he heard the sound of her engine. Disgusted with himself, he slipped back into the house before she could catch him keeping an eye out for her.

He circled the living room twice, then paused and considered. Adjustments.

Romance.

That was something she appeared to believe was vital in any culture. Cultures were made up of relationships, rituals and romance. Maybe he should try a small foray into that and see where it got him.

He strolled into the kitchen as she set a bag of groceries on the table. "I have your receipts for the overnight mail I sent," she told him.

"Good." Since he wanted to anyway, he brushed a hand over her hair.

She gave him an absent smile, and turned away to put a quart of milk in the refrigerator. "There were some letters in your post office box." Frowning, she rubbed at her temple where a tension headache nagged. "I must have left them in the car."

"No problem." He leaned down to sniff the side of her neck. "You smell great."

"I what? Oh." She patted his shoulder, reached for the bag of new potatoes she'd bought for dinner. "Thank you."

Determined to make an impression he dug a little deeper. What was it women always...ah! "Have you lost weight?" he asked, feeling truly inspired.

"I doubt it. Probably gained a couple if anything." She

ook coffee out of the cupboard and prepared to brew a fresh pot.

Behind her back, Del narrowed his eyes. Since words weren't getting him anywhere, he'd move straight to deeds.

He scooped her off her feet and started out of the kitchen.

"What are you doing?"

"Taking you to bed."

"Well, really. You might ask—and I haven't finished putting the groceries away."

Del paused at the bottom of the steps and stopped her mouth with his. "In certain cultures," he said when he eased back, "women indicate their desire for intimacy by stocking the pantry. I'm merely picking up on traditional signals."

Amusement nudged at the gnawing worry inside her. "What cultures?" she demanded as he continued up the steps.

"Mine. It's a new tradition."

"That's so cute." She nuzzled at the side of his throat. "I think you missed me."

"Missed you? Did you go somewhere?" When she huffed out a breath, he tossed her on the bed. When she bounced, he rolled his shoulder. "Got a twinge from hauling you up. Maybe you have gained a couple pounds."

She shoved herself up on her elbows. "Oh, really?"

"That's okay. We'll work it off." And he dived on her.

Her first reaction was laughter. Playfulness wasn't his usual style, and it caught her off guard. As he rolled her over the bed, she forgot to be worried.

"You're heavy." She shoved at him. "And you haven't shaved. You have your boots on my clean linens."

"Nag, nag, nag," he said, and dragging her hands over
her head, took her mouth with his.

He felt her pulse jump, then race, and her hands go
limp in his. Her body gloriously pliant.

He skimmed his lips over her jaw. "You were saying?"

"Shut up and kiss me."

He cuffed her wrists with one hand, used the other to
unbutton her shirt. "So, are you indicating your desire for
intimacy?" He trailed a fingertip down the center of her
body, toyed with the hook of her slacks as he watched
her face. "Just want to get my signals straight."

Her breath was already backing up in her lungs. "Your
pantry's been stocked since I got here, hasn't it?"

"That's a good point." He lowered the zipper, brushing
his knuckles over the exposed skin. "Had the hots for me
all along, haven't you?"

"If you're going to be arrogant—"

"Maybe you were hoping I'd come into your room one
night," he continued, and traced the dip between her center and her thigh. "And do this."

"I never..." Her hips arched, her breath hissed out as
he cupped her. "Lord. Del."

"Let me show you what I thought about doing."

Keeping her hands pinned, he touched her, unerringly
shooting her up into an intense climax, muffling her
shocked cry with his mouth as her body bucked. When
her breath sobbed, he closed his teeth over her breast,
torturing the sensitized point through the cotton of her bra.

He nudged the straps down, nibbled his way over the
slope of her shoulders, almost delicately, while his hand
roamed, exploited and plundered.

She went wet and wild beneath him. Unable to find her
balance, she shuddered, then spiked, then floated down.

again only to have him fling her ruthlessly over the edge one more time. Her hands strained against his grip. And the helplessness added a layer of panicked excitement over shattered senses.

Her body was molten, and she trembled from the heat that slathered her skin and burned in the blood. Still she arched to him, desperate for more.

She heard his voice, the words thick and soft.

"I'll owe you for this," he said and snapped the bra in two with one rough tug.

Then his mouth, his teeth, his tongue, found flesh. The moan wrenched from her gut as her system erupted.

"Let me go. Let go of my hands. I need to touch you."

"Not yet, not yet." It would end too soon if she touched him now. He hadn't known he could arouse himself to a frenzy just by arousing her. He wanted her weak and wrecked and wailing.

And he wanted to take, take, take.

When he felt her go fluid beneath him, when he felt release pour through her and leave her lax, it still wasn't enough.

He tore the panties away, feeling a dark satisfaction at hearing the delicate fabric rip. Then he drove her back to madness with his mouth.

Finally, when she thought there could be no more, he filled her. Her hands slipped off his damp shoulders, her mouth lifted urgently to his.

And she wrapped herself around him like a vine.

"Mon amour. Mon coeur," she murmured mindlessly as they tumbled over the brink. *"Toujours mon amour."*

They slept, sprawled over each other like exhausted children. And when they woke, steamed the walls in his

394   *Cordina's Crown Jewel*

narrow shower as they took each other again under the hot spray.

Realizing he was taking an unprecedented step—a day off—Camilla packed a picnic and cajoled him into sharing a very late lunch by the pond.

She didn't have to do much cajoling. Picnics, he thought, were romantic. And romance was the current name of the game.

She looked happy, he mused. Relaxed. Her face glowed, her eyes were soft. If he'd been an artist, he'd have painted her now and titled it Camilla Content.

He didn't feel foolish—or not very—telling her so.

"That's just what I am. I love this place." She stretched out on the bank, stared up at the powder-puff clouds. "It's so quiet, it seems as though there's no one else in the world." She turned her head to smile at him. "Perfect for a hermit."

"I'm not a hermit." He polished off the last of the fancy triangular shaped sandwiches she'd put together. "I just don't like people around."

"I like people." She rolled onto her stomach. "They're often so much kinder than you expect," she added, thinking of Sarah. "But sometimes, if you don't have a place to be alone—or to be quiet—you forget that and only see the demands, the responsibilities, the obligations people mete out."

"If you don't have a place to be alone, you don't get anything done."

"You have such purpose, your own purpose. That's a gift. Not everyone does." Her eyes clouded. "Some of us fumble around looking for one, and end up with so many we realize, all at once, we haven't got any at all."

"You don't strike me as a fumbler."

"Hmm. Sometimes efficiency is just as much of a flaw. Without that quiet time, you stop seeing the flaws, and the virtues. You can forget, not just who you are, but who you want to be." She smiled up at him, then turned over again to rest her head on his lap. "So I like this spot, because it's helped me remember."

"And who are you, Camilla?"

She understood he wanted an answer—a real one. But she found she couldn't speak and irrevocably change this moment. So she evaded. "A woman who won't forget again." She picked up a plum, took a bite, then held it up to him. "I like being alone with you, Delaney."

And she would give them the rest of the lovely, lazy day before Camilla de Cordina joined them.

He wanted to be patient, but patience wasn't his best skill. He'd thought, been sure, she'd been ready to confide in him. What did a man have to do to pry that woman open? he wondered. Most people spilled their guts at the least provocation.

But she just made vague philosophical statements, an occasional wistful one. And clammed up.

It was grating, but he was going to have to press. To do that he was going to have to make it clear that they were…that he was…

He'd never in his life told a woman he loved her. He'd gotten through his entire adult life without it being an issue, much less a problem. Now it was both.

He could march into the kitchen and blurt it out and be done with it. He equated it to ripping off a bandage in one painful jerk. Or he could ease them both into it, stage by stage—like lowering yourself into a cold pool inch by inch so your body adjusted to the shock.

I like having you around, he could say. Maybe you should just plan on staying.

He could let that settle awhile then move up to the I-care-about-you level. She'd have something to say about that. She *always* had something to say. Who would have believed he'd like listening to her so much?

But in any case, he thought, drawing himself back to the point, when they'd finished hashing through all that, he could just finish it off.

"I love you." He winced at his own muttered voice, shot a look toward the kitchen. It didn't even *sound* like him, he decided. The words didn't seem to fit his mouth.

"I love you," he tried again, and exhaled. Easier that time.

"Now, tell me what kind of trouble you're in, I'll take care of it and we'll move on."

Simple, he decided. Direct and supportive. Women liked supportive.

God. He was going to need a good shot of whiskey to get through it.

"I know it's late." Cocking the receiver on her shoulder, Camilla looked down at her wrist before she remembered her watch was gone. A quick glance at the kitchen clock had her calculating that it was after one in the morning in Cordina. No wonder she'd woken Marian.

"No problem. I was only sleeping."

"I'm sorry. Really. I just had to tell someone."

"Okay, let me pull myself together. Are you coming home?"

"Soon. I promise."

"You missed the first fitting for your ball gown. Your dressmaker is seriously displeased."

"Ball gown?" She drew a blank before it clicked in. "Oh, the Autumn Ball. There's plenty of time. Marian, I'm in love."

"You say that now, but if you'd heard the woman gnashing her teeth, you'd...what? What?"

"I'm in love. It's wonderful. It's terrifying. It's the most incredible thing that's ever happened to me. He's perfect. Oh, he's the most irritating man half the time, but *like* that. And he's so smart and so funny—and very committed to his work."

"Camilla."

"And he's very attractive. I know that's just surface, but isn't it nice to fall in love with the inner man and have the outer man be gorgeous?"

"Camilla."

"He's in love with me, too. He's coming around to that, though it might take just a little while longer to—"

"Camilla!"

"Yes?"

"Who is he?"

"Oh, he's the man I've been working for here. Delaney Caine."

"The archaeologist? You fell for Indiana Jones?"

"I'm serious, Marian."

"Well, does he at least look like Indiana Jones?"

"No. Hmm, actually perhaps a little. But that's not the point. This isn't a game or a movie, it's my life. And this is something I want, something that feels very right."

"I can hear that. Cam, I'm so happy for you. When will I meet him?"

"I don't know exactly." Gnawing over the question, she wrapped the phone cord around her fingers. "That's

part of the problem. After I explain things, then I hope
we can make arrangements for him to meet the family."

"Explain things?" There was a long pause. "You mean
you haven't told him who you are?"

"Not yet. I didn't expect this to happen, did I? I
couldn't anticipate it. And then I wanted…" She trailed
off warily as she heard Del heading into the kitchen.

"Camilla, how could you let things go so far and not
tell him? If the man's in love with you—"

"I don't know that," she murmured in French. "Not
for certain. I didn't intend for it to be complicated."

She cleared her throat as Del took the whiskey bottle
from the pantry. It wasn't possible to ask him to hurry
or to cut Marian off, so she continued the conversation in
French, keeping her voice as mild as she could manage.

"Marian, I had a right to my privacy. I could hardly
stay here, if I'd announced I was a member of the royal
family. The whole point of this was not to be Camilla de
Cordina for a few weeks."

"The point seems to have changed."

"Yes, I know that, but I'd hardly be staying here if
people knew who I was. The cabin would be surrounded
by the media, and that, if you recall, was what sent me
off in the first place."

"If you think the man would call reporters—"

"No. No, of course I don't think that. And I didn't call
to argue with you, Marian. I did what I had to do, what
I thought best, for me. As to the rest." She slanted a look
toward Del as he poured whiskey into a glass. "I'll deal
with it."

"I'm your friend, Camilla. I love you. I just don't want
to see you hurt or disappointed. Or exploited."

"I don't intend to be. Tell the family I'll be home soon."

"And your dressmaker?"

Camilla sighed. "Inform Madam Monique that Her Highness will not disgrace her at the Autumn Ball. Go back to sleep, Marian."

She hung up, opened the refrigerator for a cold drink while Del stood swirling his whiskey in the glass. "I hope you don't mind me using the phone."

"No, I don't mind."

"I reversed the charges."

"Good. I'd probably have gotten a jolt if I'd noticed a call to Cordina on my phone bill next month."

"Yes, I imagine so. I…" She trailed off, and the hand that had lifted for a glass fell to her side again.

"Je parle francais aussi." Del lifted the whiskey to his lips as she turned to face him. "Your Highness."

Chapter 9

She knew her color faded. She could feel it drain and leave her face cold and stiff. Just as she could feel her heart leap into her throat and fill it with pounding.

Because of it she instinctively straightened her spine.

"I see. You didn't mention it."

"Must've slipped my mind," he said evenly. "Like being a member of the royal family of Cordina slipped yours. Just one of those stray details."

"My lineage never slips my mind. It isn't allowed to. Delaney—"

"So what's all this?" He gestured with the glass. "Your little version of the princess and the pauper? Taking a few weeks, slumming with the hoi polloi."

"You know better. You can't think that."

"Let's see, what should I think?" He lifted the whiskey again, splashed more in the glass. He couldn't precisely pinpoint why he wanted to heave the bottle against the wall. Or more, why he resisted. "What, are you hiding out from a lover? One a little too anxious to get his hands on the crown jewels?"

"That's unfair. I have no lover but you."

"Not for the past couple of weeks anyway. You should've told me I was having sex with a princess. It might've added a nice flair."

Her lips wanted to tremble, so she firmed them into a hard line. "And that's unkind."

"You want fair? You want kind?" His voice changed from dangerously soft to viciously sharp. "You've got the wrong guy, sister. Somebody plays me for a fool, I get pissed."

"I didn't play you. I never intended to—"

"To what? Cut the crap, Camilla. You don't do anything you don't intend. You came in here because you wanted to play pretend for a while, and amuse yourself with the locals while you were at it."

"That's not true." Her temper started to build to match his. "And it insults both of us."

"You're insulted." He slammed the glass down before he did throw it. "You come into my place and pretend to be someone you're not. You lie about who you are. About what you are. Virginia farm girl, my ass."

"My father has a farm in Virginia." She shouted back because she was too frightened to do otherwise. "I've lived there half the year all of my life."

"And the other half in the palace. Well, I guess the tiara suits you better than a straw hat."

"Yes. No!" Struggling through the anger and panic, she dragged a hand through her hair. "We have a farm in Cordina. My mother—"

"Your 'French' mother," he said coolly.

"You said France, I said Europe." But it was weak, and she knew it. "Delaney, I'm exactly the same person I was ten minutes ago. I only wanted the privacy of—"

"Privacy? Give me a break. You slept with me. You made damn certain you'd sleep with me. What, looking for a change of pace from the purebreds? You get points for nailing stray Americans on your little adventure?"

Her color came up now, flaming into her cheek. "How dare you! You're crude and vile, and it's despicable to turn something lovely into something cheap. I won't have this discussion, nor explain myself to you while you're in this impossible mood. Move aside."

"You don't give commands here, Princess." He grabbed her arm before she could stalk by him. "You used me."

"No." Tears wanted to brim, wanted to fall. "Not the way you mean. Del, I only wanted a place to be. I only wanted some time."

"You got a hell of a lot more, didn't you? Playtime's over, Your Highness. You're going to do more than explain yourself."

"Let me go." She drew on all of her composure and command, and eyed him coldly. "I have nothing more to say to you now. Let me go."

"Oh, I will. All the way. I guess we've said all there is. You can pack your bags and run away, since that seems to be your pattern."

The temper and shame that warred within her were no match for the grief. "You want me to go?"

"You got what you came for, didn't you? I'll make it easy for you and get the hell out of your way."

Her breath hitched as he started for the door. "Del. Please, don't. I love you."

The pain stabbed through him. The words snarled out of him as he tossed them at her, though they were pure truth. "You're breaking my heart, sister," he said, "try that line on someone who's stupid enough to believe it. And get the hell away from me." He left and slammed the door behind him.

He tromped through the forest for an hour, thinking vicious thoughts and cursing all women. He stalked the woods another hour as the flames of his temper banked to a smoldering rage.

In love with him? What a crock. She had a lot of nerve pulling that routine on him. She'd been about to pour on the tears, too. He'd seen that coming. Thank God he'd gotten out of there before the floods hit.

He just couldn't stand weeping females.

Well, she'd pulled every other trick out of her hat. Excuse me, he thought bitterly, make that crown. Why not tears?

And for what? So she could have a couple weeks to indulge herself. Cinderella in the wilderness?

He stopped, rubbing at the ache in his gut as he stared out over the pond.

I love this place.

He could hear her saying it, see the easy pleasure in her face as she lay on the grass beside him.

So she had an appreciation of nature. Big deal.

Haven't you ever needed to just breathe?

He remembered her saying that, too. That first day, standing beside him with all that tension in her face, in her voice. As if she'd been standing on the edge of something and fighting to hold her ground instead of leaping over.

Okay, so maybe she had some problems. Who didn't? But that didn't excuse what she'd done. It had all been a pretense, right from the beginning. And she'd let him fall in love with her—let him fall into that cage without warning him it had a trap door to nowhere.

She had to pay for that.

He turned, headed back toward the cabin. Okay, he'd let her explain—not that he was buying any of it. Then...

Then he'd figure out what the hell to do next.

With his head down and his hands in his pockets, he didn't notice her car was gone until he was nearly at the back door. For nearly a full minute he stared blankly at the spot where it had last been parked.

Then he was bolting into the cabin, charging up the stairs.

Her clothes were gone. He flung open both closets as if she might have put them back in the spare room just to make him sweat. She'd even taken the pots and tubes from the medicine cabinet.

On a tearing fury, he searched the cabin for a note. But there was nothing.

He couldn't say she'd gone without a trace. She'd left the candles, the little bottles springing with wildflowers. Her scent, everywhere, was already haunting him.

So, she'd pulled up stakes, he thought. Just because he'd yelled at her and told her she could pack and run away. If the woman couldn't stand up to a fight...

No, better this way, he reminded himself. No point in dragging it out. She was heading back to where she belonged to where she'd been headed all along, and he could get back to work without having her distract him every five minutes.

He prowled over to his notes, picked up one at random. After tossing it down again, he dropped onto the couch to brood.

She'd come back. He talked himself into that, particularly when he got just a little drunk. She was just off in a snit, that was all. Women had snits, didn't they?

His two hours stomping through the woods was a natural expression of justifiable aggravation. He didn't go off in snits.

In the morning, suffering from a surprisingly nasty hangover, he convinced himself he didn't want her to come back. He liked his life the way it had been before she'd plunged into it. And he didn't like, not one damn bit, this sensation of loss and misery. Which was, no question about it, completely her fault.

By the second day, he was edgy and busily working himself into a temper again. She had absolutely no business running off before he'd finished yelling at her. But it was just like her, wasn't it, to stick that chin out, shoot that nose in the air and flounce off. He should've recognized it as princess behavior from the get-go.

When she cooled off and came back, he had a great deal to say to her.

Why the hell hadn't she come back?

Didn't matter to him, he reminded himself and struggled to concentrate on his work. He had plenty to do to keep himself occupied while she was off sulking. In fact, maybe he'd just pack up and take himself back to the dig. It was where he belonged anyway.

And it gave him a hard, rude jolt to realize he'd planned to take her with him. He'd wanted to show her the place, to watch that interest and intellect shine in her eyes when she got her first look at his pet project.

He'd wanted to share that with her—and that was terrifying. He'd wanted to share everything with her. He couldn't believe how much that hurt.

Just as he sat, unsteady in the knowledge that she really wasn't coming back, he heard a car coming down the lane.

He *knew* it! He sprang up, fueled with relief, pleasure, fury, and had reached the door in one leap before he stopped himself. This was not the way to handle it, he decided, or her. He'd *wander* out, casually. Then he'd let her apologize.

Feeling smug, and generous, he stepped outside. Everything inside him sank when he saw it wasn't Camilla climbing out of the car. It was his parents.

"Surprise!" Alice Caine ran toward the porch in her ancient and sturdy boots. Her hair, a streaky mess of mouse-brown and gray was, as always falling untidily from beneath a scarred bush hat. She was trim as a girl, with a face splattered with freckles and lined from a life in the sun.

She leaped on her son, gave him a slurpy, smacking kiss on the cheek, then immediately turned to her husband. "Niles, let the boy get the bags. What's the point in having a big, strong son if you can't use him as slave labor? How's the shoulder, Del?" she asked him. "And the rest of it?"

"Fine. It's fine. I wasn't expecting you."

"If you had been, it wouldn't be a surprise." She tipped down her dark, wire-rim glasses. Though she grinned, she was sharp enough to have seen her son's shocked disappointment when he'd stepped out on the sagging porch. "Got some coffee?"

"Sure. Sure." Ashamed of himself, he bent down—she was such a little thing—and gave her a quick hug.

"Drove three hundred, fifteen miles today." Mumbling in his public school English accent, Niles Caine finished noting the mileage in his tattered book as he crossed to his son. "Made good time."

He was a big man, tall and dashingly handsome at sixty-seven. His hair, a mop of it, had gone shining silver, and his eyes, green as his son's, were jewel sharp in his tanned face. He tucked the book into the pocket of his faded shirt, then gave Del a crushing bear hug. "How's the shoulder?"

"Fine. Better. What's up with your dig?"

"Oh, we're just taking a break. Clear the mind." Alice said it airily, one warning look at her husband, as she strode into the house. She stopped dead, fisted her hands on her narrow hips. "Del. You've got a woman."

"What?"

"Look at this. Flowers." She arched her brow at the wildflowers tucked into bottles. "Scents," she added, sniffing a bowl of potpourri. "Clean." She ran a fingertip over a tabletop. "Definitely a female on the premises. Where is she?"

"She's not here."

Ah, Alice thought. Poor baby. "Niles, my hero, would you run into town and get me some ice cream?"

"Run into town?" He stared at her. "I've just got here. I haven't so much as sat down yet."

"You can sit down in the car on the drive to town."

"Woman, if you wanted ice cream, why didn't you say so when we were still in the bloody car?"

"I didn't want any then. Something with chocolate." She rose on her toes to kiss his scowling mouth. "I've such a yen for chocolate."

408 Cordina's Crown Jewel

"Flighty, fluttering females," he muttered, and stomped back out to the car.

Alice simply walked to the couch, sat and propped her boots on the table. Smiling, she patted the cushion beside her. "Sit. Coffee can wait. Tell me about the woman."

"There's nothing to tell. She was here, she was a constant annoyance. Now she's gone."

Cranky, wounded bear, she thought indulgently. Just like his father. "Sit." Her voice firmed—she knew how to handle her men. "Why did she leave you?"

"She didn't leave me." His pride pricked, he dropped onto the couch. "She was just working for me, temporarily. Very temporarily," he muttered.

And at his mother's long, patient silence, he cracked. "I kicked her out. If she's too stubborn to come back...I don't need her underfoot anyway."

"There now." She patted his head. "Tell Mommy all about the horrible girl."

"Cut it out." But his lips twitched.

"Was she ugly?"

"No."

"Stupid then."

He sighed. "No."

"A cheap floozy."

Now he laughed. "Mom."

"That's it then." She slapped a hand on his thigh. "A cheap floozy taking advantage of my poor, sweet-natured, naive little boy. Why, I'll fix her wagon. What's her name? I'll hunt her down like a dog."

"She's fairly easy to find," he murmured. "Her name's Camilla. Her Royal Highness Camilla de Cordina. I could strangle her."

Alice tossed her sunglasses and her hat on the table. "Tell me," she said. So he did.

She listened while he worked himself back and forth through temper, into misery and back into temper again. So often, she noted, he had to leap up to pace the room just to keep up with himself.

His description of Camilla—except for the irritating, interfering nuisance portion—jibed with the lovely note she'd received some days before from Her Serene Highness Gabriella.

A gracious—and clever—note, Alice mused, one that acknowledged Gabriella's gratitude to Delaney for his hospitality to her daughter. Alice hadn't been sure if having anyone consider her son hospitable was more of a surprise than learning he was being so with a member of Cordina's royal family.

But she was a woman accustomed to thinking on her feet, and adjusting in midstride when necessary. The contents of the note had caused Alice to drag her husband from the Arizona dig and head home to see for herself just what was what.

Now that she'd seen, she had a very good idea just what was what.

What came through, in huge, neon letters to her mother's view, was that her son was completely, pitifully in love.

And it was about damn time.

"So she left," Del finished. "That's for the best all around."

"Probably so," Alice agreed calmly. "It was short-sighted of her to deceive you. Certainly she should've felt comfortable—frankly even obliged—to be forthcoming with you after you told her your own lineage."

"Huh?"

"Obviously a viscount is lower in rank—considerably—from a princess, but she should've had the courtesy to trust you as you trusted her." Delighted by her son's blank face, Alice crossed her booted feet at the ankle. "You did tell her your father is Earl of Brigston—and you are Viscount Brigston."

"It didn't come up," Delaney said, then added with more heat "Why would I?" as his mother simply watched him coolly. "Who remembers anyway? I never use it."

Unless it suits you, Alice thought. But it was enough, she decided, that she'd planted that little seed. "There's your father, back with the ice cream. Let's have some with our coffee."

She gave her son a day, partly because she simply enjoyed him, and partly because she knew he had to chew on things. She debated how she'd tell him she'd been in communication with Camilla's mother.

"He might get his back up all over again," she mused as she cast her line into the pond. "It would be so like him." At her husband's grunt, she turned to where he sat, papers scattered over his lap and the ground. "Pay attention, Niles."

"Hmm? What? Damn it, Alice, I'm working."

"Your son's work."

"Just leave him alone. A man should handle his own affairs without any interference."

"Hah. So you said to me thirty-three years ago this coming winter. Look where it got you."

"Got me you, didn't it?"

She grinned out over the water. Two peas in a pod, she decided. Her men were two very stubborn peas.

Before she could decide how best to handle things, the matter was taken out of her hands. Del swooped through the woods, making enough racket to scare away every fish for ten miles, and scooped her right off her feet.

"We've got new funding."

"Good thing, because we're not getting any fish for dinner." Still she hugged him. "That's wonderful, Del. Who?"

"I don't have the details—just got the call from the university. I've got to get back to the dig. Sorry to run out on you like this."

"Don't be." She tucked her tongue in her cheek. She saw how it would work now. Perfectly. "Give us a call once you're settled."

"Will. Have to pack."

That evening, while her son was—very likely—steaming over the idea that his funding was being generated by the interest and influence of a young princess, Alice sat and composed a tidy and formal note to Her Serene Highness Gabriella de Cordina.

The Earl and Countess of Brigston, along with their son, Lord Delaney, Viscount of Brigston, were very pleased to accept her gracious invitation to the Autumn Ball in Cordina.

"It's insulting." Camilla waved the latest communication from Del. "Rude and insulting and just like him."

Gabriella sat calmly, fixing simple pearls at her ears. Guests who had been invited to stay at the palace for a time before and after the ball, would be arriving shortly. "It sounded perfectly polite and informative to me, darling."

And she found it very telling that in the month she'd been back in Cordina her daughter had lost none of the heat where Delaney Caine was concerned.

"That's because you don't know him," Camilla raged on. "Insufferable is what it is. Reporting to me as if I were some sort of accountant. Dollars and cents, that's all. He doesn't tell me anything about the finds—the things he'd know I'd want to know. And see how he signs them? Dr. Delaney Caine. As if we were strangers. He's detestable."

"So you've said." Gabriella turned on the chair of her dressing table. Her hair was swept back from a face her husband told her grew more lovely with each year.

She didn't believe him, but it was nice to hear. Her eyes, the same tawny gold as her daughter's were quietly sober and showed none of the humor and anticipation she felt.

"I'm sure he's grateful for your help in funding the project, Camilla. You parted on such bad terms, he probably feels awkward as well."

"He should feel awkward. He should feel sorry and small." She whirled around her mother's lovely room. Stared out the window at the stunning view of the gardens, the bright blue sea beyond. "I didn't get the funding for him in any case. I got it for the project. The work's the priority. It's an important find and it deserves to be completed."

And her daughter's interest in the work hadn't waned in the weeks since she'd been back. If anything, Gabriella reflected, it had increased. She'd spent hours with books, had gone to the university to speak to professors who were knowledgeable, had raided their library for more books and documents on archaeology.

She'd neglected none of her duties. It simply wasn't in Camilla's makeup to do so. There were times Gabriella wished she were less dedicated. Even though she'd been worried, she'd been pleased when Camilla had taken those weeks for herself.

Her own heart had hurt when her little girl had come home with hers broken. She was grateful their relationship was such that Camilla had confided in her. About falling in love—and becoming Delaney's lover. It helped a woman, Gabriella knew, to talk to a woman.

And now, though she knew her daughter suffered, part of her rejoiced that Camilla's heart was constant. She was still very much in love. Her mother, with a little help, intended to see she got what she wanted. Even if it meant a little—very little, she assured herself—finagling.

She rose, crossing to her daughter to lay her hands on her shoulders, a kiss on the back of her head. "Love isn't always polite."

"He doesn't love me." Camilla hurt still, sharply. "Mama, he looked at me with such contempt, turned me out of his life with less compassion than you would a stray dog."

And should answer for it, Gabriella thought fiercely. She was counting on her daughter to see that he did. "You weren't honest with him."

"I was trying to be honest with myself. If I was wrong, there still should've been room for... It doesn't matter." She straightened her shoulders. "I have my interests and duties, and he has his. I wish this ball were over and done."

"When it is, you'll go on your first dig. It'll be exciting for you."

"My mind's full of it." Ruthlessly she folded Del's

formal letter, set it aside. As she would, she promised herself, set thoughts of him aside. "Imagine me, studying artifacts from the Lower Paleolithic in France. Dr. Lesuer has been so generous, so forthcoming. I'll enjoy working with his team and learning from him. But now, I'm behind schedule. Sarah Lattimer will be here in a couple hours. I believe I told you about Sarah—the shop keeper from Vermont who was so kind to me?"

"Yes, you did. I'm looking forward to meeting her."

"I want her to have a spectacular time. Aunt Eve's going to give her a tour and she'll have a chance to meet Uncle Alex before the ladies tea tomorrow."

"I need you to greet some of my personal guests with me—the Earl and Countess of Brigston and their son. They should be here within thirty minutes. I'm entertaining them in the Gold Parlor on arrival."

"Yes, I remember." She glanced at her watch. "I don't suppose you could have Adrienne fill in for me."

"Your sister's in the nursery with young Armand and the baby. I won't keep you above fifteen minutes," Gabriella promised.

"I'll be there. I'll just adjust a few things in my schedule." She started out, came back and picked up Del's letter. "I need to have this filed," she murmured, and hurried away.

Exactly twenty-nine minutes later, Camilla dashed down the main staircase. Preparations for the Autumn Ball—and all the events leading up to and following it—were well underway. The *regisseur,* the palace manager, would overlook no details. And should he, her aunt's eagle eye would scope them out.

Her Royal Highness, Princess Eve de Cordina was Chatelaine of the palace, and a woman who stood beside her husband as he ruled the country. But she often had her own opinions about matters of state, and had her own career apart from her royal duties. Her Hamilton Company of players was a world-renowned theatrical group and she was also a respected playwright.

Her example served to remind Camilla that with ambition, work and brains, a woman could do anything. Even be on time—barely—to meet guests when her plate was overfull.

She was nearly at the base of the steps when the man jogging up to her caught her by the shoulders. He was handsome as sin and smelled comfortably of horses.

"What's the hurry?"

"Uncle Bennett. I didn't even know you'd arrived." She kissed her mother's youngest brother on the cheek. "And already visited the stables."

"Bry and Thadd are still out there," he said, referring to his two young sons. "Hannah's around here somewhere. She wanted to talk to Eve. And look at you." He ruffled her short hair. "Very chic."

"How was your trip to England?"

"Successful. I found the perfect mare to breed with my stallion."

"I want to see her and all the rest of you—but later. I'm late."

"What's this about some American who needs a good ass-kicking?"

She rolled her eyes. "You've already seen my father."

"On the way in from the stables. I volunteered to hold his coat."

"I don't think you'll have the chance. I don't see the ass he'd like to kick being within striking distance any time in the near future. *A bientôt.*"

"But—" Puzzled, Bennett watched her dash off. Someone had their information skewed, he mused, then began to smile as he climbed up the steps, hoping to search out his brother and harass him for details.

Knowing Reeve MacGee, Bennett doubted that Camilla's father had the wrong data.

Camilla slowed to a dignified if brisk walk as she moved through the palace. Flowers, fresh and elaborate, speared and spilled out of vases and urns. Her heels clicked efficiently on the sparkling marble floors.

The occasional servant paused to bow or curtsy. She greeted most by name, but continued on. She hated being late.

By the time she made it to the Gold Parlor, she was. By six minutes. Because she heard the low murmur of voices, she took another moment to smooth her skirt, her hair, take a breath and fix a welcoming smile on her face.

When she stepped in, she saw her mother was already seated in one of the conversation areas, pouring tea from one of the Miessen china pots into cups for a middle-aged couple.

The woman caught her attention first. Such an intriguing look, Camilla thought. Lovely in a unique way, and casually disheveled. She wouldn't have called the baggy tweeds fashionable, but they certainly suited the woman.

The man rose as she approached. She started to speak, to apologize for her tardiness in greeting them. Then couldn't speak at all. He was, she thought, stunned, an older and more distinguished version of Del.

She needed to find a way to get the man off her mind, she ordered herself, when she started seeing pieces of him in dashing and dignified English earls.

"Camilla, I'd like to introduce you to the Earl and

Countess of Brigston. Lord and Lady Brigston, my daughter, Her Royal Highness Camilla de Cordina.''

"Lord and Lady Brigston, I apologize for not being here with my mother to welcome you to Cordina. Please, sit and be comfortable. I hope you enjoyed your trip.''

"We're delighted to be here, Your Highness.'' Alice smiled as she curtseyed, then shook hands with Camilla. "As is our son. May I present Lord Delaney, Viscount Brigston.''

Her thoughts whirled as Del moved from the far window and crossed the room toward her. Her heart beat too quickly—first with the sheer joy of seeing him, and then with confusion. And lastly, with anger.

Viscount Brigston, she thought. What was this? How did the American scientist become a British aristocrat? The nerve of him.

She inclined her head, coolly, then lifted her chin. "My Lord," she said in a tone frigid as winter.

"Madam,'' he returned, and with annoyance clear in his eyes, took her offered hand and kissed it.

She got through it. Camilla was too proud, and too innately well mannered not to. But the following thirty minutes were torture. She held up her part in conversation. Which was more, she thought darkly, than Del managed. He barely grumbled monosyllables, and only when directly addressed.

Why did he have to look so big and handsome and *male?* The suit and tie should have dwarfed him somehow, or tamed him by a few degrees. It did neither.

"My son,'' Alice said at one point, "is delighted and grateful for your assistance in funding the Bardville Project, madam. Isn't that right, Del?''

He shifted in his chair. "I've relayed my appreciation, and the team's, to Her Highness via letters and reports."

"Yes, I received one of your...letters just this morning, Lord Delaney." Camilla smiled with her eyes frosted. "How odd you didn't mention you'd be traveling, and so soon, to Cordina."

He wouldn't have been here if he'd had any choice, he thought. His mother had hounded him like a she-wolf and all but dragged him to the plane by his ear. "I wasn't entirely sure my schedule would permit the trip."

"We're so pleased it did," Gabriella broke in, warned by the battle-light in her daughter's eyes. When Camilla's temper rose too high, her tongue could be lethal. And rash. "So that we can, in some small way, repay you for the hospitality you offered Camilla in your home in Vermont. A lovely part of America, I'm told. I regret never having seen it for myself."

It was a toss-up, Gabriella decided, who looked more shocked by her easy mention of their prior relationship, the princess or the viscount.

Both gaped at her while she sipped her tea. She thought—was nearly certain—she heard the countess muffle a squeak of laughter.

Now, she would see how long the two of them could manage to continue to behave like polite strangers.

"Camilla has developed a keen interest in your field, my lord," Gabriella continued. "It's always rewarding for a mother to see her child so enthusiastic."

"And equally rewarding for a child to entertain her mother," Camilla said with a perfectly pleasant smile—one with an edge only her mother could see. "What an...interesting surprise for you to have invited Lord Delaney and his parents without mentioning the plans to me."

"I hoped it would be, and that you'd be pleased to offer Cordinian hospitality." It was said lightly, but with underlying firmness.

"Of course. Nothing could please me more than repaying Lord Delaney for...everything."

"I'm sure you'd like to rest a bit after your journey," Gabriella said to Niles and Alice as she rose. "Camilla, perhaps you could show Lord Delaney the gardens."

"I'm not—" Del began, then ground his teeth at his mother's killing glare. "I wouldn't want to put you out."

"It's no trouble at all." Gabriella laid a hand, a heavy one, on Camilla's shoulder as she passed.

Trapped, Camilla got to her feet, braced herself as her mother breezily led Del's parents away then turned to face him. "First, let me make it perfectly clear that I had no idea you would be here, and if I had I would have done everything possible to be absent from this welcoming party."

"That's clear. If I could've gotten out of making this trip, I would have. Believe me."

"Second," she continued in the same cool and mannered tone, "I have no more desire to show you the gardens than you have to see them. However, I've less desire to distress my mother or your parents. Ten minutes should do it. I'm sure we can tolerate each other for that length of time. My Lord," she said in a hiss.

"Don't start on me." He rose as well, then found himself talking to her back as she strode to the terrace doors on the other side of the room.

When she sailed out, he jammed his hands into his pockets and followed. It was going to be, he thought, a very long four days.

Chapter 10

In the third floor guest wing, Alice paused at the entrance to the suite of rooms they'd been given for their stay in Cordina.

It was time, she decided, to test her impressions and instincts regarding Gabriella de Cordina.

"I wonder, ma'am, if I might have a moment of your time. In private."

"Of course." Gabriella had been calculating her options and considering how best to handle her guest since she'd first set eyes on the woman. In her opinion, Alice Caine preferred the direct approach. And so, when possible, did she. "We'll use my sitting room. It's very comfortable, very private."

As she led Alice through the palace, to the family quarters, she spoke of the history of the building, the art collection. She kept up the polite tour chatter until they were comfortably behind closed doors in her elegant rose and blue sitting room.

"May I offer you some refreshment, Lady Brigston?"

"No, ma'am, thank you." Alice took a seat, folded her hands. "We are, obviously, both aware of the relationship between our children, and the unfortunate way that relationship was left late last summer," she began.

"Yes. Your son was very kind to provide my daughter with shelter."

"I beg your pardon, but that's nonsense. He didn't do it out of kindness, or at least only partially. He isn't unkind, he's just boneheaded."

Gabriella sat back. "Lady Brigston...Alice," she responded warmly, pleased that her judgment about the woman had been on target. "I wasn't certain I was doing the right thing for Camilla by inviting your family—and by not telling her of the invitation or about your son's title. It was self-serving of me. I wanted to give her time to search her heart, and I wanted to gauge her reaction for myself when she saw your son again. The minute I did, I knew I'd done the right thing after all."

"You saw the way they looked at each other—well, before their backs went up."

"Yes, I did. They love each other, and they're both letting pride get in the way."

"It's more than pride with Del. He's so much like his father. Toss him some old bones, and he can give you chapter and verse on the woman who owned them three thousand years ago. Give him a flesh and blood female, and he's clueless. It's not that he's stupid, ma'am—"

"Brie," Gabriella interrupted.

Alice took a breath, settled more comfortably in the chair. Like her son, she knew the formalities of protocol—and like her son found them mildly foolish. She was glad

Her Serene Highness felt the same way. "Brie. He's not stupid. He's just a Caine. Through and through."

"I don't like to interfere in the lives of my children," Gabriella began.

"Neither do I. Technically."

They said nothing for a moment, then both began to smile. "Why don't we have a small glass of brandy," Gabriella suggested.

It helped, Alice thought, when you could see the woman your son loved in her mother's eyes. And you liked them both. "Oh, why don't we?"

Pleased, Gabriella rose to fetch the decanter and pour the snifters herself. "I do have an idea, which while not— technically—interfering, may help things along a bit. My sons would call it double-teaming."

"I'm all ears."

Ten minutes later, Alice nodded. "I like your style. Good thing, since we're going to be in-laws." She glanced toward the window when she heard raised voices. "That's Del—booms like a bull when he's mad."

They rose together, moved out to the balcony. In tune they linked arms as they looked down on their children. "They're arguing," Gabriella said with emotion thickening her voice.

"It's great, isn't it?"

"We shouldn't eavesdrop."

"We're just standing here, taking some air. We can't help it if they're shouting at each other."

"I suppose not."

Even as she inched out a bit more, Gabriella heard her sitting room door open and slam shut.

"Is that jackass Caine here yet?"

Mortified, Gabriella closed her eyes, then turned back

is her husband came to the open doorway. "Reeve," she murmured.

"You must be Camilla's father." Delighted, Alice stepped forward, pumped his hand. "I'm the jackass's mother. We were just pretending not to eavesdrop while they yell at each other in the garden. Care to join us?"

He stared, a tall man with silver shot black hair, as his wife began to laugh helplessly. "Well, hell," was all he said.

She hadn't intended to argue. In fact, Camilla had ordered herself not to rise to any bait he might cast. The jackass. She swept him along garden paths as if they were on a forced march, and took none of the pleasure she normally did in the scents, the textures, the charm.

"We're particularly proud of our rose garden. There are more than fifty varieties represented, including the climbing specimens trained on the fifteen arbors in what is called *La Promenade de Rose*. The less formal beds at the far edges add charm, I think, to elegance."

"I don't give a hang about the roses."

"Very well, we'll continue on to the walled garden. It's a particularly lovely spot where—"

"Let's just cut it out." He took her arm, pulled her around.

"I have not given you leave to touch me, sir."

"Tell that to somebody who hasn't seen you naked."

Her color came up—fire under cream—but her voice remained cold. "Nor do I care to be reminded of my previous poor judgment."

"Is that what it comes down to, poor judgment on your part?"

"You're the one who ended it."

"You're the one who took off."

"You told me to go!"

"Like you ever listened to a damn thing I said. If you'd been honest with me from the beginning—"

"You dare?" Incensed, she yanked her arm free. "Honesty, *Lord* Delaney?"

He had the grace to flush. "That has nothing to do with anything. I didn't tell you I had chicken pox when I was ten, either, and it's just as relevant."

"Your title is hardly a rash."

"It's just a title, something I inherited from my father. It doesn't—"

"Ah! Titles, lineages, don't count when they're yours, only when their mine. You asinine jerk."

"Just watch it. Just watch it," he ordered. "It's not the same, and you know it. I don't think of myself that way. I don't use the damn thing, and don't remember it's there half the time. I don't live in a palace and—"

"Neither do I! I live on a farm! This is my uncle's home. You say you don't think of your title half the time. I have no choice but to think of mine every day—with every public move, and most private ones. I wanted time, a little time to live as you live, to have what you take for granted. Freedom. So I took it," she said passionately. "Right or wrong, I took what I needed because I was afraid I might…"

"Afraid of what?"

"It doesn't matter now. It's no longer an issue. We'll consider it bad luck all around that I ended up where I ended up during that storm."

She drew herself in. "Now, I won't embarrass my uncle or the rest of my family by arguing with one of his guests, however insufferable. While you're here, I suggest we do our best to stay out of each other's way.'' She turned her back on him. "I have nothing more to say to you.''

"Some hospitality—Cordinian style.''

Shocked to the bone, she whirled back. "My mother—'' she nearly choked. "My mother offered you and your family an invitation to our country, to her brother's home. You will receive every courtesy—publicly—from my family and from me. In private…'' What hissed through her teeth was an insult more usually heard in a French gutter than a palace garden. Del only raised his eyebrows.

"Nice mouth, Your Highness.''

"And now, there is nothing more to be said between us.''

"I've got plenty to say to you, sister.''

His tone, the term, made sentimental tears want to rise in her throat. Turning her back on him, she did what she could to force them back. "Sir, you are dismissed.''

"Oh, stuff a sock in it.'' Out of patience, he spun her back around. Then froze when he saw the sparkle of tears. "What are you doing? Stop that. If you think you're going to pull out the waterworks to make me feel like a heel, think again.''

He took a deliberate step back from her as he searched his pockets. "Look, God. I don't have a handkerchief, so snuffle it back.''

"Go away.'' She was no less appalled than he when a tear spilled over. "Go inside, go back to America, or go to hell. But go away.''

"Camilla.'' Undone, he stepped toward her again.

"Your Highness.'' Formal in company, and avidly curious, Marian stepped onto the garden path. "I beg your pardon, but Miss Lattimer has arrived. She's been shown to her rooms.''

"Sarah?" Surprised, Del stared at Camilla. "You invited Sarah to the palace."

"Yes. I'll be right in, Marian. Thank you. If you'd please show Lord Delaney to his rooms, or anywhere else he'd like to go? Please excuse me, My Lord."

"My Lord?" Marian studied him carefully when Camilla walked quickly away. She was torn between wanting to level him for hurting her dearest friend, and sighing with sympathy over the misery so plain on his face. "May I show you the rest of the gardens?"

"No, thanks. Unless you've got a handy pond or fountain I can soak my head in."

Marian only smiled. "I'm sure we can accommodate you."

He wondered if he'd be doing everyone a favor if he did leave. His mother would be furious, his father baffled. And they would both be embarrassed, but Camilla would, obviously, be relieved.

And he wouldn't have to see her, look at her and try not to remember how she'd looked wearing jeans and a T-shirt while she fried up eggs. Not that she looked anything like that now.

She was polished and sparkling and elegant as the diamonds he'd seen winking at her ears. And just, he tried to convince himself, as cold.

But it occurred to him that he couldn't let her chase him off—the way he'd chased her. He'd stay, if for no other reason than to prove to her what spine was.

It wasn't hard not to get in her way. The palace was a far cry from a five-room cabin in the Vermont woods.

And he couldn't claim not to be enjoying himself, on some level. He liked her brothers, her cousins. It was like watching a pack of handsome, elegant wolves run just short of wild.

As an only child, he'd never been exposed to big, boisterous families. Which, he soon discovered, was what they were under the titles and polish. A family. Closely knit enough that he had trouble remembering who was sibling, who was cousin.

Several of them talked him into going down to the stables—and a hell of a horse palace it was. The minute they discovered he could ride, he was mounted up.

That was how he met Alexander, Cordina's ruler, and his brother, Prince Bennett, Camilla's uncles. And her father, Reeve MacGee.

"Sir." One of the young men—he thought it was Dorian—grinned and made formal introductions.

Del shifted in the saddle. He'd been taught, of course, but months—years—passed without him needing the protocol. He didn't like having to dig it up—and cared less for the sensation of being dissected by three pair of coolly measuring eyes.

"Welcome to Cordina, Lord Brigston," Alex said in a smooth, faintly aloof voice. "And my home."

"Thank you, sir." Del managed what passed for a bow while mounted on a skittish horse.

"We're pleased to have you, and to repay you in some way for the hospitality you showed my niece." There was a subtle and keen edge under the courtesy. Alex made certain of it.

"That horse wants a run," Bennett said because he felt a tug of sympathy. Poor bastard, he thought. Outnumbered. "You look like you can handle him."

Del felt the quick slice of Alex's words—like a nick from a honed fencing sword. He preferred shifting his gaze to the more friendly brother. "He's a beauty."

"We'll let you enjoy your ride. I'd be interested to speak with you regarding your work," Alexander added. "As it's become so much a passion of Princess Camilla's."

"At your convenience, sir."

Alex nodded, then continued to walk his mount toward the stables. After a glance of some pity, Bennett followed behind him. Reeve turned his mount until he was side by side with Del.

"You," he said, pointing at his sons, his nephews. "Take off." Then, turning to Del, he continued, "It's time you and I had a little chat," he said as the echo of hooves faded in the race up the hill. "I'm wondering if you can come up with a good reason why I shouldn't just snap your neck."

Well, Del thought, at least there was no need for protocol and politics now. The man looked like he could give the neck-snapping a good shot. He was fit, broadshouldered, and his hands appeared to be rough and ready.

And he looked to Del more like a soldier than any farmer he'd ever come across.

"I doubt it," Del decided. "You want to do it here, or somewhere more secluded where you can dump me in a shallow grave?"

Reeve's smile was thin. "Let's take a ride. You make a habit out of taking stray young women into your house, Caine?"

"No. She was the first. I can promise she'll be the last."

The day was warm, but breezy. Del hated the fact that he was sweating. The man had eyes like lasers.

"You want me to believe you took her in out of the goodness of your heart. You had no idea who she was— even though her face is plastered on magazine covers, in newspapers, on television screens all over the world. You had no intention of exploiting her, of using her influence for your own gain. Or of trading off the press with stories about how you took her to bed."

"Just a damn minute." Del reined to a stop, and now it was his gaze that bored heat. "I don't use women. I sure as hell couldn't have used her if I'd tried because she'd have kicked me in the teeth for it. I don't have time for gossip magazines or television, and I wasn't expecting to find some runaway princess stranded on the side of the road in a storm. She said she was low on funds so I gave her a place to stay and a job. I didn't ask her a lot of questions or pay much attention."

"Well, enough attention, apparently, to take her to bed."

"That's right. And that's nobody's business but ours. You want to kick my ass over that, you go ahead. But you start accusing me of taking what we had between us and turning it into some cheap splash for the media, I'm kicking yours right back."

Right answer, Reeve thought. Exactly right. He shifted in the saddle. The boy had guts, he decided, pleased. But that was no reason not to torture him. "What are your intentions toward my daughter?"

The angry flush faded until Del was sheet pale. "My— my— What?"

"You heard the question, son. Roll your tongue back in your mouth and answer it."

"I don't have any. She won't even speak to me. I'm staying out of her way."

"Just when I was beginning to think you weren't a complete jackass after all." Reeve swung his mount around again. "Give that horse a good gallop," he advised. "And don't fall off and break your stiff neck."

As he rode back to the stables, Reeve thought the conversation might not have been precisely what his wife had meant when she'd asked him to have a man-to-man talk with Del. But it had certainly been satisfying.

Camilla would have enjoyed a good gallop herself. But the ladies' tea required her attention and her presence. As the weather was fine, the party was spread over the south terrace and the rose garden so that guests could enjoy the views of the Mediterranean and the fragrance of flowers.

Her aunt had opted for casual elegance so the pretty tables were covered with warm peach cloths and set with glass dishes of deep cobalt. More flowers, cheerful tropical blooms, spilled out of shallow bowls while white-coated staff poured flutes of champagne as well as cups of tea. Each lady was presented with a silver compact etched with the royal seal.

A harpist plucked strings quietly in the shade of an arbor tumbled with white roses.

Her aunt Eve, Camilla thought, knew how to set her stage.

Women in floaty dresses wandered the garden or gathered in groups. Knowing her duty, Camilla moved through the guests while she nursed a single glass of champagne. She smiled, exchanged pleasantries, chatted, and shoved all thoughts of Del into a corner of her mind, then ruthlessly locked it.

"I've barely had a moment with you." Eve slid an arm through Camilla's and drew her aside.

She was a small woman with a lovely tumble of raven hair that provided a exquisite frame for her diamond-shaped face. Her eyes, a deep and bold blue, sparkled as she nudged Camilla toward the terrace wall.

"Not enough time now," she said in a voice that still carried a hint of her native Texas drawl, "but later I want to hear about your adventure. Every little detail."

"Mother's already told you."

"Of course." With a laugh, Eve kissed Camilla's cheek. Gabriella had done more then tell her—she had enlisted Eve's help in the matter of prying and poking. "But that's secondhand information. I like going to the source."

"I've been waiting for Uncle Alex to call me out on the carpet."

Eve lifted an eyebrow. "That worries you?"

"I hate upsetting him."

"If I worried about that, I'd spend my life biting my nails." Lips pursed, Eve glanced at her perfect manicure. "Nope. He has to be what he is," she added more soberly, and looked out to the sea that lay blue against the edges of her adopted country. "So much responsibility. He was born for it—and bred for it. As you've been, honey. But he trusts you—completely. And he's very interested in your young man."

"He's not my young man."

"Ah. Well." She remembered, very well, when she'd tried to convince herself Alex, heir to Cordina, wasn't hers. "Let's say he's interested in Lord Delaney's work— and your interest in that work."

"Aunt Chris was a tremendous help," Camilla added,

glancing over toward Eve's older sister. She wasn't technically Camilla's aunt, but their family was a very inclusive one.

"Nothing she likes better than a good campaign. That comes from marrying the Gentleman from Texas. The senator was very pleased to discuss the Bardville Research Project with his associates in Florida."

"After Aunt Chris talked him into it, and I'm very grateful to her. She looks wonderful, by the way."

"Like a newlywed," Eve agreed. "After five years of marriage. She always said she was holding out for the perfect man. I'm glad she found him. Whether it takes fifty years or five minutes," she said, giving Camilla's hand a quick squeeze, "when it's right, you know it. And when you know it and you're smart, you don't take no for an answer. Something like that is worth fighting for. Well, back to work."

Camilla stopped by the tables, found a precious three minutes to speak with her young cousin Marissa. She watched her sister, Adrienne, sit and with apparently good cheer, talk with an elderly Italian countess who was deaf as a post.

Hannah, her uncle Bennett's wife, gestured her over to a shady table where she sat enjoying tea and scones with Del's mother.

"Lady Brigston and I have a number of mutual acquaintances," Hannah explained. "I've been badgering her about her work, and now I'm dreaming about running off to dig for dinosaur bones."

There had been a time when, as a British agent, adventure had been Hannah's lifework. But as a princess, and mother of two active sons, she'd traded one kind of adventure for another.

As an agent, she'd had to deliberately downplay her looks and bury her love of fashion, now she could indulge them. Her dark blond hair was sleeked back in a twist. Her sleeveless tea dress showed off athletic arms and was the same vivid green as her eyes.

"I'd like that myself." Smiling, Camilla obeyed Hannah's signal and sat. "Though I imagine it's hard, tedious work. You must love it," she said to Alice.

"It's what I always wanted to do—even as a child. Other girls collected dolls. I collected fossils."

"It's so rewarding," Camilla commented, "to know, always, what you want, and be able to work toward it."

"Indeed." Alice inclined her head. "And tremendously exciting, I'd think, to discover an advocation along the way—and work toward it."

"Oh. Would you excuse me a moment?" Recognizing her cue, Hannah rose. "I need to speak with Mrs. Cartwright." She exchanged a quick and telling look with Alice—and got out of the way.

"Your family, if I may say so, Your Highness, is wonderful."

"Thank you. I agree with you."

"I'm, as a rule, more comfortable in the company of men. Simply don't have much in common with females. So fussy about the oddest things, to my mind."

The hand she waved had nails that were short and unpainted. She wore only a simple gold band on her ring finger. "But I feel very much at home with your mother, your aunts," she went on. "It's no wonder I'm already so fond of you."

"Thank you," Camilla said again, a little flustered. "That's very kind."

"Are you very angry with my son?"

"I—"

"Not that I blame you," Alice went on before Camilla could formulate a diplomatic answer. "He can be such a...what's the word I'm looking for? Oh, yes. Bonehead. Such a bonehead. He gets it from his father, so he really can't help it. He must've given you a terrible time."

"No. Not at all."

"No need to be tactful." She patted Camilla's hand. "It's just we two, and I know my boy in and out. Terrible manners—partially my fault, I can't deny it. I never was one to bother about the niceties. Outrageous temper— that's his father's—always booming around. Forgets why half the time after the explosion—which is annoying and frustrating to the other party. Don't you think?"

"Yes—" With a half laugh, Camilla shook her head. "Lady Brigston, you're putting me in an awkward position. Let me say I admire your son's work—his approach to it and his passion for it. On a personal level, we have what you might call a conflict in styles."

"You have been well raised, haven't you?" Gabrielle had warned her it wouldn't be easy to chip through the composure. "Do you mind if I tell you a little story? There was once a young American girl, barely twenty-one with her college degree hot in her hand. She had a fire in her belly, one burning ambition. Paleontology. Most thought her mad," she added with a twinkle. "After all, what was a young woman doing fiddling around with dinosaur bones? She wheedled her way onto a dig—this particular dig because the man in charge was someone who's work—his approach to it and his passion for it— she admired."

She paused, smiled and sipped her tea. "She read his books, read articles on or by him. He was, to her, a great hero. Imagine her reaction when he turned out to be this big, irritable, impatient man who barely acknowledged her existence—and then mostly to complain about it.''

"He is like his father," Camilla murmured.

"Oh, the spitting image," Alice acknowledged with some pride. "They sniped at each other, this rude man and this brash young woman. She did most of the sniping as he was so thickheaded most of her best shots just bounced off his skull. It was utterly infuriating.''

"Yes," Camilla said almost to herself. "Infuriating."

"He was fascinating. So brilliant, so handsome, so—apparently—disinterested in her. Though he began to soften, just a little, toward her as she was damn good at the work and had a sharp, seeking mind. Caine men admire a sharp, seeking mind.''

"Apparently."

"She fell madly in love with him, and after getting over being annoyed with herself over that, she put that sharp mind to work. She pursued him, which flustered him. He found all manner of reasons why this shouldn't be. He was fifteen years older, he didn't have time for females and so on. She had a few quibbles herself. This Earl of Brigston business just didn't fit into her Yankee system very well. It might have discouraged her, but she was stubborn—and she knew, in her heart, he had feelings for her. And since the title came with the man, and she wanted the man, she decided she could live with it. So what could she do but seduce him?''

Because Alice looked at Camilla for agreement, Camilla nodded obediently. "Naturally."

"He stammered and stuttered and looked, for a delightful few moments, like a panicked horse caught in a stable fire. But she had her way with him. And three weeks later, they were married. It seems to be working out well,'' she added with a little smile.

''She was an admirable young woman.''

''Yes, she was. And she gave birth to an admirable, if knot-headed son. Do you love him?''

''Lady Brigston—''

''Oh, please, call me Alice. I look at you, and I see a young woman, so bright, so fresh, so unhappy. I know my place, but I'm looking at Camilla, not Her Royal Highness.''

''He sees the title, and forgets the woman who holds it.''

''If you want him, don't let him forget. You put flowers in his house,'' she said, quietly now. ''I never remember to do that sort of thing myself. You know he kept them, after you'd gone.''

Tears swam into her eyes. ''He just didn't notice them.''

''Yes. He did. Part of him wants to step away from you and bury himself in his work again. I imagine both of you—being strong, capable young people—will do very well if you go your separate ways. But I wonder what the two of you might do, might make, if you break through this barrier of pride and hurt and come together. Don't you?''

Yes, Camilla thought. Constantly. ''I told him I loved him,'' she murmured, ''and he turned me away.''

With a hiss of breath, Alice sat back. ''What an ass. Well then, I have one piece of advice. Camilla. Make him crawl a little—it'll be good for him—before he tells you the same. I have no doubt you can manage it.''

* * *

Del suffered through a formal, and to his mind interminable, dinner party. He was seated between the deaf Italian countess and Camilla's sister, Adrienne. The single advantage was that Camilla's father was seated well across the enormous dining room.

It would, he decided, be more difficult for her dad to stab him with his dinner knife that way.

By the time the main course was served, he'd reversed his initial impression of Adrienne as a vapid if ornamental girl. She was, he realized, simply an incredibly sweet-natured woman who was both blissfully happy and quietly charming.

Her help with the countess saved his sanity. And when Adrienne glanced at him, a quick sparkle in her eyes, he saw some of Camilla's sly humor.

He found himself telling her about some of his work as she asked questions specifically designed to encourage it. It didn't occur to him until later that her talent was in drawing people out.

"No wonder Camilla's so fascinated." Adrienne smiled. She had, he'd noted, her mother's soothing voice and her father's sizzling blue eyes. "She always enjoyed puzzles—and that's your work, really, isn't it? A complex puzzle. I was never very good at them. Will you go back to Florida soon?"

"Yes, very soon." He shouldn't be here at all, he told himself.

"When my children are a bit older, we'll take them there. To Disney World." She looked across the table at her husband.

It was that look he'd think of later as well. The sheer

contentment in it. The look that had been missing from Camilla's face, he thought, except for the briefest of times.

It had been there. He remembered it being there, when she'd stretched out on the bank of his pond. *Camilla Content,* he'd called her. And then she'd been gone.

Chapter 11

For a princess she worked like a horse. It made it difficult for a man to manage five minutes alone with her to apologize.

Del wasn't sure exactly what he was apologizing for, but he was beginning to think she had one coming.

Guilt—a taste he didn't care for—had been stuck in his throat since he'd seen that tear run down her cheek. Adding to it were various members of her family who were so bloody friendly, or gracious—or both at the same time—he was beginning to feel like a jackass.

Even her mother had cornered him. If that was an acceptable definition of being taken gently aside to be given a warm and graceful expression of her gratitude for opening his home to her daughter.

"I know she's a grown woman," Gabriella said as she stood with him on a rise overlooking the gem-blue waters of the Mediterranean. "And a capable one. But I'm a mother, and we tend to worry."

"Yes, madam." He agreed, though he'd never consid
ered his mother much of a worrier.

"I worried less when I knew she was with someone
trustworthy and kind—who she obviously respected."
Gabriella continued to smile, even when he—quite visi
bly—winced. "I'd been concerned about her for some
time."

"Concerned?"

"She'd been working too hard for too long. Since the
death of my father, and her own blossoming, you could
say, there have been more demands on her time, her en
ergies."

"Your daughter has considerable energy."

"Yes, as a rule. I'm afraid she's been more exposed to
the appetites of the media in the last year or two than
anyone could be prepared for."

Could he understand? Gabriella wondered. Could any
one who hadn't lived it? She hoped he could.

"She's lovely, as you know, and vibrant—as well as
the oldest female of her generation of the family. The
media's pursuit of her has been voracious, and I'm afraid
it cost her, emotionally. Even physically. I know what it's
like. I used to slip away myself. There are times the need
to be away, even from something dear to your heart, is
overwhelming. Don't you think?"

"Yes. I have Vermont."

Her face went soft, and bright. Yes, she thought, he
could understand. "And I had my little farm. Until, I
think, very recently, Camilla hadn't found her place to be
away. To be quiet, even if it was just inside her mind.
Thank you." She rose up and kissed his cheek. "Thank
you for helping her find it."

He might have felt lower, Del thought when the

parted, if he crawled on his belly and left a slimy trail behind him.

He had to talk to Camilla. Reasonably. Rationally. There were questions now, and he wanted them answered. It seemed only right a man should have some answers before he did that crawling.

But every time he made some subtle inquiry about her, he was told she was in a meeting, taking an appointment, engaged with her personal assistant.

He wanted to think all this meant manicures or shopping or whatnot, until Adrienne corrected him. "I'm sorry, were you looking for Camilla?"

"No." It felt awkward lying to that soft, pretty smile. "Not exactly, madam. I haven't seen her this morning."

Adrienne cuddled her baby daughter. "She's doing double duty, I'm afraid. My oldest isn't feeling quite well, and I don't like to leave him. She's filling in for me at the hospital. I was scheduled to visit the pediatric ward, but with little Armand so fussy, I wanted to be close."

"Ah…I hope he's all right."

"He's napping now, and seems much better. I thought I'd bring the baby out for some sunshine before I went back up to check on him. But Camilla should be back in an hour. No," she corrected. "She has an appointment with Mama regarding the Art Center afterward. I know she normally deals with correspondence midafternoon, though where she'll find the time today is beyond me."

She kept the soft smile on her face and the delighted laughter inside. The poor man, she thought, was so frustrated. And so in love with her sister.

"Is there something I can do for you?"

"No. No, madam, thank you."

"I believe Dorian escaped down to the stables," she

said kindly. "Several of the guests are making use of the horses, if you'd like to join them."

He didn't, but wished he had when he was summoned by Prince Alexander.

"Lord Brigston, I hope you haven't been neglected since your arrival."

"Not at all, Your Highness."

The office reflected the man, Del thought. Both were elegant, male and polished by tradition. The prince exuded power along with dignity. His hair was black as night and threaded with silver. His aristocratic face was honed to sharp angles. Dark, his eyes were equally sharp and very direct.

"Since the Princess Camilla has expressed such a keen interest, I've studied some of your work. My family's interests," he said in a tone smooth as a polished dagger "are mine. Tell me more about this current project of yours."

Though he resented being made to feel like a student auditioning, Del obliged. He understood perfectly, and knew he was meant to understand, that he was being measured and judged.

When, in twenty minutes, he was graciously dismissed Del wasn't certain if he'd passed the audition or if he should keep a wary eye out for the executioner.

But he did know the back of his neck prickled as the image of an ax poised above it hovered in his mind.

Any man, he decided, who considered—however remotely considered—becoming involved with a member of the royal family of Cordina needed his head examined While it was still safely on his shoulders.

Del had always considered himself perfectly sane.

To stay that way, he decided to escape for a couple of

hours. It wasn't a simple matter. A man couldn't just call a damn cab to come pick him up at the palace. There was procedure, protocol, policy. In the end, Camilla's older brother Kristian casually offered him the use of a car—and a driver if he liked.

Del took the car and skipped the driver.

And came as close to falling in love with a place not his own as he'd ever in his life.

There was something stunning about it—the tiny country on the sea. It made him think of jewels—old and precious ones passed down from generation to generation.

The land rose in tiers of hills from the lap of the sea. Houses, pink and white and dull gold tumbled up and down those rises, jutted out on the promontory, as if they'd been carved there. Flowers—he'd been paying more attention to them since Camilla—grew in abundance and with such a free and casual air they added immense charm to the drama of rock and cliff. The fronds of regal palms fluttered in a constant balmy breeze.

The sense of age appealed to him. Generation by generation, century by century, this small gem had survived and gleamed, and clung to its heart without giving way to the frenzied rush of urbanity, without exploiting its vast and staggering views with skyscrapers.

He imagined it had changed here and there over time. No place remained the same, and that was the beauty of man. And when man had wisdom along with invention, he managed to find a way to preserve the heart while feeding the mind.

The Bissets, who had ruled here for four centuries, had obviously been wise.

He stopped on the drive back, along the winding, rising road, to study the place of princes. It was only just, he supposed, that the palace stood on the highest point. It faced the sea, its white stones rising from the cliff. It spread, even rambled with its battlements, its parapets and towers harking proudly back to another age. Another time.

Wars, he thought, and royalty. Historic bedfellows.

Even in modern times a small, ugly little war had been fought here. When he'd been a boy a self-styled terrorist had attempted to assassinate members of the royal family. Camilla's mother had been kidnapped. Her aunt, then simply Eve Hamilton, had been shot.

He realized now that he hadn't considered that, or how such a history so close to the heart could and did affect Camilla.

Still, she hadn't let it stop her from striking out on her own, alone, he thought now. It didn't stop her from coming back here, to the castle on the hill, and taking up her family duties.

The country, the family, was at peace now. But peace was a fragile thing.

He imagined those who lived inside understood the palace had been built for defense. And his archaeologist's eye could see how cagey the design. There could be no attack from the sea, no force that could breech the sheer rock walls of the cliffs. And the height, the hills made it all but impregnable.

Its port made it rich.

It had also been built for beauty. He considered the quest for beauty a very human need.

Standing where he was, he wouldn't have thought of it as a home, but only as a symbol. But he had been inside, beyond those iron gates. However powerful, or symbolic, or aesthetically potent, it was a home.

Perhaps she lived a part of her life on a farm in Virginia, but this place, this palace, this country, was very much her home.

It had to be obvious to both of them that it couldn't be his.

When he drove back through the gates, passed the bold red uniforms of the palace guards, a cloud of depression came with him.

"He's in a horrible mood," Alice confided to Gabriella when they stole five minutes in the music room. They huddled close, as conspirators should. "Apparently he went out for a drive and came back brooding and snarly. It's a good sign."

"Camilla's been distracted and out of sorts all afternoon. It's going perfectly. Oh, and my spies tell me Delaney asked about her several times this morning."

"The best thing was her being so busy and unavailable. Give that boy time to think."

"He won't be able to think when he sees her tonight. Oh, Alice, she looks so beautiful in her gown. I was at her last fitting, and she's just spectacular."

"They're going to make us beautiful grandchildren," Alice said with a sigh.

He didn't like wearing black tie. There were so many pieces to it, why a man needed all those pieces where a shirt and pants did the job was beyond him.

But he'd made up his mind to leave in the morning, so that was something. He'd already come up with the necessary excuse for his early departure—an urgent e-mail from the site.

No one would know the difference.

He'd fulfill his obligation tonight—for his parents—

find a way to apologize or at least come to terms with Camilla. And then get back to reality as soon as possible. He wasn't a man for palaces. Digging under one maybe— now that could be interesting.

All he had to do was survive the sticky formality of one more evening. He was sure he could manage to slip out early from that event as well. In the morning, he'd pay his respects to his hosts, then get the hell out of Dodge.

Only one little chore had to be done first. He had to— in all good conscience—express his appreciation for the help in funding to Camilla. Face-to-face, and without the stiffness he'd fallen back on in correspondence.

That had been small of him and unworthy of her gesture.

Dressed, and wanting nothing more than to get the entire ordeal over with, he joined his parents in their sitting room.

"Well, hell, look at you." It was a rare event to see his mother elegantly attired. He grinned, circling his finger so that she turned. The simple black gown showed off her trim, athletic figure, and the Brigston pearls added panache.

"You're a babe," he decided and made her laugh.

"I figure I can stand these shoes for about an hour and a half, after that, it's anybody's guess." She walked over to straighten her husband's formal tie.

"Don't fuss, Alice. I'm getting rid of the damn thing at the first opportunity." Still Niles smiled as he leaned down to kiss her cheek. "But the boy's right. You are a babe."

"This 'do' will be crawling with babes. Speaking of

which," Alice said casually to her son, "have you seen Camilla today?"

"No."

"Ah, well. You'll see her tonight."

"Right." With hundreds of people around, he thought. How the hell would he manage to say what he had to say—once he figured out what that was—when they were surrounded? "Let's get this over with," Del suggested.

"God. Just like your father." Resigned, Alice took each of her men by the arm.

Guests were formally announced, then escorted to the receiving line. The bows and curtsies went on endlessly in Del's estimation. Then he got his first look at Camilla, and forgot everything else.

She wore a gown the same tawny gold as her eyes. In it, she was iridescent. Luminous. It left her shoulders bare, nipped in to a tiny waist, then simply flowed out with what seemed like miles of skirt that shimmered like sun-drenched water in the elegant light of countless chandeliers.

White and yellow diamonds sparkled at her ears, dripped in complex tiers toward the swell of her breast. And fired in the tiara set on the glossy cap of her hair.

She was, in that moment, the embodiment of the fairy-tale princess. Beauty, grace and elegance, and all of them bone-deep.

He had never felt so much the frog.

But he thought—hoped—he'd managed to roll his eyes back into his head by the time he reached her.

"My Lord."

"Madam." He took the hand she offered, sliding his thumb over her knuckles. Had this woman actually scram-

bled eggs for him? If this was reality, maybe all the rest
had been some complex fantasy.

"I hope you'll enjoy your evening."

"I wasn't planning on it."

Her polite smile never wavered. "Then I hope you
don't find it overly tedious."

"I need five minutes," he murmured.

"I'm afraid this is an inconvenient time. Let go of my
hand," she said in an undertone as his grip tightened.
"People are watching."

"Five minutes," he said again and their eyes locked,
then he reluctantly moved up the line.

Her heart might have raced, but she continued to stand,
smile and greet guests. The combination of willpower and
breeding stopped her from giving into the towering urge
to crane her neck and find Del in the crowd moving into
the ballroom. Curiosity pierced with a splinter of hope
made her almost ill by the time her aunt and uncle opened
Cordina's Autumn Ball.

He'd looked at her—hadn't he—as he had at odd moments in the cabin. As if she were the center of his
thoughts.

But, as she and her cousin Luc crossed the floor for
their first dance, she had no time for private thoughts.

When the palace opened its doors for a ball, it opened
them wide and with brilliant ceremony. Glamour was allowed full sway here and given the satin edge of pomp.
Waterfalls of chandeliers showered light on dazzling
gowns, glittering jewels, banks of sumptuous flowers.
Frothy champagne bubbled in crystal.

On the terrace beyond there was the seductive glow of
candles and torchères. Hundreds of antique mirrors lined

the walls and threw back reflection after reflection of gorgeously gowned women and elegantly garbed men as they spun around the polished floor.

Jewels flashed, and music soared.

Camilla danced, for duty and for pleasure, and then for love with her father.

"I watched you and Mama."

"Watched us what?"

"Dancing just a bit ago. And I thought, look at them." She pressed her cheek to his. "How can anyone look anywhere but at them. They're so beautiful."

"Did I ever tell you about the first time I saw her?"

Camilla leaned back to laugh into his eyes. "A million times. Tell me again."

"It was her sixteenth birthday. A ball, very much like this. She wore a pale green dress, not so different from what you're wearing now. All those billowing skirts that make a woman look like a fantasy. Diamonds in her hair, the way they're in yours tonight. I fell in love with her on the spot, though I didn't see her again for ten years. She was the most exquisite thing I'd ever laid eyes on."

He looked down at her daughter. "Now I'm dancing with the second most exquisite thing."

"Daddy." She took her hand from his shoulder to touch his face. "I love you so much. I'm sorry you were mad at me."

"I wasn't mad, baby. Worried, but not mad. Now as far as that jackass you were with—"

"Daddy."

The warning light in her eye had him glaring right back at her. "I have one thing to say about him. He has potential."

"You don't really know—" She broke off, narrowed her eyes suspiciously. "Is this a trap?"

"I used to worry that some slick-talking pretty boy was going to come along and sweep you off before you realized he was a jerk. Well, you certainly can't call Caine slick-talking or pretty."

"No, indeed."

"And since you already know he's a jerk, you're in good shape," he added, making her laugh. "I want you happy, Cam. Even more than I want to keep my little girl all to myself."

"You're going to make me cry."

"No, you won't cry." He drew her close again. "You're made of sterner stuff than that."

"I love him, Daddy."

"I know." Reeve's eyes met Del's across the crowds of dancers. "Poor son of a bitch doesn't have a prayer. You go get him, honey. And if he doesn't come around quick enough, let me know. I'd still like a reason to kick his ass."

"Make up your mind, Delaney."

"About what?"

Alice took the wine she'd asked him to fetch. "Whether you're just going to scowl at Camilla half the night, or ask her to dance."

"She hasn't stopped dancing for two minutes all night, has she?"

"It's part of her job. Or do you think she likes dancing with that pizza-faced young man with the buck teeth who's stepping all over her feet? Go. Dance with her."

"If you think I'm lining up with half the men in this place—"

"I'd say you'd lost your wits," Alice finished. "Go, cut in. Another minute with that clumsy boy and she'll have a permanent limp."

"All right, all right." Put that way, it was like doing her a favor. Sort of like riding to the rescue, he decided as he saw—quite clearly—the wince flicker over her face as her feet were stomped on again.

Feeling more heroic with each step, Del threaded through the dancers. He tapped Camilla's partner on the shoulder, and moved in so smoothly he surprised himself.

"Cutting in." He whirled Camilla away before the boy could do more than gawk and stammer.

"That was rude."

"Did the trick. How're your feet?"

Her lips twitched. "Other than a few broken toes, holding up, thank you. You dance quite well, My Lord."

"Been a while, but it comes back to you, Madam. Either way, I couldn't be worse than your last partner. Figured you needed a break."

"Rescuing the damsel in distress?" She arched her eyebrows. "Really, twice in one lifetime. Be careful or you'll make it a habit. You said you needed five minutes with me—and that was nearly two hours ago. Did you change your mind?"

"No." But he was no longer clear on what to do with five minutes. Not now that he was holding her again. "I wanted to... About the project. The funding."

"Ah." Disappointment sank into her belly. "If it's business, I'll see that Marian schedules an appointment for you tomorrow."

"Camilla. I wanted to thank you."

She softened, just a little. "You're welcome. The project's important to me, too, you know."

"I guess I get that. Now." He had only to angle his head, dip it a little, and his mouth could be on hers. He wanted, more than anything, to have one long taste of her again. Even if it was the last time. "Camilla—"

"The dance is finished." But her gaze stayed locked with his, and her voice was thick. "You have to let me go."

He knew that. He knew exactly that. But not quite yet. "I need to talk to you."

"Not here. For heaven's sake, if you don't let me go you'll have your name splashed all over the papers tomorrow." She smiled, gaily.

"I don't give a damn."

"You haven't lived with it all your life, as I have. Please, step back. If you want to talk, we'll go out on the terrace."

When he relaxed his grip, she eased away, then spoke clearly and in the friendliest of tones for all the pricked ears nearby. "It's warm. I wonder, Lord Delaney, if you'd join me for some fresh air? And I'd love a glass of champagne."

"No problem."

She slid an arm through his as they walked off the dance floor. "My brothers tell me you ride very well. I hope you'll continue to enjoy the stables while you're here." She kept up the casual chatter as he lifted a flute of champagne from a silver tray and offered it.

"Do you ride, Madam?"

"Certainly." She sipped, strolled toward the open terrace doors. "My father breeds horses on his farm. I've ridden all my life."

A number of other guests had spilled out onto the terrace. Before Camilla could walk to the rail, Del simply tugged her arm, the wine sloshing to the rim of her glass as he steered her briskly toward the wide stone steps.

"Slow down." She paused at the top. "I can't jog down stairs in this dress. I'll break my neck."

He took her glass from her, then stood restlessly by as she gracefully lifted her billowing skirts with her free hand. At the base of the steps, he set the champagne— barely touched—on the closest table, then continued to pull her down one of the garden paths.

"Stop dragging me along," she hissed. "People will—"

"Oh, lighten up," he snapped.

She grit her teeth as she struggled to maintain her dignity. "See how light you are when gossipmongers in ten countries are tossing your name around tomorrow. In any case, I'm wearing three-inch heels and five miles of skirt. Just slow down."

"I don't listen to gossip, so I won't hear them tossing my name around. And if I slow down too long, somebody's going to jump out of some corner with something for you to do. Or to fawn and scrape. Or just say something so they can say they've spoken to you. I want five damn minutes alone with you."

The retort that rose to her lips faded away.

Sparkling silver luminaries lighted a path that was already streamed with moonlight. She could smell the romance of night jasmine and roses, hear it in the pulse and pound of the sea. And her own heart.

Her lover wanted to be alone with her.

He didn't stop until the music was barely more than a murmur in the distance. "Camilla."

She held her breath. "Delaney."

"I wanted to—" She wore moonlight like pearls, he

thought, too dazzled to be astonished by the poetic turn of mind. Her skin was sheened with it. Her eyes glowed. The diamonds in her hair sparked, reminding him there was heat inside the elegance.

He tried again. "I wanted to apologize for... To tell you—"

She didn't know who moved first. It didn't seem to matter. All that mattered was they were in each other's arms. Their mouths met, once, twice. Frantically. Then a third time, long and deep.

"I missed you." He pulled her closer, rocking when she was locked against him. "God, I missed you."

The words seemed to pour into her. "Don't let go. Don't let me go."

"I didn't think I'd ever see you again." He turned his head to race kisses over her face. "I didn't mean to ever see you again."

"I wasn't ever going to see you again first," she said with a laugh. "Oh, I was so angry when I got that letter. That stiff, formal, nasty letter: 'We of the Bardville Research Project wish to express our sincere appreciation.' I could've murdered you."

"You should've seen the first draft." He eased back enough to grin at her. "It was a lot...pithier."

"I'd probably have preferred it." She threw her arms around his neck. "Oh, I'm so happy. I've been trying to figure out how to live without you. Now I won't have to. After we're married, you can teach me how to read one of those lab reports with all those symbols. I never could..."

She trailed off because he'd gone so completely still. Her soaring heart fell back to earth with a rude and painful thud. "You don't love me." Her voice was quiet, scrupulously calm as she eased out of his arms. "You don't want to marry me."

"Let's just slow down, okay? Marriage—" His throat closed up on the word. "Let's be sensible, Camilla."

"Of course. All right, let's." Now her tone was terrifyingly pleasant. "Why don't you go first?"

"There are... There are issues here," he began, frantically trying to clear his jumbled brain long enough to think.

"Very well." She folded her hands. "Issue number one?"

"Cut that out. You just cut that out." He paced down the path, back again. "I have a very demanding, time-consuming profession."

"Yes."

"When I'm in the field, I usually live in a trailer that makes the cabin look like a five-star hotel."

"Yes?"

He bared his teeth, but snagged his temper back at the last minute. "You can't stand there, with that palace at your back while you're wearing a damn crown and tell me you don't see there's a problem."

"So, issue one is our different lifestyles and separate responsibilities."

"In a nutshell. And neatly glossing over the tiaras and glass slippers. Yeah."

"Glass slippers?" That snapped it. "Is that how you see me, and my life—as one ball after the next, one magic pumpkin ride? I have just as vital a role in the world in my glass slippers as you do in your work boots."

"I'm not saying you don't. That's the whole point." He tugged his formal tie loose and dragged it off. "This isn't what I do. I can't strap myself up like a penguin every time I turn around because you have a social obligation. But you should have someone who would. And I'm not asking you to chuck your diamonds to live in camp in the middle of nowhere. It's ridiculous. It would never work.''

''That's where you're wrong. My father was a cop who wanted to farm. Who wanted, more than anything, peace and quiet and to work on the land. My mother was—is— a princess. When they met she was the chatelaine of this place. She had taken up the responsibility as hostess, as ambassador, as symbolic female head of this country when her mother died. But you see, they loved each other so they found a way to give to each other what they needed, to accept the responsibilities and obligations each brought with them, and to make a life together.''

Her chin was up now, her eyes glittering. ''They make me proud. And I'm determined to be every bit the woman my mother is. But you, you with your excuses and your pitiful issues, you're not half the man my father is. *He* had courage and spine and romance. He isn't intimidated by a crown because he respects and understands the woman who wears it.''

She swept up her skirts again. ''I would have lived in your trailer and still have been a princess. My duty to my name—and yours—would never be shirked. It's you who doubt you could live in this palace and still be a man.''

Chapter 12

He hated one single fact the most. She was right. Under all the issues and trappings and complications, he'd been…well, he didn't like the term intimidated. Leery, he decided as he stalked around the gardens as he was wont to stalk around his forest in Vermont. He was leery of linking himself with the princess.

He'd been paying attention in the weeks they'd been apart. He'd seen her face and name splashed over the media. He'd read the stories about her personal life, the speculations about her romantic liaisons.

He knew damn well she wasn't and hadn't been having some hot affair with a French actor as all the articles had trumpeted. She'd been too busy having one with a half-American archaeologist.

Besides, anyone who knew her could see the actor wasn't her type. Too smooth for Camilla.

And that was part of it. The stories, the innuendoes, the

outright fabrications were, for the most part, written by people who didn't know her. Who didn't understand how hard she was willing to work, or her devotion to her mother's country. Her great love of her family, and theirs for her.

They saw an image. The same one he'd let himself be blinded by.

But damn it all to hell and back, the woman had leaped from possible, tentative relationship into marriage so quickly it had been like a sucker punch to the jaw. She didn't give a guy a chance to test his footing.

All or nothing with her, he thought darkly as he jammed his hands into his pockets and reviewed the situation.

First, he finally figures out he's in love with her, then he gets poked in the eye with the fact she's been lying to him. Before he can clear his vision on that, she's long gone. So what that he'd told her to go.

Now, after he'd realized the whole situation was totally impossible, she had to stand there looking like something out of a dream and make him see just how much he'd be losing. And just when he'd started to think maybe, maybe, with time and effort, they could get back what they'd had, she kicked him square in the teeth with marriage.

Yeah, give her a month in a trailer in Florida, toss in a few tropical storms, knee-deep mud, bugs the size of baseballs, and...

She'd be great. He stopped dead in his tracks. She'd be fantastic. She was the kind of woman you could plunk down anywhere, in any situation and she'd find a way. She just kept hacking and prodding and fiddling until she found the way.

Because that was Camilla.

He'd fallen for that, he realized. Before he'd fallen for the looks, the style, the heat, he'd lost his head over her sheer determination to find the answers.

And he was letting a minor detail like royal blood stand in his way.

He wanted the woman, and the princess came along with her. Not half the man her father was? Oh, she'd tried to slice him up with that one. He didn't have courage, backbone. He had no romance?

He'd give her some romance that would knock her out of her glass slippers.

He turned, stormed halfway back to the ballroom before he stopped himself. That, he realized, was just the sort of thing he was going to have to avoid. If this relationship was going to have a chance in hell of working he was going to have to think ahead. A man went charging into a palace ball, tossed a princess over his shoulder and started carting her off, he was going to get them both exactly the sort of press she hated.

And likely end up tossed in some dark, damp dungeon for his trouble.

What a man had to do was work out a clear, rational plan—and carry it out where there were no witnesses.

So he sat down on a marble bench and began to do precisely that.

He got rope at the stables. There were times, he was forced to admit, where being a viscount came in handy. Stable hands were too polite to question the eccentricities of Lord Delaney.

He had to wait until the last waltz was over, and guests were tucked in to bed or were on the other side of the palace gates. That only gave him more time to work out logistics—and to wonder what his parents would do if he ended up breaking his idiotic neck.

He knew where her room was now. That had been a simple matter of subtly pumping Adrienne. He could only be grateful her windows overlooked the gardens where there were plenty of shadows. Though he doubted any guards who patrolled the area would be looking for a man dangling several stories up by a rope.

Even when that man swore bitterly when he swung, nearly face first, into those white stone walls. Rapelling down from the parapet had seemed a lot easier in theory than in fact. He was fairly proficient at it from his work, but climbing down a building at night was considerably different. The cold reality had him swinging in the wind with scraped knuckles and strained temper.

He didn't mind the height so much, unless he thought about the possibility of it being his last view. And all, he mused as he tried for a foothold on a stone balcony rail, because she'd pinched at his ego.

Just couldn't wait until morning. Oh, no, he thought as his foot skidded and he went swinging again. That would've been too easy, too ordinary. Too sane. Why have a civilized conversation in broad daylight and tell a woman you love her and want to marry her when you can do something really *stupid* like commit suicide on the bricks below her bedroom window?

That made a statement.

He managed to settle his weight on the rail, and catch his breath. And the rising wind swept in a brisk September rain.

"Perfect." He glanced up to the heavens. "That just caps it."

While the sudden downpour had rain streaming into his

eyes, he swung out again, kicked lightly off the wall, and worked his way down to Camilla's private terrace.

The first bolt of lightning crashed over the sea as he dropped down, thankfully, to solid stone. He fought with the knot of the thoroughly wet rope he'd looped around. It took him two drenching minutes to free himself. Dumping the rope, he pushed his sopping hair out of his eyes and marched to her terrace doors.

Found them locked.

For a moment he only stood, staring at them. What the hell did she lock the balcony doors for? he wondered with rising irritation. She was three stories up, in a damn palace with guards everywhere.

How often did she have some idiot climb down the wall and drop on her terrace?

She'd drawn the curtains, too, so he couldn't see a bloody thing. He considered, with a spurt of cheerfulness, the satisfaction of kicking in the doors.

There was a certain style to that, he thought. A certain panache. However, that would likely be squashed when alarms started to scream.

Here he was, wet as a drowned rat, on her terrace. And the only way to get in was to knock.

It was mortifying.

So he didn't knock so much as hammer.

Inside, Camilla was using a book as an excuse not to sleep. Every fifteen minutes or so, she actually read a sentence. For the most part, one single fact played over and over in her head.

She'd handled everything badly.

There was no way around it. When she stepped back to look at the big picture, Del had reacted exactly as she'd expect him to react. She had leaped, heart first, into an assumption of marriage.

She'd have been insulted if he'd been the one doing the assuming.

Did love make everyone stupid and careless, or was it just her?

She sighed, turned a page in the book without particular interest. She'd bungled everything, she decided, right from the beginning. Oh, he'd helped. He was such a…what had his mother said? Bonehead. Yes, he was such a bonehead—but she *loved* that about him.

But the blame was squarely on her head.

She hadn't been honest with him, and her reasons for holding back now seemed weak and selfish. His anger, and yes, his hurt, had so shattered her that she'd turned tail and run rather than standing her ground.

Then he'd come to her. Was she so steeped in her own self-pity that she refused to acknowledge that no matter how much pressure had been put on him, he'd never have traveled to Cordina unless he'd wanted to see her?

Even tonight he'd taken a step. Instead of taking one in return, she'd recklessly leaped. She'd taken for granted that he'd simply fall in line. Obviously she was too used to people doing so. Wasn't that one of the reasons she'd taken a holiday from being the princess? Had she learned nothing from those weeks as just plain Camilla?

It wasn't just marriage that had caused him to balk. It was the package that came with it. She closed her eyes. She could do nothing about that—would do nothing even if she could. Her family, her blood, her heritage were essential parts of her.

And yet, she wouldn't want a man who shrugged off

the complexities of her life. She couldn't love a man who enjoyed the fact that they'd be hounded by the press.

So where did that leave her? Alone, she thought, looking around her lovely, lonely room. Because she'd pushed away the only man she loved, the only man she wanted, by demanding too much, too fast.

No. She slammed the book shut. She wouldn't accept that. Accepting defeat was what had sent her running from the cabin. She wasn't going to do that again. There *had* to be an answer. There had to be a compromise. She would...no. She took a deep breath. *They* would find it.

She tossed the covers aside. She'd go to his room now, she decided. She'd apologize for the things she'd said to him and tell him...*ask* him if there was a way they could start again.

Before she could leap out of bed, the pounding on her terrace doors had her jumping back with her heart in her throat. She grabbed the Georgian silver candle-stick from her nightstand as a weapon, and was on the point of snatching up the phone to call security.

"Open the damn door."

She heard the voice boom out, followed by a vicious crack of thunder. Astonished, still gripping her makeshift weapon, she crossed to the doors, and nudged the curtains aside.

She saw him in a flash of lightning. The furious face, the dripping hair, the sopping tuxedo shirt. For a moment she could do nothing but stare with her mouth open.

"Open the damn door," he repeated loudly. "Or I kick it in."

Too stunned to do otherwise, she fumbled with latch and lock. Then she staggered back three steps when he pushed the doors open.

"What?" She could do no more than croak it out as he stood, glaring at her and dripping on the priceless rug.

"You want romance, sister." He grabbed the candle-stick out of her numb fingers and tossed it aside. It looked a little too heavy to risk any accidents, and he had enough bruises for one night.

"Del." She backed up another two steps as he stepped forward. "Delaney. How did you...your hand's bleeding."

"You want backbone? You want adventure? Maybe a little insanity thrown in?" He grabbed her shoulders, lifted her straight to her toes. "How's this?"

"You're all wet," was all she could say.

"You try climbing down the side of a castle in a rainstorm, see what shape you end up in."

"Climb?" She barely registered being pushed across the room. "You climbed down the wall? Have you lost your mind?"

"Damn right. And you know what the guy gets when he breaches the castle walls? He gets the princess."

"You can't just—"

But he could. She discovered very quickly that he could. Before she could clear sheer shock from her system, his mouth was hot on hers. And shock didn't have a chance against need. A thrill swept through her as he dragged her—oh my—to the bed.

He was wet and bleeding and in a towering temper. And he was all hers. She locked her arms around his neck, slid her fingers into that wonderful and dripping hair, and gladly offered him the spoils of war.

Her mouth moved under his, answering his violent kiss with all the joy, all the longing that raged inside her.

The storm burst through the open doors as she released

him long enough to tug at his sodden shirt. It landed, somewhere, with a wet plop.

He was surprised his clothes didn't simply steam off him. The heat of his temper paled with the fire that she brought to his blood. So soft, so fragrant, so wonderfully willing. Her face was wet now with the rain he'd brought in with him. He could've lapped it—and her—up like cream.

Undone, he buried his face against her throat. "I need you, damn it. I can't get past it."

"Then have me." Her breath hitched as his hands roamed over her. "Take me."

He lifted his head, looked down at her. Her eyes were dark now, tawny as a cat's. And as her hands came up to frame his face, she smiled. "I've waited so long for you," she murmured. "And I didn't even know."

To prove it, she drew his mouth down to hers again.

Everything he felt for her, about her, from her, bloomed in the kiss. She trembled from it, and the quiet hum in her throat had his pulse bounding.

That long, white throat fascinated him. The strong slope of her shoulders was a wonder. Damp with rain now, the thin night slip she wore clung provocatively to her body. He took his mouth, his hands over the wet silk first, then the hot, damp flesh beneath.

She moved under him. A graceful arch, a quick shiver. Slowly first, savoring first, he explored, exploited. Excited. When her breathing was thick, her eyes dreamily closed, he dragged her to her knees and ravaged.

He'd catapulted her from quiet pleasure to reckless demand so that she floundered. Drowned in him. Those hard hands that had been so blissfully gentle were now erotically rough. Bowing back, she surrendered to that hungry mouth. Moaned his name as he tore reason to shreds.

She went wild in his arms. As her need pitched to meet his, she tore and tugged at his clothes. Kneeling on the bed, they clung, flesh to flesh, heart raging against heart.

Once more, in a flash of lightning, their eyes met. Held. In his, at last, she saw all she needed to see. And it was she who shifted, taking him in. Wrapping her legs around him to take him deep until they both trembled.

"Je t'aime." She said it clearly though her body quaked. "I love you. I can't help myself."

Before he could speak, her mouth covered his. What was left of his control snapped, whipping his body toward frenzy. She met him, beat for frantic beat. When she closed around him, he swallowed her cry of release. And emptied himself.

"Camilla." He couldn't think past her name, even as he slid down her body to nestle between her breasts. He felt her fingers stroke through his hair and wanted nothing more than to close his eyes and stay steeped in her for the rest of his life.

But his gaze skimmed toward the terrace—and the rain cheerfully blowing in the open doors and soaking floor and rug.

"I didn't close the doors. We're starting to flood. Just stay."

As he rolled away, she watched him lazily. Then she bolted up as he started to cross the room. "No! Wait." She scrambled out of bed, snatched the robe that had been draped over the curved back of her settee. "Someone might see," she muttered, then, with her robe modestly closed, hurried to close the doors herself.

Control, he thought as he watched her draw the drapes.

Even now. A princess couldn't walk around naked in front of the windows—not even her own. And certainly couldn't have a man do so.

She turned, saw him eyeing her speculatively. "The guards. Guests," she began, then dropped her gaze. "I'll get some towels."

While she walked into the adjoining bath, he untangled his damp tuxedo pants. They were ruined, he decided, and would be miserably uncomfortable. But if they were going to have a conversation, he wanted to be wearing something besides his heart on his sleeve.

She came back, got down on her hands and knees and began mopping the floor. It made him smile. Made him remember her in his cabin.

"I have to be practical, Delaney."

His brows drew together at the strained edge in her voice. "I understand that."

"Do you?" She hated herself for wanting to weep now.

"Yes, I do. I admire the way you manage to be practical, self-sufficient—and royal."

Her head came up slowly. She eased back to sit on her heels, and the look of surprise on her face was enough to have him shoving his hands in his wet pockets. "I admire you," he said again. "I'm not good with words, these kinds of words. Damn it, do you think I'm an idiot? That I don't have a clue what kind of juggling act you—your whole family—has to perform to be who you are and manage to have any sort of life along with it?"

"No." Looking away from him again, she folded the damp portion of the rug back, then dried the floor beneath it. "No, I believe you understand—as much as you can. Maybe more than another man might. I think that's why, in some ways, we're at odds."

"Why don't you look at me when you talk to me?"

Struggling for composure, she pressed her lips together. But her gaze was level when she lifted her head again. "It's difficult for me. Excuse me a moment." She rose, and shoulders straight as a soldier's, carried the damp towels back to the bath.

Women, Del thought, were a hell of a lot of work.

She came back, went to a small cabinet and took out a decanter. "I think some brandy would help. I was wrong," she began as she poured two snifters. "Tonight in the garden, I was wrong to say those things to you. I apologize."

"Oh, shut up." Out of patience, he snatched a snifter out of her hand.

"Can't you at least pretend to be gracious?"

"Not when you're being stupid. If I want an apology, you'll know it." She'd beat him to the damn apology. Wasn't it just like her? He paced away and though he didn't care for it, took a slug of the brandy. "When you're wrong, I'll let you know it."

He spun back, temper alive on his face. "You hurt me." It infuriated him to admit it.

"I know. The things I said—"

"Not that. That just pissed me off." He dragged a hand through his hair. "You lied to me, Camilla. Or the next thing to it. I started counting on you. And I don't mean to clean up after me. I started thinking about you—about us—a certain way. Then it all blew up in my face."

"I handled it badly. It was selfish—I was selfish," she corrected. "I wanted some time—then more time—to just be. I ran. I told myself it wasn't running away, but it was. Last summer, it was all suddenly too heavy, too close. I couldn't..."

"Just be?"

"I couldn't just be," she said, quietly. "Last summer
here was an incident with the press. Not much more,
really, no less than so many others the past few years. But
t had been building up inside me, all of it until it just got
o be too much. I couldn't eat. I wasn't sleeping well, I
ouldn't concentrate on what I was meant to do. I…"

"No, don't stop. Tell me."

"This incident," she said carefully, "wasn't so differ-
nt from others. But while it was happening I could hear
myself screaming. Inside. I thought—I knew—that unless
 got away for a while, the next time it happened, the
creams wouldn't be just inside. I was afraid I was having
ome sort of breakdown."

"Camilla, for God's sake."

"I should've spoken with my family." She looked back
t him because she'd heard that unspoken question in his
hocked tone. "They would have understood, supported
ne, given me time and room. But I just couldn't bring
myself to confess such a weakness. Poor Camilla, who's
•een given every privilege in life, and more—so much
nore—the unquestioning love from family, is suddenly
oo delicate, too fragile to deal with the responsibilities
nd difficulties of her rank and position."

"That's malarkey."

The term made her laugh a little. And steadied her. "It
lidn't feel like it at the time. It felt desperate. I was losing
myself. I don't know if you can understand that because
ou know yourself so intimately. But I felt hounded and
unted, and at the same time so unsteady about who I
vas, inside. What I wanted to do with my life beyond
vhat I was supposed to do, beyond duty. I had no passion

for anything, and there's a horrible kind of emptiness to that.''

He could imagine it—the pressures, the demands—and the nerves of steel it took to be who she was. The courage, he thought, it had taken to break from all that to find the woman inside.

"So you took off, with a couple suitcases in a rental car, to find it?"

"More or less. And I did find it, though as I said, in the end, I handled it badly."

"We handled it badly," he corrected. "I was over my head with you, and that was when I thought you were a weird rich chick in some kind of trouble. When I found out, I figured you'd used me for some kind of a lark."

She paled. "It was never—"

"I know that now. I know it. I had feelings for you I've never had for anyone else. I'd worked myself up to tell you—and came into the kitchen and heard you talking on the phone."

"To Marian." Eyes closed, Camilla let out a long breath. "The timing," she murmured, "couldn't have been worse. I'm surprised you didn't throw me out bodily."

"Thought about it." He waited until her eyes opened, met his again. "It felt better when I sat around feeling sorry for myself. It took me a while to start considering what it's like for you. The people, the press, the protocol. It's pretty rough."

"It's not all that bad. It's just that sometimes you have to—"

"Breathe," he finished.

"Yes." Tears swam into her eyes. "Yes."

"Don't do that. I can't have a rational conversation if

you start dripping. Look, I mean it. Plug the dam. I've never told a woman I love her, and I'm sure as hell not going to do it for the first time when she's blubbering.''

"I'm not blubbering." But her voice broke on a sob as joy leaped into her. She yanked open a drawer, tugged out a lace-trimmed hankie and wiped at tears. She wanted to leap again, just leap. But this time, she knew to keep quiet. "So, tell me."

"I'll get to it. You're not fragile, Camilla."

"Not as a rule, no."

"Cordina's crown jewel. I've been catching up on some magazines," he said when she stared at him. "A jewel has to have substance to keep its shine. You've got substance."

"That," she managed to say, "is the most flattering thing you've ever said to me."

"That's just because you're used to men telling you you're beautiful. And I like your family."

"My family?"

"Yeah. Your mother's an amazing woman. I like your brothers, your cousins. Still haven't quite figured out— for sure—which is which, but, I like them. And your sister's sweet." He paused. "I meant that in a good way."

"Yes." Camilla smiled a little. "She is, very sweet."

"Your aunts, uncles, they're interesting people. Admirable. I guess that's where you get it. Had some trouble with your father. But I figure if I had a daughter and some guy was... Well, it's natural for him to want to kick my ass for putting hands on what's his."

"He likes you."

"He'd like to roast me over a slow fire."

"He thinks you have potential."

Del snorted, paced, then glanced back at her. "Does he?"

"Yes. Of course if you make me unhappy, that slow fire could still be arranged. But I don't mean to pressure you."

"You're a clever girl, princess. Sharp, sexy mind. I could get past that face of yours, but your mind kept hooking me in." He gestured to the thick book on archaeology resting on her nightstand. "So you stayed interested?"

"Yes. I want to learn. I really loved working with you."

"I know."

"I find the work fascinating. Not just because of you, you know. I want to learn for me first. I needed something for myself. Something that pulled at me, from the inside. Something beyond what's expected—must be expected of me because of my position. I wanted to find my passion, and thanks to you I did. I'm making arrangements to join Dr. Lesuer on a project in France."

"Yeah, Lower Paleolithic." Del shrugged. "He's good. Hell of a teacher, too. He's got patience. I don't. It'd probably be less complicated to work with him. Then again, it'd be a shame for you to miss following through on Bardville."

She took a deep breath. "Are you suggesting that I join the project?"

"I've been thinking about outfitting a new site trailer. The old one's a dump. And I need to oversee a lot of lab work. It'd probably be practical to rent a house near the university. Maybe buy something."

The pressure in her chest was unbearable. It was wonderful. "It's understood in my family that when one of us takes a career, or makes a personal commitment, his or her official duties can be adjusted. Tell me.''

"Listen, I'm going to complain every time I have to gear up in some fancy suit—and you'll probably throw my own title in my face when I do,'' he said, walking to her.

"Naturally.''

"But I'll carry my weight on what you bring to the deal, and you'll carry yours on what I bring.''

She closed her eyes briefly. "Are you asking me to ma—''

He cut her off with a quick, warning sound. "You've got some looks, don't you?'' He lifted her chin and cupped her face. "Some fabulous looks. You know, I don't care how many times this face of yours is splashed over magazines. I don't care about the gossip and bull written in them, either. That kind of stuff doesn't matter to me. We know who we are.''

Tears clogged her throat, shimmered in her eyes again. Nothing, nothing he might have said could have told her more clearly he believed in her. "Oh, Delaney.''

"I don't have a ring for you right now.''

"I don't care about that.''

"I do.'' Funny, he thought as he lifted her hand, studied those elegant fingers, that he would feel it was important. "I want you to wear my ring.'' His gaze shifted to hers and held.

"If you don't want me to cry again, you'll hurry up.''

"Okay, okay. Try to give a woman a little romance.''

"You climbing down the palace walls is about all the romance I can take for one night. Thanks all the same.''

He grinned. "I'm crazy about you. Every bit of you, but especially your smart mouth.''

"That's lovely. But I could probably stand just a little more romance than that, if you can manage it."

"I love you." He took her face in his hands. This time when a tear slid down her cheek, he didn't mind. "Camilla. I love who you are. I love who we are when we're together. I love the woman who mopped my kitchen floor and I love the woman I waltzed with tonight."

Joy soared inside her. "Both sides of that woman love all the sides of you. You make me happy."

"Marry me. Make a life with me. You won't always be comfortable, but you sure as hell won't be bored."

"I'll marry you." She touched her lips to his cheek. "And work with you." And the other. "Live with you. And love you. Always," she murmured as their lips met.

"Come back with me." He pulled her close and just held on. "We'll work out the details—whatever has to be done. I don't want to go back without you."

"Yes. I'll arrange it." She tightened her grip. "We'll arrange it."

"I'll carve out some time off—whatever we need to deal with whatever we have to deal with."

"Don't worry." Here, she thought, was her passion, her contentment and her love all wrapped in one. "We'll work it all out. When there's a question, we'll find the answer."

She rested her head on his shoulder, smiling as she felt his lips brush over her hair. The most important question, she thought, had been asked. And answered.

* * * * *

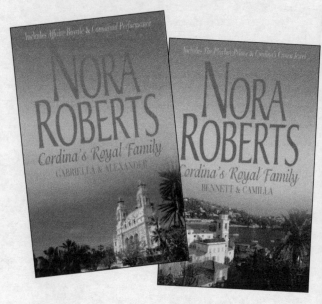

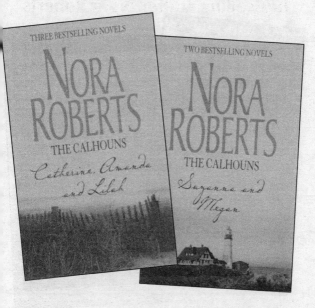

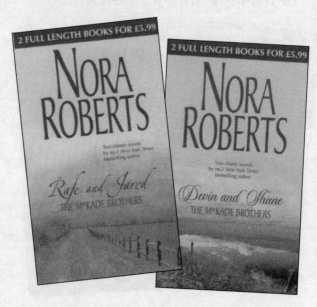

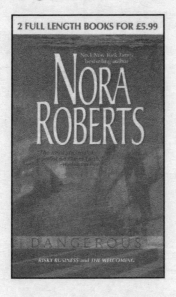

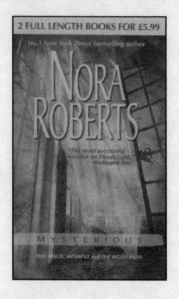